THE
LOST
GIRL
OF
BERLIN

BOOKS BY ELLA CAREY

Beyond the Horizon
Paris Time Capsule
The House by the Lake
From a Paris Balcony
Secret Shores
The Things We Don't Say
A New York Secret

THE LOST GIRL OF BERLIN

ELLA CAREY

Bookouture

Published by Bookouture in 2021

An imprint of Storyfire Ltd.
Carmelite House
50 Victoria Embankment
London EC4Y 0DZ

www.bookouture.com

ISBN: 978-1-80019-217-1
eBook ISBN: 978-1-80019-216-4

For my son, Ben.

"*No one keeps a secret like a child.*" Victor Hugo

"*I am the enemy you killed, my friend.*" Wilfred Owen

Part One

Chapter One

Kate

Berlin, March 1946

The jeep's brakes shrieked through the ashen city. Kate squeezed her eyes shut. The primitive scream keened like a dying eagle over the icy streets of Berlin, and she laced her fingers around the wooden bench in the back of the vehicle, bracing for the chilling clash of metal hitting metal, the thin whine of sirens in the white cold air. The sounds that sang of her father's fatal accident ten years ago, the sounds that would haunt her until the day she died.

The jeep that held the cache of war correspondents halted in the snaking traffic, its yellow headlights beaming into the afternoon mist. And when there was no crash and no siren and the jeep remained at a standstill, Kate allowed herself to breathe.

She bit her tongue and forced her memories back, focusing on the ruins of an old mansion opposite the vehicle.

The garden would have been beautiful once. Boxwood and evergreens were all draped in snow and the decorative front gate was swung open as if preparing to invite guests inside from the Berlin cold. Before the war, the red-brick, pillared house would have been warm and enticing, guests stepping over the threshold into the grand entrance hall, rubbing their hands in front of a roaring fireplace, laughter rippling through the richly decorated rooms. After dinner, there might have been dancing, girls resting their heads on young men's shoulders, while upstairs, children cut out paper dolls and jumped on featherbeds before sinking in between silken sheets and reading fairy tales.

Now, on the pockmarked front steps of the mansion, there sat a little girl.

Instead of a cashmere coat of the softest navy blue with two rows of shiny buttons and a pair of sturdy leather boots, the child wrapped her stick-like arms around her shapeless, dirty brown shift. Her feet were pressed into a pair of ragged brown moccasins, her dust-caked legs poked out like a fragile bird's. When her blue eyes caught with Kate's in the fading light of the afternoon, they held her still and Kate reached her hand to cover her mouth.

The child's eyes were startling blue, a pair of endless pools, drawing Kate into her life, her misery, in the endless Berlin winter that attacked the people of this city like a wild beast and drove them into their houses. Inside, the windows were boarded up with no panes, and the walls and ceilings filled with cracks and holes, covered with paper and rags through which the wind whistled and surged until the old and sick froze to death in their beds.

"Let me out, driver!" Kate's voice jolted into the icy air, her breath white and curling, only to drift hopelessly around the back of the driver's implacable neck, the whirr of the jeep's engine as it trundled forward, drowning her shouts. She tried to stand up in her seat, pushing forward past her fellow American correspondents, reaching to tap the driver on the shoulder, only to be thrown back down again, with an unceremonious thump on the hard wooden bench that made do for a seat.

Rick Shearer reached out to steady her. He held her arm until she was safely seated. The jeep lumbered on.

Kate threw her hands up in frustration, but Rick's intelligent brown eyes were full of understanding underneath the snap brim of his fedora hat.

Hopelessly, Kate tried to mouth something at him, and he nodded, while Kate cast about wildly. Where in this no man's land were they? Every street was unrecognizable—strangled with broken cables and water pipes sticking out of the ground like monsters. She folded her arms around her own too slender frame and settled back down, hollow hopelessness shrouding her like some worn old blanket.

Would the tiny ghosts of this war ever find peace?

On this journey across war-torn Europe, Kate had seen the concentration camps, the ovens that bore silent testimony to the deepest horrors that humankind could inflict on one another. She'd witnessed men and women crawling out of cattle cars to huddle by the railway tracks in Krakow, and she'd stared helplessly at potbellied, starving children in Rome.

Nothing could provide her with immunity to the devastation of war. She would never be blind to the horrors the Nazis had wrought during the last years.

On the vehicle went and they pounded past a park, its benches stripped bare of their wooden seats, torn apart for firewood in a hopeless attempt to heat Berlin's homes.

When the jeep came to a rattling stop outside the war correspondents' ramshackle hotel, Kate wrapped her scarf over her mouth against the pungent air, even now still ripe with decay and death and the stink of burnt-out buildings. She tucked her short dark curls into her woolen lined hat and adjusted the jacket she wore as her official war reporter's uniform.

Harvey Milton pushed open the chipped door of the old hotel they were staying in, a decrepit building that had miraculously survived the Allies' bombing. The overwhelming smell of boiled cabbage, the smell Kate had come to associate with this godforsaken place, met them in the street, but Harvey flashed her one of his famous wide smiles, his pearly white teeth bright against his naturally tanned skin, and waited for her to pass. Harvey always looked as if he'd stepped out of a hot shower, with his blond hair slicked back, despite the rigors of their European tour.

Kate swung around, unable to bear going into the cold, miserable building just yet, unable to rid herself of the image of the little girl.

And then, she stopped. *She couldn't bring her papa back, but she could save that orphan from freezing to death in the cold.*

Kate strode down the frosty road, only to sense Rick Shearer walking beside her, keeping pace, step for step, the GI boots they'd been told to bring on this all-male, except Kate, reporters' delegation of nine months over thirty-five thousand miles beating out a tattoo on the street.

Kate kept her gaze forward, passing the rows of silent women who toiled on the sides of the streets in the seemingly hopeless task of tidying away all the mess, still working in the gathering darkness with their bare hands to break up the mountains of rubble. There was no one else to repair the damages of war, with the men too exhausted to help and the government gone.

"Kate. I know what you're doing."

"She won't survive the night." She would not be swayed on this.

"They won't let you tell her story. You know that." Rick's voice, rich and sonorous, trained by radio journalism, sounded like a song from home in these haunted surrounds. Kate pushed aside familiar intruding thoughts of Manhattan and bright lights and life being lived and people dancing in the streets back home because the war was finally done.

She trudged on, her fists tightening into balls in her leather gloves. "It's not about the story, Rick." The moment Kate had laid eyes on the child, she'd wanted to know how the girl had come to be sitting on the steps of that ruined home, but she would not exploit her story. She wanted to help her. And she did not expect a soul to understand why.

Rick's expression darkened, eyes searching her face, until finally, he nodded, rubbed a hand over his stubble flecked chin, and walked by her side.

She'd already been told the story she *was* keen to write about the relationships between German women and American GIs stationed in Germany would not happen, because American news managers were not interested. It did not put American soldiers in a good light. She'd been told by a US colonel that chaos would result if the wives of American soldiers visited their husbands in Germany and were to learn that German *frauleins* had been scrounging army rations and warm places to sleep alongside affections from the American military since VE day. She would not give up on this story as well.

Next to her, Rick strode on in the cold, eyebrows furrowed, his expression unfathomable.

Kate rounded corners, relying on the sharp sense of direction she'd developed while touring so many broken European cities in the past devastating months. She moved past ruined homes while hollowed-out German men wandered the streets, two of them dragging tree branches to light fires to keep their families alive.

Tree branches meant they must be approaching the park near where she'd seen the child. When she finally came to a standstill outside the once grand home, the little girl still sat on the steps, her head in her hands.

Kate hesitated, her own warmly gloved hand resting on the stone wall out front.

"You speak German." She turned to Rick, her breaths coming in fast, uneven gasps. A bitter flurry of wind ruffled her jacket, and her gaze flew to the ill-dressed child. "She will have been sent away to the countryside for the war, and returned home, only to find her family are all gone."

A small kitbag sat by the young girl on the front step.

"She'll be sent to a children's camp for refugees and will likely die." They were in the Soviet zone. So that meant Soviet orphanages. Kate shuddered, and placed her boot on the front step. The child looked like an urchin, but had this house once been her home?

Rick laid his gloved hand over hers. Kate met his eye, startled at the gesture, even though they'd become close friends these past months, finding a kinship that Kate appreciated because some of the other correspondents refused to take a woman on tour seriously, viewing her as either an unnecessary distraction and ignoring her, or trying and failing to flirt with her.

She'd learned to stand her ground back home already, having worked in print journalism and radio in Washington DC before the chance to tour came up, and she'd jumped at this, desperate to escape the memories that preyed upon her in New York. Perhaps, she'd thought, witnessing the aftermath of war would help her heal from the guilt that had enveloped her since her father's tragic death.

Rick trudged up the front steps of the house, his boots crackling on the snow. In front of them, the house loomed, there was no front door, and through it, there was nothing, it was all bombed out.

And looking at the freezing child, Kate's fingers felt too hot in her warm leather gloves.

Rick advanced toward the little girl; Kate next to him now. Above, there was no second story to the house. It had just been sliced away like a guillotined head. Opposite, the sounds of girls and boys sledding in the park, all wearing leggings and hoods, threw some sense of normality into this ghostly place.

Leaning down, Rick talked to the girl in soft German. She seemed to contemplate this for a moment, then looked up, her extraordinary blue eyes locking with Kate's like they had when they'd landed on her before.

Rick murmured gentle words in German, but the child only watched Kate. Slowly, she held out her hand. She bent down close to the girl and, in a quick movement, scooped her up into her arms. Silently, the child lay her head on Kate's shoulder, and Kate, closing her eyes a moment, patted the little girl's head, a strange sense of stillness spreading over her. It was a feeling she'd forgotten all about.

She had been able to do something. She had been able to help.

Rick's brown eyes were serious. "She's mute."

"Pick up her kitbag, please, Rick."

Rick shook his head. "Kate…"

"Just pick it up. I'm not leaving her alone out here."

The girl tucked her head into Kate's chest, her long bare legs dangling toward the mud-caked street. Kate treaded gingerly back down the narrow flight of steps, avoiding slipping on the treacherous ice and snow.

Rick only shook his head, before hauling the child's kitbag over his shoulder, pulling down his hat, and turning around, his footsteps cutting hollow notes into the desolate streets.

As if in unspoken complicity, they had avoided the main thoroughfares back to the Allied zones and wound a wide circle around the Brandenburg Gate. Kate trudged alongside Rick through the Soviet-controlled parts of the city. They climbed up the back stairs of the old hotel, a strange, silent party, avoiding the ancient cage-like lift and the watchful eyes of other reporters and official Allied personnel.

Now, an hour later, the girl lay motionless on Kate's narrow bed, her small, forlorn shape buried underneath the rough gray blanket that was standard issue here. Kate's cheeks burned red after being out in the cold, and were still rosy in the freezing air that the hotel's ancient heaters could never combat.

She peered out the window as night fell over Berlin, waiting for Rick to return.

Jumpy, Kate started at a knock on the door. And waited. Three taps and then a break, then two, then one. She slipped across the room and let Rick in.

In his hands, he held three mugs of thick broth. Germans were existing on potatoes, cabbages, bread and preserves, nary enough calories to support a child, let alone a fully grown adult. But in the American- and English-occupied hotels, there was enough food to go around, even if cabbage and potatoes were the main fare, along with stews made of tough, wizened meat.

He tended to the child, stirring her awake, his hands cupping the enamel mug while she took tentative sips, before settling down on Kate's creaking bed and sitting the child up on his knee while she looked at him, her huge eyes even rounder and bluer under the stark light bulb that swung from the cracked ceiling. Her face was streaked with dirt, and her long blond hair hung to her thin shoulders in matted tufts and knots. Her feet were bare and filthy and rich with dried blood, her mud-caked shoes lined up under the little desk beneath the window where Kate wrote her newspaper stories.

Rick talked to her in soft, soothing German.

"How old do you think she is?" Kate whispered, her chest aching for the little girl.

Rick rubbed the heel of his hand against his forehead. "Ten, perhaps. If that."

Kate placed her mug down on the chipped windowsill and paced. "She can have my broth when she is done." She turned again to face Rick. "I'm thinking about how to get her to safety, and I don't know how to do it, Rick."

"All those posters of lost children out in the streets," Rick said, frowning.

Kate shook her head. "I'll stay in Berlin if I have to, until she's safe. I'll join you in Nuremberg once I'm done."

"No, Kate." His face rose to meet her gaze, his eyes carrying the weight of seriousness that lingered over everyone here. "I won't leave you here. It's too dangerous to be alone."

Kate glanced up at the ceiling a moment. "It's not about me; we can't leave the child alone," she said. "She'll end up in a Soviet orphanage." She looked down at the girl and shuddered at the thought. "I am certain she'll make her way back home if we let her out of our sight. But I can't stand her sitting there waiting for family who are never going to come back. She'll get picked up, the streets are thick with dangerous people, or she'll freeze to death if she tries to make a bed among the rubble in that destroyed house."

Kate's shoulder burned with the close memory of the child's weary head resting there. She'd never forget the comfort of the soft rise and fall of the girl's chest against her own heart.

The child lay back on the bed and closed her eyes, and when Kate tried to place her own mug of soup in the little girl's tender hands, the child put up a hand—*enough*.

Kate tucked her under the blanket and turned out the lamp by the bed.

Rick raked a hand through his dark hair; he tilted his head to one side. "A few of us are having a drink in Harvey's room." He lowered his voice. "She needs quiet, dark. Sleep. Come and sit with us, Kate."

Kate looked at the child doubtfully. "I'm not experienced with kids, in fact, normally I'm not particularly drawn to them, but this one? The way her eyes caught with mine." Kate clasped her hands together. "It was as if her expression held the agony of every kid I've seen on tour."

"Come and have a drink," Rick said, suddenly reaching out and squeezing Kate's shoulder.

She startled at his touch.

"The floor is going to be hard tonight," he said.

"Oh, fiddlesticks to that." Kate ran a hand through her dark curls. She sighed. "There has to be some way of finding out whether she has friends or family alive."

Rick held the door open. "We'll worry about that tomorrow. You've done all you can for tonight."

Chapter Two

Kate

Berlin, March 1946

In Harvey Milton's room, Kate slid down on the bare floorboards next to Leonard Andrews, the hard-bitten forty-something full-time reporter for the *Washington Post* who took everything they'd seen on tour in his stride. He'd simply stay quiet, his eyes flashing in cynical recognition of human nature in wartime.

Leonard poured a slug of red wine into a cracked mug and handed it to Kate, his red stubby fingers inflamed from the relentless cold. Len's detachment had impressed Kate at first, she'd even tried to emulate it as a way to cope, but as the tour had wound on, she'd realized more and more that even while she would always be professional, she could never disengage from the people who inspired her stories.

Opposite her, Joe Ackerman, the young red-headed reporter who was on contract with CBS, sent her a crooked smile. He'd tried flirting with Kate in Krakow, but she'd been so shaken by what she'd seen that she'd hardly noticed him, and he'd given up.

Rick stretched his long legs out next to the black-haired Californian, Walter Puglisi, who wrote for the *Los Angeles Times* and reported for NBC. Walter sat with his eyes closed, leaning his head against the wall.

On Kate's other side, Rick's fellow Harvard graduate, Harvey Milton, sat, hands folded between his knees. Harvey was as keen and hard-working as Rick was laid-back and steady. Talk was Harvey would be up for a media executive role once they got back home. He certainly made no secret of the fact that he was eyeing a post in New York at one of the top radio stations or newspapers, and his ambition knew no limits.

All the reporters on tour were on full-time contract except for Kate, but she was used to working freelance; unlike her male colleagues, she'd never once been under contract even though she'd been working as a political correspondent for seven years. Now, at least, she earned twenty-five dollars if a story of hers got published by the Western News Union, whom she'd fought hard to persuade to send her on tour. But only if the story was syndicated to weekly newspapers across the United States.

When she did get a story published, the payment went straight to her mom back home in New York for safekeeping. Kate's accommodation and food were all paid for by the government while she was on tour, and she'd saved every dollar she'd earned so far.

She let the men's conversation drift around her, finding herself curiously drawn to the neat way Harvey kept his room. Next to his typewriter sat one of the two pairs of sunglasses they'd all been told to pack for the trip, along with his supply of copy paper, a notebook and a few sharp pencils sticking out of a chipped red mug. She wondered if he ironed his underpants. Kate grinned and took a sip of brandy, the liquid burning down her throat.

Harvey's compulsory box of Lux soap flakes was stored under the thin muslin curtains. His clothes hung on a row of hooks along the wall, and his rucksack was stowed under the desk, his GI boots lined up in perfect formation by the chair.

"Guess you've made a real home here, Harvey," she said, her words flickering beneath the soft conversation in the room.

Harvey sent her a smile through the smoke haze. "I can make a home anywhere, Kate. It's a knack I have." His expression changed. "But I get the feeling you aren't so happy with the end of the war."

"The end of war won't mean the end of suffering, as so many Americans think." Kate felt a warmth, despite her misgivings, at the expression on his eager, boyish face.

Harvey tilted his head to one side. "At least the Soviets won't let the Germans starve like the Nazis did."

Kate let out a short laugh. "How can you ignore what's under our noses, what we're seeing out there in the streets of Berlin? No, the Soviets will let the Germans starve just as well as we will. If not, better."

Harvey's face crinkled into a frown.

Kate lowered her voice. "The tales of astounding horror during the Red Army occupation of this city toward women are slipping under the radar."

Harvey's brow knitted.

Kate sighed. "We can't ignore the facts. What happened to women and children under the Soviet watch? They are too scared to come forward, particularly in the Soviet-occupied sector of the city. And for good reason. You know as well as I do that there are tales of Russians raping thousands of German women during the invasion, talk of all German women aged between fifteen and fifty-five having to get tested for venereal disease."

Harvey was quiet.

"The Soviets may well hide the stories, but a source has told me that there have been nearly one thousand women who have asked for an abortion here since last June. It is brutal. Just because this happened to German women on the other side of the battle lines, does that make it any less horrific?"

A muscle tweaked in Harvey's tanned cheek. "My loyalty is only to America. I find it's simpler to think that way."

Kate's brow tightened and she shook her head. "Seeing war-torn Europe has left me with an abiding disgust for war, Harvey. I think we should be allowed to report the truth of the effects of it. Deeper, human stories. I believe folks back home would care if they knew.

But we can't demonize the victors, according to the news agencies back home. We're not being allowed to tell a balanced truth."

Harvey poured another glug of wine into her mug. "All our countrymen want to do is get back to normal." He sighed. "My folks in Cleveland say they just want to go fishing, live without blackouts. Do normal things. They don't want any more horror stories to read about."

The soft chatter of the other men filtered around them.

Kate shook her head. "I think that we Americans have an obligation to help our neighbors overseas. We haven't brought democracy to half of Europe anyway."

Harvey lowered his voice. "Democracy doesn't mean a thing to the starving man in the street, Kate."

Kate leaned forward. "The point is, the surrender of Germany didn't bring peace for the Europeans. We can't just ignore what is going on here. We should *all* be willing—Americans too—to make sacrifices to avoid another, far worse war in the future. At home, we need to think about going without to help the starving, suffering people in other countries. The children here, orphaned. Women. If we all did our bit…"

Harvey stubbed out his cigarette in a chipped ashtray on the floor. Outside, rain started pouring down in torrents, lashing at the windows. *Thank goodness the little girl was safe and warm in Kate's bed.*

"I can't see a way of doing that."

Kate eyed him. "The United Nations. One united front to work together and provide solutions that are well thought out and democratic. Ideally, there would be one united convention that believed in peace to unite us all. It's our only way of preventing another disaster of catastrophic implications on an unimaginable worldwide scale ever happening again."

Kate was aware of the other men's chatter coming to an end, aware of Rick's eyes on her, aware of his hand reaching out across the floor toward her.

Kate felt a sudden urge to check on the German orphan.

She eased herself up to standing. "Goodnight," she said. "Goodbye until the morning. Sleep well, everyone."

The men said goodnight as she walked out, closing the door, Rick's eyes burning into her back as she left.

Back in her hotel room, the child slept, the soft rise and fall of her skeletal frame the only indicator that she still lived. Kate slipped across to her desk, propelled by a strange energy after her conversation with Harvey. She had suspected for a long time that Harvey lived in a simple, optimistic world. His fellow Harvard graduate, Rick, was an altogether more complicated man. Kate had fought her attraction to Rick from day one of the tour, but she wasn't interested in a relationship. Trusting people, like she'd trusted and loved her father, meant endangering them.

If Americans knew what was going on here, they would sympathize. But how to get past the gatekeepers? The editors who insisted on filtering the truth? Kate slipped a fresh ream of paper into her typewriter and glanced over her burgeoning story, the pages she'd already written laying on her desk, the truth splattered all over them, staining the post-war copybook, tarring it with a brush that no one knew of back home.

Her words flashed straight back at her. The Allies' deep, deep hatred for Germans in the aftermath of war was going to leave a raft of innocent orphans who'd been born under the Nazis, only to be faced with Soviet leadership that was about to whisk them out of sight like unwanted flies. They were already eyewitnesses to a brutal war. And yet, with "freedom" too many of them still had no parents, no possessions, and no homes.

Kate's eyes scoured her sentences, her stark descriptions of children who had been separated from their families, and now, after the invasion of the Red Army in Prussia, they'd been left to roam through the unforgiving German forests in order to survive. It was going to be impossible for families to reunite, and these children's fates hung in the balance, most of them ending up in Soviet children's homes. In the face of the new and divided Germany, some would attempt to flee across borders but would be unable to survive the terrible journey to other countries on their own.

Kate tucked a pencil behind her ear, returning to the keys, more words tumbling out to the accompaniment of the child's soft stirrings behind her, of how many of these children had witnessed their parents and grandparents succumbing to starvation, and those memories would stay with them like scars. She wrote that most of them probably did not even have the dignity of knowing whether or not their parents were alive, some of them witnessing their beloved parents, uncles, aunts, grandparents, being sent away on death marches, and in post-war Europe, innocent children's German nationality was a stain.

But editors back home had already told her that orphaned German children were not part of the post-war discourse.

When Rick knocked his soft code on the door, Kate gathered her story and hid it in the briefcase on the floor. He stood in the freezing hallway, rubbing his hands together, peering inward to the little body nestled in Kate's bed.

Kate glanced up and down the empty corridor. She'd become used to looking out for unexpected eyes watching every move since she'd arrived in Europe. "The child is sleeping. Come in, Rick," she whispered.

He stepped in, standing in the shadows close beside her. Kate felt her cheeks flush. In the narrow room, she folded her arms around her body, a sudden, unexpected shiver passing through her. Rick smelt of soap, and cigarettes and wine, and she closed her eyes a moment to settle herself.

"Don't take this the wrong way, but you can have my room if you want it. You need to sleep tonight." His voice was so close, she could have reached out and touched the words as they left his lips.

"I'll be fine here with her." She would not leave the child alone.

The girl stirred and let out a little sigh.

Rick's eyes held with hers a moment, darkening, before he pulled his gaze away, glancing toward the closed door. He lowered his voice to a mute whisper. "Things aren't as hopeless as you make them out to be, you know."

Kate took a step back. He'd heard her conversation with Harvey.

"Getting the truth through back home or saving this poor child?" she whispered, still staring up at him.

He held her gaze in the dark. "Both."

Feeling exhaustion sinking in, she slid down to sit on the floor.

He sat down next to her; his hands folded loosely in front of him. "But you are right, people at home need to know what's going on, because if they did know, I believe they'd act differently too."

Kate rested her chin in her hands. "The latest thing, so I'm told, is that some papers are only accepting positive news stories." She turned to him, incredulous. "Editors say the war is done. That folks don't want anything negative. They have moved on." She studied the floor. "But how can that possibly be? If people saw this…" She waved her hand about the room.

"I agree. We all need to look beyond our own noses, *Katia*." Rick's tone was low and firm.

Kate started at the way he spoke her name. It was the way her father had pronounced it when she was a little girl, *Katia*, the Italian name her Italian parents had given her, not realizing that her school friends in New York would anglicize it the moment she walked into class. She'd not been Katia since she was five years old. When she'd asked her father to stop using her Italian name, he'd looked at her sadly and had called her Kate after that.

She reached for a shawl that she kept on her bed to wrap herself up warmly under the single, inadequate blanket on the freezing Berlin nights. Now, she drew it around her shoulders, imagining it still held the scent of her mother's lavender laundry powder.

Rick yawned, exaggerating the exhaustion that lined his handsome face, the faint traceries around his brown eyes, and the paleness of his formerly tanned cheeks. Kate knew she could look little better.

"I've missed connections with some of my editors," Kate said, "so I don't know which of my stories have even been published at this point. What's more, my checks all go to my mom, so I have no idea what's getting syndicated in the newspapers and what's not." She circled her finger on the dusty wooden floorboards. "But I'm determined to keep sending my more in-depth articles back home." She looked up, holding his gaze. "Even if no editor will take them on."

"I wouldn't expect anything less," he murmured, his words hanging in the shadows.

His eyes crinkled.

There was a silence.

"You're missing home?" he said, his voice cracking on the upswing.

Her heart beat a little faster under the warm shawl. Home was complicated. "I'm getting letters from my mom, sporadically."

But not her little sister. Not Bianca. They'd hardly spoken since their papa died. Kate fought hard to bite back the memories of how close their childhood was, how they'd grown up sharing the same room, whispering secrets to each other every night that they solemnly promised would not go any further, holding each other through thunderstorms and counting the seconds after the lightning struck, freezing winter nights when Kate read her sister stories by the light of a torch under the bedclothes while Bianca snuggled up next to her. Summer days spent out in New York, swinging their arms while their papa walked them to the museums, or to Washington Square Park. But that was all gone now. Gone for good and replaced with the very deepest of wars.

Rick pulled out a cigarette holder, silver, and offered her one. "This experience," he said, "being in the aftermath of war. Smelling it, and seeing it, and walking in its reprehensible footprints. It will stay with me when I'm back in the States."

"I know," Kate said. She refused the cigarette.

The little girl sighed and turned in her sleep.

"Who drew out the debate champion in you?" he asked, lighting up and regarding her through the smoke. "Harvey looked mighty downcast after you were done. You don't want to annihilate him, you know. But I liked the way you challenged him."

A small smile escaped from Kate's lips. "It was my papa."

Rick's expression grew more serious. "Your dad?"

"He was a school teacher, after migrating to New York from Italy with my mom before the Great War."

Rick nodded, not asking her about the way she'd spoken of her dad in the past tense. Instead, he watched her intently, and she took this as a sign from him to talk on.

"He came to America as a stonemason, worked in Connecticut for a time, then went back to university... NYU, and trained as a high-school teacher while working shifts at the shipyards on the weekends."

"He sounds very special."

Kate shot him a sideways look. "Papa taught me to take an interest in the world, to understand how politics underline everything there is." She let out a short sigh. "He was my best friend. When he died, I..."

Rick was quiet. The expression on his face was hard to read. Rick didn't indulge in gossip. That was something she'd realized from day one. He noticed everything; she saw that. But he kept his cards close to his chest and was respected and trusted by everyone.

"My dad was killed ten years ago, in the winter of '36." She still winced at the hateful words.

"I'm sorry, *Katia*." He leaned forward, resting his cigarette between his legs.

Kate drew her arms around her knees. "He stepped out to go to the store. To buy *me* a ream of paper for an assignment." She took in a shaking breath. "I asked him to go." She caught Rick's gaze. "He was hit by a car going too fast."

And then, her little sister, Bianca, had blamed Kate. Thrown herself into a passionate fury and blamed her older sister.

Next to her, Rick stared straight ahead, a muscle twitching in his cheek.

Kate looked up at him. "And you?" her words were almost lost in the quiet. "Who encouraged you to go into journalism?"

"My mom," he said softly. "She loves history and follows politics like a demon." His expression softened. "I have her to thank for throwing every book at me under the sun when I was growing up." He tapped her on the knee. "But I'll tell you one thing, Katia, I would have liked to be up against you in debate. I wonder who would have won?"

Kate leaned back against the wall, playing with the fringes of her shawl. "If you'd been there, I would have made sure I won at all costs." Slowly, she lifted her eyes to his.

He let out a short laugh, his eyes lighting up, intent on her. "Well," he whispered, "We'd see about that."

Kate flushed, looking away from him. Her eyes caught on the child's old hessian kitbag, and then, her hands stilled on the shawl.

Rick followed her gaze.

"We'll have to search her things," Kate said. She'd avoided opening the bedraggled bag. Her inbuilt respect for property belonging to others had stopped her brazenly searching it and looking for information about their strange little guest. But, if they were to help her, they had no choice. If she was carrying any identity papers, they'd be invaluable in assisting the child.

"Yes," Rick said. "She's too young to have a *Kennkarte*."

Kate reached for the little girl's knapsack. One of the green identity papers that Nazis had issued to all their citizens would have helped, no matter what sickening distaste Kate felt for the things. But Kate pulled out only three items from the child's bag: an old, moth-eaten sweater, an empty brown paper bag that only held a few biscuit crumbs, and a worn-down pencil that had been chewed at the top.

Kate stood up, tucking the single blanket over the sleeping child. How long had she been searching for her family? What unimaginable experiences had she endured? The fact that the little girl had made it to her house showed a determination Kate admired. Kate knew she had to finish the child's quest. She had to find her a safe haven, in spite of the dangers that were everywhere in this hellish place.

Outside, rain thundered on the windowpane. Kate turned to Rick, her eyes locking with his. She'd miss his companionship when they returned to America. Rick held eye contact with her, before Kate gave out a huge yawn. He reached an arm around her shoulder, and, her eyes searching his face a long moment, she shuffled downwards and leaned against his shoulder, her eyes closing, while he stroked her head. It seemed he wasn't interested in anything more than friendship either. Which was a relief.

Finally, she succumbed to the waves of sleep.

Chapter Three

Kate

Berlin, March 1946

Dawn cast a gray, pearly light over Berlin and Kate opened her eyes, sitting up and stretching her aching body, stiffened from a night on the hard floor. She'd ended up sleeping with her head in the crook of Rick's shoulder, glad of the soft sound of his breathing and the warmth of his woolen sweater under her head when she'd woken in the night. Now, he'd gone, and the room felt empty and hollow, save the little girl still sleeping.

Kate stood up and moved to check on the child. It was touching, the way the orphan had trusted both her and Rick. She smiled as she remembered how Rick had spoken in soft German on the steps of her ruined family home. Kate had distinctly heard him say, *Amerikanisch*, and that was when the little girl had come forward into Kate's open arms.

A note caught Kate's eye on her desk, dust motes floating in the cold air above it.

Katia,

I've gone to try and sort something out for our little friend. Trust me, I have an idea that just might work, but I may not be back until this afternoon. Keep her safe and stay in the hotel.

Rick.
PS. I am glad you slept.

*

The yellow sun glinted through the dull gray clouds by mid-morning, a pale weak orb whose rays would only provide the dimmest of warmth. Kate straightened the pages on her desk, her neatly typed story growing nicely.

The hunk of bread that she'd saved for the child from her own breakfast sat alongside a couple of slices of liver sausage, likely made of wood shavings, and a glass of milk, along with a treasured apple, something that Kate knew would never reach the hands of starving German children who were out in the Berlin cold.

As they'd traveled through the coldest countries of Europe during the desolate months of December, January and February, she'd felt so disheartened at the sight of people in cities queuing for food, women in old pinafores doling out soups from enormous canteens for the crowds of starving citizens, their freezing fingers wrapping around broths fortified with oatmeal. It was only in the rural areas that farmers had stockpiled food legally, making preserves from their own fruit trees, pickling their own vegetables.

But survival in the cities had relied largely on the black market under the Nazis, and now the British and American authorities were cracking down on black markets, checking farms, and stopping cars that moved past checkpoints.

It was as if the whole nation was exhausted, its citizens only grateful that the countries whom they'd fought against were now providing them with a means of survival.

Kate checked on the still sleeping child. The dirt that streaked her cheeks seemed more ingrained in daylight. Her blond hair was matted and greasy, sticking to her head in knotted tufts. The little girl did not look close to waking, so Kate collected her bath towel from where it hung over the end of the plain iron bedstead, folded it over her arm, and went down the corridor to the women's restroom that served this floor of the hotel.

After showering quickly, letting the trickle of water soak her glossy dark curls, and rubbing her hair and body dry as best as she could with the scrap of a towel, Kate checked up and down the empty corridors.

It should be safe to allow the orphan to wash.

Back outside her room, she turned the key in the lock, only to stop, starting at the sight of the little girl sitting up in bed, her legs tented in a mound under the blanket, eyeing the breakfast that Kate had left for her on the table by the bed.

Kate clasped the large key to the room in her hand. She chatted softly in English and gave the child the extra bread she'd saved, and the awful sausage, which the girl ate quickly and efficiently after her soup. Kate held out her towel and made washing movements with her body. Solemnly, the little girl placed her mug on Kate's desk and followed Kate out of the room.

The child walked trustingly; one hand tucked into Kate's underneath the harsh light of the bare light bulbs that swung in the ghostly corridors of the hotel.

Kate handed the child soap and a clean towel, and the girl's eyes caught with Kate's. She disappeared inside the bathroom and closed the door.

Kate hovered. If anyone caught her, she'd have explaining to do. Still, no one came down the hall. Kate leaned against the wall and waited. After several minutes had passed, she knocked on the door and heard the efficient, unspoken response, the sound of the bath plug being pulled.

How long had it been since the little girl had enjoyed a wash? It was impossible to imagine what she could have endured while trying to get home, in the winter, in the forests, trying to find her family, all alone. What had the child's life been like before the war? Before Hitler took over this country and terrified his citizens into obedience? If the house where they'd found the girl was any indication, she must come from a wealthy family, but their home was smashed up, the family nowhere in sight, and all that was left was a lost little orphan.

Kate jumped at the sound of the door handle turning and drew a hand to her mouth when the girl appeared, her body scrubbed clean, her blond hair wet from the shower, sticking to her head and rendering her already huge eyes even bigger than before. And when she sent Kate a sudden, tentative smile, Kate let out a little cry of relief. She reached out her hand, and the child took it, curling her roughened fingers around Kate's.

Kate had taken her bedding down to the hotel laundry, exchanged it for fresh sheets and a clean blanket, and she'd exhausted every resource she knew for entertaining a child who both spoke a foreign language and did not speak. They'd played several games of tic-tac-toe, drawn pictures together, looked out the window while Kate attempted to chat in soothing tones about what they could see, about what Berlin must have been like before it was destroyed, before finally, the girl had fallen asleep against Kate's shoulder again, her hair streaming down her back now, her face scrubbed clean. She was beautiful.

When a cold, leaden rain started beating against the window, Kate shuddered to think how many hundreds, thousands of other children were still out there in the freezing cold.

Rick's knock finally sounded at the door around noon. Kate rushed to open it, only to stand back, stifling a gasp. Her eyes flew from handsome Rick to the woman next to him. She wore a thick fur coat and a fur hat, her burgundy hair falling in dressed waves around her shoulders.

Kate folded her arms around her old sweater, and stifled the burning, inexplicable urge to tell Rick that this woman may be glamorous but she was not right for him.

Silently, she stepped aside to let the handsome pair into her humble hotel room.

Chapter Four

Kate

Berlin, March 1946

Kate draped one arm over the girl, tucking the child's head into the crook of her shoulder. The jeep rattled along the outskirts of Berlin, Rick at the wheel, his friend, Claudia, by his side. Kate gazed out the window at the still, silent German farmland. The child had fallen into an exhausted sleep. Trees dotted the hushed, eerie landscape, their leafless branches silhouetted against the gray afternoon sky. Out here, the fields seemed imbued with a deep sense of loss and mourning, a melancholy was set deep into the silent surrounds.

Kate stayed quiet, and Rick and Claudia's soft chatter in German was all at once comforting and chilling in the confines of the vehicle. The intonations of the language that all Americans had learned to revile and fear these past seven years sounded strange coming from someone Kate was being encouraged to trust. Here they were, reliant on a German woman to help save an innocent child. And she wasn't just any child. Kate had felt deep affinity the moment she laid eyes on the orphan, and over the past twenty-four hours, she'd felt a warmth, almost a love, opening inside her chest, something that had been absent for a decade.

The little girl had made her feel alive again.

The jeep moved through war-torn, desolate villages, and when they passed by a signpost to Bergen-Belsen, Kate's stomach sickened, but she refused to turn her gaze away.

She was still haunted every night after their tours of the concentration camps. Images of the millions of innocents, taken as Nazi prisoners, forced to work themselves to the bone in the death camps, their skeletal, emaciated frames pushed to the end as they strove to carry out all the hard labor that was necessary for the Nazi's war machine.

What had it all been for?

Claudia turned to the back seat, her beautiful face searching the still, mute orphan. *Who knew what this child had seen?*

Kate shivered and drew her jacket closer around her body.

"Thank you for taking care of the little girl," Claudia said. She spoke without accent. Her English was cut from an expensive-sounding cloth.

"It is nothing," Kate said. She tightened her grip on the girl's shoulder.

Claudia's gaze moved to the girl, her eyes softening. "I understand that it must be hard for you to entrust her to a stranger," she said.

All Kate could do was nod. "Yes." Claudia didn't know the half of it. Rick had assured her that Claudia was reliable, an old friend, his family had known Claudia's all his life. Claudia, he said, would leave no stone unturned to find the child's family. But once they came to the woman's home, Kate promised herself if there was any question in her mind, she wouldn't leave the child alone with her. She'd insist they turn right around and go back to the American zone in Berlin.

The child stirred. She reached out and placed her small hand in Kate's, her huge eyes luminous.

Claudia said something soothing in German, and the little girl buried her head in Kate's side again. Kate closed her eyes. The child had come to trust her. She bit back ideas of taking her home to America. That was crazy, and yet, what was not crazy in this godforsaken place?

Kate stroked her little friend's head.

"You are worried?"

Kate sent Claudia a strained smile. "I have grown fond of the child."

Claudia's beautiful green eyes were sad. "My sister lost her husband during the war, so her two children are with us in our home just outside our town, Celle. My papa will adore her. She will have playmates. We will take care of her. Please, understand she will be well looked after."

Kate caught Rick's gaze in the jeep's rearview mirror, his dark eyes were unfathomable. "She will be safe, Katia," he said.

Kate's hand stilled on the girl's shoulder. "She will need time before she is ready to talk. Please, she needs patience and understanding."

"Believe me, Papa has all the patience in the world," Claudia said.

Kate chewed on her lip.

Rick's eyes flashed with her own in the rearview mirror again. "Katia, my family used to come and stay here with the Schroders between the wars. Claudia's dad was a role model to me. Perhaps more so than other people..." Rick's voice trailed off, and he cleared his throat.

Kate clung to the child. Rick had only mentioned his family once. Last night, and then, he'd only talked of his mother. As a group, she and her fellow correspondents seemed to tread carefully around each other, not opening up about their private lives. Despite all they'd experienced together, they'd kept things professional among themselves. But Rick's past, his family, his life outside being a journalist... it would be good to know more.

"And then," Claudia picked up the story, "I went to study in America for university, and Rick and I were both at Harvard together."

"I see." She was being a little daft about Claudia. Kate knew that. And yet, the way the child had placed her hand so trustingly in hers... and now she had to leave the orphan with strangers.

Strangers whom Rick trusted, Kate reminded herself sternly. Strangers who were those very folks she'd spent yesterday evening trying to convince Harvey were deserving of American help and sympathy.

But as they passed through a tiny bombed-out village, Claudia's conversation took a sudden change of direction.

"My town," Claudia said, in soft, halting English, "Celle, was spared any major destruction during the war, unlike these villages we are passing through now." Nothing was left except for empty shells where cottages had once lined a narrow street and, instinctively, Kate tucked the child's head back under her arm.

"You were very fortunate, Claudia." Kate drew in a breath at the sight of an old leather suitcase half buried in the snow and strewn among the tufts of tangle-weed on the edge of the road. *There'd been too many one-way journeys in this country during the war.*

"My sister, Papa and I survived only because my father was a musician, a composer and opera conductor," Claudia said. "Papa still went to Berlin and Hannover to work. Hitler kept the opera houses open during the war, and Papa never had to fight. He was, on occasion, drafted as a radio operator. He mastered the Morse code. The rest of the time, he still conducted." Claudia lowered her voice. "Papa was no resistance fighter. He was a genuine pacifist. Thankfully something Hitler never knew."

Kate still gazed out the window. *All those Jewish musicians, taken away forever, never to lift an instrument again, and your papa was able to work.*

When they entered Claudia's hometown of Celle, Claudia pointed out shops, houses, in German, talking animatedly to Rick, whose eyes crinkled at the sides. They passed by exquisite, medieval half-timbered houses, built with traditional, high-pitched roofs.

"We are nearly at my home now." Claudia turned around excitedly and spoke to the little girl.

The child sat up, one hand still holding Kate's as she peered out the windows of the jeep at the obviously prosperous streets.

And why had this town survived when so many others were utterly destroyed?

"While my hometown only suffered one attack last year, something happened here that was… unspeakable," Claudia said, seeming to read Kate's mind.

Kate tensed. She leaned forward in her seat.

"In April last year, a train," Claudia went on, her voice barely a murmur in English, "on the way to Bergen-Belsen, containing prisoners was bombed here in Celle. It was a train with dozens of cattle cars. But we knew that the train did not contain cattle. It contained people—people wearing the gray-blue stripes of the concentration camp uniforms. Four thousand people destined for Bergen-Belsen."

Kate checked the orphan's face for a reaction, cautious in case she understood even a smattering of English, but the child was silent, her eyes staring straight ahead, seemingly impervious to the sound of Claudia's words as they rolled on.

They turned out of the historic center, traveling along a road overhung with skeletal trees, where the houses were larger, set back from the road with gardens half covered in snow, far more prosperous than those packed tightly in the town overlooking the cobbled squares.

"Three squadrons of the United States Air Force attacked the trains," Claudia continued, "bombing the train tracks and the buildings of the train depot. They did not realize that thousands of people were crowded inside the freight train."

Kate drew a hand to her mouth.

"*Claudia…*" Rick warned.

"No, continue," Kate said. She ran a jerky hand through her hair. The chance to talk properly with a German citizen who had not been commandeered for an interview was rare.

Claudia turned around in her seat. "I understand that you are horrified by the suffering of my fellow Germans, but it's also important to understand that even this small town has a terrible burden of guilt."

Kate nodded slowly, holding the other woman's gaze. "Go on."

"The United States, in their B-26s, as well as bombing the train filled with prisoners being shunted to Bergen-Belsen, also bombed one of the nearby trains at the depot, which was filled with ammunition, and one of that train's cars exploded. German SS guards opened machine-gun fire on the attacking planes, and also shot any prisoners trying to flee."

Kate took in a shaking breath. "Did you say *four thousand* prisoners were in the trains?"

"About two thousand of those were killed in that one attack, just near here, instantly. The others, many of them starving, escaped."

Rick turned into a driveway, bringing the jeep to a stop outside an old manor house, its soft pink façade glittering in a burst of late-afternoon sunlight. Kate gazed up at the beautiful, three-story house, with rows of white-painted windows looking out over a circular drive, the gravel neatly raked.

Beyond this, a large garden was dappled with snow, and the first glimpses of daffodils poked their heads through the freezing earth, snowdrops bobbed under a huge tree, while a glistening stream ran through the garden, its bubbling sound the only accompaniment to the stillness of the afternoon.

"I was in the kitchen when the first lot of bedraggled, bloody prisoners dressed in striped prison garb approached the house from the woods." Claudia pointed toward the garden, with the towering tree and the snowdrops. "I ran out and administered first aid to as many as I could. Some of them were so scared and shocked that they ran further away from Celle, trying to escape." Claudia lowered her head. "Our very neighbors drove the escaped prisoners away. People I have known since childhood picked up guns and shovels and chased them, hounding them until they fell, and then killing them. The SS guards also opened fire on them. Then, the four hundred or so remaining of the four thousand were rounded up and marched to Bergen-Belsen."

Kate stayed quiet. Rick placed his hands on his knees, staring out at the lovely garden. It still seemed impossible to imagine such cruelty in this beautiful place.

"It was my neighbors, Kate, the people I know, who hunted them out." Claudia's voice was devoid of emotion, but her expression held the gravity of an entire generation.

Kate leaned closer to Claudia, suddenly reaching out a hand to the German woman and stroking her shoulder.

"I hope you will understand that Papa, my sister Greta and I will give your little orphan a home, solace, and peace," she said. "I know you care about her. And I want you to know—you can trust us."

Kate tried to say something, but her throat closed over, and instead, she found herself unable to speak. Silently, she nodded. It was all she could do.

Claudia turned her gaze toward her beautiful home, wiping a stray tear from her cheeks. "You are going to Nuremberg tomorrow?"

Kate nodded again, dumbly.

Claudia cleared her throat. "This was the darkest time in our history. We are honored to bring this little girl into our home, and to try and put things right, at least for her."

"I understand," Kate whispered. *More than you realize.*

Her hand still clasped in the child's; she could hardly bear to leave her.

But she must.

Rick opened the car door, letting in a flurry of cold air.

Kate was silent as she climbed out of the jeep, waiting and watching while the child looked up at the grand manor house. In the soft afternoon light, the pink-painted façade of the old family home looked nostalgic, as if from a fairy tale.

Such beauty never belonged inside the Third Reich.

The child drew close to Kate again, burying her head in Kate's trouser leg.

And then a man in his sixties appeared on the front steps, holding out his arms to Rick. Claudia's papa.

Kate shaded her eyes against the sudden streaming of the sun through the branches of the trees, while a breeze whispered from the forests that surrounded this old German family home. The child did not move, instead threading her little hand around Kate's leg, her grasp on Kate's trousers intensifying.

While Rick hugged Claudia's papa, the old man holding Rick at arm's length, his eyes misting over, Kate crouched down, Claudia next to her, gently disentangling the child's hand from her leg. "You will be safe," she said to her little friend, and Claudia translated her words into German. "I promise. These are friends of Mr. Rick's, and look, you will have a beautiful house to live in, and children to play with, and food to keep you warm and help you grow."

Rick and Claudia's father came down toward her, making introductions.

"We cannot stay, I'm sorry," Rick said, when Claudia asked them to stay for dinner. "We have to return the jeep, and we have a very early departure for Nuremberg in the morning." He pressed his hands into Claudia's papa's hand, and tears streamed down the old man's face freely now. "We will meet again. And it will be in better circumstances, Georg."

The old man hugged him tightly before letting go.

Rick came back to stand by Kate, and gently he placed an arm around her shoulder. "You can thank Kate for saving this child. She insisted."

The old man blew Kate kisses in an eternal language that would never be stymied by wars. When two children, dressed in red coats and bright matching mittens, came skipping out the front door, only to come to a sudden halt in front of Claudia and her guests, they studied the child who stood so close to Kate.

Claudia bent down and spoke to her nieces in German, inclining her head toward the orphan.

Kate fought to slow the beating of her heart, until slowly, both the children came forward to the orphan child and held out their gloved hands to her.

Kate stood in silence, freezing white air curling from her lips, Rick's hand still softly draped on her shoulder, giving it a little squeeze. And around them, only the sound of the brook bubbling away contentedly broke the soft melody of the surrounding forest.

Solemnly, the child took one last look at Kate, and stepped forward to stand with the other children, her old kitbag hauled over one shoulder, and Kate fought the lump in her throat.

"We will make a new life for her," Claudia said, suddenly reaching out and taking Kate's hand. "Papa, Greta and I will take care of her, and we will leave no stone unturned to find out who she is."

The child turned her huge eyes to Kate once more, and one of the other children leaned down, whispering something in her ear. The orphan sent Kate a final searching look.

"Go, my little friend," Kate said, sending the child the bravest smile she could muster, her heart ripping out of her chest. It was as if this one orphan represented every innocent person she'd seen on this trip. "God protect you," she whispered to herself.

But then, suddenly overwhelmed with sadness, knowing she'd never likely see this little girl again, she leaned down and held out her arms, desperate to feel the warmth of the child near her one last time.

And the child threw herself into Kate's outstretched arms, tucking her face into Kate's hair. And Kate closed her eyes and held the little girl close. "You, for me," she whispered, "are a symbol of the future. Go, lead a wonderful life. An unlimited life and believe in hope."

Kate held the child at arm's length, and suddenly, she turned to Claudia, her voice coming out urgently. "Claudia, if you discover her family are in the Soviet-occupied territories…"

Claudia nodded, her expression darkening. "I understand. I will do everything I can to help them."

"If you have to… get them out," Kate's voice shook. "Forgive me. I have seen too much, and yet I have experienced nothing compared to you."

Rick kneeled down next to Kate and stroked the child's head.

"You have our word," Claudia's papa said, reaching forward and laying a hand on Kate's shoulder.

The little girl followed the other children up the steps into her new home, her haversack swinging, trusting them.

Rick took Kate's hand in his, and she swallowed hard as she watched her little friend disappear inside the house.

Rick maneuvered the heavy jeep down the driveway, the tires crackling on the gravel. Kate found herself staring at the brook, its water running clear as transparent silk, rushing over little rocks. They drove down the road with its strange, gnarled trees, and grand houses hidden behind large gates. The air of desolation and tragedy out here in this countryside was overwhelming.

Rick's gaze flickered toward her. "You all right?" he murmured.

She nodded, but her stomach lurched, filled with pictures of prisoners running down this very road, stragglers, who for no reason had been ripped out of their homes, pulled from their families, and herded like cattle to the slaughterhouse. And just at the moment they thought they had escaped, their own countrymen had turned on them. It was unthinkable.

"Tomorrow, we go to see the very worst of them on trial," she said. "The men who ordered everything. All of it."

Rick reached his hand across the seat, only to draw it back when Kate huddled further against her window. "Are you okay, Katia?"

He slowed the jeep as they neared the outskirts of the impossibly pretty town, driving by the last of the traditional village houses with their high, sloped roofs.

"We have to be okay, Rick," she whispered. "For the sake of everybody who died here. Don't you see?" She turned to him; her face streaked with tears. "We have life, and that is a gift that has been taken so brutally from so many these past years."

"And you have saved one child and given her a wonderful new start," Rick whispered. "Saving one life is something mighty in the face of all this death."

Kate's expression softened, and his brown eyes lingered on hers, crinkling into a warm smile.

"That makes you a very special person, Katia," he said.

"Oh, I don't know," she whispered.

"I do," he said.

The last of the afternoon light started to fade, and a pearly twilight settled over the desolate, haunted countryside as he turned the jeep away from Celle into the gathering dusk.

Chapter Five

Kate

Nuremberg, March 1946

The bar at the hotel in Nuremberg was swarming with newspaper-men. Kate slipped onto a high stool between Rick and Harvey Milton and ordered a martini. It was all she could do to put today's journey out of mind; the first half in a train, the second in a rattling old bus. The ruins of the old town of Nuremberg were breathtaking. Bombed and burned-out houses hit first by the RAF, then by the Americans, who had smashed everything from the moats to the quaint towers that were old before America was even begun.

In the crumbling city that used to feature on Christmas cards, chimneys stuck up out of nowhere, hollowed-out windows were like blackened eyes, piles and piles of rubble were swept away into dry mountains of dust. And over the whole city there still hung the echoes of hundreds of thousands of voices shouting "*Sieg Heil!*" along with the sounds of marching feet. It was impossible to imagine the Nazi ghosts of this town ever being laid to rest.

Kate had tossed and turned all night in the hotel back in Berlin. She'd woken in a hot sweat, searching and scrabbling in her bed for the orphan in her blankets. Her dreams were broken by visions of the little girl lost. Kate had sat up in bed, hating that the child had been left to wander the silent forests of her bleeding country alone.

How could the men on trial tomorrow pay for what they'd done?

"So. We've made it. Last stop. We did it." Harvey's hair was slicked back and his eyes bright. He leaned his forearms in their shirtsleeves on the crowded bar. "What's your plan, Kate?"

"I'm going back to Washington."

Rick's hand stilled from pushing a cardboard coaster around in circles on the wooden bar.

Kate leaned closer to Harvey and held her drink aloft. "Writing longer stories, something more comprehensive. I'm done with the lack of authenticity in what we have to write here."

Harvey flashed her a smile. "Honey, every print reporter's known since 1940 that radio is the way to go. Radio City. New York's where it's all happening, Kate. It'll be a gas."

Kate blew out a sigh and cupped her hands under her chin. "You forget," Kate said. "I'm a woman. 'All the jobs,' as you put it, will go to the men."

Rick's brows knitted, and he frowned into his beer.

Harvey nudged Rick. "And you? Going up for an executive role at Radio City too? Going to give me some competition, are you? A run for my money?"

"Not likely." Rick tipped his beer back and took a long drink. He placed it back down carefully and turned to Harvey. "I'm a reporter through and through. Executive roles hold no interest for me."

Harvey's eyes widened a moment, but then he put on his famous grin again. "Well. All I can say is that's good for me. 'Cos I'm certain that if you and I both went for an executive role; you'd win hands down."

Rick pushed back his bar stool and stood up, clapping Harvey on the back. "You can keep your executive roles, Harvey." He eyeballed the other journalist. "And you know why."

Harvey tweaked the straw in his drink, his cheeks reddening, eyebrows up to his hairline.

"I'm hitting the sack," Rick said. "Night, Kate. Harvey." He nodded and walked off.

Kate opened her mouth, but nothing came out. Harvey peered down into his drink, and she felt a light tap on her shoulder.

Leonard Andrews was right by her side, his button eyes scrutinizing her, his hair combed back over his balding head. He eased his frame onto Rick's bar stool.

"Kate, what're your plans for tomorrow?"

Kate sent him a resigned smile. "Guess I'll be writing up an unpublished storm in the Palace of Justice, Len."

Leonard sent her a sad smile. "Joe's come down with the flu and he's contracted to report on Goering's trial for CBS radio."

Kate stilled. *Goering.* Whoever covered his trial for CBS would be syndicated all over America.

"He's laid up in the hotel and won't be out for at least a week. You interested in covering for him?"

Kate placed her martini down on the bar. Harvey's words rang in her ears. *Radio.* Was she shooting herself in the foot ignoring that medium's phenomenal growth?

Len leaned in closer to her. "I put a good word in for you, and they've agreed to let a woman cover it. Although..."

Although. Kate folded her arms and waited for the catch.

A woman's laughter rang through the bar. Only a handful of women were here alongside the male reporters, but they were working behind the scenes, producing, editing, secretarial roles.

"The program managers stood adamant that a woman's voice would not carry authority in a man's field."

Kate swallowed her own dry laugh.

"But I insisted that you were exceptional, and finally they relented."

"Well then. Thanks, Len."

"They say they'll let you cover the story as long as you understand this is a fill-in for an emergency, and nothing more."

Kate pushed back her bar stool. "I'll be ready at eight a.m. sharp."

Len looked at her, his eyes narrowing in appreciation. "You know, taking on assignments that others are forced to give up could be a smart plan."

Kate sent him a wan smile. "Well, Len, you might be right there."

The following morning, Kate was at the courtroom door of the Medieval Palace of Justice, guards checking her identity card, hurrying along with her fellow war correspondents in American, British and French uniforms up the makeshift wooden steps to what she was certain was going to be one of the most harrowing experiences of her life.

Inside, she settled in the press gallery, sitting down on a hard wooden bench. The courtroom was filled with the hum of the ventilating system, and the murmur of hundreds of voices. Fluorescent light bulbs lit the room, and the dock and judges were especially illuminated for the photographers and newsreel cameramen by powerful floodlights.

But Kate's eyes flew to the prisoners' dock. And stilled. Seeing the culprits of Hitler's regime sitting there was like one of those visions that comes between waking and sleep. She only wished that, were she to close her eyes, the last six years of the world's history would be obliterated for good.

And yet, here they were, right in the same room as Kate. The Nazi architects of the Third Reich sitting in two rows: some in brown suits, some in military uniform, mouths set, arms folded, all men. Implacable. Not one of them showing any remorse, guilt or sadness.

And in the front left-hand corner sat the worst of them all. Goering, one arm resting over the back of the wooden docks as if he was entitled to do what he liked. As if he was running his own trial.

These, the men who had turned Europe into the raging mess that Kate had witnessed in the last ten months. Burned-out homes, human beings crawling around like rats in the merciless cold out there, the unspeakable misery. And these men had caused it all.

Extermination camps, mass executions, carnage, fatal psychological effects.

And in the end, one innocent orphan girl who seemed to represent it all.

Kate's hands shook uncontrollably in her lap.

"Attention in the court!"

Everyone rose. Kate's stomach dived as the four judges and their deputies emerged in single file from a door in the main wall of the hall in black gowns.

Only the Russians stood out in uniform.

Rick's hand touched her shoulder a moment.

They all sat down, and the silence was only broken by the sharp, punctuated answers of those on trial, the cold questioning of the attorneys.

Throughout the entire proceedings, one question haunted Kate like a refrain: *how could they have done what they did?* And one thought dominated her mind: *Hitler's ghost was in this room overseeing them all.*

Goering, famed for being charming and confident, sat mocking and aloof the entire time. The man didn't flinch. He looked like he owned the place.

And when called, Goering said he was so devoted to Hitler that he would do it all again. His ugly, licentious face seemed to gloat, and the entire room turned cold.

Kate could not look at him. *How can we both be human?*

After the last day, Kate sat down in the makeshift CBS studio, put on her headphones and read her story, her voice deliberately deepened, and every trace of her New York accent removed.

Never in the history of mankind have individual men been accused of so many and such terrible crimes as the defendants at Nuremberg.

Today, Hermann Goering, the most famous survivor of the Third Reich, seen as a crafty and clever defendant, who many thought had initially outfoxed his prosecutors, failed, as a politician, as a soldier and as a man.

Goering showed himself as Hitler's companion, a former Reichsmarschall, and wearer of the Grand Cross. He was known to be vain, conceited, a striver for popularity, untruthful, inaccessible, greedy and with an ego that was unquenchable.

No one could have demonstrated this more clearly than he did on the witness stand here in Nuremberg. Believing himself to be descended from the Nibelung, and the true descendant and heir of some superior, supreme race of human beings, his testimony was full of the reprehensible euphemisms that the Nazis adopted as subterfuge for their unspeakable crimes against their fellow human beings.

We have heard Goering's catalog of crimes and it is truly terrible: the murder of millions under the disguise of a final solution, the courtroom sitting in silence while they were told that for the Fuhrer, Goering had built up the Gestapo, created the first concentration camps, and was one of the five important leaders at the Hossbach Conference in 1937, when Hitler announced his plans for war.

Goering commanded the Luftwaffe during the attacks on Poland, and during all the attacks that followed. He made many admissions during the trial to the use of slave labor.

He ordered the special treatment—murder—of Polish workers in Germany.

He was active in the pillaging of occupied countries.

He persecuted Jews, not only in Germany, but in the occupied countries, and he was instrumental in extending anti-Jewish laws in those occupied countries of the Third Reich.

Goering instructed Himmler and Heydrich to bring about the final solution to the so-called "Jewish question" within the German sphere of influence in Europe.

As the driving force of the horrors inflicted by the Nazis, he was second only to Hitler himself.

Goering was the leading personality in wars of aggression, both as a political and a military leader.

At the beginning of the trial, Goering declared himself not guilty of the charges laid against him, including the new charge of "crimes against humanity" for atrocities committed by a power against its own citizens.

For nine days, he was given a chance to speak without interruption. He appointed himself as representative of all the others accused, and undertook to fill their common background, and to relate the historical political events as he saw them, the beginnings of Hitler and the National Socialist Party, the Munich Putsch, the struggle for power.

His own statements, in which he tried to hide his guilt, only served to establish his true culpability. Indeed, no one could find excuses for the evidence presented against him.

When the exasperated American chief prosecutor Robert H. Jackson threw his earphones on the table and stood, he criticized Goering's arrogant and contemptuous attitude toward the tribunal.

Goering attempted to hit back with a few shabby, childish evasions about having not known what was going on in the camps, but was easily proved to have committed a terrible

*catalog of crimes, having a disastrous effect on Germany,
Poland, Hungary and France, along with every other country
invaded by the Nazis.*

*He was found guilty on all four counts of the indictment:
conspiracy, crimes against peace, war crimes and crimes
against humanity.*

Kate took off her earphones, walked out of the temporary studio,
ran to the nearest restroom, and was violently, crushingly, sick.

That evening, Kate sat with Rick, Harvey and Leonard Andrews
in the beer-stained bar. The chatter of newspapermen was subdued
after Goering's horrific trial, and the air around the small round
tables hung heavy with a film of thick cigarette smoke, the pearly
wall lights indistinct and blurred.

When a CBS programmer swiveled to the bar next to them, he
ordered a strong whiskey and turned his attention to Kate. "Miss
Mancini?" He leaned down and shook Kate's hand. "Your radio
coverage has been picked up by North American News Alliance
for distribution all over America. You've filed the first report back
home on Goering's trial. It will be your biggest story from post-
war Europe. I think congratulations are in order. You're clearly a
special lady!"

In spite of the horror that still overwhelmed her after sitting
through the trial, Kate raised her glass along with the men.

"You should get the pick of any job you want once you go back
home," the programmer said.

"I have no illusions about what to expect when I get back to
America," she said. "But I hope to get a contract." Although, her
hopes were not high. Talk was that women were being told to stay
home and have babies now the war was done. The men were back,
and they needed jobs more.

The programmer started chatting with the others, and Rick, next to her, softened his voice. "Katia, well done, you're a natural on radio, you know."

Kate sent him a sad smile; Goering's contemptuous face imprinted onto her mind.

He tilted his head to one side. "Come to New York," he said. "Radio City." He barely whispered the words.

She lifted her head, shaking it slightly. "Radio City?"

Rick moved a little closer. "Not just that, Katia, sweetheart."

She startled at the endearment.

"Rick, Kate?" Leonard placed his hand on Kate's shoulder, and she tore her gaze away from Rick. "What are you doing talking by yourselves? Come and be sociable. Join the conversation."

But Kate pushed aside her glass of Riesling. What had she been thinking? She'd let her guard slip and she was flirting with her friend. It wasn't on. Couldn't happen. She'd been more than aware of her own treacherous heart's responses when Rick was in her hotel room on the night the orphan came to stay. And she'd been so exhausted, she'd let herself sleep on his shoulder.

But that was enough. More than enough. Promises to herself about getting involved with men after her dad was killed aside, no woman in this industry could afford a relationship. Everyone knew a woman reporter who was with a guy, or married, or who even had the hint of an engagement hanging over her had far less chance of getting even casual work than a single girl, and as for getting a contract, she may as well hang a noose around her neck and declare herself dead as fall in love.

She knew of female reporters back home who took off their wedding rings before they went into the male-dominated newspapers and studios, hiding their marital status so they could keep working and not jeopardize their careers.

Kate said her farewells to the men and wound her way out of the crowded bar.

But as she walked through the smoke-filled room, she sensed Rick's eyes lingering on her and she blushed again at the way he'd looked at her, at the way she'd felt when he'd leaned a little closer.

Hands wrapped around her waist, she came to a stop at the old creaky elevator that led up to her hotel room.

Kate took the stairs instead, let herself in and leaned against the door. Falling in love with Rick was not an option.

She had to let him go.

Chapter Six

Frances

Connecticut, USA, March 1946

Frances slowed Cinnamon to a trot, ducking her head beneath the overhanging branches at the edge of the woods as the horse made her way into the fields outside Farmington. Even after an hour out riding, the delicious, dewy, early-morning air was still invigorating, and a soft mist hung over the glorious, country Connecticut vista that spread out ahead. The sound of Cinnamon's hooves crunching on old leaves and the sight of the daffodils and freesias poking their heads through the rich earth that lined the pathways through the forests caused Frances' spirits to soar in spite of the turmoil she felt inside.

She let the mare have her head, urging Cinnamon into a gallop up the wide fields that ran in the dip below Woodlands. She only reined the horse in at the spot where the field rose, affording her a view of her beautiful home atop the hill outside of Farmington, patting her and talking in the soft way she loved, the mare's sides heaving, ears pricked up and flanks beaded with sweat.

Even now, Frances still adored the sight of her glorious home. The architect who had designed Woodlands right outside one of the most picturesque towns in historic Connecticut must have been a genius. The white-painted mansion, with its rows of windows, shutters thrown wide, and its elegant verandahs with their white porticos blazed out as a symbol of gilded age prosperity, a neoclassical triumph. It was a gorgeous house, and after thirty-four years of marriage, Frances never failed to be thankful that it was hers to call her own.

She let Cinnamon walk up to the white farm gate that divided the field from the garden, once her sunken garden, which, before the war, had been filled with pink, white and mauve flowers, their upturned faces twinkling toward the sun, borders running along raked gravel pathways that were studded with follies, a summer house, a pigeon coot, and a little playhouse for the children, as well as rustic wooden benches dotted to make the most of the view over the valley below.

But since the war began, they'd let the garden grow over, due to labor and supply shortages, and now, only the follies sat, strange and forlorn, in the lawn that had run wild and was thick with neglected grasses and weeds.

Frances drew Cinnamon around to the stables, dismounting, loosening her girth and removing the saddle and bridle, washing her and brushing her down before leaving her in her stall with a good trough full of hay.

She made her way across the back stable yard into the kitchen.

Mrs. Hall, bustling away at the coffee pot, eggs bubbling in boiling water, toast crisping and bacon sizzling in a pan, looked up at Frances, tucked a loose strand of gray hair back into her bun and smiled, her reddened cheeks flush from bending over the wood-fired oven.

"Morning, ma'am," she said. "Looks chilly out there."

"But once this mist lifts, it's going to be a glorious Saturday." Frances smiled. "Good morning, Mrs. Hall, that all smells delicious."

Once Frances had showered, and dressed in a pair of camel trousers and a cashmere sweater, her dark hair pulled into a loose chignon, her brown eyes made up with a little mascara and the muscles in her slim legs still tingling from her morning ride, she slipped along the long gallery that ran the length of the entire second story of her home, passing her late father-in-law's collection of Impressionist art, before winding her way down the grand staircase, past the ballroom into the light-filled breakfast room.

Willard was already at the table. He had the newspaper open. Her husband hardly looked up when she entered.

"Good morning, darling," she said. In spite of his recent coolness, she placed a kiss on her husband's cheek, allowing herself a delicious, and yet, slightly nervous anticipation of the thought of their weekend together.

She'd invited Eloise and Teddy for dinner, and Rick would be home tomorrow, at last, if her calculations were correct. She was sure the thought of seeing her son home was helping lift her mood this morning, rendering her happier than she'd been for months. After all, her adored boy had been traveling through a war-torn landscape, and deep down, she'd been more than unsettled ever since he announced he was leaving ten months ago. He'd returned from military duty aboard a ship in the Pacific, staying in New York for only three months, before he set off on this war correspondent mission.

The fact that he was finally returning to America in one piece was a huge comfort, not that she'd admitted her deep fears to a living soul. But she knew she was lucky. Oh, she knew that.

"I thought we might go for a walk through the woods this afternoon, followed by a visit to that new gallery on Farmington Avenue?" she said. In fact, the gallery was the initiative of her oldest friend Bernice, but Willard didn't need to know that, not yet. Once he was there and he'd fallen in love with some of Bernice's excellent acquisitions, he'd be sure to support her and buy something, even if it was just a little painting to hang in a quiet spot at Woodlands somewhere.

Willard remained focused on his paper.

Frances poured coffee, collected a boiled egg, toast, bacon and some fried tomatoes from a ceramic dish and slipped into her seat at the table opposite her husband, the man who used to call her every lunchtime on a weekday while he was down in New York, then again, when he was about to leave his office in Manhattan, often arriving home bearing flowers and a small bottle of some lovely new French perfume at the end of the week.

Or he would invite her down to New York, impromptu, because he'd managed to get tickets to Broadway. Here sat the man who used to rush home every Friday evening after a week away to see his children, providing the whole family with a largesse and a wonderful sense of humor that they all adored. Tickets to Europe, flights to the Caribbean, nothing had been off the agenda, and she'd adored every minute of being married to him.

Until the last few months.

At first, Frances had put the sudden change in Willard down to Rick's leaving, again, after his tour of duty in the Pacific in the navy. He'd hardly arrived home before he turned around and disappeared. She supposed that was her fault, that Rick had not gone into the family bank, because she'd encouraged him to follow his passion for history and politics from a young age, buying him books, reading with him, discussing the newspapers, taking him to debates in New York.

And she also suspected that, deep down, Willard envied Rick; she knew that her husband recognized that their son was, in fact, brighter than he. Worse, she'd also suspected for a long time that Willard might resent her, Frances, for also being more intellectual than he was.

When she truly forced herself to think about it, Willard's withdrawal had been gradual, not as sudden as it seemed. Once, when Rick was eighteen, Willard had told her that he felt like Frances and Rick were a team of two.

But in the last few months, things had come to a head. Willard had completely disappeared. In body he was sometimes—not often—here. In spirit, he was always somewhere else.

Willard removed his thick linen napkin from his lap and folded it, along with his newspaper. He frowned a moment, his graying eyebrows knitting together across his still handsome face, before pushing his chair back and moving to the large bay window at the end of the breakfast room, staring out at the garden and the fields beyond. "I'm going back to New York," he said.

Frances placed her coffee cup down, an all too familiar pain piercing her belly. "But Eloise is bringing Teddy tonight, dear, and they'll be so excited that Rick's on his way home. I'm not sure, but he might even arrive back tomorrow. Surely you want to be here for that? And it's the weekend, Will." The way she'd always shortened his name still rolled off her tongue, as it had done for all her adult life.

Willard remained faced away from her, his tall frame stolid, unmoving, his hands on his hips. When he finally circled back around, his blue eyes were unfathomable.

"I don't want to feel that I can't go into work on a weekend," he said.

Frances bit on her lip. She did not understand what was going on. Could not get through to him. Had lost the best friend she'd ever known. Pushing the sear of disappointment back down, she nodded politely.

Being married was her life, her family, her world. If she risked her marriage, and upset Willard, she could lose everything she valued the most in her life.

"I see," she managed.

Willard's expression darkened. "I hope when Rick returns, that he'll have seen some sense."

Frances sat up, eyes widening.

Willard stalked toward the breakfast room door. "You heard me. I'm expecting that he'll come and join us at the bank. The lark is over. He can do something sensible now. I'll organize to have him trained up for an executive role. I'm sick of it."

Frances checked the response that wanted to come hurling out of her mouth. "But I think he will stay with political journalism," she said. "Don't you?"

Willard stopped by the open doorway, resting his hand against the creamy painted frame a moment. He lowered his head, staring at nothing. "You have no idea, do you? He'll never make any money. We've indulged it long enough." Willard ground out his words. "You've indulged it, Frances. Indulged him. He needs to grow up."

Frances placed both forearms on the table. She contemplated the now blue, blue sky. Suddenly, all the promise the morning had held had turned sour, and she let out a heavy sigh.

"If he'd gone to business school, he'd be working with me." Willard's voice pierced the pretty room.

Frances looked away, heart beating wildly. She still did not understand what had gotten into her husband. Still worried that she was imagining his cold treatment of her.

"I won't be back until next Friday evening." Willard looked past her, through her, as if she were not in the room at all. "Why don't you go visit your parents in Cleveland? You could take a vacation for a couple of weeks."

And with that, he turned, and strode out the door.

Later that morning, Frances stood up from the little rose-colored velvet stool at her dressing table. She'd sat here staring at herself in the round mirror for at least half an hour or more. *Was she too old? Too dull? Why was he so suddenly angry with her?*

And yet, she reminded herself, stopping halfway across her bedroom, the chintz four-poster bed sitting as pretty as ever on the soft, creamy carpet, she'd been trained. Trained, like so many girls of her generation, to put her husband first. And she was doing that, was she not? In fact, she'd followed every single darned letter to the rule.

At the expensive private school for girls to which her parents had sent her, bastion of the elite families, famous for educating girls who'd married politicians, international businessmen, European royalty, many of whom had suffered—oh, they had suffered at their husbands' hands… Nothing had been drummed into them harder or more repeatedly than the importance of not upsetting one's husband, of letting him make the decisions, have his way, do what he wished, and above all else, to always maintain social niceties and *never* complain about him with one's friends.

The importance of keeping up appearances was paramount. Gossip was rife. And one did not wish to be the subject of it. So, she'd stayed silent about her unhappiness these past months.

But things had also changed since she was a girl. During the war, women had stepped up and run those businesses that men used to control entirely on their own, they'd manned government agencies, served in the armed forces, driven trucks, repaired airplanes, flown those very airplanes all the way across the country, and still managed their homes, kept their husbands.

Frances had set up a hospital in Farmington for returned, injured veterans, and she'd worked there every day. Now, she was as good as a fully trained nurse. Quietly, so as not to upset Willard with her deep interest and understanding of foreign politics, gleaned from reading history books at school when she should have been embroidering, she'd read every newspaper she could get her hands on at the hospital and followed the war with great interest, her heart in her mouth.

She'd kept her opinions to herself, not raised her thoughts on the war's end and the outcome for Europe, once, with Willard. She'd behaved by the book.

She'd long ago given up any aspiration she might have had to study history and politics properly, to get a job in a related field, like so few women, but some, indeed, had done.

Frances had done everything for her family. So, why was her husband so angry with her?

She simply did not know. She stumbled on the edge of her carpeted floor.

Should she be talking to a divorce attorney?

Because her fairy-tale life had become a nightmare.

Chapter Seven

Frances

April 1946

On Sunday morning, Mr. Hall brought the telegram to Frances in her morning room. She'd paced the grounds after her early ride, laughed politely with Eloise and dear Teddy, with whom her daughter was so obviously, deliriously in love, over breakfast, sat upright in church, and fooled everyone.

Except, it seemed, her oldest friend, the one who had never married, the friend who had sat by while Frances' life went from strength to strength. But Bernice had quietly stuck with her own dreams; first, a swish interior design business funded by the inheritance her father had left for her, now a small art gallery in Farmington, international travel, and a charming apartment in the Upper East Side. Alongside her busy life, Bernice had been a sort of surrogate aunt to Frances' children. A pseudo member of the family who it was acknowledged would always remain that way.

Bernice sat forward in her chair in Frances' morning room, still decorated with the pink cabbage roses that Frances' late mother-in-law had favored.

"Rick is on his way?"

Frances nodded, her eyes scanning the message. "He'll be home for lunch." She placed the telegram down on the coffee table, crossed her legs and folded her arms, repressing her fears at how Rick would find his family. Because Rick picked up on everything.

He'd know instantly that something was wrong. It was one of the things she adored about him.

Bernice threw a glance toward the open door. She had come clean and said she'd been worried about for Frances for months. "Darling, I think you should have Willard followed."

Frances stood up. She moved toward the gilt clock on the mantelpiece, a delicate, filigreed, gorgeous confection lined with mother-of-pearl. In silence, she shook her head. "I could never do that. I would feel disloyal. There really is nothing wrong."

What she was determined to do was get through to Willard. Save their marriage, because she couldn't bear to break not only her own heart but Eloise's and Rick's too. Frances bit on her thumbnail, something she hadn't done since she was a girl and her mother had punished her, telling her she'd look like a tramp with bitten-back nails.

"I haven't heard any rumors," Bernice went on. "But... you are in agony."

Frances blanched. *Was she so transparent?*

"No talk of an affair, darling. Back in New York," Bernice said.

Frances reddened. She couldn't manage him having an affair. Couldn't bear it. This entire thing was preposterous.

But they'd been warned as young girls to stay silent and sit it out if it happened.

And happen it did. All the time.

And yet, she and Willard had always been different. She was different. She'd taken care of herself.

He loved her. He used to tell her all the time.

Her Willard would never, ever humiliate her.

Frances looked into the huge mirror above the fireplace. Behind her, she saw Bernice raise one of her blond brows. Her old friend sighed and crossed her legs, encased in black woolen trousers, her shoulder-length blond hair sitting softly to her shoulders.

Frances paced to the window. And then, the sound of a car engine! *Rick*. Rushing she knew not where, Frances drew her hand to her mouth, covered it, let out a little squeal, and ran out to the hallway, while Bernice drew out her silver cigarette case, lit up, and moved to the window.

In the grand entrance hall, Frances fumbled with the locks on the enormous front door, the sun beaming through the fan-shaped window onto the black and white marble tiles, and right when Rick turned off his engine, she barreled out onto the circular driveway and straight into her son's arms.

Thank goodness. Thank goodness her boy was home.

He held her, before finally drawing away, eyes crinkling at the sides. "So, Mom, how are you?"

Frances stiffened.

She held her chin up. "Fine," she said. "Everything is perfectly fine." She linked her arm with Rick's and walked with her son toward their adored family home, their Labradors bounding around them on the sweep of the gravel drive.

Chapter Eight

Kate

New York, April 1946

Kate stood in the kitchen of the one-room apartment on a corner of Ninth Avenue that she was about to call home. A studio was all she could afford in Manhattan right now, and she'd persuaded herself that it was all that she needed. Fact was, the place was a bed of luxury after the dingy hotel rooms she'd lived in for the past ten months. And in any case, she swore she would never complain about anything at home again after she'd witnessed the deprivations that raged across Europe, and the hardships folks there were facing as they struggled to stay alive.

Outside, the sounds of hooters and buses rang through the warm spring air. Kate had wandered around Manhattan like a woman who'd landed from another planet when she first came back, awestruck by the city's unscathed landmarks, like St. Patrick's Cathedral, whose fine towers stood in perfect, unblemished majesty for all to admire. She'd stood in amazement outside the great hotels, the Waldorf Astoria rising to lofty heights, with its starlight roof and its flags flying, as if there'd never been a war.

She'd wandered alone and unsettled through Broadway after dark, unable to shake her sense of wonder at the crowds in furs gathering outside the Metropolitan Opera House, the queues of carefree folks waiting for the Rockettes show at Radio City. Heard folks chatting about the formidable excitement of ice hockey matches in Madison Square Gardens, basketball.

She'd walked along the bridges that spanned the mighty New York rivers, all intact. Chinatown, with its old-world customs, the dragon parades, dances and rituals, the exotic, wonderful food. The Metropolitan Museum of Art, Coney Island with its giant Ferris wheel taking people hundreds of feet in the air. Hot dogs, peanuts, soda pop. Folks swimming in the ocean, and finally, she'd gone on a ferry to eyeball the Statue of Liberty, that symbol of peace and democracy standing over it all. She'd wanted to see it. Wanted to know that it was still there.

Now, she studied her kitchen, its tiny, rattling cooking range stuffed into a dank corner alongside an old sink stained with rust and a few cupboards that she struggled to close. Lucky she was not the domesticated type. She'd probably only fix herself ham and eggs in here.

Down the end of a short hallway, past the one closet which would have to hold her clothes, whose doors creaked something awful when you opened them, there was a tiny bathroom, and in front, one dusty room that she'd scrub from top to bottom and would double up as sleeping quarters, living room and dining room. The narrow old front window overlooked the rusted steel rungs of the building's fire escape. It was not a home, but thinking back on the fact of the orphan sitting in front of her bombed-out house in Berlin, Kate would never take this for granted.

On her first night, having cleaned the studio from top to toe, scrubbing out the oven and the cupboards, Kate sat cross-legged on her bed and looked around, satisfied. Her mom had given her some faded old Turkish rugs for the floors, her bookshelves were freshly dusted, polished and stocked with her favorite books, some of them her papa's, on history and politics. She'd draped her sofa and soft armchair with one of her mom's old shawls and a pile of bright cushions, perfect for curling up in when she wanted to read.

Now she had a home, she had to focus on her biggest problem. She was reaping the cost of being away for nearly a year, and with no full-time association with any news outlet and bills to pay, she only had enough saved up to last her a few months.

She'd so far had rejections from every newspaper in New York. No one wanted to hire a woman. In 1945, all the jobs had gone to men.

She turned to the newspapers spread out over her bed. She had to face up to the facts. Every newspaper told the same story. Technology was moving fast. Americans were beginning to get radios into their cars, thirty-four million people in the population had radios in their homes, and there was talk that television might start coming into play soon. She'd have to try and get a job in radio. She'd have to trade on the fact she'd reported on Goering's trial and she'd been the first reporter to do so in the US.

Pencil stuck behind one ear, dark curls looped up atop her head, the floral print dress she wore tangled up around her bare legs, Kate started typing up an application to CBS.

The following morning, Kate woke with her sheets a tangle around her ankles after she'd thrown her bedding off during the night. Every night since Berlin, she'd woken with the same nightmares, whether she'd been in her childhood bed back in the Village with the sound of her neighbors' radios chattering through the thin walls, or whether she'd been in the drab hotel in Nuremberg. She'd woken, shaking, with visions of the little orphan girl.

Now, she rubbed her sleep-deprived eyes, yawning, and stretching, moving toward the kitchen to make her morning coffee. She'd fought hard to try and let Germany go. And yet, it seemed that no matter how hard she tried to resist responding to the notes Rick had sent her, inviting her to catch up for a drink, knowing that he was not good for her, no matter how she tried to take the toughened attitude toward life, she couldn't sway her thoughts away from the mute German child.

When there was a knock on the door, Kate moved toward it, resting her head against the locks. "Who is it?" she asked, keeping her voice low, hoping, irrationally, that whoever it was would go away.

"It's me," her mom said. "What are you doing? You only just woken up? It's almost ten o'clock!"

Kate sighed and unlocked her door, pulling the catch, and stepping aside for her mom.

"You have just woken up! Look at you!" Livia Mancini stood, arms folded across her tiny frame, dressed in a tight-fitting mustard pullover and a toning brown-and-orange checked skirt. Her short legs were stocking free, because they were still hard to get, but her shoes were polished, and she smelled of perfume and her dark hair was freshly washed and waved.

Kate moved by her into the kitchen. "Coffee, Mama?" she spoke. She couldn't shake how her mom resembled Kate's sister, Bianca.

The less said about that the better right now.

"I've had my coffee," Livia said. She took a turn around the room, stopping to straighten the newspapers that Kate had left strewn on the sofa last night, tidying up Kate's notepad, surveying her typewriter on its desk. "I took the train up here during my break. Took an extra half-hour, which they owed me."

Kate didn't doubt they did. The school in Lower Manhattan where her mom worked was only a ten-minute train ride, but Kate knew how they valued her. She was the person on the end of most of the incoming calls to the school. If a child was sick, parents called Livia; if they were worried about their daughter, it was Livia they wanted to speak to. She'd worked there tirelessly in office administration, while Kate's dad had taught history to the seniors.

Kate moved to the window, hugging her arms around her pajama-clad waist, staring down at the buses, and the yellow cabs lining the street.

"I brought you this," Livia said.

Kate turned. Her mom was burrowing in her neat leather handbag. Finally, she produced a letter, battered, the top corner slightly ripped.

Kate took in a breath. Livia handed it to her, and Kate's fingers froze at the sight of the multitude of stamps. *Germany.*

It was postmarked Berlin, and Claudia's loopy scrawl was vivid and unblemished, Kate's mom's address written in blue fountain pen ink.

"Oh!" Kate managed, reaching for it with shaking hands.

"Have you got a letter opener?" Livia said, hands on her hips, her Italian accent curling through the tiny room.

Kate's eyes rounded and caught with her mom's. *Her orphan.* She might have worked hard to push intrusive thoughts of Rick and their friendship and how she missed him and how he made her feel alive right out of her head, but that little girl. She had to know what had happened to her. And Claudia's letter felt like a connection to something so distant-seeming that she barely remembered it. Claudia's letter felt like a long-lost connection to that life.

"No opener," she managed.

Livia dug through the kitchen and came back with a slim knife. She held it out for Kate, and hands shaking, breath hitching, she sliced the thin paper open, and pulled out the pages inside.

Livia busied herself in the kitchen.

As the aroma of coffee seeped through the room, and the sounds of her mom pulling open drawers, finding a bread knife, plates, and toasting Kate's day-old Italian loaf in the toaster, opening its little doors every now and then to check on progress, Kate sank down in her sofa, curled her knees up underneath her and read.

Berlin, April 1946

Dearest Kate,

It is only weeks since we met, but it feels like months since our little friend began staying with me, with Papa, my sister and my nieces here in Celle. It is so sweet, the way they have taken to her, as I have too. I think she is about ten years old. It breaks my heart that we do not know. And it appears we have little chance of finding anything out about her in the near future. All I have been able to do is learn more about these war orphans in general. Now that I have done that, I will try to piece together her story.

With the weather improving now, she takes great delight in collecting the eggs with Papa in the morning, and she's a solemn little helper in the kitchen at mealtimes. She seems to enjoy nothing more than standing on a stool by my side while I cook, and she patiently hands me the ingredients that I need when I am ready for them. Sometimes, I let her stir cake mixture with a wooden spoon or beat fresh eggs. I think she must have done this before, but I do not know. Before the war took everything from her, the only life she knew.

Oh, Kate, I have no qualms that she is intelligent, but she will not speak, and we cannot coax her to do so. The other thing is sometimes we are finding broken-off chunks of bread in her bed in the mornings. I think she is so used to starving that she is taking food scraps to bed with her. It is heartbreaking and yet understandable, poor little girl. We never chastise her for such things.

Apart from that, there is something of great importance I need to tell you. We found, hidden deep in the pockets of her ragged dress, a photograph of another child.

Kate paused, taking the cup of coffee that Livia held out for her, thankful for her mother's silence while she read this letter that meant everything to her. She closed her eyes a moment, the tears that threatened to prick her eyelids stinging, and read on.

It was a small black-and-white photograph of a little boy. When Papa tried to ask her who he was, she buried her face in a cushion and after that, would not come out of her bedroom for a whole afternoon. I suspect he was her brother. And this lead is the only one we have.

What's more, I've spent several hours combing the newspapers and getting in touch with my contacts in journalism in Berlin to try and find out how we go about learning who she is.

The situation is worse than I thought, Kate. I suspect she is one of the children who was caught in the German territory that has now been ceded to Russia. There are stories of tens of thousands of these children roaming the forests and swamps. The Russian citizens are forbidden from taking them in. So many city children were sent to what are now Russian parts of Germany during the war to avoid the Allied bombing raids on the German cities, particularly in the last two years when the Allied campaigns stepped up.

Kate brought her hand to her mouth. Dear goodness. Please, they had to find out who she was.

I have learned that our little girl would have been prohibited from speaking German in the Russian-occupied territories immediately after the war. Even her German name would be risky. It could be that she only managed to hide the photograph of the little boy, after any other photos, letters or relatives' addresses were taken from her and destroyed.

She's lost her identity, she's too scared to speak, but she's managed to survive. What's more, I suspect she managed to get back home to Berlin, in the hope that she'd find her parents there, only to discover they were gone.

I am only guessing, Kate, but I think this might be what has happened.

What I do know is that those orphans who did not make it out of Soviet-occupied territories were sent to Soviet homes run by the Soviet military in the Soviet occupation zone. There are stories of German children traveling in freight trains without any straw to sleep on, for up to four nights, most of them more dead than alive by the time they came to the Soviet homes. There, they are being forced into Soviet-run orphanages or adopted by ardent communists.

Kate, you and Rick have saved this little girl from this fate. Bless you.

I will leave no stone unturned to try and piece together her story. And I will let you know how I get on. As soon as she is able, I will have her write to you. I am sure she will never forget you. I am certain you will always remain in her heart.

Send my love to Rick,
Claudia

Kate's eyes rose to meet with her mama's. And she placed her mug on her coffee table. Weeping, she buried herself in Livia's arms.

Chapter Nine

Kate

New, York, April 1946

A week later, Kate sat in a crowded diner in Midtown with Harvey Milton, amidst the clatter of cutlery and plates and the good-natured shouts of waiters rushing around in the smoke-filled restaurant with its clean white tiles and its mirrors lining the walls. She'd bumped into Harvey right out in the street, and he'd insisted on catching up with her that very moment and buying her lunch. Outside, a warm spring breeze danced through Midtown, sending folks' coats flying out behind them, while flotsams of paper, blossom and dust swirled in the wind.

Seeing Harvey, sitting opposite her with his Brylcreemed hair, his square-cut fingernails and his neatly pressed shirt, only served to remind her of how good things were here in America. Outside the picture windows, yellow taxi cabs lined the streets, and young couples walked hand in hand, the girls with bright red lipstick and the boys with that certain swagger and New York style.

But Kate had avoided both Rick and Harvey these past months, like a woman running from a bomb. Every time she thought of Rick, her senses stirred, and she felt agitated. That was no way for a woman who wanted to get ahead in a male-dominated occupation to be when she was trying to get a contract.

"I'm sorry about the rejection from CBS," Harvey said.

Kate pulled her latest rejection back across the table. She glanced at the words that had found her staring out the window most of last night, coffee in hand, fear for her future starting to curl around her insides.

Dear Miss Mancini, we have a long list of women applicants, and little chance to use them. I am afraid that your name cannot be put near the top of the list.

She'd sent out a 78mm audition platter about women in the news, along with her application, but CBS had shipped it right back. Even though she'd been the first American reporter to file on the trial of the most significant Nazi criminal still alive in the world today, she still wasn't worthy of a job.

And yet every man on the tour of Europe had a contract. Harvey was reporting, and on top of that, he was waiting for news on two executive roles at New York radio stations.

"Rick's at the *New York Times*," Harvey said, his eyes searching her face with sympathy. "He's been asking after you."

Kate turned away. She folded her arms and let the room blur into a haze.

"He says it's like working in a garage sale," Harvey went on.

Kate nodded. "Does he."

"The place is full of shouting, phones ringing, typewriter keys clanging, calls for the copy boys." Harvey chuckled. But then, he was silent. He lowered his voice. "Kate, you okay?"

Kate took in a breath. *Darn it. She wanted to see Rick. She missed him. But she also wanted a job.*

A woman in a red polka-dotted dress gesticulated with a cigarette, smoke plumes blowing around at the table next to them.

"He says he can't get hold of you."

Kate bit on her lip. She turned back to Harvey, holding her head high. "Oh, you know how it is."

Harvey tilted his head to one side. "He was worried about you, Kate. We all are." Harvey lowered his voice. "Talk is, men are even cleaning down the desks in the newspapers these days. Answering the phones." He ran a hand over the stubble on his chin, a frown shadowing his features.

"I don't want to answer phones," Kate said.

Harvey leaned his forearms on the table. "You're a great journalist, Kate."

She raised a brow. "I would be if I could grow a mustache."

A waitress brought their desserts, rice pudding for Harvey, and wheat cakes with maple syrup for Kate.

Kate sighed and picked up her spoon. She toyed with the perky little cake. "From what I can see, nearly all the women who have managed to get jobs in public affairs programming are only behind the scenes." She raised her gaze to Harvey. "They're getting roles that don't carry the prestige of being on the air."

Harvey shook his head and dipped his spoon into his pudding.

Kate focused on her dessert. Last night, she'd ended up having a good old cry.

Suddenly, Harvey put down his spoon. "Why don't you go see Hilary Winthrop at WNYR?"

Kate sent him a glance. "Hilary Winthrop? How do I get a meeting with her?" The woman was a radio legend. She'd worked her way up from a maid-of-all-work role in a fledgling radio station in the early thirties, to head of women's and children's programming at New York Radio, otherwise known as WNYR, just as all radio stations had a four-letter acronym. And Hilary Winthrop was also famous for being tough.

Harvey grinned at her. "I have an inkling she just might talk to you, Kate. If you call her."

Slowly, a smile spread across Kate's face. "Well, then, Harvey. I'll have to see about that." And she dipped her spoon into her cake, her appetite suddenly reawakened.

*

One week later, Kate waited for her appointment with Hilary Winthrop on the fourth floor of Radio City. She'd written to her, and had been invited in for a chat.

When Miss Winthrop's secretary ushered Kate through the door to the well-known programmer's office, Miss Winthrop, a tall spare woman, with dark hair turning gray, and a quantity of freckles, reached straight across the desk and grasped Kate's hand with a firm shake.

"I've heard of you, of course," Miss Winthrop said. She adjusted her glasses on the end of her long, patrician nose, and sat down. Her well-cut dark suit could have belonged to a man if it weren't for the calf-length tailored skirt. "Your report on Goering was exceptional. And you'd done a little radio work before the war?"

Kate felt her tension ease. Miss Winthrop had done her research, and that meant Kate didn't have to start on the wrong foot, explaining who she was, or why she was here. "Local independent stations in Washington. I've never had a contract, but I've freelanced for several years, and have always been busy." *Until now.*

Miss Winthrop nodded. "History and Politics major at NYU. A considerable body of stories published and several syndicated across the country. Well done. And a particular interest and expertise in foreign affairs."

Kate sagged with relief. Having someone acknowledge her and show an interest in her credentials without instant dismissal was something she'd begun to think would never happen again.

"I have a passion for history and politics, and a deal of experience reporting on international public affairs after my ten-month tour around post-war Europe writing for North American News Alliance."

The older woman leaned forward in her chair. "I suppose you've come to me because you've heard that I'm willing to help other women. I always encourage younger women in radio."

"I was recommended to write to you, and I thank you for talking with me. The truth is, no one seems to want to hire a woman right now."

Miss Winthrop looked contemplative for a moment. "Well, my interests for WNYR reach out to our listeners as well. I like to treat not only my staff, but both my male and my female listeners, with respect, both equally as intelligent people who are interested in world affairs."

Kate sent the older woman a smile. "Surely the modern woman deserves to hear her news delivered by another woman, just as a man deserves to hear his news from a man. And in time, I hope that more men will be open to hearing their news read by a woman as well."

Miss Winthrop toyed with her silver pen. Her hazel eyes darkened. "Right now, most network officials are willing to take advantage of a woman's talents and dedication to the job, but they are unwilling to give them the same job duties or pay as men."

Kate stayed quiet.

"My biggest programs are 'The World of Women,' where we interview famous women from all around the world, 'Auntie Margaret,' who keeps our listeners abreast of women's events and happenings in New York, homeware exhibitions and fashion shows that sort of thing, and 'Cousin Jenny,' whose recipes are fast becoming a staple all over the country, let alone New York. Cousin Jenny's new cookbook is doing just grand. I've got several other shows, grandmotherly types, you know the sort of thing."

"I see." Kate chewed on her lip.

"I don't do soap operas, we have a different programming department for those, but they hire women actresses to do the voices, of course. I never broadcast myself if I can help it. My voice is too rough, but I'm very keen to bring people in who would widen the horizons of the listeners to the microphone. I'm dedicated to keeping my women listeners tuned in." Miss Winthrop sat back in her chair, arranging her hands in front of her chest. "You know, on the day of President Roosevelt's death, I had a bit of a lucky break. I rounded up and had on the air, three significant women to commentate. I am trying, Miss Mancini. But it's an uphill battle to get our senior executives to consider women political reporters. I'm afraid it's impossible at the moment."

Kate bit back the outpouring of frustration she felt. She'd already given up on writing longer stories, now was she to give up on any political reporting as well?

Not likely.

She turned her focus toward Miss Winthrop.

"I know what it is to be surrounded by men, and to succeed," the older woman added. "My great interest and belief in radio is what keeps me in the job. I still do a good deal of radio listening, and while I keep executive hours, I get up at 5 a.m. to get in two to three hours work before breakfast, both listening and preparing, and I sit on several boards." She leaned forward.

Kate nodded. "So, you work twice as hard as any man."

Miss Winthrop sent her a smile. "That's what I'm saying. You see, I don't have a wife to go home to, so I can." She eyed Kate. "Nor do I have a husband for that matter. I couldn't do both my career and marriage."

"I understand." Kate held the woman's gaze, certain not to give away a flicker of a doubt about the fact she was *fully a*ware.

"How about I hire you freelance? I won't be able to give you a contract, because the network will oppose that. You'll have to work on stories about and for women. Fashion shows, and the like."

Kate nodded professionally but her heart plummeted to her shoes.

"That would be a very good opportunity for me, Miss Winthrop," she said, her lips forming a tight smile. She waited a beat and weighed things up. Last night, she'd sat over her bank accounts for hours, knowing they didn't add up. She had to get some form of work. "Miss Winthrop, I'll report for you. I'm at your service and am thankful for the opportunity to learn and work with you."

Miss Winthrop laid down her pen. "The first thing I want you to cover is a forum about how to get a husband." She held Kate's gaze.

Kate clasped her hands in her lap. *Oh, you are kidding me, what a pain in the neck.* "Well, I'm sure I can get that done for you." She gritted her teeth and smiled and smiled ever so politely.

The older woman started tidying papers on her desk, reaching for a notepad.

Kate gathered her handbag, stood up, straightened her blue two-piece suit.

And then, Miss Winthrop looked up at her. "Miss Mancini, I'll struggle to get your voice on air in any capacity that is not a woman's story. You'll have to adjust to how things are in New York these days. Now the war is over, jobs for women aren't on the agenda."

Kate simply nodded at her.

She walked out into the WNYR suite of offices, pushed the glass doors open onto Sixth Avenue and marched home, and refused herself an inch of self-pity. She refused to think of Rick reporting for the *New York Times* and she refused to feel sorry for herself. Things were not so bad. *Think of that orphan. Think of what she's been through.*

Chapter Ten

Bianca

New York, May 1946

Bianca ran her appraising eye over Marshall's gray flannelled suit. She'd aired it especially for him overnight. She handed him a brown paper bag containing corned beef and pickle sandwiches on fresh white bread, a slice of homemade cherry pie and a flask of iced tea. Marshall leaned down and kissed her, and Bianca kicked up her back heel, reveling in the feel of his hands lingering around her waist before running down over her rounded hips, so perfectly emphasized by the peplum waist on her dress.

"See you tonight, sweetheart." He took a step toward their charming front garden in Forest Hill Gardens, Queens, disappearing across the neatly mowed lawn to the garage on the edge of the street that was a bowery of vivid green trees.

"You'd better leave, or I'll drag you back inside," Bianca called. She batted her eyelashes, her pretty black eyes dancing with delight.

Bianca trailed her fingers over her polished front door.

The perfect family, the perfect husband. She'd be the perfect wife. It was the dream she'd held onto after her own family had fallen apart at the seams. Her sister, Kate, whom she'd grown up with, idolized, adored all her young life. All her young life, she'd only wanted to be like Kate.

But then, their adored papa's tragic accident when he went out the door at Kate's bidding to buy her some paper for one of those stories she always wrote set off a sudden, great and uncontrollable screaming pain, flaming Bianca into a passionate anger toward her sister that she'd never known she could possess, fanning the agony of her deep-held fear that her father had, quite simply, loved Kate best. Worshipped her intelligence, just like Bianca did.

Bianca's papa had been killed because of his devotion to Kate. He'd been the light of the family, the kindest man, who'd made them laugh every day since she could remember.

Bianca had shouted at Kate. Yelled at her. Blamed her relentlessly.

And every time Kate had tried to reach out to Bianca since, complimenting her when she got her first job, sending a telegram from some far-flung, war-torn city to congratulate Bianca on her wedding, secretly, Bianca had relished the messages. But then some old dark demon inside her would question whether Kate's sentiments were genuine.

It wasn't until after the war that Bianca had seen any chance of meeting her perfect guy. The guy who would love her and accept her for who she was. The guy who wouldn't walk out into the street one day at Kate's bidding and get knocked dead by a car, even though Bianca worried sick every time Marshall left the house in case an accident should befall him like it did her papa.

She had been determined to find the man who'd love her exactly as she was, not compare her to Kate. The guy who would not care two hoots about her sister.

When the government had switched their propaganda from encouraging women to work in factories and businesses to instructing them on providing an immaculately clean house, producing cookies and greeting their husbands every evening effortlessly with dinner on the table, Bianca knew her own time had come.

The moment she'd laid eyes on handsome Marshall Green at a dance in Midtown, she'd noticed how he stood out, a good head taller than the other guys in his group, dark hair all Brylcreemed, black eyes that matched hers. He looked like a guy who had moved on from the war. He looked like a guy who knew what was what.

And when he'd danced with her all night and bought her two glasses of punch, taking her elbow and leading her around the room, laughing with her girlfriends, and offering to accompany her home in a yellow cab which he'd paid for, she knew she'd met the one.

Invitations had come for dinner along with bouquets of flowers at the grade school where she taught class. Her little first-graders had watched with wide eyes while she'd opened the tiny white envelopes that accompanied the bright blooms, her cheeks turning pink and her pearly teeth showing in the hint of her smile.

And then, secretly, hoping for her dreams to finally be realized, even while Kate roamed around Europe, sending Bianca and her mom letters from places with names that had been emblazoned all over the papers for the last six years—Dunkirk, Sicily, Normandy, Belorussia, Krakow, Berlin—Bianca had started buying bridal magazines.

And now Bianca's house was strewn with glossies that said how women would be expected to nurture families as America moved toward the new decade. Sometimes, when Bianca was straightening her growing collection, which she'd sit and read during her breaks from cleaning and baking and shopping for Marshall's dinners, something deep inside wondered whether she was trying to prove something, still. Prove that she could do what Kate could not. But she stamped those intrusive thoughts right down.

Bianca clicked closed the front door of the mock-Tudor house that she shared with Marshall in the very suburb where he'd grown up. She turned around and surveyed her formal sitting room, bending down to pick up an imaginary ball of fluff from the wall-to-wall pale green carpet, before standing up and admiring the get-up with its woodsmoke-gray wallpaper with chalk and white flowers imprinted on it, commodious cupboards and open shelves painted to match, white ruffled curtains that draped to the floor, shining mahogany furniture placed just so, and beyond, the dining table, the garden.

It didn't hurt that her husband's family owned a wallpapering and curtain business. Marshall would always keep their home up to the look of the minute.

And today, Marshall's mother, Florence, and his beautiful sister, Patricia, were coming for morning coffee and Bianca had hardly slept for nerves. Florence lived right around the corner in a classic colonial mansion in the heart of the neighborhood. Her dinner parties in her exquisite home with its hand-painted murals and stunning central staircase were legendary. Florence Green knew everyone that mattered in the neighborhood, and Bianca admired her so very much.

In fact, Florence and Patricia had become the role models that Bianca'd never had. Patricia constantly socialized with the other fashionable young moms in the neighborhood, her life a whirl of well-mannered daytime parties stocked with punch and cookies, tennis games and calisthenic classes, baby showers and toddler play dates.

Surely, an invitation for Bianca to be included had to come soon. *Didn't it?*

Bianca, her heart stirring with anticipation at her mother-in-law's kind visit to her home, checked the time on her sparkling oval filigree watch and moved through the dining room to the kitchen beyond, grabbing the floral coverall she wore most of the day while Marshall was at work, now she had given up teaching because she was married. Of course, she whipped the pinafore off at five o'clock sharp, because if Marshall were to come home and see her dressed in it, she'd die with embarrassment on the spot.

Bianca started clearing the little table in the breakfast bay in back of the kitchen, tidying away the gracious setting that she'd risen early to set out for Marshall.

Fruit, cereal, eggs, toast, jelly and coffee, along with another extra round of toast and milk were all ready for him the moment he walked into the kitchen every day, seven days a week. Even though she'd been married three whole months now, she still took delight in the way he appeared like a miracle in the mornings, all freshly showered and scented with aftershave, his hair combed back and his cufflinks shining under the beautifully bright fluorescent lights of their gorgeous renovated 1909 home.

Bianca cleared away the low pot of ivy, her centerpiece for breakfast, along with the nine-inch plates she'd carefully placed on the center of the two breakfast mats made of oyster straw, the plates one inch from the edge. She washed them all up in her sparkling new sink.

Two hours later, to a T, there was a delicate knock at the front door. Marshall's mother, Florence, stood resplendent in a black straw picture hat decorated with enormous white roses, a ruffled blouse spilling out from her black suit, the skirt flaring out below the knee in the latest, softer post-war style, and an entire fox's fur draped around her arms. She stepped over the threshold into the living room without waiting for an invitation, the heels of her patent leather pumps pressing tiny button shapes into Bianca's carpet.

Bianca found herself transfixed by the little dead fox's head; its glazed eyes seemed to follow her as Florence paraded around the room.

Bianca barely had time to air-kiss her mother-in-law before Marshall's sister, Patricia, appeared, discarding her white gloves and handing them to Bianca, sashaying so elegantly into the house in a pink suit with white piping around the hem of the softly swaying skirt, the sleeves, and the edges of the jacket. Her blond hair was piled up on the crown of her pretty head in the latest fashion, and she settled down on one of Bianca's sofas, handing Bianca her mother's crocodile purse and her own white leather bag.

Bianca rushed to the spare bedroom and placed her guests' possessions on the beautifully made-up bed, not stopping to admire the craftsmanship, even though her fingers itched to do just that.

She'd been so worried about today that she'd risen at 5 a.m. to scrub down her front steps, because she'd woken with a start, remembering how Florence had commented that you could tell how a woman kept her entire house by the state of her front doorstep.

Bianca wrung her freshly manicured hands, took a deep breath and walked back across her living room, achingly aware of her mother- and sister-in-law's eyes on her.

"Cloudless iced tea?" she asked, her voice horribly high-pitched. She poured generous glugs into sparkling glasses, splashing a little over the sides and forcing herself not to grab one of the glasses and down the lot in one gulp. She'd added cherries frozen in ice cubes, and now, hands shaking, her focus determinedly on what she was doing, she placed a sprig of mint on the edge of each glass, setting the drinks on small plates and passing them around, clinking in the strange silent atmosphere of her dear living room.

"Thank you, dear," Florence said, and Bianca almost collapsed with relief.

"Refrigerator cookies, anyone?" Bianca asked, sounding like an opera singer out of tune. "You see," she garbled on. "You can have fresh cookies every day, once mixed. You slice off a batch as needed, and slip them in the oven, and presto!"

"Well, I wouldn't know about baking," Patricia said. "The maid does all the cooking at home."

Bianca flushed pink, the heat rising all the way up her neck. "You shape them into a firm roll and wrap them in waxed paper," she managed.

"And when does your sister return?" Florence asked. "The one in Europe that you told us about?"

Bianca clasped her shaking hands in her lap. *Oh no, here we go.* Why was Florence remotely interested in her sister?

"Switzerland, wasn't it, dear?" Florence went on.

Kate was back, but the last real details Bianca had heard were when her mom had read out a letter from Germany, in which Kate had written in great depth about how the German people were all struggling for food—a handful of potatoes, a loaf of bread, a few lumps of coal, some cigarettes, no fuel, no light, no jobs, and how they were starving, freezing, and desperate. It had given Bianca the shivers.

There was a terrible silence.

"Yes, I believe she was visiting Lake Lucerne," Bianca said. The lie slipped off her tongue like ice cream down a child's chin. "With friends, such elegant friends you couldn't imagine, you know. She's such a lady."

Florence's brown eyes narrowed. "But I thought she was an educated woman." She uttered the phrase as if she wanted her dead fox to spark into life and gobble Bianca up. "A career woman who had taken the liberty of traveling alone. Very unbecoming."

Bianca reddened. "Oh, my, no. Whatever made you think that?"

Florence stroked her fox. "Well, girls won't be straying so far from home now in any case. Women's colleges are going to have a distinctly feminine curriculum from now on. And quite rightly too. It's all over the magazines. I would never have allowed Patricia to travel overseas alone. And after that ghastly war! Unthinkable."

Bianca rolled her earrings around and around in her ears. "Well, Kate was not alone, I guess."

"Now the war is over," Florence went on, holding court, "women's colleges will mostly only offer the applied arts, ceramics, weaving, textiles, and flower arrangement. So I'm sure your mother will be relieved."

Bianca sat horrified while Patricia crooned in agreement with her mom.

"I've always said the college years should be the preparation for the major performance, which is the task of creating a good home, and raising good children." Florence folded her flawless white hands in her lap.

Bianca shot her mother-in-law a desperate look. "I never wanted, for myself, to have any education that would upset my future marriage. "

"Patricia *adores* arranging flowers," Florence went on. "It's such a wonderful art. A relief to see that women will be looking and behaving like women again." She cleared her throat and picked up a cookie, taking a bite.

"Yes," Bianca whispered, her poor heart sinking to her shoes. "Of course."

"Girls must do their bit to repopulate." Florence adjusted her fox.

Oh, heavens to Betsy. I must have a baby! That's what she wants. Slowly, Bianca's hands moved to her own waistline. It had taken a mighty effort to get the dress on this morning. She'd had to use a coat hanger to zip it up. Bianca was suspicious. She'd felt slightly nauseous for a couple weeks. If she were pregnant, Florence would have to accept her. *Wouldn't she?*

Patricia sighed and looked at her watch. "You know, we really should be going, Mother. I need to get changed before today's luncheon party."

Bianca reeled. Marshall's family couldn't leave yet, it would be a disaster. Marshall had kissed the nape of her neck last night and told her how important it was to him that she got in with Patricia and his mom. Got *in* with their circle, he said, not just *on* with them. And Bianca knew the difference. She had to be accepted if their marriage was to work. And she did so love Marshall.

Bianca's background was not his fault. He'd told her how he hoped she'd get an invitation to one of Patricia's events out of today's effort. He'd been so sweet and charming about it.

Bianca closed her eyes.

And Florence's tone was pure steel. "I see family as sort of corporation, Bianca. You have to cultivate it. And to that end, I always protect mine."

Bianca wanted to sink into her sofa and never come out. She'd never be accepted. What would it take to be included by her new family?

Florence stood up and flicked her fox over her shoulder. She simply held out a hand for her crocodile handbag.

Bianca let out a little moan and shot out of her chair and dashed to the spare room, standing with her back against the wall, chest heaving, stomach roiling. She took in some more deep breaths.

In a flurry, she gathered the bags and rushed back out to the living room.

"Goodbye," Patricia said, pulling on her gloves and taking her bag from Bianca without so much as a glance in her direction.

Bianca stood in the background, almost biting her lip through.

Patricia linked her arm through her mother's, who raised a brow to the ceiling, and turned away with her nose in the air and her pink suit swishing around her legs.

Bianca stood in the doorway watching them leave and she bit back the tears that threatened to spill down her cheeks. And fought the overwhelming desire to flee back to the Village and throw herself into her mom's arms, into Livia's warm embrace.

Chapter Eleven

Bianca

New York, May 1946

That night, Bianca lay in bed, her head in the crook of Marshall's shoulder. She traced a finger across his chest in the dark. She'd spent the afternoon scrubbing the bathroom in order to get over this morning's disastrous visit with her in-laws, and she'd spent two hours preparing their evening meal—ham shank served with beans and a My-T Fine Vanilla Pudding, which she'd made out of meringue and a mound of soft pudding on top, completed with a spoonful of bright-colored jelly. But she'd struggled to fight back her tears.

It was the one thing she could control. Housework. But fury and passion burning underneath all her scrubbing, it had been the picture she'd kept hidden in her bedside drawer, of she, Kate and their neighbor and childhood friend Natalia Morelli, sunbathing in the vegetable garden in the Village, that had finally broken her down in tears in her pinafore. She'd only taken it out for one look.

It was just that she was so lonely. That was all. She'd tried so hard to fit in, done everything by the book, and yet, still folks around here ignored her. Still, nary an invitation came. And girls in this neighborhood socialized. She knew that, oh yes, they did.

Just not with her.

And then, scrubbing brush in hand, hair scooped up into a tight turban around her head, she'd sat back on her heels by the bath.

It was because she was Italian.

She'd gazed, this afternoon, at the photo. Tom Morelli, Natalia's brother, had been the local heartthrob, and Bianca had let the tears fall down her face at the memories of how things used to be. How she and Kate had swooned over Tom, daring each other to go knock on the Morelli apartment door and see if he'd answer, applying ridiculous makeup on their faces, stealing their mom's lipstick and slathering it on to try and attract his attention.

Well. That was all before their papa was killed. Before the war took Tom away to Italy. He'd gotten engaged to some chef in the Upper East Side, lucky girl, and now, Bianca was alone out here in Forest Hill Gardens and she'd gone and got the very opposite of the life Kate would approve of, and Natalia was working at Albertina's deli, with no plans to get engaged at all!

But it would all work out. Like Papa used to say, all's well that ends well.

She rolled away from Marshall, frowning into the darkness of the silent, still bedroom. Back in the Village, there was always the sound of a neighbor's radio blaring through the walls. You could hear folks chatting. You were never alone back at home.

Unless… She placed her hand to her belly. What if she was right? What if she were pregnant? She'd be like Patricia. With children. Surely, everyone would love her if she produced a baby. Her mama. Marshall's family. All of them.

Bianca sat up.

"Marshall?" she whispered into the cool night air.

"What is it, baby?"

She turned around and propped her head up on her elbow. "You know how I told you that this was my dream? Marrying and having a family?"

He reached out, tucking a strand of her hair behind one ear.

"Well, I think we might be moving one step closer to that." She dropped her voice even more.

She saw his eyebrows knit closer in the dark.

"I think I'm having a baby."

He lay back on the pillow, hands behind his head. He let out a slow whistle. "Is that true?"

Bianca ran her hand over his cheek. "You're excited, Marshall?" she said.

"A kid? Of our own!" His eyes widened and he let out a slow smile. "Well, I just wasn't expecting it so soon, honey. But, how wonderful."

She bit on her lip. "The government are expecting women to put their husbands first and to stay home and bear their children, did you know that?"

Marshall pulled her back down onto his chest. "Well, I like the sound of the government's thinking, baby." He started stroking her hair, the tip of his thumb tracing idly down her neck, across her collarbone. "Come here," he murmured, drawing her face up to his. Marshall pulled her even closer and started slipping the strap of her nightgown down.

And Bianca closed her eyes at the feel of his touch on her skin. And right then, she pushed all thoughts of Patricia, and Florence, and Kate and the Village, and how darned lonely she was right out of her head, because a baby had to fix *everything*.

The next morning, Bianca stepped out of the doctor's surgery and stopped dead, right in the middle of the street in front of the building.

Suddenly, overwhelmed by a surging desire to avoid going home to her empty, silent, immaculate house, Bianca took a swift about-turn. Overcome with a shocking homesickness, and overwhelming desire to find out what she might see if she went back to the Village this minute, she trotted toward the railway station. *Because the fact was, she simply needed to get out of here.* And the thought of home, and her mom's cooking—real cooking from scratch, not the fancy modern packet meals that Marshall insisted on—just set her senses reeling. She knew she shouldn't think this way, because she had a beautiful house in Queens, but right now she just wanted to be home.

Bianca sagged with relief back in Greenwich Village as she was jostled up the steps of the station, making her way to MacDougal Street with its hotchpotch of row houses, washing strewn out of windows, the sounds of Italian women singing and calling to one another ringing through the air.

One hand tucked into her coat pocket, eyes shining with unshed tears, wearing as much false confidence as she could bear, Bianca clasped her key ring and slipped up the steps of her childhood home. She let herself in the chipped, flaking, beloved front door and made her way straight in, through the old narrow hallway, to the first-floor apartment where she'd grown up, calling for Livia.

Calling for her mom.

Instinctively, she went to the kitchen in the back of the tiny flat because Livia was usually there, humming and cooking, her tiny frame at the stovetop, a beloved recipe book open on the windowsill among her pots of herbs, while the aroma of freshly chopped tomatoes, and bright green basil and cheeses and garlic wafted through the apartment. Bianca wanted to sit down and gossip with her old neighbors, her dearest old friends over a plate of cannoli, the deep-fried pastry tubes piped full of creamy ricotta that all the moms and nonnas made with such love and flair around here.

Seeing the room empty and still, Bianca pulled aside the net curtains that framed the window overlooking the back yard, her face splitting into a teary grin at the sight of them all; Livia and Natalia's mom, Gia Morelli, kneeling among the vegetable patch, Natalia and their other childhood friend, Elena, sunning their legs on the path. She pushed aside the stab of relief she felt that Kate hadn't chosen today to drop by.

The spring day was uncommonly warm, and Bianca threw off her expensive hat and tugged away the new gloves that Marshall had bought for her, flexing and stretching her fingers in turn.

He'd declared that the old things she'd worn for teaching and flitting around the likes of Italian tenement houses were only fit for the trash. Bianca had urged him to reconsider throwing out the outfits she'd carefully made herself, sitting sewing with Livia during the darkest evenings of the war, while Kate was working in Washington, their blackout curtains tightly closed, the radio chatting away like some crazy house guest.

It had just been the two of them. And she'd taken her home for granted. Always, always, wanting to get out of here.

So, they'd all gone. All her old things, the clothes she and Livia had made. Marshall had said his mother had donated them to the poor. And when Florence had swept in and decorated their house, telling Bianca she had the expert eye, like a lamb, Bianca had complied. She'd let Marshall and his family, with their superior standing, tell her exactly what to do. She knew the sick feeling that accompanied her mornings was not all the fault of the pregnancy her doctor had just confirmed. Surely, things would get better once Marshall's family all heard this news.

Bianca tapped on the back window, and when Livia turned, startled, to stare, her brown eyes widening in astonishment, Bianca blew her mom a kiss and a wave.

Shedding as much as she could of her Queens finery, shedding as much as she could of Bianca Green, Bianca slipped into her old pair of garden shoes that Livia still kept in the broom cupboard, grabbed an old cardigan of her mom's and opened the half-glass back door that led out of the tiny, bright kitchen and shaded her eyes against the glorious spring sun.

In a flash, her old friend, Natalia, was up and running toward her, pulling her into a hug, holding her at arm's-length, her intelligent brown eyes taking in Bianca's white face.

"Son of a monkey! You look like you need a gigantic slice of cassata. What have you been eating? Breadsticks and peanuts?" Natalia said.

Soon, Gia, Livia and Elena were crowded around her.

"Looks like she's seen the Washington Square Park ghosts, if you ask me," Elena added, her strong features curling into a frown. "Come here, you." She pulled Bianca close.

Bianca forced her gaze away from them, her two oldest friends, toward her mother's black eyes, which were crinkling in concern; Natalia's mom, Gia, quietly taking in everything.

Bianca closed her eyes against the sound of them all chattering at once, reveled in the way they elongated their vowels, rolling their r's in the way Bianca had tried so hard to rid herself of.

She swallowed the thick lump that formed in her throat. "It's all peachy. It's terrifically swell."

All that effort that went into the wedding. She couldn't say a thing. She'd have to go back to Queens, and she'd have to pretend it was all okay for the rest of her life.

But for now, Bianca stood back, overwhelmed with hunger pangs now she was home and out of that artificial environment out in the suburbs. She was certain she could smell *Pasta alla Norma*, pasta with eggplant, basil, garlic, fresh tomatoes and ricotta. And she'd hazard a guess it was Elena's mom cooking their family lunch. She closed her eyes at the thought of them all sitting around the table in the kitchen later on, laughing, talking over each other, passing around the crusty Italian bread, bowls of fresh pasta bright and colorful, and plenty of wine.

"I could murder a plate of—"

"Fresh brioche and granita," Livia said, wiping a hand over the apron she wore. "You wait right there, and I'll bring some out, darling. You need feeding up." She tutted and swept off inside.

Bianca stood helplessly while Natalia and Elena eyed her expensive dress.

Most of the girls around here would give anything to be living in a grand home like she was.

In what seemed like a flash, Livia had spread a red-and-white checked tablecloth on the round wrought-iron table that one of the elderly members of the community had made years ago, and they all settled down around it, Bianca's eyes drinking in the fresh, round brioches, the crisp lemon granita, the pot of freshly brewed coffee.

She'd forgotten how her mom and Gia could conjure everything out of nothing. Perhaps it had been the war that had done it, those dark days during which they all hid their Italian pride away, cultivating this garden, folding in on themselves like doves tucking their heads under soft wings, while Mussolini tried to march his Fascism all over their home country, and the local elderly faces had turned pale with shame. So many of them had lost relatives back home. So many of them had lost sons who had never come back to New York.

Perhaps, also, that deep shame in her nationality during the war was partly why she'd allowed Marshall and his all-American family to completely strip her of her Italianisms, of her past, Florence declaring to Marshall one night when Bianca had overheard that the only way his marriage would work would be if they kept Bianca's heritage quiet.

When had she become ashamed of her home country? Who had put such a notion in her head?

"You do look peaky, Bianca. Are you sure everything's as peachy as you say?" Natalia asked, her pretty eyes serious.

"Let her have her coffee, Natalia," Gia warned her daughter.

Bianca buttered her brioche, taking in a bite of the bread and closing her eyes at the softness, the sweet dough against her tongue. "If I have to boil one more corned beef, bake one more brisket, or suffer through any more My-T-Fine Vanilla Puddings, I think I'll go stir-crazy." She attempted a smile. "I sure do miss the food around here."

Livia's face clouded, and she looked with concern at her daughter.

Bianca, suddenly overwhelmed with shame at her outburst, couldn't bear to worry her mom. "Well, here's news. I'm having a baby," she said, placing her coffee cup down, reaching for the cool, tangy granita, turning her spoon in its depths. She raised her face to them all and smiled them her perfect lie. "So, isn't that grand?"

"*Santa Madonna*," Livia murmured. "Sufferin' succotash! Darling, what wonderful news!" She pushed back her chair and clasped her hand to her chest.

Bianca swallowed, but the granita stuck in her throat.

"Holy moly," Elena said. She downed her espresso, tipping back her head and slamming her cup down on the tablecloth. "Well. I'll be godmother. Don't you forget me."

Natalia placed her coffee cup down ever so slowly. "Congratulations, honey," she breathed.

"I'm so very happy for you," Gia said.

Bianca gaped down at her half-empty plate, while the garden all around her swayed in the soft spring breeze. "You are pleased?"

"Thrilled," Livia said. And then she chewed on her lip. "It's just, you'll be so far away."

Bianca nodded, head up and down. She'd have to go back soon. Go to the butcher. Have dinner ready after Marshall returned from his Saturday golf before he fell into bed, and then tomorrow, they'd get up all over again and go to the Episcopalian service with his family. There'd be lunch at Florence's home afterward and none of them would talk to her. If she were lucky, she could dash out alone to the nearest Catholic church for evening Mass.

Bianca let out a half-smile. "I'm very lucky. Marshall is…"

Livia's face crumpled. "I always thought my grandchild would be raised near home. You know? With us all around her to cheer her on. But I'm happy for you, you know that, darling."

Gia reached out and rubbed Livia's back, and Natalia and Elena exchanged a glance.

Bianca bit on her lip. She fidgeted, her fingers interlacing themselves into a mighty knot in her lap. "It will all be fine, Mama," she said.

Livia stood up and moved to stand behind Bianca, leaning down and placing her cheek against her daughter's. "You'll have Marshall's family right around the corner. You've really gone out and found your dream, sweetheart. I'm proud of you."

"Yes," Bianca said. "Yes, Mama." Tears threatened to spill down her cheeks, and she took a great, gulping breath.

"Oh, Bianca," Gia Morelli murmured softly, taking one of Bianca's hands in her own reddened palm. "It will all be fine."

Would it? And suddenly, Bianca fought an overwhelming and strange urge to hug her big sister, Kate. She wanted to hug her big sister and have things go back to how they used to be before Papa died, because Kate was the only one she knew who'd have the heart, the courage, the intelligence, and perhaps, *the education*, darn it, to stand up for Bianca out in Queens, to help her make it, in what should be her perfect life.

But things were so far gone between them. There was no way she could reach out to Kate after the way she'd yelled at her, no way that she could hope that things would ever go back to the way they once were.

Chapter Twelve

Kate

New York, May 1946

Kate made her way up Sixth Avenue to Radio City. She pushed open the swinging glass doors at the entrance to the tall skyscraper, registered with the man behind the glass counter in the grand foyer, and took the elevator up to the fourth floor to WNYR. She grasped her small briefcase, with her draft story on the marriage convention she'd endured a couple days back folded neatly inside.

She'd sat through the entire excruciating convention at the Waldorf Astoria, while a panel addressing hundreds of hopeful women told the room how sixteen million women over the age of seventeen in America were still unmarried, and that the days of a girl sitting on her front porch waiting for Mr. Right to come along were well and truly gone. A girl had to go out and find her husband. And she had to adopt strategies if she was going to land herself a suitable man.

Kate had sat there, poleaxed, making notes in horrified silence, clenching her pen until her knuckles turned white, while the so-called experts—a male doctor, the director of a modeling agency, a happily married housewife, a socialite, the editor of a women's magazine and an eligible bachelor—had all dispensed advice to the eager girls in the room, finishing up by telling everyone that the one key thing to landing a husband was *never* to let any man believe a woman's career was more important than he was.

Kate had sat up studiously typing her story in her little apartment, pushing aside her annoyance, thoughts of her own baby sister and *her* suitable husband going through her mind. Kate felt the inclination to just get on the train and go see Bianca so very often, to see how she was doing, what her life in the suburbs was really like. But she held back, still unsure, Bianca's harsh and hurtful words ringing in her ears, even so long after they'd been said.

And yet, here she was, stuck writing for the very young women who would end up exactly like Bianca was, while the powerful, horrible stories which she knew Americans needed to hear were the ones she'd not been allowed to tell.

Hilary Winthrop came into the reception area of WNYR with its modern, low seating and its glass tables set with newspapers and magazines. The older woman held out a hand in greeting and ran her eyes over Kate's slim-cut navy suit of rayon crepe.

Kate was mortified to see that Hilary was dressed in almost exactly the same outfit as her. She'd admired Hilary's understated way of dressing and had ended up copying her!

She'd rushed to get dressed this morning, sipping down fresh coffee, after another night assailed with horrific images of what she'd seen in Germany. Bathed in sweat, her stomach sick to the bone, she'd lurched out of bed and stumbled to the kitchen for a glass of water, needing the simple fact of a light on to repel the horrendous memories, Berlin with its bombed and burned-out houses, the merciless cold, the unspeakable misery. And that little girl who couldn't speak.

Kate's memories of Germany were more real than any dream. They haunted her in the twilight zone between waking and sleep.

But now, Hilary swept her down a long corridor and Kate had to try to focus on what was in front of her and let Germany go, if only for a few hours.

"When you came in last time, you didn't get a tour, Kate. Would you like the tour we give all our new employees?"

"Yes, please, Miss Winthrop," Kate said, refraining from point-ing out she was not an employee of the station, she did not even hold a contract.

"Call me Hilary, if you please."

Hilary took her past the closed doors that lined both sides of the long wood-paneled hallway, some rooms with lights overhead that read "ON AIR." Hilary swept on, but Kate took in the photos that lined the corridor, photos of WNYR's radio stars, broadcasters, actors and actresses in the stations' soap operas who graced the airwaves and were becoming household names across the United States.

"I know you've had more experience in print journalism than radio," Hilary said, taking a clipboard from a boy with a pencil behind the ear and leading Kate further into the station's depths. "But we believe here that radio knows no limits, and what goes on in the world goes on in every American living room, thanks to radio."

"It sure is something else," Kate said, stepping aside for a group of suited young men to pass them by.

"Hard to believe radio started in a shed in Pittsburgh with the first radio studio," Hilary said, "when you see us now in the Rockefeller Center."

Kate sent Hilary a smile, and Hilary led her into a large room with a selection of straight-backed chairs set out in rows.

"This is one of our observation galleries, Kate, and an audience can watch a show being recorded right down there." She pointed at the studio, visible through an oversized glass window below. The studio, which was empty, sported a single microphone hanging in mid-air. "As you know, our programs are not broadcast from here but sent by wire to the transmitter station, located outside New York, from where they are actually put on air."

Hilary held the door open for her, and next, she led Kate to another wide window set into the corridor. Through the window was a black control board lined with knobs and buttons that stretched along the back wall of the entire room. Two men sat behind it.

"Here," Hilary said, "is our master control board. Every program is wired through this to the transmitter."

Kate watched the two men operating the master control panel a moment. It was all very modern, and exciting.

"This way, Kate."

They passed by the huge scheduling room, where a weekly board outlining each day of the week and each program the station was airing was attended to by another two young men. Then, Hilary let Kate take a quick look inside a conference room, where there was a rectangular table, and ten leather chairs set around it. Scripts sat ready for the next meeting of the department conference heads, the first step in the creation of any program the station aired.

Just then, Hilary stepped aside for three men to enter the room.

Kate started when Harvey stopped right in front of her, his face breaking into his trademark grin.

"Hello, there, Harvey," Kate said, returning his smile. *Could he get her some work that was more reflective of her training? Oh, she hoped so.*

"You know Mr. Milton, our new Head of News and Special Events?" Hilary asked.

Kate regarded Harvey and raised a brow.

"She sure does know me," Harvey said. "We were on the same delegation of correspondents that toured post-war Europe for ten months. Delighted to see you here, Kate. And I'm doubly delighted that you're working with Miss Winthrop."

The other two men went inside the room.

"What are you working on now, Kate?" His tawny eyes crinkled.

"I'm reporting on…" She turned to Hilary, a faint blush stealing across her face. *What* was she doing? The realm of women's stories still seemed alien and strange to her.

"Auntie Margaret's show," Hilary said. "We're doing a series of segments on women after the war, Harvey."

"Excellent!" Harvey smiled.

Kate stared at him. Oh, for some of Rick's sardonic wit right now!

"You wanted to write some in-depth pieces while we were away," Harvey said. "And I remember one of your interests was women's stories. Women in Germany. So, women in America. Perfect!"

Kate wanted to throw her hands in the air.

"I'm very excited to introduce Kate to our women listeners." Hilary sounded so genuine.

Harvey's enthusiasm had always been infectious, but right now, Kate only wished she knew how she could catch his bug.

Harvey patted Kate on the shoulder. "Well, I guess I'll see you around the traps!" he said.

Kate's chest heaved up and down. She shot a glance toward Hilary, suddenly overcome with a bursting need to at least try. "*Harvey?*" she said.

He turned around, and the other two men raised their heads across the room and focused on her too.

Kate was acutely aware of Hilary right behind her, but she plowed on, regardless. She couldn't let any opportunity go to waste, and here was one right in front of her eyes. "I'd particularly like to report on the UN Security Council sessions on talkback. Are there any opportunities for me to apply for such work here?"

Hilary went very still.

Harvey's tone was even. "Kate, I know how passionate you are about politics. And I do understand where you are coming from."

But the other man frowned at Kate, his graying eyebrows knitting together. "Why, the only women we have on air apart from our soap opera stars are Auntie Margaret, Cousin Jenny, and Joyce Jordan, who addresses questions as to whether women can possibly be things like doctors and women at the same time. Outside of women's issues, the answer is no." The man sent her a tight smile.

"We also have Sarah McNillis, our fictional grandmother who interviews housewives," Hilary said. "And then, there are our gossip shows, but that's about it for women, Kate."

But Kate stood her ground with the older executive. "I have an honors degree in political journalism from NYU, and nearly a year's experience reporting direct from Europe through North American News Alliance, as well as three years freelance in Washington. If you have any openings, sir, I'd love to apply."

The older man smiled, showing his slightly pointed teeth. He returned to the papers he'd been studying on the table. "Thank you, dear. Enjoy working with Hilary. Please leave the men's stories to the men. Right now, we need to plan a program with a panel discussing whether science can bring world unity, with participants from Harvard, a Nobel Peace Prize Winner, the Science Editor for the *Times*, and a Pulitzer Prize-winning *New York Times* journalist."

Kate lifted her chin. "Well, I would love to be a part of that, and I'm as passionate and knowledgeable about world affairs as any male journalist."

Out of the corner of her eye, she saw Harvey look down at the ground.

"I said no," the older man said, his tone moving from patronizing to angry. "We would never consider a woman for such things. Our male listeners don't want women. Now, please go back to your *women's* show."

How dare he! She'd left one war zone and walked headlong into an equally insidious one at home!

But the senior executive walked right across the room and closed the door in her face.

Kate turned on her heel, nostrils flaring, face reddened, and pounded down the hallway after Hilary.

"Management has a real attitude sometimes," Hilary confessed, once they were well away. "But, unfortunately, all our heads—programming, artists' services, publicity, press division, scripts—will choose men over women for reporting roles, because they still maintain a woman doesn't sound as authoritative, and they say both men and women listeners want men informing them of hard news stories. It's just the way it is."

Kate shook her head. "I'm sorry, but I can't believe it. When were stories divided between women and men?"

Hilary kept walking. She stopped outside a closed studio door at the very end of the long hallway.

"Here we are," she said, changing the subject. "Auntie Margaret's ratings are outstanding. She's the highest-rated women's talk show in New York right now. Welcome to her studio, Kate."

Kate stepped inside, greeting the sound engineer and Auntie Margaret, a woman in her forties with a savvy eye, loads of blue eyeshadow and blond hair that curled short at the collar of her red dress secured with a patent leather black belt.

Two microphones hung in the studio, and Auntie Margaret handed Kate the edited version of the script she'd written and sent in last week, the copy of which sat in her handbag right now. Kate looked over the redrafted version and cleared her throat. "Hang on…" She hadn't written a word of this.

But Hilary had disappeared. Auntie Margaret popped her headphones on, indicated to Kate to do the same, and the sound engineer carried out his soundcheck, telling Kate to move closer to the microphone.

After Auntie Margaret introduced her, Kate took her cue and a deep breath, and plowed into the story she had not written and would never write.

> *Hundreds of hopeful girls were lined up at the Waldorf Astoria, eager to get some answers to the one question that is on all unmarried women's lips, because every girl across the nation has only one goal in their lives: to find a man.*

It is no secret that the desire to marry and raise children comprises the formula for female contentment, and this was proven true when this week's convention quickly became one of the most popular events the Waldorf Astoria has held since the end of the war.

So, what did the panel of experts—a doctor, a magazine editor, a contented housewife, a socialite and one of the most eligible bachelors in New York—have to say to the hundreds of wide-eyed young hopefuls who sat in anticipation like a gaggle of eager starlets? After a war when proposals were made on dance floors with dashing men in uniforms asking girls to marry them after a whirlwind romance, women are left asking, if that has all gone, then what next?

This vital question was hotly debated, but by the end of the day, the unworldly, yearning audience came away with some very valuable tips indeed:

Every panelist agreed that young women's choice of employment was key. Getting a job in a medical, legal or dental office, or becoming a nurse or an airline stewardess was top of the list, because girls in those professions have very high marriage rates. When girls are on their way to these jobs, they were advised, don't sit by yourself on the train, or next to another woman. Why not bite the bullet and sit next to an eligible man instead?

And if he speaks to you, be nice to him, because you just don't know who he is.

Now, if you can't work in one of these highly coveted areas, then ask your friends who do if there are any eligible bachelors in their offices, and if there are, don't be shy, learn to paint and set up your easel right outside those premises, or, better still, outside a medical school, or a legal school, or, if you prefer, attend night school with men.

Next, you need to ask yourself, are you rooming with the right girl? If your roommate is a sad girl, then don't room with her anymore, instead, take a holiday to Europe and vacation at small hotels where you're more likely to meet eligible men.

Once you've found your dreamboat, you need to look good for him. Remember, always ask your man what he'd like you to wear and let him be the authority on your perfume. Wear high heels most of the time, they're sexier! Take good care of your health and don't tell him about your allergies. Men don't like girls who are ill.

And most of all, never let him believe your career is more important to you than marriage, although you could point out to him that the death rate of single men is twice as high as married men.

Well, that rounds up all the advice we have for you today, ladies. Good luck with finding, attracting and landing your man! Always remember, don't marry him if he has too many loose buttons!

Ten minutes later, Kate walked down the corridor with Hilary, not knowing whether to laugh or cry. But she accepted the check that Hilary handed to her over her desk and thanked the program director.

"Well done, Kate. You have a charming, natural speaking style that is well suited to Auntie Margaret's show. I'm sure her listeners will be eagerly awaiting your next story, and I can offer you another opportunity that I'd like you to file next week."

Kate sent Hilary a polite smile. "My story was heavily edited. The angle I took was completely cut."

Hilary spread her hands on her desk. "We can't take political angles when it comes to women's stories."

Kate sighed. "Why are women not supposed to take an interest in politics?" She shook her head. There were so many examples, so many things going on in the world outside the realm of the domestic arena, that women should know about. So why not target their programming? Why censor it so heavily? "Don't you think WNYR's women listeners would be interested in concepts such as the Iron Curtain, and how this divide in political thinking might impact the world in the coming years?"

Hilary started shuffling papers on her desk. "We want you to report on women's hair during and after the war. You can mention hats if you like."

Kate sat back in the seat. "Please, Hilary. If women can't report on 'men's' shows, then why can't we bring general stories into women's shows?" *Enlighten me. Tell me why women wouldn't want to be kept informed about talk of the US carrying out atomic tests on the Bikini Atoll, or the fact that thirty million people are starving in China? Because I sure would like to know!*

"I'm sorry, Kate. We just don't have those topics on our agenda. The other thing that is of interest is that Tupperware is being sold in department stores and hardware stores." Hilary frowned, "And something a little more controversial. I'm really very uncertain as to how our listeners are going to react."

"Oh?" Kate folded her hands in her lap.

"A French designer is said to be releasing a very controversial bathing suit. It's quite risqué. Of course, during the war, our bathing suits became smaller and smaller, and were made of two pieces of fabric, to accommodate wartime restrictions, but I feel what the French are proposing is going to take things to the next level." Hilary rolled her eyes. "Typical."

"Astounding." There was to be no talk of atomic tests for her. Only swimming costumes.

Hilary raised a brow and handed over the brief for the story on women's wartime hair.

Kate scanned the page in her hand and simply nodded. She loosened the collar of her white business shirt, thanked Hilary and walked out into the New York sunshine.

Chapter Thirteen

Kate

New York, May 1946

The night after her show on getting a husband was aired, Kate stayed up late, wearing a pair of old blue jeans and a soft knit sweater, her legs curled under her on the sofa and a cup of coffee warmed her hands.

She listened to the radio for hours, to all the stories that she wanted to hear. The in-depth discussion forums about the impact of Winston Churchill's speech in Missouri in March, where he had coined the phrase "Iron Curtain" to describe the divide between communism and democracy, three talk shows outlining some of the potential dangers of the expanding Soviet Union and then a panel about the strikes of two hundred and fifty thousand railroad workers here in the United States, leaving thousands of commuters stranded, and the effects of that on the economy, and how President Truman was threatening to use the government to operate the railways and draft the striking workers into the army.

Finally, well after midnight, she turned off her bedside lamp and fell into a troubled, haunted sleep.

Kate stepped into the crowds the next evening after a day spent researching the new French swimsuits, which were named after the coral reef in the South Pacific where the new nuclear bomb had recently been tested. She was writing about the bikini after all, but not in the way she'd planned. She held her hat on her head in the swift breeze, her head filled with what she'd heard from a fashion designer, three young models and a department store head, only to feel the tap of a hand on her shoulder. An all too familiar frisson passed through her as, slowly, she turned around.

"Kate."

Rick. Right here underneath his favorite fedora hat. He looked even more Humphrey Bogart than usual here in New York, with his brown eyes crinkling, and that look that could see straight through a girl. But he looked a little troubled as well, as if something was perpetually on his mind.

Kate sighed and shielded her eyes from the late-afternoon streaks of sunlight that beamed between the skyscrapers, the New York street sounds of car engines and beeping horns and folks shouting and rushing footsteps all a whirl.

She'd *have* to make an excuse. If she was to open the floodgates to her complicated feelings about the man standing in front of her again, she'd be gone.

"I'm sorry," she said. "You'll forgive me, you've caught me at a bad time, and I have to go write up a story for the morning broadcast." She winced at the irony of her words.

But Rick tilted his head to one side and looked perplexed. He'd gotten a bit of a tan from being home in the spring sun, and he crinkled his brown eyes in a smile.

He raised a brow. "I've been trying to contact you, Kate. Harvey told me how you were working at WNYR."

She turned away and pressed her lips together.

"Katia?" Gently, he turned her back to face him.

No. She swallowed hard.

"Let's catch up. Let me take you out for dinner. It would be good to talk."

She sighed, the ridiculous research she'd done weighing heavily in her bag. "I don't know, Rick."

"You've got better plans?" he said, his eyes scouring her face. His brows furrowed and he flinched, his shoulders drooping. And she knew she couldn't lie to him.

"Only if you include going home and sticking my head in the oven. I've been researching a story on swimwear all day. And my next gig? Women's wartime hair." She shook her head.

He held out his arm. "How about we talk about it over a martini." He tilted his head and sent her a smile.

Nothing more than a drink and a meal. *Nothing more.*

"Where do you feel like going?"

"Nothing fancy," she whispered. "We never did fancy, did we?"

He cracked a smile. "I think we could change that. Come on." He stood there with his arm out, all hers to take.

And Kate knew that if she laid her hand on his arm, then those feelings that she'd fought so hard to bury would come rushing back up to the surface.

But here he was, and here she was. And somewhere, deep inside, she knew if she told him to go away, she'd regret it for the rest of her life. So, she slipped her hand into his arm, breathing shakily at the poignancy she felt when they walked up the street together, not in Berlin, not in some far-flung, decrepit city ravaged by war, but at home. Their home. New York.

And she knew she couldn't feel more at home with him by her side if she tried.

He stopped outside a tall, arched entrance down Sixth Avenue toward Bryant Park. "I've wanted to try Josephine's since I came back from Europe."

He drew Kate aside from the front door, with people bustling in and out and an immaculately dressed young woman greeting people just inside.

"The owner was Head Chef at Valentino's, before setting up her own restaurant once the war was done." He held open the tall glass door for her once he had the chance and it was quiet.

"Well, I'll never," Kate murmured, distracted from her worries about Rick by the sight before her eyes. "I do believe this is the restaurant owned by the wife of my old childhood friend Tom Morelli. I'd heard she was a pretty determined sort of girl."

Rick paused a moment. "The owner's called Lily Morelli. You know her husband?"

"Yes, I do. But I haven't seen him in an age... since I moved to Washington, and then the war hit." Her mom had told her all about Tom's adventures during the war, and how he'd bought the thriving deli, Albertina's, while his wife had started up her own restaurant on Sixth Avenue. But she'd never imagined she'd have a hope of affording to eat here. She stopped. "Rick, you certain this is okay? I mean, we can go somewhere simple."

Rick shook his head and took off the fedora. "You deserve a treat," he murmured, his eyes flickering over hers. "And it's no problem, Katia." His expression softened.

Kate felt herself blush something terrible. Heavens to Betsy. Five minutes in and her heart wanted to jig away up the street.

Inside, the beautiful space bustled with waiters bearing delectable-looking food on white plates, and folks chatted and laughed as if there'd been no war at all. Tall arched windows and high ceilings lent a spectacular air to the room, and next to the bar, a massive stained-glass window was surrounded by beautiful art deco plaster decorations.

"Why, it's like something out of Vienna, or bohemian Budapest, very Art Nouveau," Rick said softly.

"It's a dream," Kate breathed, but Rick didn't hear her, and she drank in the gorgeous surrounds. Tom's wife must have a real flair for design, or she'd hired someone who did. Behind the bar, a huge landscape mural ran the length of the wall, and in front of it, marble-topped tables lent an unmistakably European air. Brass chandeliers glittered overhead, and folks sat at curvy banquettes set into the walls, as well as at the tables in the main dining space.

Rick spoke to the woman on the front desk, on which an old photograph of a smiling, beautiful woman sat in pride of place. Kate wondered who she was but kept her questions to herself while the hostess consulted her bookings for the night, reached for a couple of menus and led them to a secluded banquette set deep into the restaurant.

Kate slid into the velvet seat, sinking into its depths and marveling at how quiet it was at their table, given the restaurant seemed almost full.

"How did you manage this?" she asked, while a waitress unfolded thick linen napkins over their knees and handed them drinks menus. A waitress… even Kate knew that was unusual in a fine restaurant. Usually, waitstaff were exclusively men in New York.

She looked around the restaurant. The place was all staffed with women. But Rick had opened the drinks menu. And Kate simply shook her head.

"I wonder how hard Tom's wife had to fight to get all this," Kate mused, cupping her hand in her chin, not sure whether to linger her gaze on the gorgeous restaurant or, were she totally honest, Rick.

Rick ordered a bottle of champagne and poured her a glass. "I know someone else who shares a similar determination," Rick said. He held his glass up to toast hers. "I hope this inspires you and proves to you that you can get there too."

Kate eyed the champagne.

Rick sipped his champagne, his eyes on hers, their expression more serious. "Remember our little German friend?"

Kate's hand stilled. "You have news? Oh, Rick, you cannot believe how much I think of her."

"I do." He pulled an envelope from his jacket pocket and handed her some thin, almost transparent writing paper.

Kate reached out for the letter before Rick had the chance to hand it across. She leaned over it, needing to know, to understand what was going on back in Germany, and most of all, yearning to find out whether the child had a name, a story, any family she could call her own.

Dearest Rick,

I fear that this orphan's story is going to be worse than I imagined. And the more I am learning about the plight of the children in my homeland, the more I fear for what she has endured. Still, she will not speak, still, she stays silent, while my two nieces, sheltered and protected by a loving family, nevertheless try to bring some warmth into this poor child's days. They don't understand why she won't speak, but we all know one thing, she has lost faith in the world, and for that reason, she will not trust even us with her precious words but continues to hold it all in, by herself, locked away somewhere she dare not tell.

I hate to think what she is enduring in her mind.

I am certain that the only way to bring her peace is to help her feel safe enough to trust us with her story. Rick, every day you have no idea how thankful I am for what you and Katia did for this little girl.

I am learning terrible, tragic stories, how so many children in my homeland have no parents, no possessions, no place to call home. Millions of them, sharing this terrible predicament. I fear the child in our midst, the little girl for whom you, Katia and I care so deeply, has witnessed humanity at its very worst.

While I am unable to coax her to talk, I have made a little progress. I wanted to share this with you.

I have discovered the United Nations Relief and Rehabilitation Administration is trying to assist refugees driven from their homes. They employ skilled workers and volunteers to organize and care for these displaced people and I've talked to them and sent them the child's photograph, and the photograph of the little boy that I found hidden deep in the pockets of the clothes she was wearing when you brought her here. While the UN are mostly placing refugees in displaced persons camps, they are also helping to find family members, to discover if they are still alive, and then to identify what to do next.

When I made contact with their headquarters in the American Zone of Berlin, they explained to me the intense devotion that is needed to engender trust within these children again, as we do not know whether the child might have been a forced child laborer, a survivor of a concentration camp, or, as my theory was, a child sent to Eastern Prussia and then forced out when the Soviets came through.

They told me to give her a sense of security and an understanding that she is wanted and loved in the hope she might tell us her tale, and who she is.

All I want to do is listen to her story. We are continuing to give her plenty of food, clothing and love.

When it has come out, I will tell you.

Until then, stay safe, Rick.

My dearest thoughts,
Claudia

A bolt of sadness pierced Kate's heart. "Oh, my dear," she said. "Bless her." She pulled out her handkerchief, grief, guilt, sadness overwhelming her. Why was she even worrying about her own problems, when the gorgeous child who'd placed her hand so trustingly in Kate's could not even voice hers? "I shouldn't have come home and left her. I should have brought her to New York!"

Rick reached his hand under the table, and softly, took hold of Kate's. She took in a breath at the intimate gesture, another little jolt of electricity shooting up her arm. Despite her nerves being on fire, she didn't pull away but leaned in a little closer to Rick, ridiculously glad of his presence now as her mind turned back to Berlin.

"I hate to think what she must have endured," Kate said.

She looked down at the table, the voices around her suddenly turning to a blur.

"*Katia*," Rick said, gently lifting her chin.

She bit on her lip, her senses going crazy at his proximity. Somehow, the little girl seemed to embody all the devastation that Kate had witnessed in Europe, and at the same time, the child was deeply associated with Rick. It was all confusing, how full of emotion Kate's time with the child and Rick made her feel. It was as if for that twenty-four hours looking after the orphan, and being with Rick, she'd really lived for the first time in many years.

"You saved the child's life," Rick said softly.

Kate felt a sudden shiver run through her. Sitting here, so close with Rick, was as if she were back in Germany again. She sent a worried glance around the restaurant, the sense of imminent danger and heightened nervousness that she thought she had conquered suddenly returning, that feeling she thought she'd discarded ever since she left Europe and came home to New York.

"*We* saved her life," she whispered.

Rick squeezed her hand.

It wasn't until their entrées arrived, Paupiettes of Sole with Sauce Veronique for Kate, and Breast of Chicken Virginia with Sugar Cured Ham and Juniper Berry Sauce for Rick, that he dropped his second bombshell for the evening.

The fairy lights in the restaurant twinkled to life as twilight fell over Manhattan, and Rick let Kate help herself to the side dishes, tiny sauteed string beans, small roasted potatoes, before he spoke.

"I've been offered my own radio slot at WNYR," he said.

Kate's hand stilled over her plate.

"*Afternoons with Rick Shearer*. Every weekday at 5.30 p.m."

She nodded, trying to stem her disappointment. It was a prime-time slot. Of course, he'd been offered it. Why not? He was a terrific journalist.

It was just that she'd worked equally hard to be as good. And she was already at the station.

"How nice for you," she said. "Congratulations, Rick." The executive had warned her the day she'd read her story on the husband forum; they didn't want women telling important news stories. The listeners didn't like it. *But the executives clearly didn't like it even more.*

She tried to take in the exquisite plate of food.

"I haven't accepted the job, Katia," he said, his voice impossibly close.

She turned to him, astonished. "But you must. Take it. It's a perfect chance."

"No," Rick said, shaking his head, his eyes narrowing. "I don't want to damage your career."

Kate picked up her fork and took a bite of the delectable food. She closed her eyes in delight at the perfect balance of flavors that melted in her mouth.

Rick was quiet next to her, and while she savored the beautiful food that Tom's wife had created, a realization dawned. If a woman chef, and the owner of this restaurant, had risen to the top of her profession in the notoriously male-dominated world of haute cuisine, then, she, Kate Mancini, must not give up, no matter how hard things were. And if that little orphan girl could fight her way back home, and find a loving home, and people to take care of her, then she had to push on and fight too.

There had to be a way.

She just had to work out what it was.

Chapter Fourteen

Kate

New York, May 1946

Later, her taste buds still dancing with the taste of Lily Morelli's signature honey, pear, caramel and chocolate tarte Tatin, which had oozed the most decadent and wickedly velvety chocolate sauce, Kate allowed Rick to walk her home. The petits fours they'd had with their coffee were worthy of being on display in a patisserie window in Paris, they were so intricately formed—tiny pink meringues filled with cream and little red chocolate hearts perched on their tops, miniature mille-feuilles filled with raspberries and cream, and tiny pastries topped with coffee icing and pecans, along with exquisite bite-sized lemon tarts and chocolate truffles.

They came to a stop outside Kate's building, the sounds of the busy New York night all around them, cars hooting, folks laughing and lights flashing.

"I'd forgotten how wonderful New York can be. I'd forgotten about the magic," Kate said, drawing her light coat around her, looking up into Rick's eyes.

He'd put his fedora back on. "You deserve all the magic in the world."

"Yes, but I'm here, safe, and I only wish I could do something, anything for our little orphan," she said, folding her arms around her waist now, looking down at the ground. "I hate feeling so useless. I just don't know what I can do to help."

He stepped closer to the door to her building, shielding her from the steady flow of folks walking up and down the busy sidewalk. "I have an idea."

She looked up at him.

"How about we send her some toys? Come shopping with me tomorrow? I know how to cheer her up."

"But the cost of postage."

"I can run to that," he said. He spoke the words quickly, and Kate chewed on her lip. She couldn't afford such a thing.

"Are you sure?" she said. "Where would we go?"

Rick's eyes lit up and he tilted his hat at her. "Why, F.A.O. Schwarz, of course. Where else?"

"Fifth Avenue?" Kate said. "But isn't that mighty expensive? Fancy German toys and handmade this and bespoke that?" She held her hand to her mouth, suddenly aware of her faux pas. German toys going back to Germany?

"I don't think they would have been manufactured in Germany," Rick said, his voice gentle. "Let's say with confidence we'll be sending her gifts from the USA." He took a step closer to her, ostensibly getting out the way of a woman with a pram passing by.

Kate closed her eyes against the feel of him so close, fighting the urge to wind her arms around his neck.

She searched his face. "I think it's a grand idea. I can only contribute something modest, but—" she said finally.

He placed a hand on her arm. "Kate. It's no problem. But I would love you to choose, as you two had such a connection. What time suits you tomorrow?"

"Well, once I've filed my vital story on French swimwear, I should be available around noon."

He nodded. "See you then." And with that, he winked at her, and disappeared into the crowds.

Kate stood still for a while, before reaching in her bag for her key. What *was* she doing? She didn't know, but when it came to that orphan child, she was going to do it anyway.

The following day, the sun was high in the sky and the Central Park end of Fifth Avenue bustled with folks strolling up and down the street, dressed to the nines, women in pearls and high heels, men in sharp suits and felt hats. It always felt like an event coming up here, and as Kate walked toward the iconic toy store on the corner of Fifth and 58th Street, her heart skipped a beat when she saw the handsome man waiting there for her.

The great glass doors edged in shining brass were swept open for them before Kate had a chance to greet Rick. She raised a brow at his tailored suit, and when he took off his hat inside the famous toy store, his hair was all styled and nothing like the ruffled way he'd kept it on tour.

A store attendant approached them, held out his hand and shook both of theirs. "Can I help you today, sir, and madam?"

Kate looked down at her own pale blue dress, belted at the waist with a simple fabric knot. She removed her hat and pulled off the unaccustomed white gloves she'd put on in a flurry back home. She darted a nervous glance around the store filled with exquisite teddy bears, from ones you could hold in the palm of your hand to giant lifelike stuffed toys, and rows and rows of miniature toy cars and dolls of all shapes and sizes on display behind glass cabinets. Soft music played and staff helped well-to-do-looking customers who held wicker baskets.

"We'd like to purchase a selection of toys for a very special child. And I want them sent to Europe," Rick said.

Kate's grip on her gloves tightened. Did Rick realize what that was going to cost? But he moved forward with confidence while the store attendant collected two large wicker baskets, gave one to Rick and asked him if the lady would like one too.

Ricks' expression clouded. "I think we can ask the lady herself, don't you?" he said.

The young man reddened.

"Oh, never mind," Kate said. She accepted the basket, her eyes wandering around this place of magic. It was as special as the restaurant that Rick had taken her to last night, and as she glanced around the gorgeous space, she noticed one thing. None of the toys had price tags on them. They'd have no way of knowing what things cost.

But Rick was waiting for her to lead the way with the attendant. And Kate swallowed hard and walked alongside the young man. Had Rick, like her, saved all his income from the tour? Clearly, money was not a problem. She knew that men earned three times the money women did for exactly the same work, but she had no idea how a journalist could afford to come and shop at places like this.

Rick stopped at the first glass cabinet. It was filled with board games. The soft hush of piped music and well-dressed Uptown folks chatting with white-coated store attendants was only broken by the occasional child's squeal.

Kate hovered next to him. The lack of price tags was mighty worrying. But Rick pointed at a game of tiddlywinks, the box decorated with a great big heart. "How about one of those?" he said.

The attendant drew out a pencil and a notepad and started making a list. "All our toys out here are only for display," he said to Rick. "I'll make a list; we'll package your selection up for you and send it on its way this very afternoon." Clearly, he'd decided Kate wasn't worth addressing in her simple frock.

She clutched her empty basket and eyed the board game. How much would that cost? She couldn't let Rick bear all the costs, but she needed to be careful. Hilary was not giving her enough work to constitute anything like a full-time income.

But then, her eyes landed on a gorgeous teddy bear up ahead. While Rick was looking at a phonograph, complete with six records of popular tunes, Kate wandered up to the next glass cabinet, her heart warming at the sight of the plush teddy bear. His mouth was turned upward in a friendly smile, and his arms and legs were moveable. His button eyes just kindled with warmth and he looked as soft and huggable as cashmere. The little girl was so affectionate. Kate was certain this fellow would bring her cheer.

"How much for this darling thing?" she asked the man.

His nose tilted upward, and he barely hid his flinch. "That," he said, "is a Steiff bear. I'm afraid I'd have to check the cost. It's a golden-brown excelsior-stuffed mohair teddy bear. His head swivels and his nose and mouth are hand-embroidered. His limbs are disk jointed, and in his ear, he has the original metal button with the word 'Steiff' on it. He's from the 1920s and was made in Germany. You have excellent taste, madam." He looked at her doubtfully.

"We'll take one," Rick said.

Kate gasped. "Rick?"

But he shook his head. "This is for a child who is inexplicably dear to us both," Rick told the attendant.

"Yes, Mr....?"

"Never mind that," Rick said. "We'll definitely take the bear. Now, Kate. Is there anything else you think the child would fancy?"

Kate cleared her throat and shook her head. *Not unless you want to send yourself mighty broke.* "I don't want you spending too much," she murmured.

The store attendant didn't bother hiding the way his eyebrows raised this time.

"Katia," Rick murmured, "I promise you. It's fine. I have plenty of savings. I just want the child to feel loved. That way, we might have a better chance of helping her. The bear is a part of that." He sent her a crooked smile, and Kate felt herself blushing something awful, while her heart took on a wild dance.

"So." Rick turned back to the attendant. "The game of tiddly-winks, the bear, and the phonograph. And one more thing," he said.

Only one more?

Rick held out his arm for Kate. "This wooden block set of the New York skyline. Look at it, Kate. It's wonderful." His eyes crinkled as he looked at the tiny wooden, green-painted trees, the ribbons of blue river, the exquisitely carved and decorated skyscrapers, the Empire State Building, the train lines, the beautifully decorated wooden houses that looked just like the ones in the Village where Kate had grown up.

Kate leaned in to take a closer look. The set was entrancing. And so perfectly New York. "Oh," she breathed. "How magical."

"It's made of beech wood," the attendant said.

Rick's face broke into a grin and he winked at her. "Katia," he said, his voice soft. "Let's send her something that will bring her closer to us."

He spoke to the store attendant, went over to the counter to sort out the account, and wrote out Claudia's address in Celle on a piece of paper.

Kate was right next to him; she opened her purse.

"Kate, I won't hear of it," he said. "Honestly, it's fine."

She shook her head.

"I promise," he went on, thanking the attendant and tucking her hand into his arm. "Darling, when you have a full-time contract at WNYR, and I'm certain you will one day soon, you can take me out to dinner, and I'll gladly accept, but for now, I want to put this child's interests first, and I want to let her know that we..." he stopped just at the front door of the store. "I want her to know that we care. That we love her." His voice was so soft it was almost indiscernible.

As Kate stood by him in that enchanted store, while outside Fifth Avenue with its mansions that once were the homes of the most successful dreamers in the world, and its exquisite storefronts and its skyscrapers standing tall, she simply nodded.

He was right.

And she was glad he was sharing some of this magic, the magic of New York that was only for the privileged few, with a little girl who had lost everything, and who had as much right to joy in her life as anyone else.

Chapter Fifteen

Rick

New York, May 1946

Rick stepped into the hushed lobby of the limestone clubhouse on Park Avenue, his feet echoing on the marble floor underneath the spectacular coffered dome. He signed himself into the members' book, the silver pen that the receptionist handed him cool and smooth against his fingertips, still roughened from years away at war.

The scent of bespoke cigars wafted out from the card room nearby, mingling with the freshness of the roses that were arranged on the table in the center of the entrance. Rick paused a moment, reflecting that he had not stepped inside the famous club which his grandfather and father viewed as a second home since the war had started. Rick knew he was hardly recognizable as the man he'd been before his tour of duty, before the war correspondent's tour that had changed his life.

The unmistakable sound of his father's laughter rang out from the famous lounge and writing room that ran the length of the club's Park Avenue façade. Rick ran his hands down his suit, automatically checking that everything was pristine. Even though Rick had adhered to the club's strict dress code, Willard Shearer was a stickler for appearances, and the last thing Rick wanted to do was give him a reason to complain.

Not today, of all days.

In the lounge, settled under the decorative ceiling that was designed like a billowing festival tent, several middle-aged and elderly men were dotted around in groups, legs crossed elegantly in the finest tailored suits. In here, the perfume of roses was replaced by the spicy aroma of Colonia and Blenheim Bouquet, the classic men's fragrances that gentlemen of society preferred.

Rick's father gazed toward him, Willard's expression flickering with that slight disapproval to which Rick had long become resigned. Willard stood up and excused himself from the group of gentlemen with whom he was sitting, reached out his pristine hand, shook Rick's formally, and ushered him to a quiet set of wingback chairs in a secluded spot by one of the tall windows overlooking the street.

Rick settled down opposite his father, eyeing the folks out there in the warm sunshine wistfully, suddenly wanting to jump onto one of the crowded buses on Park Avenue. He turned to face Willard.

"Thank you for joining me," Willard said, his sardonic tone matched by the way he raised one of his gray eyebrows. He waved to the waiter who was hovering by the door and ordered a whiskey and sour. He accepted a cigar from the proffered box.

Rick ordered a gin and tonic, refused a cigar and sat back in his seat, tapping his fingers on the leather handles. "I had my own reasons for coming here, to be honest," Rick said.

"I imagine you did." Willard cut his cigar and held its tip above and near the flame of the cedar spill, rotating the cigar so that the tip was equally heated.

Rick watched until there was a glowing ring all the way around the cigar's tip and the edges were thinly blackened. He'd learned at a young age not to speak to his father while he performed any of his rituals. Only when Willard raised the unlit end of the cigar to his lips and took his first puff, did Rick open his mouth. "But I came to see how you were too. How are you?"

Willard gazed across the room, narrowing those blue eyes in the way he did when he was distracted, which was much of the time. "Perfectly fine. Why do you ask?"

Rick leaned forward, cradling the gin in his hands, not entirely unused to his father's defensive stance.

Willard swiveled his head back to face Rick. "I suppose you've spoken to your mother. Is that why you are here?" He shook his head. "I wouldn't take what she says seriously."

How could his dad ever think she would open up and talk? Frances always avoided anything remotely unpleasant when it came to friends and family, and it was something Rick loved about her. His mother refused to indulge in gossip as so many in their circles did, preferring, instead, the newspapers, world events, history, politics, books, but as he'd grown older, Rick realized his mother's refusal to discuss her feelings were also the result of a harmful restraint on her part.

"Is anything going on?" More to the point, *what* was going on? When Rick had returned home to Woodlands, he'd been alarmed at the change in his mom. She was stick-thin and pale. And she was afraid of something, Rick was sure of it. He'd learned to observe her acutely at a young age, because of her tendency to stay quiet.

"What makes you ask if there is anything amiss?" Willard's tone and his blue-eyed gaze were mild.

"You tell me." Rick bit back his frustration.

"I don't see that it's necessary to share personal details with you. There are limits."

Rick smiled into his glass of gin. "Well then." He lifted his head. "I will start by sharing something myself. I trust you won't view my doing so as some form of weakness."

A muscle flickered in his father's cheek. "Go on."

"I would like, that is, I have met someone of whom I've grown very fond, and I'd like to bring her home to meet you and mother."

"Are you serious about this someone?" Willard dropped his voice.

Rick held his father's gaze. "I think it would be wise for her to meet you all before it becomes serious, Dad. In fact, I'd like to bring her as a friend so that she knows what we're about before I ask her on a date."

Willard was silent.

"I care about her too much not to tell her about… us. To be honest, I want to give her a chance to know the truth about me, and if she wants to get away quickly, she can."

Willard puffed on his cigar. He indicated with it. "She's not from the families, I take it."

Slowly, Rick shook his head. "She's not from our circles."

"Where did she grow up? Go to school?" His questions were brief, typical, expected.

"The Village. NYU. She's a journalist."

Slowly, Willard lowered his hand over the ashtray, flicking his cigar into the silver dish. "Does she have a name?"

Rick narrowed his eyes. His father had connections. If Rick mentioned Kate's name, he knew Willard would have someone check her out.

"I would appreciate your confidence in my ability to make my own choices before I tell her your name. And a promise you won't go investigating. There's nothing to find."

Willard returned to his cigar. "Don't be so naïve, Rick. There's always something. Everyone has a story."

Rick's expression was tight.

"Whoever she is, she'll see Woodlands and want an engagement ring on the spot."

"I'd hoped you'd changed. I'd hoped the war had changed things, Papa. Surely…" Rick's voice cracked and the old endearment that he used to use when he was a child slipped out.

"Let me tell you one thing, and one thing only," Willard said, leaning closer, eyeing Rick through the smoke haze. "It takes a certain type of girl to be able to handle our life. Woodlands. The way we live. The bank. No ordinary woman will manage. When you inherit—"

"Stop." Rick's leg started to jig up and down, fast on the floor, like it used to when he came home from boarding school and had to have excruciating discussions about his future with his father. He tried to take in a deep breath, but his throat caught.

Willard narrowed his eyes into two mercurial blue slits. He dropped his voice to the tone of a barely-there whisper, but his words spoke louder than if he'd shouted through a microphone. "Your mother grew up in the right circles. She knows how to handle herself in every single area that is required. Choosing anyone from a different background will be a disaster. I trust I make myself clear, and the answer is no. What's more, I've indulged this journalism idiocy up until now, and I've been more than generous with your selfishness." Willard waved his cigar in the air. "But I'm not having some laughable liaison in the family on top of it. Some woman who will bring us all down. The Village? Forget it. Forget you ever met her."

"I'm not doing that." Rick rubbed his brow, a headache starting to form behind his temples. Right now, the thought of stalking out to get some fresh air was more than tempting. He glanced around the old-fashioned, quiet club, flooded with memories of brandy in chipped mugs on cold hotel room floors, his friends sitting around with him talking about things that did matter, not excluding people who deserved better, or in Kate's case, people who deserved only the best. The question was not so much whether she was good enough for his family, but whether his family were good enough for Kate.

There was a cough from behind Willard's high-backed leather chair. Willard swiveled his head around and Rick raised his eyes. He'd been so caught up in his father's outburst that he'd not noticed the club staff member sidling up close to them.

"Phone call for you, Mr. Shearer," the man said.

Willard's hand stilled, his cigar poised mid-air.

"Miss Daisy McKinnon," the man said. "In booth three." The staff member reddened slightly and cleared his throat.

Slowly, Rick leaned forward in his seat. "Daisy McKinnon?" he breathed. "The Broadway actress. Now why would she be calling you?"

Willard's eyes flashed to the right. "There are two types of women. One for marriage, one for affairs. You need to learn the difference."

"I take it this is the woman for whom you have broken my mother's heart. I'm leaving, Father. I cannot sit in the same room as you." He threw his napkin down on the table and was turning away when his father reached out, laying a firm hand on his arm.

Rick pushed his father's hand back, stood up and walked out of the club, loosening his tie and hardly acknowledging the doorman who swung open the heavy wooden doors at the entrance to the exclusive, all-male club.

Rick was ashamed of his father. He was ashamed of him for his mother's sake, and now, for Kate's. What had either of them done to deserve being treated with such utter contempt?

And that begged another question. A question that had whispered quietly in his ear for months, only to beam a warning more brilliant than any lighthouse after this disastrous encounter with his father. A relationship with Kate could send both her and him sailing headlong toward deadly, treacherous rocks.

Rick stood in his apartment on Central Park West that evening, still dressed in the suit he'd worn to the club. He'd pounded around Midtown after his encounter with his father, head down, scowling, before finally winding up in a diner near Radio City, where he'd ordered barbequed ribs and coleslaw, washed down with a beer. He'd bumped into a couple of journalism colleagues, who'd managed to take him out of his foul mood for a couple hours.

But now, hands buried in his pockets, tie loose, top button of his shirt undone, Rick looked fixedly out the huge picture windows of his apartment's living room, at the dark expanse of Central Park, the tracery of lights that wound around the pathways shining in the endless dark, and the twinkle of lights on the skyscrapers on the East Side of the park forming geometric patterns that had fascinated him when he was a kid and had stood staring out the windows of apartments like the one he now owned.

It was all right for some.

Kate's view was of a fire escape.

Daisy McKinnon. He knew the name. She'd been linked to a series of high-profile businessmen, and clearly Willard Shearer was the latest in a long line.

What a cliché.

And his father had put him in an impossible position; either he'd have to lie to his mother and keep his father's indiscretion secret from her, or he could tell her, and break her already hurting heart.

Rick turned and strode through his luxurious living room, his fingers brushing the cream art deco chairs with their black piping and matching velvet buttons that were scattered with silk cushions, all set on luxurious cream rugs. He flicked on one of the tall lamps, sat down on a sofa, crossed his legs and picked up the phone from a low coffee table, a crystal vase of brightly colored hydrangeas having been placed there by the maid.

No. His father should be the one to tell his mom the truth. It was not Rick's job to do such a thing.

Rick went to his desk and reached for a sheet of embossed writing paper. The family's embossed writing paper. The paper that Willard took such pride in when he sent his little missives off to society friends, men at the club, extended family. It was all a farce.

Rick twisted the lid on his fountain pen and began writing to his father, informing him that it was Willard's obligation to tell Frances what was going on.

Once he had the letter tucked into his jacket pocket, addressed to his father at the club, Rick moved to the phone and picked up the receiver. Only to place the phone down again, bringing his hand up to rub his chin. Kate couldn't afford a phone. He couldn't even call her.

He frowned, tapping his polished shoe on the rug. He gazed through the living space, beyond the sweeping staircase that led to the suite of four bedrooms on the floor above, to the vast dining room, with its dazzling art deco light overhanging the polished walnut table that ran the length of the floor-to-ceiling windows that brought the park almost inside, the leather upholstered chairs, and the huge kitchen beyond which was up to the minute with marble benchtops. His father had commissioned several pieces of modern art which were backlit on the walls, along with sculptures which Rick knew would be worth a fortune one day.

He'd been given the apartment for his twenty-first birthday.

What would Kate think? Was he being fair to her in even considering it? Because Rick knew his entire family would not take to her background. In fact, they'd make things as difficult as possible for her.

Even, possibly, his mom.

He leaned forward, hands dangling between his knees. Damn it. He would never want to cause Kate to suffer in any way. But he'd fallen for her, he knew the signs. When half the guys on tour had tried chatting her up, he'd taken a different stance. Offered Kate friendship, because he thought she'd appreciate it. But then, his genuine regard and respect for her gumption coming on a tour for ten months as the only woman journalist in a group of men had grown and overwhelmed him.

He'd asked her about herself, and they'd talked, and gradually the mutual respect and interest in him that she'd showed, in turn, had caused him to care, deeply, especially when he saw the way she felt so strongly about the Europeans, the United States' former enemies, who were suffering so badly as they passed through all the devastation of the Second World War.

While the other reporters had taken a hard-bitten approach, some even throwing sardonic comments around about the Germans getting their just deserts, Kate had shown the most empathy he'd seen in a person in a long time, and he adored her for it. Not to mention, she was startlingly attractive, funny, hard-working, well-educated and intelligent. He liked her. And then, that night when she'd curled up and slept next to him on the floor...

He slumped back in the chair. He should not offer himself to her. She'd hate all this. Wealth. Privilege. Snobbishness. He knew her well enough to know that.

Rick picked up his keys and strode toward the front door. He'd go for a walk. Clear his head for the second time that day. Because there was something else that was bothering him deeply as well: he couldn't bear the thought of ending up like his father.

Today's encounter with Willard had brought that home to roost and it wouldn't go away. Heaven help him if he ever treated Kate, or a woman of her or his mother's integrity, like Willard was treating his mom.

Rick stopped in the entrance hall by the front door, standing in the echoing, silent space. *Had his father ever felt the way he felt about Kate right now about his mother?* What had happened to Willard? What had turned him into the lesser man who was clearly lying to his family? And would the middle-aged Rick be immune to such weakness...

No, he couldn't risk Kate's heart with his own flawed heritage.

Rick flicked off the light in the entrance hall. He stood in the dark a moment, hands clenched by his side.

Shutting the door softly, he strode out into the anonymous New York night.

Chapter Sixteen

Bianca

New York, June 1946

The table was set, the candles were lit, and the hors d'oeuvres were arranged on a platter. Bianca surveyed her afternoon's handiwork, nerves mingling with anticipation at what the evening might bring. Apple and salami porcupines, chicken livers and bacon, cocktail sausages, blue cheese and minced onion spread on potato chips, celery stalks stuffed with cream cheese, and stuffed olives and bacon all sat ready to be passed around to the dinner guests. The fact that one of those dinner guests was Kate was something Bianca was forcing herself not to panic about.

Her hopes for tonight were a long shot, she knew that, but if she didn't take the opportunity to try and bring Kate back into her life right now, she, Bianca, might just go under. Her doctor was talking about tranquility pills as soon as her baby was born, and Patricia and Florence were still cold toward her, still excluding Bianca from every social occasion on their calendars and only tolerating her at family occasions when Marshall was around.

If Bianca couldn't be fully recognized as a part of Marshall's family, she'd bring her own family into Queens instead.

Bianca removed her apron and patted her freshly coiffed hair. Thank goodness her nausea had started to ease up, because the smell of her Easy and Elegant Ham with its side of creamy mashed potatoes would have sent her reeling a couple of weeks back. Now, her waistline was still trim and the new blue dress that Marshall had bought for her to cheer her up swirled to her knees. She took in a deep, steadying breath at the sound of the doorbell ringing.

The moment her mom had mentioned that Kate was researching a story on women's wartime hair, Bianca had seen her chance. She had called Kate and offered to help, having finally made one new friend named Betty at calisthenics who used to work as a hairdresser before her children were born. When Bianca had asked Betty and her husband for dinner, playing up the fact that Kate might just mention Betty's name on the radio if she helped out with the wartime hair story, Betty had jumped at Bianca's dinner invitation and offered to bring along her hairdressing friend, Ruth.

Then, with a stroke of genius and an impulsive dismissing of the consequences, Bianca had invited Marshall's partner, Roy Hammond, tonight as well. Marshall's business partner was a keen golfer, and a regular, wealthy, single guy who was a dear. Roy would be perfect for Kate. He'd tolerate her quirks and even liked reading the occasional book. He had a nice home around the corner that was just waiting to be filled with children and laughter.

If Kate was writing about womanly topics now, did that mean Bianca's sister was finally thinking of settling down? And if Kate moved out to Queens, well then. Florence and Patricia wouldn't have a hope of looking down their noses at Bianca's big sister. Everyone knew that Kate could out-debate a congressman.

Bianca opened her front door wide. She'd not realized the importance of her own family until she'd joined Marshall's.

Kate stood in a belted green dress, her curls pulled back from her face with a couple of tortoiseshell combs. She was turned to face the lush green, freshly mown lawn with its edges neatly trimmed and tidied, just like every other house in Forest Hill Gardens.

When Kate turned to face her, Bianca stopped frozen in front of her sister, memories of that awful day Papa died hitting her on every side. For a second, Kate did the same. The awkwardness between them still hung like a soiled sheet on a washing line.

"Bianca," Kate said.

Bianca stepped aside for her sister to enter her home. "Hey," she said. Was this going to be harder than she'd thought? She was such a whizz at imagining how her life should be. If only reality would at least try to match up.

"Looks like you've flown away and landed in the pages of *Inside My Home* magazine." Kate stood with folded arms in the living room.

Bianca brushed away sudden tears that threatened to spill down her cheeks. It had been happening lately, the urge to cry. She nodded bravely and invited her sister to sit down.

An hour later, everyone sat around the dinner table and Bianca handed around her platter of hors d'oeuvres. Roy Hammond and Marshall had made the cocktails, while Bianca was only sticking to tomato juice, and now the two of them were deep in a conversation about golf with Betty and Ruth's husbands, which was not quite to plan, but Betty and Ruth seemed keen as anything to talk to Kate about hair.

"I'm impressed that you work in a radio station," Betty said, eyeing Kate over her dry martini, her own auburn hair falling in waves to her shoulders and her brown eyes sparkling. "But I don't miss my work in hairdressing one bit."

"Oh my, no. Me neither," Ruth said. She helped herself to some celery stuffed with cream cheese and popped it into her rosebud-shaped mouth, her artfully made-up blue eyes dancing with interest.

"Well, that's grand for you," Kate said.

Bianca chewed on the tip of her thumb. She'd forgotten how stubborn Kate could be.

Once things were done with the hair story, Bianca was planning to get Kate and Roy to sit by each other after dinner on the large sofa. She even hoped that Ruth, Betty and their husbands might have to leave a little early so that she and Marshall could go make coffee in the kitchen while Roy and Kate became better acquainted. She would encourage him to stay and smoke a cigar with Marshall. That's what she'd do.

Sometimes Kate just didn't know what was good for her and she needed a little nudge.

"Once you get married, you'll understand," Betty said. She sent Kate a knowing smile.

"I'm afraid I can't comment on the marriage state." Kate's tone was even. She reached for her handbag, which she'd hung over the back of her chair, and pulled out a notebook and pen. "How about you tell me more about wartime hair? It's very kind of you to help me."

Bianca chewed on her lip. *Let's just get the hair part of this out of the way already and move to the main event!*

"Oh, you see, women wanted their hair cut shorter," Betty said, flicking back her waves. "An awful shame if you ask me, because I love long locks on a girl, but, you see, too many accidents were happening in factories, and so Veronica Lake cut her long hair short as an example. Then other American women were happy to follow her."

Kate wrote a few notes down. "I see. And now?"

"Now," Ruth said, running a hand through her own rich auburn curls, "folks want to leave the drabness of war behind them. Because that's what it was, *drab*."

Kate looked up sharply. "I can assure you that's the last word most women would use about the war. Maybe," she said, arching her brow, "it was only drab for some?"

Bianca's hand froze above her neatly crossed legs.

Ruth's blue eyes rounded. "Well, we are starting to get new hair products again, so we can all move on."

Kate contemplated Ruth a moment, then shook her head and went back to her little page full of funny notes.

Bianca smiled bravely.

Marshall let out a peal of laughter at something Ruth's husband said. Marshall was supposed to be encouraging Roy to notice how gorgeous Kate was. She sent him a kick under the table, but he didn't even as much as register her sharp little shoe.

"So how have things changed then, now this drabness, as you call it, is done?" Kate asked.

"Generally, side parts are in fashion, and turbans are out," Betty said. "During the war, women used to wear turbans, pinned their hair into curls, then they could shake things out, spruce up and dress their hair for a night out afterward. They had to wear their waves soft though, nothing like the crisp crested waves of the twenties and thirties."

Kate wrote, her brows knitting together.

Bianca sighed and went out to get the entrées served up.

"But bone-straight hair's not fashionable at all, that hasn't changed," Betty was saying when Bianca came back out with her ham.

No one faltered in their conversations even when she laid perfectly arranged plates of elegant ham and mashed potato in front of them. Only Marshall looked up and blew her a kiss.

Bianca sighed. Suddenly, her appetite dimmed. And she couldn't even have a glass of wine. She grimaced at the tomato juice.

"You need waves and curls to achieve the lift. You use your pin curls to style it into rolls and waves, and to brush it smoother for soft movement," Ruth said.

Kate ran a hand through her own natural curls.

"Kate has fine natural waves," Bianca said. "She'll never have to have a perm. I was always the one who had to sleep while my hair set."

"You could do a lot more with your curls, Kate," Betty told her. "You should go see Silvio on Austin Street, when you have a chance."

Kate demurred. "Well, I'm not so sure…"

"Oh, you should, yes, do," Ruth agreed. "There's nothing like a good gossip with Silvio. He'll tame those wayward strands of yours into submission, Kate. You'll be a different girl when you come out. Might just help you catch a husband." Ruth sent Kate a wink. "I know it's hard these days. So many girls, not enough men. After the war."

Bianca swallowed. *Wow.*

Betty looked thoughtful. "You should roll your hair, you know, dear. That would go a long way to helping you attract a man. You could do with a rat."

"A *rat?*" Kate said.

Bianca covered her mouth with a hand.

Kate sat back in her seat; hands pressed against her narrow waist. "The only rats I've seen lately have been in sewers."

The men turned silent at that, and Bianca folded her hands in her lap. *Kate. Honey. Please no. If you're moving to more womanly topics, let's not mention the sewers.*

Ruth looked confused. "What? No, silly. I mean a hair rat, you know, made from old stockings stuffed with more old stockings and used to bulk out hair rolls." She looked at Kate as if she'd landed from Mars.

Bianca took a harder look at Kate. She needed a makeover. She should have thought of that! Roy wasn't even giving her a second glance. Bianca's shoulders slumped. All her cooking gone to waste…

Kate picked up her pen and started writing again. "And what about accessories? You know, other things to put in your hair, apart from the… rat."

The men started talking golf again, and Bianca hid her groan.

"Slides and combs like those Bakelite ones you have in your hair work well, and grips and combs are awful popular," Betty said. "Some girls are lucky enough to own real tortoiseshell combs from their grandmas. We used a lot of hairnets in the salon to keep the back of the hair neat, and sometimes, we added braids during the war. That was fun."

Bianca saw the way her sister was struggling with this. It seemed now Kate was the one who was hopelessly misunderstood. In the modern world, her ambitions were out of step. Everyone was having babies. No, serious intervention was required.

"But the most important thing of all during the war was the victory roll," Ruth said. "It's a tight sausage at the back of the hair that is rolled upwards. Or you can tie the top of an old stocking right around your head like a headband and roll the hair over it."

Kate put down her pen. "I'm sure the listeners will be mighty fascinated with all of this."

"Oh, it is fascinating," Betty assured her. "Hairdos are the bee's knees."

"Apart from being married," Ruth said, sending Kate a pointed look. "Good hair attracts a good man. It's all in a good cause, isn't it, girls?"

"Sounds like a plan to me, girls." Marshall winked at Ruth.

And Roy chuckled next to him, while Ruth turned a becoming shade of pink.

But Bianca saw how Kate reached for her wine and raised her eyebrows to the roof.

"Now," Ruth leaned forward. "Let's get to the real point. Why hasn't a pretty girl like you got a husband?"

And all the men went quiet.

"Well," Marshall said. "You couldn't have a lovelier, more attractive woman."

And Kate turned bright red.

This was Bianca's cue. "My lovely sister just has to find the right man who is deserving of her," she said firmly. Avoiding Kate's eye. "Now, if you'll excuse me, I'm going to clear up the entrée plates. Why don't you all enjoy some more wine while I get the Lemon Meringue Pie?"

"What a marvel you are," Ruth's husband said.

Marshall refilled glasses and the conversation drifted away from Kate.

And Bianca smiled prettily at everyone and went out to her immaculate kitchen. She rinsed and stacked all the dirty plates, her heart beating in triumph. This was what Kate should be doing, having a home, hosting friends, entertaining, having babies alongside her. And if Bianca had her way, she'd be doing so mighty soon. If Bianca could set up Kate with Roy, well then. She'd be the happiest girl in the world.

Or the second happiest.

The happiest girl would be Kate.

After most of the dinner guests had gone, Bianca lay stretched out on the sofa, her shoes kicked off. Kate perched on a chair opposite, cradling a cup of coffee, and Marshall and Roy had gone into his study to smoke a cigar.

"Are you happy out here, Bianca?" Kate asked.

Bianca tensed. Did this mean that Kate was interested in moving out here too? She could hardly dare to hope, but she could also hardly contain her excitement that Kate might be open to what Bianca had in mind for her.

"Of course," she said. Now was her chance. "What do you think of Roy?"

"The wallpaper guy?" Kate's eyes rounded.

Bianca held her sister's gaze. "Come on, Sis," she said, trying one of the endearments for her sister she'd not used since that awful night. "Wallpaper guys aren't so bad. And the girls were right tonight. You can't live in the past. We need to find you a husband. And…" Bianca would play her strongest card. "I miss you. Truth is, I'd love to have you around out here."

Kate's hand stilled over the coffee cup.

Bianca waited. *Now what?* Her heart pounded with anticipation.

She wanted Kate close, despite the last few years. Maybe, because of them. Because she'd realized that pushing through life alone was so much harder than it was with family close by. Without her sister. But maybe she'd always known that. Seen how empty things would be right at the time of Papa's death and panicked, while not realizing that blaming Kate for the loss of their father was doing her more damage than it was doing to Kate.

Kate turned quiet, and all Bianca could hear was the sound of her sister's soft breathing and Marshall and Roy's muted chatter in the study.

Bianca stretched her foot out, sliding her toes along the velvet cushion. "It's not the same, being out here without you, without my own sister. I miss you." Her voice cracked.

It was true. She'd idolized Kate when she was small. Always wanted to be like her. Kate had been as much a part of who Bianca was as she was herself when they were young.

She had identified herself in relation to Kate. Always. Having Kate around had been like breathing. She wanted her big sister back, especially now she was having a baby.

It was terrifying. She was scared.

"What do you think of him, Roy, I mean?" Bianca asked, her voice quiet. "Could you go out with him on a date if he asked?"

Kate looked off to the side. "Me, with a wallpaper guy?" She covered her mouth with her hand and, to Bianca's horror, stifled a laugh. "Oh, Bianca, honey. For goodness' sake!"

And suddenly, something in Bianca flipped. She had tried and Kate was going to humiliate her. What about those times Kate and she had promised each other, when they were little, how they'd always look out for each other and would never be apart? Those times when Kate had protected Bianca from the taunts at school, standing in and fighting for her. She'd been the best big sister in the world. Bianca knew how Kate's tough, protective streak had sparked. She'd protected Bianca. And she knew Kate would always stand up for what she believed in.

Who or what was she protecting now?

Of course, things had changed when Kate became fascinated with politics and studying and being best in class when she turned thirteen.

Bianca remembered that year well. Teachers at high school had recognized Kate's talent, they'd called Papa in, a history teacher himself, and he'd taken Kate under his wing too, spending hours reading and talking with her on weekends.

Bianca had been left unmoored, like a little boat lost out at sea. So, she'd decided to write her own life story, make up her own dreams that were the opposite of Kate's. What else could she have done?

But now, it hit her. She'd wanted *Kate's* love back, even when Papa died.

That was why she was so angry.

Because she'd worshipped her big, brave, huge-hearted sister like no one else on this earth.

"Being married, having kids and a family, Katy," she whispered, her insides stirring.

Kate's head lifted at her use of the name she'd called her until she turned thirteen.

"Surely that's better than trying to be a man," Bianca said. "Katy, please? I'm having a baby and I want you around. And I'd love it if you'd consider marrying and settling nearby. Our children will be cousins. They could be close, like we were, once..."

Slowly, Kate looked up. "Sorry, Bianca, I didn't mean to upset you. I was just surprised to hear you'd think to set me up with someone like Roy. But you think I want to be like a man? You think that's what I'm about?"

Bianca's heart beat wildly. Kate *had* to come around. She had to.

"Please," Bianca said, her voice tiny. "I need you out here. Will you just think about it?"

"Bianca, honey, I love you," Kate said. "But you need to let me live my own life. You belong out here, but I don't. I don't want to give Roy false hope, so I think it would be best if I went back to the city before he and Marshall come back in here." Kate sighed. She raked her hand through her curls.

Bianca bit back the tears that threatened to spill down her cheeks. She wrapped her arms around her waist, her stomach fluttering. She gnawed on her lip to stop it from trembling. She'd tried to be honest, and she'd gone too far! *Why were she and Kate like two straight lines that couldn't connect?*

Bianca shook her head, horrified. "No, please…" The tears she'd fought sprung to life at the backs of her eyes.

She had everything she'd ever wanted, and yet it felt like nothing. It was all so empty.

Why?

"I'm sorry, Bianca." Kate came over, rested her hand on Bianca's shoulder, gathered her coat, her shoes, and slipped out the door.

Later that night, after Kate had gone, and Roy had left too, oblivious of Bianca's shattered hopes and dreams, Marshall sat down in his favorite armchair and turned the radio on. "You're whistling Dixie trying to put any sense into your sister's head, honey," he said.

Bianca just stood in the middle of the room, achingly aware of the mess in the dining room, the kitchen, and the living room that needed to be tidied up.

The sound of Marshall's favorite radio station rang through the otherwise silent house.

Chapter Seventeen

Kate

New York, November 1946

"Phone call for you, Kate." Tom Morelli came through from the kitchens in back of Albertina's, his deli in the Village, wearing a white T-shirt and a black apron over faded blue jeans.

Kate looked up at her old childhood friend and neighbor, a large serving spoon filled with olives poised in her hand. The back-to-back shifts she'd been working in Tom Morelli's deli since August while filing two women's stories a week for Hilary Winthrop were paying the bills and she appreciated her old friend employing her.

"For me, you say, Tom?" She sensed her godmother, Gia Morelli, Tom's mom, moving to her side behind the busy counter. Kate sent Gia a grateful smile when Gia took the spoon from her hands and started serving the customer who was in front of a long line snaking through the busy store.

"Yes, call for you, Kate," Tom said.

Kate wiped her hands on a towel and wove her way down the counter, passing his sister Natalia, who was boxing up a selection of cannoli, Tom's signature rolled biscuits filled with delectable vanilla crème.

While Kate had survived these last months on meager pay from Hilary for women's interest stories, along with writing a few articles for The North American News Alliance without a contract, her fellow male war correspondents were enjoying the prestige of high-profile jobs. Kate had earned $1,456 so far this year for her writing, with $769 from NANA, but several of her old wartime colleagues were earning lavish livings with large expense accounts.

Rick had been distant with her in the last months; she'd hardly seen him apart from bumping into him at a couple bars and diners after work. Thinking this was for the best, Kate had thrown herself into her work and tried to put him right out of her head. It was only every now and then, when she was alone and quiet in her apartment, that she wondered about him. Wondered whether she'd imagined that attraction between them when they'd been out for dinner and gone to buy the little orphan some toys.

She'd not heard any more updates from Claudia, but she'd had a beautiful drawing from her little orphan friend to thank her and Rick for the toys they'd sent. Kate had sent a couple of photos of New York and a letter directly to the little girl, but she'd not heard back yet. Sometimes, she wanted to just jump in a boat, or climb on a plane, and go see her. Feel the child's arms wrapped around her neck. Bring her back to Manhattan.

But that was selfish. *What could she offer a child?*

When the steaming-hot weather had finally broken and fall descended on Manhattan, turning the trees in Central Park to a kaleidoscope of yellows and reds, Kate had done her sums and realized she couldn't afford to pay her bills without a proper journalism contract. She'd bitten the bullet and gotten a day job.

She knew she would have to make her own luck in reporting, but searching for an exclusive was proving impossible. New York was the center of journalism, everyone who was anyone in the industry was here and legions of male reporters with contracts and access to the latest news streams were already fighting for the best stories. For now, she had to make ends meet.

Kate followed Tom down the corridor to his office, where he handed her the big black telephone receiver. She'd never had a call here before. The first worry that came to mind was that something had gone wrong with her mom. *Or Bianca.* Bianca's pregnancy was advancing, and Kate worried about her carrying an unborn baby, given she had seemed so upset last time they met.

So many times, she'd gone to pick up the phone to call Bianca, only to place the receiver back down again. It seemed every time they were in close proximity, an argument would spark, whether it was about Kate's dedication to her career, her lack of interest in settling down in the suburbs, while underlying everything was Kate's guilt.

Because the fact was, she used to stand up for Bianca. Used to protect her come what may, from taunts at school, boys who showed an unwanted interest in her petite sister with the dancing eyes and lustrous black hair, even talking to teachers who had misunderstood her and treated her more harshly than she deserved.

But ever since Papa's death, Kate had reeled away from her sister, not only because Bianca had blamed her, but because she felt unworthy of being her safeguard anymore. Kate wasn't the one who could protect her family. That person had died when her father was hit by a car.

At the sound of Hilary Winthrop's voice down the line, Kate's eyes widened, and the tension eased in her shoulders with relief. Tom disappeared and she cleared her throat.

"Kate? You free to talk right now?"

"Of course, Hilary," she said, holding the phone close to her ear.

"Kate, truckers have walked off the job today all over New York. We've got all our contracted reporters out there covering it."

"Right."

"The station needs someone to cover the Big Four conference, as you will be aware that the foreign ministers of France, Great Britain, the United States and the USSR are meeting at the Waldorf Astoria today. I put your name forward to the other executives, I insisted that you were capable and, finally, they relented and said they may as well send you to cover it, because it was too dangerous for you to be at the truckers' strike."

Kate rolled her eyes. *Were they seriously worried she'd be attacked with a lug wrench?* Not that she cared, as hopefully this was her break!

"Thank you, Hilary."

Sometimes, Kate had caught Hilary looking thoughtful around her, and Hilary had made a couple of comments about how one day, she hoped Kate's skills could be put to proper use. Hilary had stood by quietly while Kate advocated for herself with the executive months ago on her tour of the radio station, but Kate had hoped that Hilary might be biding her time to see if she could help. Hilary had found her chance, and Kate was not going to waste a minute arguing.

"How soon can you get to the Waldorf Astoria, Kate?"

Kate wanted to punch the air! "An hour," she said. She closed her eyes and sent a prayer of thanks for Tom Morelli. He'd sat down with her, told her he'd seen everything there was to see when it came to a woman's struggles in a man's world when his wife, Lily, had been trying to make it as a chef. Tom had said she always had a job with him, but she could come and go at her will and he'd be there to help.

Kate reached to untie the straps of her apron.

"Don't get me wrong, Kate, our executives are still reluctant to hire women. I had to fight for you. I know you won't let me down."

Kate shook her head. "Of course not, Hilary."

"If you can cover this, and they are pleased with you, you might be able to consider yourself a regular reporter for one day, rather than a woman reporter," Hilary said.

"Well, that would be something." Kate took down the details that Hilary told her over the phone.

"I'm certain the male executives still think we women possess limited abilities and have brains too delicate to deal with the problems of the day," Hilary said when she was done giving instructions.

"Well, the Big Four conference discussing the final peace conditions of World War Two is a huge break for me, Hilary. Thank you." Kate grinned at the photo of Tom's wife, Lily, on his desk, because she was certain Lily Morelli would be punching the air right alongside her now, if she weren't buried in her kitchen, dreaming up delicious recipes.

"Oh, and, Kate, wear a simple dress with one plain necklace, and don't be glamourous. Look serious, or they won't give you another job no matter how well you do."

Kate nodded, and heaved out a sigh.

"And remember, the trick to getting listeners to pay you attention," Hilary went on, her voice low, "is to pretend you are talking to them one on one."

"Of course, Hilary," Kate said.

"Radio is an intimate medium, no matter what the topic," Hilary said. "Now, get up to the Waldorf Astoria as fast as you can!"

Kate put the phone down and hugged herself.

If a door was opening even an inch into the men's sanctum, she was going to push it as hard as she could.

The flags of the United States, Russia, France and Great Britain flew outside the Park Avenue entrance of the Waldorf Astoria. Kate showed her identification to security and was escorted by a guard through the hushed lobby, piano music twinkling, her utilitarian pumps seeming drab on the rich velvety carpet, but she'd been mindful of Hilary's advice not to look glamorous and had worn a pair of sensible shoes.

Priceless antiques sat atop gilt furniture and black marble columns lined the lobby all the way to the elevators. Kate pushed aside her nervousness at the importance of this assignment, both for the world, and for her career, and focused instead on the thrill of excitement that she'd been assigned to cover such a tremendous discussion in world history as the final peace conditions of World War Two.

The entrance to the tower apartment where the conference was being held was guarded by military police, and Kate settled in to wait, along with the other reporters assigned to the event. A press officer briefed them—inside the private apartment of Waldorf Chairman Lucius Boomer, the four foreign ministers were sat around a white pine table, deciding the final terms of peace.

That evening, Kate reported on WNYR's evening news discussion program at the studios in Radio City. Hilary had stayed back especially and watched her from the sound engineer's room, and Kate appreciated the support. She leaned close to the hanging microphone, all too aware of the weight resting on her words.

Taking a deep breath and making sure to keep her voice low and authoritative, she started to speak. "*Good evening. Today it was agreed by the foreign ministers of the United States, Great Britain, France and Russia…*"

After she finished, Hilary walked Kate out of the studios. "I only hope that we can get you more work like this on the strength of your willingness to drop everything for us today."

"Thank you for the opportunity today, Hilary. I can't tell you how appreciative I am."

"Well," Hilary smiled. "Let's hope there are many more."

Kate paused at the end of the long corridor. A photo of Rick smiled out at her from the pin-ups of WNYR's radio stars that lined the walls. He was wearing his fedora hat at a rakish angle, and his sardonic smile flashed. She missed her chats with him, if she was honest. But she wasn't game to pick up the phone and start anything up again, because to do so was playing with fire.

Above Rick's photo, Harvey Milton looked like a blond pin-up boy. His own grin was infectious, and his eyes sparkled at her.

While Rick was fast rising as one of WNYR's biggest newsmen, Harvey had shot up the ranks on another level and was continuing a meteoric rise as an executive.

Kate shook Hilary's hand. "You know I'm keen as any man." She glanced back at the photos of Rick and Harvey on the wall. "Keener."

"Don't I know it, Kate," Hilary said. She eyed Kate's simple navy-blue dress and the silver necklace she wore. "Your outfit is perfect, by the way."

Kate bit back her sigh. "Well, I'm glad of that. Thank you for everything, Hilary." She sent Hilary a warm smile.

The following week, Kate installed a phone in her studio out of her earnings from the Big Four conference. Hilary called on Monday morning just when Kate had gotten out of the shower. "You're featured in *Newsweek*," she told Kate. "Seems you made quite the splash at the conference."

Kate's hand stilled as she brought her morning coffee cup to her lips. "Are you serious, Hilary?" *Newsweek* had turned down her application just like nearly every other media outlet in New York City when she'd come home from Europe.

"*Spinster at the Mike*," Hilary read out the headline, her tone sardonic. "But they describe you as tall, lissome, with dark curls, a photogenic figure and a mellifluous voice."

Kate rolled her eyes toward her patchy kitchen ceiling. "Glad they were impressed with my political knowledge, then."

"The article goes on to say that if you'd been more glamorous, you wouldn't have got the job."

"Oh honestly! I don't know whether to laugh or cry about that."

She said goodbye to Hilary and put the phone down before grabbing her bag and rushing out the door for her shift at Albertina's.

*

That night, her new phone rang again, but this time, she started at the sound of Rick's voice. It had been months. *Why was he calling her now?*

"I'm glad you've got a phone," he said. "And I'm sorry it's taken me so long to get in touch."

He sounded odd, formal. Kate curled up on her sofa, her heart racing and her mind warning her he could have contacted her in so many other ways. He must have gotten her number from WNYR.

"How are you, Rick?" she asked.

There was a silence down the line.

"I'm well, Kate. I'm doing just fine," he said, after a silence.

Kate was quiet. She winced, floundering around awkwardly to find the right response. *What should she say to him?*

"Are you doing okay?" she asked. Darn it. They'd just covered that question.

"I am," he said, again, perfect manners not missing a beat. "And you? How are you, Kate?"

Not Katia anymore. Kate took in a deep breath. It was for the best. She'd told herself she couldn't have a relationship with him. So, she must not worry, or blame anyone but herself. Or think that this was a bad thing, their formality, his restraint. "Fine. Yes, very well."

"Well, that's good."

Kate needed to stand up and move, but the cable that connected the telephone to the wall was short and she was stuck on the sofa with her heart hammering and her mouth frozen along with her brain.

"Kate?"

"Yes?" She swallowed and took in a breath.

"Would you like to come over for dinner this weekend?" he said suddenly, speaking at the same time as her.

Kate startled. "Well, I don't know about that…"

"I've invited a few friends over on Saturday night. Some of the old gang from Europe. I thought you might like to come along and see… them again."

"Oh." Kate slumped back on her little sofa. What was wrong with her? This was a good thing. She could hardly expect him to ask her out on a date!

"It would be good for us all to catch up," he said. "And my little sister is coming along too, with her new fiancé. I think I told you about her."

Kate's stomach fluttered. "Eloise, isn't it?"

"That's right."

When Rick gave her his address, Kate held the receiver out and eyeballed it.

Central Park *West*? Central Park West bordered Central Park. The gorgeous buildings that lined that boulevard were known for their celebrity apartments with porters, doormen and concierges, not humble newspapermen. *What was going on?*

Maybe he was sharing a walk-up above some store with some other newspaper types. Rick was the most down-to-earth man she'd met in her life.

She'd imagined Harvey Milton coming from some well-to-do Connecticut family, but from what she'd learned of him, that was not the case, and the young red-headed Joe Ackerman who'd traveled with them spoke with an upscale Boston accent, but Rick? Kate chuckled. It would be a three-room walk-up, she was sure. But then, he'd thought nothing of buying all those toys for the orphan. And he'd taken her out to Josephine's at the drop of a hat.

"I'm looking forward to seeing you again," he said.

"Yes," she replied. "I hope you're well." She hit her forehead with the palm of her hand and swooned dramatically.

It must be the telephone. Definitely. She already hated the device.

*

On Saturday night at eight o'clock, Kate walked down Central Park West from the train station to the address Rick had given her on the telephone, her warmest coat bundled around her, and her scarf pulled up close around her neck. Wreaths of holly and ivy decorated the charming old apartment buildings, and the smells of roasting chestnuts filtered through the air. Sometimes, New York was a magical place.

Kate stood stock-still when she came to Rick's building. She checked the address she'd written down. A uniformed doorman in a suit with brass buttons and white gloves opened the glass double doors to the entrance lobby for her. Marble floors spread behind him for miles, and he checked Kate's name off on a ledger before escorting her to the elevators with decorative wooden inlaid doors.

Kate fought a surge of panic when the elevator started moving. Her stomach was going south while the elevator rose. Suddenly she was sure her outfit, her hair, her shoes, and her bag were all wrong.

She'd thrown every evening dress she owned on her bed after a grueling nine-hour shift at Albertina's. She'd not even thought to buy a new outfit for the dinner at Rick's house. Their get-togethers had always been so casual in Europe, sitting around on the bare wooden floors of hotel rooms and sharing a bottle of red wine in enamel mugs, and she'd feel ridiculous turning up in something formal. The last thing she wanted to be was overdressed. But when she'd laid all her outfits out, she'd not been so sure about turning up in casual attire.

She'd strode around her apartment, wringing her hands. She was *not* Rick's girlfriend and she was not trying to make an impression! No siree. *And yet...* Kate had glared at her reflection in the oval mirror by her bed.

Forcing herself to calm down, she'd stamped out her nerves, and chosen a deep blue cocktail dress that flowed gently to just below her knees. It had shoulder pads, three-quarter-length sleeves and a cross-wrapped bodice with draping that took on the look of a Grecian goddess. She'd worn it to a correspondent's function in Washington just before she left for Europe. It was professional, yet appropriate for a dinner.

She hoped.

What if they were all wearing blue jeans? If that was the case, she'd turn around, go home, get changed and come back again. That was what she'd do.

Kate clutched her matching purse, her arms encased in long deep blue gloves. She'd pulled her curls atop her head, much like the hairdos Bianca's friends Ruth and Betty had told her were fashionable for her article on wartime hair, and she'd chosen a high-necked multiple-strand necklace of rhinestones to go with the dress. As the elevator doors opened to the twelfth floor, she was certain she'd messed everything up.

She could always leave her coat on. If she didn't expire in this centrally heated building.

A vase of lilies sat on a table opposite the elevator and only two doors let off the corridor, one to the left, one to the right.

Kate closed her eyes, knocked on the door to the left, and realized that Rick's side of the building overlooked Central Park. And it appeared to take up half the floor! *What hadn't he told her about himself? He was always so understated, so self-deprecating. So, well, Rick…*

He must have some wealthy roommate. That would be it. He'd probably decided to room with Harvey, who probably owned half the station by now.

A maid opened the door, and the sounds of discreet chatter and music filtered out into the hall. The butterflies in Kate's insides turned into a hive of bees. She closed her eyes and counted to twenty to calm herself, only to hear the sound of Rick's voice, which sent her off into a frenzy all over again.

"Hey," he said. He leaned forward, gently placing a kiss on her cheek. "May I take your coat?" he asked.

Kate opened her eyes to find Rick standing opposite her dressed in a dinner suit, dark hair swept back, brown eyes, with their tawny flecks intent on her, his fingers playing at the sleeves of his tux.

"It's good to see you," he said.

Her eyes rounded and she breathed in his gorgeous musky aftershave. What had he done with the Rick she knew? And who was this guy?

She started undoing the buttons of her coat, unwound her scarf, and silently handed them to him.

"You look amazing," he breathed, finally, taking a step back. "Wow."

Kate lowered her eyes. *What was this?* He was living in a palace. It had to be some other guy's apartment. Harvey, for sure.

"Come in," he said, holding out his arm.

"You've moved in with some rich guy and gone to heaven?" she asked, gawping at the sight before her eyes, the press of his hand on her arm sending shivers up her shoulder, all the way to her neck. "This sure beats the digs we had in Europe," she managed, her voice squeaky and odd.

Rick stilled in front of her. Slowly, he turned around. "Katia," he said, his shoulders slumping. "Can we talk a moment?"

"Sure," she said. "Is everything okay?"

By way of answer, he led her through the grand entrance hall, a floating stairway made of honey-colored wood soaring up to a second floor. The floor was parquet and Kate's feet rang out loud. Modern art lined the walls and a modern marble sculpture sat on a table below a gilded mirror. Kate glanced at her reflection. Her startled eyes were the size of a pair of swimming pools.

Rick walked next to her in silence, his expression unreadable.

Kate couldn't help glancing at him, but she had to force herself not to pull him to a stop and ask him to explain.

"This is stunning," she whispered. "What a beautiful apartment."

"I'm glad you like it," he said.

That was all.

She looked up at him, her lips opening to form a question, but he went on past the staircase and led her into a smaller room, with a pair of pale velvet sofas on a soft rug, a wingback chair and deep wooden shelves line with books. A filigree clock that must have cost more than the building Kate lived in sat on the mantelpiece. And against one wall was a great mahogany desk, and Rick's typewriter sat on it, taking pride of place.

She did not have words.

"Kate?" he said, standing there, awkward. "This won't take a minute. But I wanted you to know straight away."

And right then, Kate realized what he might be talking about. And without even asking, she sank down into a velvet chair. "Our German girl," she breathed.

Rick nodded, and Kate closed her eyes.

"Just tell me," she said, all thoughts of whose apartment this was obliterated by one memory. The sight of that kid's huge blue eyes.

"I've had a telegram from Claudia," he said. "I'm afraid it's very brief, and I don't know anything other than what it says."

Kate nodded. For months she'd been worrying, sending the occasional letter but hearing next to nothing back.

"Go ahead." The feel of the girl's head resting on her shoulder, of her reaching up to hold Kate's hand, the sheer relief she'd known when the little girl had taken spoon to mouth and accepted the broth they'd given her.

Rick cleared his throat. "Kate, brace yourself. I'm afraid that Claudia's contacts in Berlin have found that the child's parents and little brother are all dead."

Kate's hand floated to her mouth. *All dead. Her family.* All killed by what? Allied attacks? An American boy her age throwing a bomb down on that little girl's home? She tried to get up out of her seat, only to sink back down again at the sound of Rick's voice going on.

"Claudia says nothing more at this stage. I don't know if she knows the details surrounding their deaths."

Kate nodded, staring bleakly at her lap.

"But here is some good news," Rick went on. "We know her name now. She is called Mia."

"Mia," Kate breathed.

"That's right, and her little brother was called Filip."

Filip. The photo of the little boy that Claudia had found in Kate's pocket. Oh, the poor child. Poor little boy...

Rick came to sit down on the sofa opposite Kate. "The last sentence of the telegram tells me they have located the child's elderly grandparents."

Hope bloomed in her chest. "Yes?" Why, perhaps she'd also have some more relatives. Cousins, aunts, uncles. "Well, that is something." Kate turned her eyes, wanting to brim over, toward Rick.

Rick sent her a tentative smile. He moved slightly closer to her, only to draw away again. "Yes. But they live in the Soviet-occupied zone."

Kate's brows drew together.

Rick looked down at the telegram. "The Soviets burned Mia's grandparents' farm, destroyed the local manor, and the village. Claudia says the only reason the child's grandmother was not raped was because she is in a wheelchair..." Rick lowered his head. "I am sorry. Claudia put it even more brutally than that. She says they are now living in a tiny village near to their destroyed farm. She says that Mia will have to return to live with her grandparents."

Kate sank back into the soft silken cushion. *Born under the Nazis, only to grow up under the Soviets.* "What can I do?"

Rick leaned forward in his seat, cupping his hands between his knees. "Kate, would you like to go to Germany?"

Kate blinked hard. "What did you say, Rick? Go to Germany?" She sat up, shaking her head at him. "And how would I get there?"

Rick scrubbed his hand over his face. "I've wanted to tell you this for some time." He stalled, as if having difficulty searching for the right words. When he spoke again, his words were slow. "And, I know that, perhaps, I should have come clean sooner."

Kate waited. Her mouth opened, but nothing came out.

"The fact is, my father is the vice president of a very large bank." His gaze clouded, and he went on in an uncertain tone. "His father was a banker, and so was my great-grandfather. My father sits on various boards, and... one of them is Pan Am. So, if you want to fly to Germany, I, in fact, can arrange to get you there. I'm sorry I didn't tell you sooner, Katia," he whispered.

Kate clutched at her purse. She took in a little breath. "So, this apartment? Yours?"

He raised his eyes to meet hers. "Yes. Mine. I didn't want to put you off. I thought you'd run a mile if you knew about... all this."

Kate swallowed. *What did that mean?* That he didn't trust her with the truth about who he was? Did he think where he came from would make any difference to her?

And yet, a hard-bitten truth ate away at her. She'd not told him that her career was too precious to risk losing for any man.

She looked down at the richly patterned rug, her shoes rested squarely on an intricate pattern of flowers that were entwined with each other in such an elaborate design that it was impossible to see where one plant ended and the other began. Her hands started moving of their own accord, smoothing out her skirt. *Mia's family all gone in a war that she hated more and more each day. Rick's family, so very privileged, one of the wealthiest and most powerful in Manhattan, if this apartment was anything to go by. Her family, she and Bianca, floundering about in no man's land.*

Rick stood up, moving across the room and crouching down next to her, his voice close. "I know it's a shock, to hear such terrible news about poor little Mia, but you know there is nothing more we can do tonight, and you need a moment to think." He held out his hand to her. "And," he whispered, as she took his hand and stood at the same time he did, "I'm sorry I wasn't open with you."

But you had no obligation to be. We aren't a couple. Her eyes raked over his face, and they stood there a moment, her hand resting in his, eyes locked. And then, slowly, he let her hand go, and stood aside for her, waiting for her to leave the room. Unless… she turned to him, but he moved past her, and it was too late. The moment was gone.

He was walking through the lobby and she followed him into a vast living room, a baby grand piano set against a huge picture window, a fireplace that was the size of Kate's entire studio with a fire crackling in the hearth, and a huge art deco sofa covered in white velvet with black piping and scattered with golden cushions set in the middle of the room.

Could she simply accept his offer, and fly to Germany at his expense?

A charming-looking couple were seated on the velvet sofa, and when Kate's eyes swept the room, there was Leonard Andrews, looking as at home as ever here with a middle-aged woman, presumably his wife, next to him on the far side of the room, and Harvey Milton chatting to them, in a black tux. Crystal vases filled with white roses sat on the polished coffee tables, along with books on art and film.

Vaughn Monroe's "Let it Snow!" played on the gramophone. As if on cue, white snowflakes started falling past the picture windows.

Kate turned to Rick, but the woman who'd been seated on the sofa along with the equally devastatingly good-looking man came toward them. The young woman's hair was dressed in soft brown waves, and the expression in her wide brown eyes was friendly. She wore an exquisite evening gown, black and strapless, and what looked like a real diamond necklace glittered on her décolletage.

"Oh, Rick, you are a dark horse. Who is this gorgeous girl?" the stunning young woman said.

"Ellie," Rick said. "This is Kate Mancini, my fellow correspondent. Kate, this is my sister, Eloise."

"Pleased to meet you, and I'm mighty inspired to hear you're a correspondent like Rick, I must say," Eloise said, leaning forward to kiss Kate on the cheek.

Kate sent Rick a quick look and saw the way he was smiling at his sister.

"I've long wished I had my brother's brains and courage. It's wonderful to meet a woman who I'm sure has both in spades."

Kate took Eloise's outstretched hand, still in a trance. *This was out of this world.* Eloise was out of this world. And Rick? How had he been able to take on a job as a lowly journalist? His mom's interest in politics aside, didn't the prodigal son have to follow in the father's footsteps? She hated to think what battles Rick might have faced. And he'd never mentioned his father. Not once. "It's charming to meet you, Eloise," she managed.

"Oh, I'm looking forward to getting to know you, Kate," Eloise said. "I'll even wager you'll tell me more about that trip to Europe than Rick has told me since he came home."

Rick raised a brow, but Eloise pressed her gloved hand to his arm. "I know. You want to protect me from all the details of the horrid war. But I can handle more than you think I can." She turned to Kate. "Do you have a brother, Kate?"

"I don't," Kate said, a tiny bit of tension easing at the girl's friendly tone, but her mind throwing out more questions. *Why would he even be interested in her?* Wouldn't he be surrounded by debutantes, beautiful, wealthy Uptown girls? "I should like to have had a brother, though." She didn't mention her sister. If she did, she didn't know whether she'd trust herself not to burst into tears. *Bianca, Mia… why couldn't she have done more for them both?* She took in a deep breath.

Eloise squeezed her hand. "I think we'll be the best of friends."

"What a lovely girl," Kate said, when Eloise went back to sit down with her handsome companion.

Rick looked at her in silence, his eyes raking her face.

Kate bit on her lip. "Rick?" she whispered.

But he turned, his arm still linked in hers. He led her across the huge room with its towering ceilings toward a quiet spot near the floor-to-ceiling windows, Central Park below.

"Kate! You look incredible." Harvey Milton was right next to them. He leaned forward and kissed Kate on the cheek. Harvey looked utterly at home and relaxed here too.

"Champagne?" Rick murmured into Kate's ear.

She nodded, feeling that old quiver at the way he leaned in close. She closed her eyes for a millisecond and savored the memories of how that used to feel. When she thought they were just a pair of normal journalists.

"How are you doing, Kate?" Harvey said, and Kate forced herself to concentrate on him. "I'm glad you're working for Hilary. I've wanted to catch up with you for an age."

"Well, I'm doing okay," Kate said. Rick moved across the room, and Kate couldn't help but notice how the cut of his suit was perfect when he moved. She swallowed. "I'd like to be writing for you as well. But I'm sure you know that, Harvey."

"I do know that, Kate," Harvey said. "And, believe me, I wish you could. I've tried to fight for a full-time contract for you with the station, but to no avail, I'm afraid."

Kate's eyes rounded in surprise. "You have?"

"Of course. But you heard what that exec said."

"And aren't you an exec too?"

Harvey smiled sadly. "I'm outnumbered, I'm afraid. But I hope you enjoyed reporting on the Big Four's conference?"

"Of course, I did, Harvey. You know that's right up my alley. It was good to report on political matters again." She had to be careful. Not complain too much. Hilary was trying to fight for her at the station too. Letting loose about her feelings could put Harvey off.

Rick was back at her side. She took the glass of champagne he handed her. They both brought their glasses to their lips at the same time.

"Just telling Kate how much I want to give her a contract as a political correspondent," Harvey said to Rick.

Rick nodded as Harvey spoke.

"You know, I understand some of your struggles, more than you might imagine," Harvey said to her, dropping his voice.

Eloise called Rick over and he excused himself.

"Oh, I doubt that." Kate sent a sardonic smile down toward the woolen carpeted floor.

"No, seriously," Harvey went on.

Kate gave Harvey Milton her attention.

"My dad was a truck driver in Cleveland, Kate," Harvey said. "And my mom cleaned hotel rooms. She was a maid. I've had nothing of the advantages that..." He glanced toward Rick.

Kate's mouth turned dry. "Yes," she said. "Yes, Harvey."

"Not that I begrudge him anything," Harvey added hastily. But he leaned a little closer to Kate. "I've worked honestly to get where I've got, and I think women deserve exactly the same opportunities as men. I don't believe in anything different. And I only hope that things change, one day, in America."

Kate looked up at him. "I'm glad to hear you hold such firm opinions, and such enlightened ones," she said simply.

"Thanks," he smiled.

Kate watched Rick as he chatted with his guests, bringing her champagne glass to her lips, enjoying the coolness of the rim against her tender skin as she let Harvey chat on about the station, about his plans, and the emergence of television in America.

"I can't imagine being on television," Kate murmured while Harvey talked. "The mediums we have to adapt to are moving so very fast."

"I agree," Harvey said. "I still like to get to the heart of a subject, and to me writing seems the only way to do that. You can approach a topic in a more individual way, and then hit with your point. But I think reporting is going to get faster and more succinct, not less. Radio has shown us that. The world, in turn, is going to start moving far faster than ever before and the way we deliver news needs to keep up."

"So, it seems..." She was glad of the distraction of Harvey's voice, but she couldn't take her eyes or her mind off Rick and his sister.

"I feel as awkward as anyone here," Harvey went on. "But I've learned to hide it. I've learned to blend in."

"I'm afraid you are better at that than I'll ever be."

Harvey was quiet a moment. "You didn't know Rick was independently wealthy, Kate?"

Kate turned back to him, raising an eyebrow.

Harvey sent her an earnest look. "His family own half of Connecticut. A grand estate in one of the most established parts of the country."

Kate drew a hand to her mouth. Her mom, Livia, took in ironing as an accompaniment to her full-time job at the school. Kate adored her mom, but neither of them would ever belong in a place like this. And Rick's family would *never* approve of her. Livia had mentioned Bianca's struggles with acceptance in Marshall's wallpaper family. Rick's family made Marshall's family look like a gaggle of geese up against the most elegant of wild swans. An Italian girl from the Village with the Shearers? She had to bite back her laugh.

"I hope you're both hungry." Rick was back beside them and Kate swiveled around. His eyes ran over Kate's face, his focus intent. He opened his mouth as if to speak, only to glance at Harvey and stop. He shuffled the sleeves of his suit jacket a little and coughed.

Kate's feelings were more than complicated, and her hands gathered around her waist at the way her stomach dipped when he was close to her.

"Come and have dinner," he said softly. "Say hello to Len and his wife, and meet Teddy, Eloise's fiancé." He held out his arm for Kate.

She hesitated for a long second while Harvey stood alongside them, before finally placing her hand in the crook of Rick's elbow, the man who was becoming more of an enigma every time they met, and the man for whom the groundswell of feelings she could not control. And yet, despite being right next to him, she felt further away from Rick than ever.

Chapter Eighteen

Frances

New York, November 1946

Frances stared at Willard across the softly lit table at Montgomery House. They'd dined here so many times over the years, and the discreet Manhattan restaurant tucked away in the Upper East Side usually felt like a home away from home for them in New York. Tonight, everything seemed perfect. Looked perfect. To all intents and purposes, she and Willard could be any handsome, wealthy middle-aged couple smiling at each other in the candlelight.

Except Frances was in agony.

How to get through to him, how to break through the invisible, formidable wall he'd put up around himself was her biggest challenge, her greatest hope, the one thing that occupied all her waking thoughts and haunted her dreams while she was asleep. And every time she mulled it over, thrashing out her options while showing the world her perfect, highly cultivated self, she always came back to one thing.

The children.

The one part of their lives that she and Willard shared equally, had in common, both loved.

"Rick is keen to bring a girl out to Ellie's engagement party," she said, her fingers swirling around her misted wine glass, the sleeves of her deep green dress floating around her wrists.

"That depends on who the girl is." Willard raised his eyes to meet hers. The startling blue chips in his irises that had once dazzled her were opaque and cold and Frances shuddered and withdrew back into her seat. "He mentioned some girl a while ago. I assumed he'd moved on and gotten rid of her. Sounded completely inappropriate."

Frances took in a deep breath. She would not react to her husband's callous words, his dismissal of a person whom he deemed was of no consequence to their family. "For a start, her name is Kate."

"What's her surname?" Willard's eyes narrowed.

"I have no idea. Does it really matter? After everything the world has been through these past years." She whispered her words. "Can we not be understanding of our only son, and support him?"

A pained expression passed across Willard's features. "Of course, it matters. It always will."

Frances' heart shrank. She wanted the world for her son. What was so wrong with that?

"She is a fellow journalist, Willard." Frances smoothed out her napkin, ran her fingers reassuringly over her wedding ring.

She still wore it. It was still in place.

For now.

"Rick says," she went on, "they grew close while traveling in Europe. He tells me that she is a very good friend, but that he would like her to know about us up front, know who we are, what she might be getting into before he… asks her on a proper date. I think he's being very sweet." *And honest.* She bit back the words that fought to flow out in a torrent, terrified to light a match to the icy war, laced with hostility that had their family, their future, hanging on a knife's edge.

A muscle in Willard's cheek tweaked. "I'm not having some woman journalist infiltrating our lives. She'll be out for blood."

Willard had never objected to *her* interest in politics and in newspaper stories. But then, like all her ideas, thoughts and feelings, she had always been discreet and never discussed such things with her husband. She did doubt that this young woman would be quite as reserved. Frances bit down on her lip.

"I'm not having some political woman at the party. She'll cause a scene and upset the guests. The answer is no, Frances."

Frances' lips curved upward as if in compliance. She took a breath. "Unfortunately, I don't think we *can* say no, though, dearest. Rick is thirty-two years old. If we do so, he may not come to the party, and that would be terrible. We don't want that." Her voice rose and she swallowed hard to beat back her distress.

Willard gazed across at the next table. A young couple, beautifully dressed, were holding hands and laughing at a shared joke.

Frances flushed. *Surely her voice had not carried?* Venting was for diaries, pillows, and long walks in the garden deadheading roses, not for Manhattan restaurants.

"Keep your voice down, Frances, for pity's sake," Willard said.

"Of course." Her cold beef tongue and sliced young fowl with potato and tomato salad was hardly touched. She'd picked at the Italian antipasto that Willard had ordered for starters and had downed two champagne cocktails before dinner while waiting for Willard in the restaurant's elegant lobby.

She hated to admit it, but she was terrified about all of this. Willard shutting her out, Rick bringing some girl Willard would take against to Eloise's engagement party, causing more division between them. And most of all there hung one great unmoving question that underlay everything. *Where would she stand, who would she be, if Willard divorced her? Who would she be if she were not his wife?*

And at the rate they were traveling, the likelihood of divorce seemed more and more plausible every time they were together.

She'd given him space, time alone, not prodded him, questioned him, remained supportive, done everything by the book. *Was there anything left of her, of the marriage they once shared?*

"How much does this journalism woman want, in hard cash, to leave us alone?"

Frances closed her eyes, her hands clutching around her stomach. The idea of swallowing any food brought bile to her throat. "Willard," she whispered. "Maybe, if you allow Rick to bring her home, you'll like her, or perhaps he'll see she doesn't fit in and come to realize she's not right."

"What are you going to do? Let this woman have the run of the house at the party and then stand by while she writes some damning article in the *New York Times*? Sit down over coffee and tell her all your secrets? You need to learn some sense, Frances."

But I have no secrets. You are the one hiding secrets. And I cannot—I will not—ask what they are. Please, Will, I am dying of love for you, even though you are so distant. Please, open up to me. Tell me what's going on.

"The Russians have agents in the country," Willard said. "Which is something you do not need to know, and should not be aware of, Frances. If she's trying to infiltrate a family like mine, then we need to be very careful."

Frances' ears burned. She reached out a shaky hand for a glass of water. Of course, she knew about the communist scare. But to admit to that now? To admit that she knew all the details, both sides, had read every opinion article as well as the hard news stories on the topic? It would cost her her marriage.

"If Russian agents were to come to Woodlands, what would they find, dear?" she asked.

"Everything," he said, eyes still blue-chip cold.

Frances spread her fingers on the table. Her sapphire engagement ring with its band of diamonds glittered in the lamplight. "It's only one party, Willard. Please. I don't want him to be shut out."

Willard refilled his glass of wine.

But when a waiter appeared at their table, a boy who looked so recently back from the war that he almost stood to attention, Willard looked up sharply.

"Mr. Shearer, sir?"

"Yes, what is it?" Willard sent a side glance toward Frances.

She arranged her cutlery to show that she'd finished her meal. Even though most of it remained untouched. If she ate, she might be sick. The unraveling of her marriage was killing her, burning out her insides and destroying her from within. She'd lost a terrible amount of weight and her stomach constantly roiled with worry. The worst part was not knowing why it was happening, knowing that everything once right was now wrong, and not understanding why. She had become an outsider to her husband's world, and she had no idea how to get back in.

The achingly young waiter held out a note on a silver platter. "Miss Daisy McKinnon is waiting for you in the front bar. She says to tell you her rehearsal was shortened."

Willard drew his mouth into a tight grimace. "You fool," he muttered under his breath. "What the heck are you playing at?"

The boy reddened and stood there as if stuck to the spot.

Frances drew her hand to her mouth, her heart clattering in her breast, fighting the urge to grab for the white napkin and bite on it, wrench it between her teeth, to stop herself from wailing, from howling.

Daisy McKinnon.

Her life had imploded with the utterance of one name.

She sat, frozen, the table, and everything on it, seeming to swirl and shimmer, unable to speak or utter a word. She took in a shuddering breath.

"Excuse me," Willard said. He stood up, elbowed the stunned young waiter out of the way and left the room.

Frances reached across the table to where the man she'd long loved had just sat, only to draw her shaking hand back to rest in her lap.

An hour later, Frances sat in a taxi driving around and around New York. She was going in circles, instructing the driver to travel around the blocks of Manhattan, because she had no idea where to go. The city lights, staring at them, had become like a mantra, a comfort, in the dark world she'd landed in tonight. Returning to the apartment she shared with Willard was impossible. Frances wanted to go home, and she couldn't.

Where was home?

Frances knew she could not be alone tonight. She yearned, now, not to have the answer, not to know about Daisy McKinnon, not to care about Daisy McKinnon, to be able to turn a blind eye to Willard's indiscretion as so many of the women in her circles did. But the fact was, she did care, she did want her family to work, and she did, in spite of everything, want her husband, and the life she loved, back.

As the taxi sat in a traffic jam on Park Avenue, horns honking and the taxi driver sitting rigid taking her she knew not where, Frances fought catastrophic thoughts of sitting like this, alone, for the rest of her life.

A light, chill rain started to fall, and the windows of the taxi turned to liquid, rendering the lights of the city into indistinct streams. "Could you take me to Central Park West," she told the driver.

"Central Park West? Sure. You're paying, lady," he said, shaking his head.

Frances slumped back in her seat. She'd not caught a taxi in an age. Willard had a town car and a driver as the director of the bank. And she supposed Daisy McKinnon was in that town car, comfortably ensconced with her husband tonight.

After Willard's rushed departure, Frances had stayed at the table and she'd requested a newspaper. The *New York Times*. And then she'd requested yesterday's paper. And the one from last weekend.

Opening that, finally, Frances had found what she sought in the Broadway Theater section. The face of a blonde girl with almond-shaped eyes smiling out at her. She was a child. The star of some new musical that was debuting later in the month called *A Family Affair*. Frances had laid the article aside, breathing, in, out, in, out, sending the waiter a watery smile when he'd come by her table. She'd fought an intense desire to take off her shoes and run. Just run out of the restaurant into the pouring rain and soak it up. All of it.

Instead, she'd sat frozen, with a frozen smile.

Was it a relief? Knowing there was a girl?

No, it wasn't. It only hurt more; the pain that pierced her insides had just become so much more intense.

She'd always been faithful.

Oh, she'd been approached by other men when she'd first started going out with Willard. Once they were going out regularly for dinner and to the theater, she'd been loyal to him and not looked at another man.

And now, he'd torn every fathom of respect for her in two.

Daisy McKinnon was playing the lead role in this musical, some girl named Sally. Daisy could sing, dance, act, flip her hair about and… make Frances' husband fall for her.

A Family Affair? Frances had wanted to slide under the table and never come out. A Family Affair! It beggared belief.

Rick had always told Frances that she was welcome anytime at his apartment, to just turn up no matter what. In fact, he'd looked at her sympathetically last time they'd met and told her she always could stay in one of his spare rooms if she was in town and the family apartment seemed too big, or if Willard was away.

And then, she reeled with horror. Did Rick already know about this McKinnon woman? Who else knew? Ellie? Teddy? Was it a running joke at the club?

No.

Frances pulled her powder compact out of her handbag, flipped it open to the mirror, and examined her face in the dim light in the back of the taxi. Her cheeks were perfectly powdered and not a drop of mascara had dripped down her face. The only thing she needed was to touch up her lipstick, so she pulled out her golden tube and applied it, closing the little round silver compact with a snap.

The taxi driver pulled up outside Rick's building.

"Thank you," she said, handing the taxi driver a fifty-dollar bill. He turned and gawped at her, but she simply climbed out the car.

Frances greeted Rick's doorman and held out her hand, allowing him to lead her to the elevators at the back of the lobby. If Rick was asleep, she'd have to check into a hotel. Frances bit back panic and fought a little tear that wanted to trace a pattern down her cheeks.

When the elevator doors opened, her stomach was roiling inside, but she held her head up, and walked straight toward Rick's closed front door.

Frances nearly collapsed with relief at the sight of Rick when he opened the front door wide. He was dressed in a tuxedo, not his dressing gown, thank goodness. He must have been out for dinner.

"Mom?" he asked, rubbing the back of his neck.

Frances leaned in for a kiss on the cheek. "I'm sorry for the unannounced arrival, dear. You see, I've come up to Manhattan and forgotten my key. Would you mind if I stayed with you tonight? I'm so sorry to be a nuisance, darling." The lies slid off her tongue like treacle dripping from a teaspoon.

Betrayal. Dishonesty. *Where did it end?*

She waited for him to step aside so she could come in, sending him a brave smile, her heart giving another little stab.

Rick tugged at his loose bow tie and stepped aside for Frances.

And right then, a tall girl appeared in the foyer behind him.

"A late-night visitor?" the girl asked, sounding amused. And then she stopped dead at the sight of Frances. "Oh! Hello," she said. Her eyes were kind, and she searched Frances' face, having the grace to blush at the sight of Frances, before she took a step back and folded her hands in front of her dress. "You must be Rick's mother. I'm so pleased to meet you." And then, she looked down at the floor. "Perhaps I should go…"

"Mom, this is Kate," Rick said. He took the girl's arm. "And no," he said, turning to her, "you don't have to go."

As if on automatic pilot, her own manners stepping in, Frances leaned forward to kiss her son on the cheek. She shook the girl's hand, unable to draw her eyes away from the fact that Kate's curls were coming loose so entrancingly from a pair of tortoiseshell combs. Her brown eyes were fringed with the darkest eyelashes you could imagine. The last thing she seemed to be was some scheming journalist.

And yet, this was the worst time to meet Kate. Frances would embarrass herself. She was still reeling from that scene in the restaurant, her heart was breaking into a million tiny shards while she stood here.

Frances tugged at her gloves and her handbag dropped to the floor with a thud.

"Mom?" Rick asked, turning away from the girl, reaching down to pick up the handbag. "Is everything okay?"

"Of course, dear," she said, her eyes swiveling to the girl.

"I'm sorry," she managed. "I should go upstairs to bed right away. I didn't mean to intrude. I apologize. You see, my key," she managed, addressing the girl now. Frances clutched at her gloves. "I forgot it."

"Come on, Mom." Rick drew her a little further into the lobby. "Come in and have a drink with us."

Frances felt a sudden giddiness.

"It's lovely to meet you, Mrs. Shearer," Kate said.

This girl seemed delightful. *Oh, how she wanted to shout her frustration at Willard right now.* "Charmed, dear," she replied. She hovered in the foyer. And worse, the sound of laughter rang out from the living room. *Oh, please get me out of here.*

"You have company?" she managed. She needed to be invisible. Everywhere she went, she needed to remain unseen. "The last person you want here is your mother."

"Oh, Mom." Rick took her by the arm and drew her toward the living room, from which the pleasant sounds of chatter swelled, and someone broke into laughter. "Eloise and Teddy are here too. Come and have a drink with us."

Frances clutched her coat. Eloise and Teddy? *No. She couldn't bear it.* Bile and panic rose in her throat.

"It's wonderful to see you," Rick whispered, taking her arm and leading her into the apartment.

Ahead, Frances saw the flicker of fire in the grate, heard the clink of wine glasses, a burst of laughter again. Young laughter. She was old. She belonged nowhere. She wanted to run upstairs, have a hot bath, and bury herself under the covers in Rick's spare room.

Perhaps, never to come out again.

"No, I am interrupting," she said, her voice sounding disembodied, strange.

Rick stopped in the quiet lobby. Kate stood next to him a moment, before placing a hand on his arm, excusing herself, and thankfully, oh so thankfully, having the courtesy to slip away into the living room.

"Mom," Rick said once Kate had disappeared, "you are family. We are a family. Never, ever feel you are intruding in my home."

Family. Frances couldn't find the words. But she looked up at her son, at her grown man of a son, standing there tall and strong. And realized somewhere along the line, Rick had grown into twice the man his father was.

And right then, Frances did something she'd never done. She let out a huge sob, and reached for the strong arm of her only, beloved son. She let herself fall apart.

Chapter Nineteen

Kate

New York, November 1946

"Do come to my engagement party, Kate." Eloise pressed her hand to Kate's arm in the foyer of Rick's apartment on Central Park West. Eloise's cashmere coat was soft against Kate's hand and her eyes still sparkled despite the fact it was well past midnight. Harvey, Len Carter and his wife had left a while back, along with the other guests, and now only Rick, Eloise and Teddy, and Rick's mother Frances lingered in the apartment saying goodbye. "You must come, dear."

"Well, that's very kind of you," Kate said. "But I wouldn't want to intrude."

"Nonsense," Eloise said. "We've had such a wonderful evening, and I can't bear not to have Rick's friends at my party. Harvey's coming, aren't you, Harvey?" Eloise sent her infectious smile toward Harvey, whose face lit up in return. "It will be such a gas. And I have a feeling that you, Harvey Milton, will be a ducky shin-cracker and all the girls will fall madly in love with you. You'll be on the dance floor all night."

Harvey grinned. "I never say no to a jitterbug, but…" he held his hands up in front of him. "I'm no jive bomber, Eloise."

"Well, I for one can't wait. It's settled." Eloise tucked her arm into her mother's. "Rick will drive you both up to Woodlands, and you must stay the night. Teddy and I want you to know that any friend of Rick's is a friend of ours and you two are just delightful."

"Thank you," Kate said simply.

"Goodnight, I'm retiring for the evening now," Rick's mother said. She kissed her daughter, hugged Rick, touched Kate lightly on the arm and slipped upstairs for the night.

The sound of Eloise's laughter rang down the hallway as she and Teddy disappeared out of sight.

Rick closed his front door softly and turned to Kate. "Thank you for coming tonight, Katia. And..." he hesitated. "Thank you for meeting my family."

"They are charming," Kate said, meaning it. "Your sister is so welcoming to your friends. And your mom was so kind to me." She glanced up the staircase where Rick's mom had just disappeared. She was lovely. But if Kate were not mistaken, she'd appeared awfully pale and drained when she arrived.

And that was none of her business.

Kate looked around for her coat.

But just then, Rick's face clouded over. He brushed an imaginary fleck of dirt from his sleeve. "Would you like a coffee?" he asked suddenly. "Can we talk?" His voice cracked on the upswing, and a silence hung between them.

A crash of thunder broke over Manhattan. They stood there, staring at each other, Kate silently counting the seconds until a flash of lightning jagged through the picture windows that were visible just beyond the stairway and the foyer.

"Well," she said softly. "I'll admit I don't fancy walking out into that right now."

Rick inclined his head. "Come and sit down, I'll fix the coffee. Make yourself at home, Katia."

Kate stopped at the entrance to the gorgeous room. It seemed so huge and empty. "You know what? I'd rather help you make coffee in the kitchen than sit out there while you slave away."

Rick raised a brow. "Well then. I think we can manage that."
He swung around on the spot and strolled back through the living
room, pushing open a paneled door to the kitchen.

Kate gasped when she stepped inside. Gleaming, floor-to-ceiling
pale green cabinets lined one whole wall of the tall room, and the
floor was tiled in a mosaic of green and white. A double-sized oven
and pull-out stovetop sat against the other wall, and the benchtops
that surrounded it were set with an array of cherry-red matching
appliances and canisters.

The whole room sparkled, and a bunch of red roses sat on the
table that was laid for breakfast already. Breakfast for two. Clearly,
someone had been working out here all night while they'd all
been enjoying their exquisite dinner and lounging by the fireside
afterwards. Kate had been so caught up in the conversations, that
she'd forgotten to even think about the waiter who'd served them
dinner, and the maid who'd let her in the door.

"Why, I've never seen anything like it," Kate breathed. She
turned to Rick.

He paused a moment, leaning against the benchtop, regarding
her. "Black or white?" he asked.

Kate stood on the threshold of the room. He'd taken off his
suit jacket and his white shirt had come a little loose. "I... drink
espresso, thanks."

He busied around at the bench. "Great," he said. When the
coffee was done, he picked up the two tiny cups and waited for
her to leave the room first. "Let's go sit by the fire and talk." His
voice was softer now.

Kate took in a breath and moved back into the dramatic living
space.

Rain beat down on the windowpanes outside Rick's gorgeous
apartment, and Kate sat, her legs curled under her on the curving

sofa by the fire. Rick sat opposite her on one of his chairs, one leg crossed over the other, his tie loose, his brown eyes thoughtful. "I really am sorry I never talked about my family," he said. "I should have done. They adored you."

Kate shook her head. "You didn't have to," she said, continuing to convince herself that she must be out of her mind to think that a guy like Rick had any obligation to confide about his family to her. But still… she quietened her troubled thoughts. "I had no idea. It was a bit of a shock." She lowered her voice. "I hope you didn't think you couldn't trust me with any confidences."

Rick met her gaze, his eyes burning into hers, searing right through her.

Kate stirred in her seat.

"I was scared, Katia. Scared it would be too much."

She tilted her head to one side suddenly glad she was sitting down. "Rick…"

He stood up, moved across to the fireplace and gazed into its depths. "It was stupid of me. I should have told you. I know my family's circumstances are extraordinary, privileged. But, out there, in Europe, it all just seemed… obscene. It didn't matter. Other things always seem so much more important when I'm with you."

Kate stood up, went over to stand by him. Gently, she turned him to face her.

His expression darkened. "All those people, in all those countries. And me, back here, with all this. How can that be fair?"

"It's not," Kate whispered. "None of it was fair. You and I *both* are so incredibly fortunate. Educated, fed, with loving families. Thank you for your help with the German child. I feel as if she, somehow, embodies everything my papa wanted to fix in the world. I feel as if she embodies hope. And I think she brought us closer together."

The muscle in Rick's cheek twitched. With a touch of his fingers, he stroked her chin. "I haven't been able to stop thinking about you. Not since Europe. And I had to invite you here tonight. I couldn't keep away."

He looked straight into her eyes. "And now? It was as I thought. My mother and sister have both taken to you immediately, as I knew they would. Katia, is there any hope that you could view us as any family, as people who live and feel and breathe, just as you do? What I'm asking you is, is there any chance you could love a man who has feelings for you that won't go away, that won't leave him, that make him want to care for you and love you? Is there any chance?"

Kate took in a breath. She gazed up into his eyes, into the face of the man who had gotten her through the most intense, the most harrowing months of her life. And as her eyes raked over his, searching the tawny flecks and the intense expression in them, she knew for certain that the thing she'd hoped for, deep down, was happening on his part too. He felt the same way.

In some way, she'd done for him what he'd done for her. Gotten him through the aftermath of war on that tour of Europe. And now, months later, they both realized that what had happened out there was not just some short-term feeling, nor was it a friendship of convenience.

It was lasting. It had gone on, despite being apart, despite both of them searching for and finding rational reasons why whatever this was between them would not work.

And right then, with Rick standing opposite her, having borne everything of himself and his family in front of her eyes, his expression so honest and sincere and intense, she knew she had to reach out to him. She knew she had no choice but to give in to the fire that fanned between them, because to ignore it would be her deepest regret.

And when her father's dear face flickered in front of her eyes, as if rendered in the flames of the fire in Rick's grate, she smiled at the memory of his life, instead of recoiling from the hurt of losing him, because he had taught her what it meant to love another person. And even though he was gone, she would never want not to have known him, even if it were only for one day.

And it wasn't her fault her papa been taken so early, just as it could never be Mia's fault that her mother and her father, and her little brother, Filip, had been torn from her arms so early too. Mia still trusted, still trusted Kate enough to place her little hand in hers.

The child had opened her heart.

And now, she couldn't let the opportunity for love go by.

"Rick," she whispered, turning her face up to his, and taking a tentative step closer.

He searched her face, and he leaned forward, his fingers gently cupping her chin, his eyes asking a question.

Kate drew close to him, closing her eyes as his lips brushed hers, softly at first, before he kissed her deeply, and all the rational questions slipped from her mind as she leaned in and gave in to the feelings that too had overwhelmed her, like nothing she had experienced ever before. Life and love had renewed themselves, and in the end, they had finally overcome death.

Chapter Twenty

Kate

Germany, November 1946

The village where Mia's grandparents lived could have once been part of a fairy tale. A cluster of small houses encircled a village square. There was a church, and a set of magnificent gates further down the road, tucked into the trees and promising the magic of a grand old manor house, only adding to the allure of old.

It was only when Kate looked closer that she saw how some of the cottages had no doors, how the wind blew through the empty rooms, and the windows were shattered like broken teeth, how the gates to the local manor house hung from their hinges, and the church's steeple was toppled to the ground and weeds grew right to the front door. A light came on in one of the houses and Kate reached for Mia's hand, closing her eyes at the way the child clasped Kate's own hand tight, just as Mia had done when they first met back in Berlin.

On the long drive from Celle to the Soviet-occupied territories, during which they'd been stopped by the guards at the border crossing and allowed to pass through because they were returning a child to her family in the Soviet zone, Claudia had talked softly of sleigh rides in the small village near here where she herself had grown up with her extended family, and how she and her sister used to hitch their sledges to passing wagons, in the hope they'd drag them through the village, how at Christmas, their mother would fill the house with the aroma of baked gingerbread cookies and spicy cakes. Every Sunday, their aunts, their uncles, their Oma would arrive for the splendid roast lunch that Claudia's mother had cooked, and her childhood was filled with summers spent at the local lake, trips to the Baltic beaches, long holidays spent sliding down the great mountain of playing sand that her father would collect for the village children each June, days spent baking mud pies and playing statues.

Carefree days. Days she talked of with a lilt in her voice and love in her heart, hoping to reassure the still silent child sitting in the back seat holding Kate's hand.

Kate shuddered. She'd stayed up long into the previous night, talking with Claudia and her papa about her worries, leaving Mia in a Soviet-run territory, before anyone really knew how controlling the Russians would be in their occupied lands. But Claudia and her papa had been adamant. The child must be with her grandparents in order to heal.

Mia's grandmother had written to neighbors of her daughter's family and their friends in Berlin once the postal service was up and running, and though the poor woman had lost her daughter, her son-in-law and her little grandson Filip, she'd been beside herself with relief to discover that Mia had survived.

They could only hope Mia would regain her confidence to talk, and she would finally tell someone the story of how she came to be sitting alone on the steps of her family home in Berlin, and what happened to her mother and Filip.

"The Soviets have commandeered the Schloss," Claudia whispered now, as they circled the square in the car that Rick had organized for them, unable to travel himself due to commitments back home. Two guards were standing, framed by the skeletal trees, stripped of their summer foliage, surrounding the old, once imposing gates.

"What will become of it?" Kate asked, her eyes drawn to the men. Impervious, upright, the representatives of yet another strict regime. Kate shuddered and stroked Mia's downy head. The child had run to her as if she were her long-lost mother, the moment she'd laid eyes on Kate at Celle. Mia had buried her head in Kate's skirt, and Kate, despite the exhaustion that threatened to overwhelm her after the long flight from New York to London, and then to Berlin, had gathered the child into her arms, closing her eyes and breathing in her warmth, her shoulders sagging with relief to feel Mia close to her beating heart again.

Claudia shrugged. "I imagine the owners of the Schloss fled, like everyone else here. I think the Soviets will have looted it, and will turn it into a school, or a hospital, or maybe some sort of training ground. Perhaps Mia can go to school there."

Kate glanced at the soldiers standing sentinel there. *Mia's playtime would always be watched.*

She drew on her gloves and helped little Mia with her scarf and her mittens. She tucked the child's long blond hair into her woolen hat, a surge of worry running through her at the feel of the child's grip tightening on her own hand. *Was she close to her grandparents? What sort of life would she have out here?*

All the way, Mia had sat in silence, all the way on this long journey through Germany, she had not uttered a word.

Claudia had told Kate how Mia's grandparents had been too infirm to leave the Soviet zone. How she'd spoken to Mia's grandmother briefly on the phone, how the woman had sounded as if she were wringing her hands with tears falling down her face when she said she'd heard no news of her daughter and her two beloved grandchildren until recently. Mia's grandparents had lost their home. They had wound up living in a small village after sending their daughter and grandchildren back what they hoped would be the Allied zone in Berlin.

"It is strange now, it almost seems impossible to reconcile the fact that Mia's mother married the heir to another Schloss, just like this one, but in a nearby village," Claudia said, frosty air escaping from her lips, her eyes beautifully made up under the fur hat she wore. "That is why they had the lovely house in Berlin, Mia's grandmother told me."

Kate swore that she detected movement in the village windows, curtains tweaking, faces appearing only to disappear if she as much as swiveled her eyes their way, and a chill passed through Kate's insides.

Was it safe to leave Mia here? What sort of childhood would she have with almost everybody gone, the only folks left being the elderly, those who were too frail to leave the village? Those who were beneath the notice of the Soviet regime, and those who were too infirm to question them.

She hated to think what the elderly, who had not fled, had witnessed here, what memories invaded their nightmares. If Mia's grandmother's experience, losing her daughter and her grandchildren was any indication, they had likely been through unimaginable horrors.

Mia's silence felt like the silence of so many German people. Too afraid to speak, too afraid to draw any attention to themselves.

Kate stepped into the small village square.

When Mia turned her huge eyes toward her, Kate nodded, patted the child on the shoulder, straightened her little woolen scarf again. The child's cheeks were plump and rosy now after months of something closer to a decent diet, and farm-fresh foods and preserves.

"That one," she whispered, indicating the ring of houses and locating the address that Claudia had given her. "That one belongs to your grandparents, Mia."

Claudia translated, and Mia gave a great shuddering sigh. Finally, turning her back on the two watchful guards outside the great Schloss gates, who appeared to be content with making them feel fearful rather than actually approaching them, Mia put her head down and walked across the square.

Kate, her heart in her mouth, trudged in silence next to Claudia, her boots heavy on the silent square. The driver turned off the car's engine, and the entire village and the surrounding countryside with its lakes and forests was bathed in an eerie quiet. The gathering twilight lent a strange softness to the air, as if the day was waiting to decide whether to move forward into the night, or to try and hang onto the last vestiges of light.

Kate had to bend her head to fit under the doorway of the tiny cottage, one of a row of small houses, where Mia's grandparents lived. She stood back on the threshold a moment, but when the old man at the door gasped, reaching for Mia with trembling hands, tears streaming freely down his weathered old cheeks from his rheumy blue eyes, Kate, heart thumping, let go of the little girl's hand.

When Mia's grandfather finally eased himself up after hugging Mia, he waved Kate into the tiny cottage. She stepped straight into a pink wallpapered living room, the lace curtains at the windows drawn for privacy even though it was not yet fully dark outside.

In the far corner, under a tall lamp with a cream shade, an elderly woman sat in an ancient wheelchair made of cane, her wispy hair held back in a loose bun, and her hands covering her mouth. And in front of her, Mia stood, her entire small body rising and falling in time with the beat of her breaths, her hat in her hand, and her long blond hair tousled.

"*Mia!*" the old woman gasped, her hands outstretched, tears falling down her lined face as freely as birds flying over an untamed beach.

And after a moment, Mia stepped tentatively toward the old woman, and rested her head against her grandmother's chest, the grandmother whose eyes were the same striking blue as Mia's own.

The old man ran his hand over his chin, and mumbled something, before bursting into tears again and saying something in German, which he repeated over and over again.

"He says that Mia doesn't recognize her grandmother," Claudia told Kate. "Because she has aged so very much since learning that her beloved daughter, Mia's mother, Gisela, is dead."

Kate stood, her own chin trembling, in the tiny room, her cheeks flushed, her knees wanting to buckle beneath her.

Mia's grandmother spoke in a keening, soft voice to the child, and Mia's grandfather talked with Claudia until they both disappeared through a little door into a small pink kitchen, where the aroma of coffee drifted out into the sitting room.

Eventually, as if it were a great, solemn occasion, Mia pulled away from her grandmother and drew Kate to meet the elderly woman.

Kate reached out a hand, and the woman clasped it, and her expression said more than ten million words.

When it was time to leave, after Mia's grandparents had insisted on serving them with mugs of warm broth, Kate fought the tears that welled behind her eyelids, and her throat was thick.

Mia. Kate bent forward, drawing Mia close, one hand stroking the child's soft head, unsure whether she would see her little friend again, because if she were deep in Soviet territory, chances were, this would be the last time Kate would get to hold Mia in her arms.

The child's grandfather pressed an envelope into Kate's hand, and she shook her head. The last thing she wanted was money, payment of some sort. But, gently, insistently, he curled her fingers over the envelope, his old eyes holding hers, and he spoke something in German.

"It's a photograph," Claudia said. "Of Mia, and Gisela, and Filip. For you to remember them by."

Kate dug her hands in her pockets for her handkerchief, her shoulders quaking, knowing in her heart that Mia needed what little family she had left now.

Kate linked her arm through Claudia's, and they moved out to the old village square, the clocktower looking over them, along with the eyes of the two watchful Soviet guards.

Chapter Twenty-One

Kate

New York, November 1946

The roads spread before them and the possibilities seemed endless in Rick's blue Alfa Romeo. Kate held onto her hat as they shot along the country roads that led toward Rick's family home in Connecticut. Golden leaves spilled along the green verges that lined the roads, and tall trees reached up to the clear blue sky. The sun sparkled on Rick's gorgeous car and, despite the fact Kate had sat every night since she came back from Germany staring out the window at Ninth Avenue and dreaming of a little village deep in Soviet Germany, it was impossible not to feel a little happiness.

She listened to Rick and Harvey talking about the music they might look forward to at Eloise and Teddy's engagement party; Frank Sinatra, Bing Crosby, Duke Ellington and Perry Como were at the top of the charts.

Rick and Kate had decided out of necessity for her career to keep their fledgling romance private, but the past few days had been glorious. Rick had pulled out all the stops to cheer her up after her trip to Germany. For they both understood that giving Mia back to her grandparents meant that the little girl, perhaps, did not need Kate anymore. It was a closing of a chapter, but one big part of Mia's private story was still hidden from them all.

In a consummate effort, Rick had taken Kate to cozy New York restaurants every night, and Kate only hoped the thrill of holding hands across tables with red-checked tablecloths while candles burned down to their wicks would never grow old for them.

Now, Rick and Harvey's chatter came to a lull, and Kate focused on the winding road ahead. Over the past week, she'd been brewing up a plan. Was now the time to raise it with the two men whom she knew would support her no matter what?

"You guys," she said. "You know, I've come up with an idea."

Rick shot a glance her way, and she only held his gaze for a split second, sending him a reassuring nod.

"What is it, Kate?" Harvey asked. His tanned hand leaned on the car door, and he tapped a little rhythm with his fingers.

"Well," Kate started. She needed to seize every opportunity she could and make them hers before this all got on top of her and she was out of the political game for good. "Hilary and I talked last week about the possibility of me having my own show, because the stories I have been filing have been popular. Hilary said they are considering me for a regular morning slot of my own on women's interests."

"Do you want to write women's stories?" Rick asked. His brow clouded next to Kate, and she took in a steadying breath.

"What if I was to interview the wives of high-profile businessmen with the angle of how the media can get more women interested in economics and politics?"

Rick stayed focused straight ahead. "That could work. As an entrance." He glared at the road. "I'm sorry this is so hard for you, Kate." His tone was formal, but Kate sensed the deep feeling for her and the frustration behind his words, and she was thankful for it.

Harvey was quiet a moment. "Why don't I pitch it to the other execs on Monday morning? And why don't you talk to Hilary then too. Hang on!"

Kate turned around to face him. He threw her one of his dashing smiles.

"In fact, why don't you do some surreptitious research this weekend? There are bound to be plenty of wives of high-profile businessmen at the party, and I'm sure you'll find one or two who'll be happy to bend your ear."

"My mom, for a start," Rick said.

"Would she mind?" Kate asked. "I don't want to bring work to a party."

Rick's eyes crinkled into a warm smile. "Kate, talking about such matters would be a relief to Mom. You have no idea how much she abhors idle chit-chat. She'd probably be your first interviewee if you asked her."

Kate felt a small thrill leaping to life. If she could present Hilary with a fully-fledged story, then her chances of scoring her own show would increase tenfold. She held onto her hat and started brewing up interview questions in her head.

Perhaps this was just what Hilary meant when she told her to find an exclusive. Perhaps all Kate's hard work could finally pay off.

"Not long to go now," Rick said.

Harvey leaned back in his seat, closing his eyes and soaking up the fall sunlight.

Kate held onto the dashboard as the car rattled on toward Rick's family home and the party she was so looking forward to attending, when she could finally meet Rick's father for the first time.

Rick turned off Farmington's Main Street and drove down a tree-lined road, its freshly mowed grassy verges fronting white painted wooden houses set behind long sweeping lawns. Golden leaves scattered to the ground from the trees that arched overhead and the fall air was crisp and fresh. Kate and Harvey had turned silent, and so, strangely, had Rick. The Alfa Romeo's engine was the only sound that rang into the quiet air.

Kate fought a piercing of nerves when Rick accelerated down a long, curving private driveway, glimpses of wooded trails through an evergreen forest on either side of the car. Berries glinted on the trees that still glistened with dew. Rick slowed as the countryside finally opened up to a broad meadow, before he rounded one more curve and came to a stop.

Kate froze. There, before them, was a white painted mansion, a grand country home that resembled a New England farmhouse on a dramatic scale. A barn was connected to it, lending it a homely air, but the old house spoke to an earlier age of gilded balls and grand estate parties. Kate had never seen anything like it before, except in photographs.

"Christopher Columbus." Harvey whistled long and low. He pulled his sunglasses off and rested them atop his head.

Kate sensed Rick turning toward her, but she couldn't tear her eyes away from the view. The more she looked, the more she was entranced, stunned, terrified.

A white marquee billowed in the breeze to one side of the house, and uniformed maids and waiters bearing flowers and trays filled with empty champagne glasses strode in and out from a side entrance of the beautiful home.

But while Kate watched, a dark reality unfurled deep down inside. The woman who married Rick and came to live here would be expected to be a full-time wife, a society host, a pillar of the local neighborhood. A journalist from the Village would never do, especially one, who had political leanings. Keeping her career and her relationship with Rick would be all nigh impossible, given the way his family lived, restrictions and expectations that women journalists stay single aside.

But she had fallen for Rick. For the first time in years, she'd met someone who had broken the hard barrier she'd put up around herself, and for the first time ever, she'd met a man who treated her as an equal, a friend as well as a girlfriend. And yet, as she took in the house, the garden, the wealth, she knew she'd never fit in here.

*

The marquee was aswirl with party frocks and women of fashion who had eschewed post-war utility trends. Kate's eyes widened at the sight of girls already wearing what was whispered to dominate the runways in Paris this winter, billowing skirts that sat just below the calves, rounded shoulders showing off décolletages. Dresses in a kaleidoscope of colors set the creamy white tent ablaze and sent a clear message to everyone here. The war was over, and it was time to celebrate.

Waiters bearing trays with dozens of glasses of sparkling champagne circled the crowds. Kate stood with Rick, Harvey and a clutch of Rick's old friends, her eyes popping at the endless array of party foods, an abundance that no citizens had been faced with during the war; tiny meatballs glazed with cranberry sauce and brown sugar, seafood cocktails with shrimp, crabmeat and crunchy vegetables from the Woodlands garden, cute little sausage-and-bacon wraps, deviled eggs, salmon dips, bacon-stuffed mushrooms and salmon mousse canapés.

On a huge table that lined one side of the marquee, folks queued with plates to dip into three cheese fondues, steak crostini, and cheesy savory party breads. Ham balls with brown sugar glaze sent a gorgeous aroma into the air. The food never stopped and when the dancing started, Rick led Kate to the dance floor and they swung around in a group, while Harvey entertained everyone to his own crazy jitterbug. Girls swarmed to dance with Harvey, and with a wink and a grin, he cut a rug with them and never showed signs of flagging at all.

And when a young trumpeter names Miles Davis stepped onto the stage with Charlie Parker's band, the room turned silent at the introspective music that set the mood for Teddy's engagement speech.

When Teddy, the tall, handsome varsity graduate from his own blue-chip family, took to the podium to speak about the lovely Eloise, the room held onto his every word before finally breaking into rapturous applause. Eloise stood next to her fiancé, her face glowing and her sapphire blue dress matching the jewels she wore around her neck and at her ears, with her parents and Teddy's parents standing close behind, their proud faces a testament to a marriage that would strengthen the future of everything they stood for and believed. Teddy already belonged to this world in a way that Kate could never do.

Later, the family and the last of the party guests sat in a living room watching the sun go down in a blaze of pink glory over the deep green forest beyond the fields. Kate was curled up on a rug, with two black-and-white family cats stretched out beside her. Idly, she stroked their soft, warm fur.

Harvey was deep in conversation with Teddy, Rick and several other young men about banking and economics across the far side of the room. Harvey really did have the knack of fitting in with anyone, anywhere. His natural charm had worked its magic on both men and women alike today, and now he was seated, leaning eagerly forward, hands folded between his knees, eyes lit up keenly as the young men engaged in a lively debate.

Willard, Eloise and Rick's father, whom Kate had only met briefly, had disappeared, and Frances sat on a chair near Kate, cradling a cup of coffee and staring at the fire, ablaze with pinecones from the nearby forests, whose scent filtered into the room with its promises of shorter days, and the festive season ahead.

"Thank you for coming, dear," Frances said, addressing Kate out of the blue.

"Thank you for having me," Kate said. "It was a wonderful party."

Frances' lips formed a quiet smile. "It was the perfect celebration for Eloise and Teddy, just how I wanted it to be." There was a wistfulness in Frances' tone, and she opened her mouth as if to say something more, only to close it with a slight shake of her head.

Kate worried about the memory of how out of sorts Frances had seemed when she arrived at Rick's dinner party, at how she was certain she'd heard his mom crying on his shoulder when she'd left them alone.

The sounds of the men's conversation seemed to float over them, and Kate felt the urge to talk to Rick's mother, get to know her.

"Rick tells me you have an interest in books, and history," Kate said, almost mentioning politics, only to change her mind.

Frances smiled. "I love to read, Kate," she said. "Although I have not had the university education that Rick tells me you have had."

"You inspired him to study politics and history at university, though, Mrs. Shearer. That is something special."

"Well," Frances leaned down, the soft folds of her taffeta skirt brushing against Kate's shoulder. "First of all, do call me Frances, and second, you know, my interest in such matters is not something I can discuss openly with people of my own class, men or women. It is simply not done."

Kate felt a little emboldened by Frances' admission to her. "But you have been able to talk of such matters with women who are *not* of your class?" she asked.

Frances' eyes lit up momentarily.

Kate suddenly felt privy to the girl Frances once was, the girl who, perhaps, harbored dreams of her own, but for whom any ambition other than marrying was a pipe dream.

"Keep this to yourself, but before the war, I presented two talks, one on women's roles in society and politics, and the other on the role of women in shaping culture and political events for the American Newspaper Women's Club." She lowered her voice. "My husband was away at the time."

Kate moved closer to Frances' seat. "You did?"

Frances nodded. "It was right before the war, in 1939, when women had only had the right to vote for less than twenty years. It seems a world away now that we've had the war and women kept the country going without men here. I was invited by my good friend, Bernice, a woman who has quite the spirit, I have to say. But now, I'm afraid that most women I know simply aren't interested in the things I find fascinating. So, I read and think in private." She sighed. "Keeping things to oneself becomes a necessity in so many ways if one is to survive in society." Frances looked at Kate curiously, and Kate suddenly felt a rush of warmth for Frances.

What else did she have to keep confidential? Somehow, it was a relief to realize that perhaps Rick's family were not all perfect.

Kate sat up, senses prickling. She had to admit, there was another reason for her interest in Frances' views. Kate had chatted with a few wives of businessmen at the party today, but it had not seemed appropriate to ask them about their political views. But Frances? Would she mind if Kate broached the subject that could help with the start of Kate's first radio show, even though Rick had suggested she talk to his mom?

"Are you saying women are not interested, or they are not encouraged to be interested?" Kate said.

"The latter, to an extent," Frances replied. She shot a look over toward the men and lowered her voice. "After the Great Depression and the Second World War, having women stay home is becoming even more the center of American life because we have been so disrupted and alienated from normality during the past two decades. Women are marrying younger than ever before, and in proportions surpassing all previous eras."

"And what do you see as the effects of women marrying so young, Frances?"

"With our women marrying at the average age of twenty, they cannot possibly have time to get an education."

"I agree with you there," Kate said. Marriage must be the cornerstone of Frances' life. How many other married women were quietly lamenting the seeming decline of women's education?

Frances sighed. "The number of female college graduates has dropped substantially since the 1920s. No, they are not being encouraged at all. It is most worrying, indeed."

"I'm interested in how the media could counter this government directive, offer an alternative point of view to women having to stay at home, to them being left out of politics entirely," Kate said.

Frances looked thoughtful. "Voices of dissent are going to be even more marginalized than ever, though," Frances said. "There is such a push in America for women to stay home and serve our men who have fought in the war, and there is such pressure for us not to countenance any questionable ideas when it comes to politics *or* family values… If one questions these things, one is accused of being a communist. I fear that we will turn from fighting the Nazis, to recruiting them."

Right then, a figure loomed behind Frances, casting a shadow beneath the cream lampshade over her head.

"Frances." Rick's father, Willard Shearer, sent a brief glance toward Kate and then turned his focus back to his wife. "I'm returning to the city. I trust that everything is in hand here?"

"Of course, Willard. Kate and I were just becoming acquainted with one another."

The flames in the fireplace flickered while Rick's father stood there unmoving. *He was returning to New York, already?* Why even she, Rick and Harvey were not rushing back to Manhattan yet. Rick had hardly spoken two words about his father. Kate only hoped he was not the direct cause of Frances' upset at Rick's apartment that night.

Frances cleared her throat, sent a nervous glance toward Kate and reddened.

Kate stood up quickly. "Please do excuse me, Mr. Shearer," she said, sensing Rick's father's cool blue eyes resting on her. "Frances, may I freshen up?"

"Of course, dear," Frances said, relief fanning her features. "Go straight down the hallway and into the door at the far end."

Ten minutes later, Kate came out of the bathroom and hovered in the long, arched hallway. The sounds of conversation drifted out from the sitting room where she'd left Frances, and occasionally, Harvey let out a delighted laugh.

When Rick's father, Willard, bolted out of the living room and strode off in the opposite direction, Kate let out a sigh of relief and started walking back toward the party, but as her footsteps echoed on the floorboards, Willard turned abruptly, and came back toward her.

"Miss Mancini."

"Mr. Shearer, thank you for such a lovely eve—" Kate began.

"Would you step into my study for a moment?"

Kate gave a little shrug and nodded. Something told her not many people turned down Willard Shearer's requests, even if they came across as rude.

She followed him into a long room. Two leather chesterfield sofas sat opposite each other on a faded Turkish rug, tall lamps supplied soft light over an antique desk that looked out the window to the meadow, a pair of deep red velvet curtains half-drawn above. A fire crackled in the fireplace, and every wall was lined with bookshelves filled with old books. It was Rick's library at his apartment in New York all over again, but on a far larger scale indeed.

"Oh, my," Kate breathed, Frances' insights lingering in her mind. Did the women of this household get to come into this wondrous space? "What heaven."

"It was my father's library," Willard said. He sounded wistful, and Kate turned to him, suddenly equally as curious about Rick's father as she was about his mom.

"Thank you for having me today, Mr. Shearer. I loved being able to be here to help Eloise and Teddy celebrate. And I'm honored to meet you, sir."

Willard Shearer moved toward the window. He did not invite her to sit down.

Kate loitered on the spot, her eyes wanting to drink in the spines of all the books lining the walls, her hands wanting to caress their covers, turn the dusty magical pages and curl up on a sofa next to the fire to read late into the night.

"Let me be frank," he said, facing out the window, his tall profile silhouetted in the shadows cast by the tall lamps.

Kate blinked.

"I do not—no, that is not strong enough, I *will* not tolerate you using my family as subjects for any political stunts you have in mind."

"But, sir—"

"My wife's interest in politics is amateur. I will not have Mrs. Shearer, or any member of my family, taken advantage of by you. I hope I make myself clear."

Kate cleared her throat. Nausea nipped her stomach, and she fought an urge to sink down onto one of the sofas. This was the last thing she intended, the last way she wanted to be viewed by Rick's family! "I have no desire to use your wife, or any member of your family, to advantage myself, Mr. Shearer. Whatever gave you that idea?" She forced herself to stay calm. Had he overheard her conversation with Frances?

He turned around and picked up a paperweight from his desk, turning it over and over in his fingers and examining it as if it held all the answers he sought. "I am not going to answer an obvious question."

Kate's lips quivered. She fought for a response. "How so?" she managed, her voice sounding crackly and tight.

"Miss Mancini, we both know that I don't have to spell things out. I'm sure you'll understand that I'm not naïve and I know where you come from. I know how... enticing..." he waved his arm around, "all of this might seem to someone of your background, of your… class and your… *nationality*." He practically spat the last word.

Kate gasped. She reached for something to hold, but her hands flailed around helplessly.

"If you have any hopes of becoming a member of this family, you can forget it. Doing so would not solve your problems. By contrast, it would only be the start of them."

And then, Kate's debating instincts kicked in. Rick's father or no, he had no right to speak to her in this way. Keeping her tone cool, she said, "And what makes you think I have ambitions of becoming a part of any other family than my own, or that I would not be as worthy as any other woman, when it came to Rick?"

"Don't make me laugh."

Papa's voice, urging her to stand tall, to stand up for who she was and where she came from. She did not need to be talked down to by a man who viewed himself as her superior, only by dint of his birth.

"Rick does not view people in terms of where they came from, but, rather, he decides who his friends are based on their character. Surely you cannot object to his having such sensible and decent judgments, especially given what the world has just been through?"

Willard let out an ugly laugh. "You think the war has changed anything? I thought you, of all people, would be aware of current affairs. No, the war has only served to strengthen the country's foundations, not sever them as you hope. The likes of you will never grace these old houses, nor these families."

Kate lifted her chin. *The likes of you*, indeed…

He lowered his voice. "Let me make myself perfectly clear. There is a codicil in my will preventing any of my children's spouses from having any share of the Shearer estates. Will you leave now? I trust that will put you off?"

Kate's lip curled, and she bit her nails into her palms. "How *dare* you," she managed, muscles quivering, her heartbeat pounding.

But it seemed Willard wasn't finished. He reached down to his desk and picked up his checkbook. "Very well. What do you want? How much to make you go away?"

Kate glared at him, heat flushed through her body, and she felt beads of sweat pearling on her lips. "I have no interest in your money. I couldn't care less about it. All I care about is my own and Rick's happiness. I had no idea he was wealthy until just recently." Her cheeks flaming, she took in a breath.

Willard's blue eyes held hers with a cold, clear gaze. "Then it's up to you. It depends how you play it. If you continue with this notion that you are somehow entitled to a relationship with my son, then you can say goodbye to your career. No newspaper will employ you; no radio station will give you airtime. Do I make myself clear?"

Kate regarded him for one, endless moment, and he stood there, unblinking, gazing right back until Kate squeezed her eyes shut. "Entitled?" This had gone too far. "And what entitles you to have any say in my career, or, for that matter, your son's happiness?"

And he dropped his voice and delivered a bomb that Kate knew she could never fight. "If you see him again, I will ruin you."

She raised her face to his gaze and folded her trembling hands in front of her. Who was this man? Who behaved like this? And how on earth did this man father a son like Rick? He was blackmailing her.

Willard was as cool as a swimming pool in November. "I'm the chairman of the board at that radio station where you work. I'm on the board of half the media outlets in Manhattan. Rick doesn't know what he's doing right now. This job, you, it's all a rehearsal for the final act. He'll realize soon enough that he needs to get an executive role if he wants to get anywhere. And to get anywhere, he needs to rid himself of you."

Kate brought a hand to her mouth. "You are behaving like some—"

"I will ruin you," Willard Shearer repeated. "You will never be employed in this country again, and you will never be seen, or heard, on any radio station, or in any newspaper for the rest of your life if you see my son again. Do I make myself clear?"

Kate's mouth fell open. "I did not come here to be insulted." She ground out the words.

But he stood there. Cold eyes, cold expression, cold heart.

A man like him could do anything if he felt like it.

And feel like it he did.

Kate turned away, her mouth working, she focused on the flicker of flames in the fireplace.

"I trust we have reached an understanding," Willard said, his voice deadly calm.

Kate's breathing hitched. Almost unconsciously, she reached her decision. She brought a hand up to her throat, to the silver necklace that Rick had bought her for the party today. Silently, she removed it and lay it down on the back of the nearest chesterfield sofa, where it glistened on the sea of rich leather, a tiny sliver of silver alone in this icy house.

Holding her head up, Kate turned around on the spot and walked out the office door, swinging it closed and standing in the hallway, leaning against the wall, her entire body rigid, her back a stiff plank, her shoulders shaking, and her feet turned to stone. She struggled to control her breathing.

Kate closed her eyes, and tried to draw in slow, steady breaths.

"Kate?" Rick was right by her side. "*Katia?*" He was close to her, his breath whispering across her face. "What on earth is wrong?"

Still with her eyes closed, Kate nodded, up and down, up and down. Sweat pooled on her forehead now, her ears burned, and the only sounds she was aware of was the crackling, burning in the hearth inside the study and Rick's voice looming in and out of the blur. She grabbed Rick's arm and glanced up at him. "I have to go. I have to go home. Now," she said.

"What? Why?" he said, resting an arm over her, leaning his hand against the wall behind her back. "Talk to me. What is wrong?"

But Kate shook her head. His father was too powerful. He'd not only make her life a misery, but he'd also do the same to Rick. Suddenly, she was overwhelmed with empathy for Frances. Her silence was the price for her marriage... and her suffering? Was that just another part of the cost? Frances had warned her even more today, she'd told Kate how she diplomatically stuck to the rules and kept her intelligence to herself. Rick's mom knew how to play the game perfectly, and yet she was married to a monster who clearly didn't care for her.

And Kate was fighting in another world, equally as challenging as the one Frances inhabited, but in a different way.

Only a handful of women had made it to the air.

She was one of them. And she wasn't giving up.

"Nothing is wrong, dearest Rick," she whispered, the treacherous words slipping off her tongue as easily as if she were smooching into a microphone at Radio City. "I feel a little tired, but that's all. I'll get a bus, a train, back to New York. You stay. Please. Just let me go home."

She'd write to him when she was back in New York. Lie to him and tell him she didn't love him enough. She was a writer after all. She'd think of something to say.

Rick's face clouded, and he shook his head in confusion. "If you are unwell, I'll call for a doctor. You should rest, darling."

"No." Kate moved past him, staring incredulously up the long hallway, while Rick stood there, bereft. Kate searched for a door, a way out. Gasping for air, she marched on regardless, up the hall, toward the front door, which loomed in front of her, a solid, empty presence. Quickly picking up her coat and bag, she pushed it open, a flurry of cold air swirled in her wake, and she slammed the heavy door behind her, staggering forward to rest her hands on the wooden balcony that overlooked the dark, misty meadow, bringing her head downwards to stop herself from blacking out.

She'd been stupid to think this would work. Stupid to think she could have both love and a career. No woman could have both. What had she been thinking? That she was somehow exempt?

No, she had to go back to where she belonged, and that, for certain, was not here.

She closed her eyes, forcing herself to replace the locked image of Willard's cold blue gaze with her own father's warm, brown eyes, the way they used to kindle to life when she walked in the door, returning to that safe place, where she'd been loved and cherished, when life seemed filled with possibilities. His laughter, his encouragement. Telling her anything was possible in New York.

She'd believed it herself.

But Papa had been wrong.

Men like Willard held all the power, from the boardroom to the bedroom, and she was a fish on a hook that he wanted to cast out to sea, as far away from his gilded dreamboat as could possibly be. Kate could either sink or swim.

Snow drifted over Manhattan on the day Kate wrote to Rick. Desperate not to have the memory of writing the letter that she deeply dreaded at home in her studio, Kate went down to the Village, to the part of New York that she viewed as hers. It was as far away from Willard Shearer's commercial world, with its wide streets and skyscrapers reaching to infinity, that she could get. Here, the snow dappled softly on the sidewalks, and there was a quiet hush in the air as folks hurried along the narrow streets, bearing children and food parcels wrapped in brown paper packages, and often speaking Italian.

The restaurants, sidewalk vendors and cafés that lined Bleecker Street were all lit up and decorated with fairy lights and wreaths of holly with red berries for Christmas, and at the market stalls, folks greeted each other by name. If Kate closed her eyes, she was certain she could smell the traditional European Christmas aromas of pine trees and gingerbread and roasting chestnuts in the pretty street.

It seemed wise to avoid Mama's house. She did not want to taint the memories of her childhood home any more than she did her little studio. Kate pushed the old glass door open in the Washington Square Hotel and made her way across the simple lobby to the hotel's small café. Unwinding her scarf in the warm air, and greeting the owner, Vincent, by name, Kate settled in a quiet booth, soft flakes fluttering down to the pavement, milling like minuscule dancers in the soft, misted air.

Kate stirred the hot chocolate she'd ordered for courage and comfort and cupped her chin in her hand. She'd tossed and turned for the past few nights, avoided answering her phone because she did not want to have to talk to Rick, had even considered going back to Willard and standing up for herself, saying she wouldn't be bullied. She'd sat up at three o'clock in the morning twice, her head spinning with plans, what to say to him, how to make him see that she truly loved Rick, that she would never do anything to harm their family's reputation and that she didn't want their money.

But, finally, she had decided that she couldn't run the risk. Willard would clearly never allow her and Rick to be together, and if she tried, she would lose her career too. She would need her work if she were forced to let Rick go.

Aching for things to be different, Kate drew her notepaper out of her handbag, pulled the lid from her pen, and, with slow, deliberate strokes, penned the letter that would break her own heart.

And outside the window, children played in the first snow of the season near the fountain and the arch in Washington Square Park, just as she, Bianca, Tom, Natalia and Elena had when they were young. Just as she had not so long ago dared to hope that she and Rick's children might have played there too, one day.

Her heart filled to the brim with more recent memories, of all the conversations she'd shared with Rick on tour in Europe, of how he'd made what was unbearable on that trip manageable, how he'd helped her rescue exhausted little Mia, supported her when she wanted to go back to Germany and see the child again, and how they had run around New York together for a precious week to help her forget.

A heaviness settling over her, Kate lifted her pen from the page, placed the letter in its envelope, and sealed it, feeling like she was sealing off a part of her heart at the same time.

Part Two

Chapter Twenty-Two

Kate

New York, June 1948

Kate's two alarm bells both rang at once, just as they did every weekday morning at 4.30 a.m. She peeled her sleeping mask from her tousled curls and reached across the bed to turn off both of the jingling clocks. If she stayed in bed one moment longer, she risked falling back asleep, so she sat up, stretched her pajama-clad arms over her head and yawned.

She padded to the tiny bathroom down the end of her corridor to shower and change. On the way past her closet, eyes still half closed, she pulled out her usual dark jacket and a pair of plain trousers, a white blouse and a pair of stockings to go with her sensible shoes.

At 5.30 a.m., she greeted the doorman in the foyer at Radio City as she did every weekday morning, rode the elevator up to WNYR and fixed herself a breakfast of toast and coffee in the staffroom.

She was always the first reporter in the studios.

Still, she did not have a contract. Still, she worked on a casual basis and ten times harder than any male reporter at the station. But now, she was a political reporter with two shows of her own and an informal arrangement to report for the United Nations every day of the week.

She'd cut her radio teeth properly with WNYR, stepping in to cover Truman's Loyalty Program, after she impressed everyone with her coverage of the Big Four conference. As tensions between the United States and the Soviet Union intensified, fear of, and opposition to, communism had become central to politics, and Harvey had trusted Kate to cover President Truman's Loyalty Security Program for the federal government to uncover security risks… meaning communists. The program was designed to root out communists and subversives from the American government and Kate knew as much about it as any male reporter in New York.

She'd followed this up with stories on growing fears throughout the public that American communists or foreign agents might infiltrate the American government.

She'd reported on the House Un-American Activities Committee's investigation into Hollywood screenwriters and directors in 1947, and as the Red Scare intensified, both the Republican and Democratic parties hammered away at the threat of subversive communism.

For months, Kate struggled to marry her faith in the United Nations with the escalating tensions between communism and capitalism, the Soviet Union and America, and within America itself. But still, she reported dutifully and professionally as she knew was expected of her. But privately, she couldn't countenance the way ordinary Americans were being rounded up and tried in this way.

In the staffroom, Kate placed her toast between her teeth, grabbed her coffee in one hand and her scripts for her morning news update in the other, which she would deliver at 7.50 a.m. before she was sent off on the train to Lake Success. There she'd report on the United Nations live in the studio for her weekday afternoon fifteen-minute broadcast which aired on WNYR and its affiliate stations.

Kate knew exactly how fortunate she was to be the only woman network reporter in the entire United States, and this was something she could not afford to lose.

That afternoon, she reported for duty at the United Nations Headquarters in Queens, where the UN had found its home at

Lake Success on the site of a plant where materials had once been made for the war effort.

Despite the growing Red Scare, Kate, in the end, had decided to hang on to her belief that the United Nations would be an instrument capable of preserving the newly won peace and of managing it by perpetrating the alliances which held after the Second World War. Out here at Lake Success, the United States had played a key leadership role in creating the post-war organization whose aim was to secure peace for generations to come and Kate was proud to be associated with the United Nations as it strove for human rights, social progress, better standards of life and larger freedoms with a framework for international co-operation that was unprecedented in human history.

Every day, she reported on the decisions of the General Assembly, which carried the weight of world opinion on major international issues, as well as the moral authority of the world community and the will of the majority of the Member States. Kate often was one of the first reporters to be privy to the decisions of the Security Council, if they were in residence, which was composed of fifteen members, and was the keystone of the organization whose primary responsibility was peace and security.

As she entered the long low building with its rows of small windows overlooking a curved driveway where the flags of all the member countries waved in the spring breeze, Kate knew today's story would focus on the dramatic events in the city she'd been so moved by when she was last there, two years before.

Berlin.

As she sat in the Council of Assembly, Kate made notes with her heart in her mouth, and her thoughts and prayers flew to Mia. Kate closed her eyes a moment and forced out images of Rick, how he'd tucked the tiny girl into his coat and carried her up the stairs to safety back in that darned awful hotel in Berlin. These days, they passed each other in the corridors of WNYR rarely, because

Kate was so often out here at Lake Success, and Rick flew between European and South American capitals as a foreign correspondent for both WNYR and the *New York Times*.

Without her, Rick's career had skyrocketed.

Later, back in the studio in Radio City, Kate glanced through her initial story of the events in Germany. The tensions between Russia and its former allies, America, Britain and France, were exploding into a full-blown crisis and it was playing out in the city of Berlin. What was more, there was a frightening paradox engulfing the United States; for all its horror, many who lived through the Second World War looked back on it as the good war. It was almost as if the war, and all its losses, had given a meaning to life.

But in its aftermath, there was a gnawing sense of anxiety, dread and frustration growing around the world. It was global in scope and its attention was riveted on Europe, and particularly on Berlin.

Kate stepped up to the hanging microphone, waited for the signal to start, and delivered her report:

> *"An iron curtain has descended across the continent,"* Winston Churchill said in 1946. Behind that curtain, East Germany, Poland, Czechoslovakia, Hungary, Yugoslavia, and the other nations of Central and Eastern Europe had come under the control of the Soviet Union and its dictator, Joseph Stalin. Now, two years later, that metaphor has become a reality as the Soviets have literally tried to cut off West Berlin, located deep in communist East Germany, with a blockade designed to starve the city into submission, no matter the costs.
>
> The Soviets have now closed the main road to Berlin, and there are concerns that all road, river, barge and rail traffic into the city will be halted in the coming months.

They know very well that a blockade is an act of war.

The blockade has left West Berlin with about a month's supply of food and coal. The United Nations Security Council is still sitting to discuss the ramifications and how to supply West Berlin, without letting the entire city fall into the hands of the Russians. The Security Council is giving, and will continue to give, every consideration to practical measures to relieve the urgent humanitarian situation in Berlin, and several proposals are being considered today.

Kate closed her eyes a moment. Those words… *humanitarian situation.* She thought of the little girl with bright blue eyes. *Mia.* Kate had kept up the letters to the darling girl, and she'd been sending copies of all the *Anne of Green Gables* books to the child, one a month. But, deep in her heart, she always worried. Worried that the world did not know enough about what was really going on behind the Iron Curtain.

No one really knew what the life of one little child might honestly entail in Soviet Germany. And, to all intents and purposes, that little girl was not yet speaking. Mia was still only sending Kate pictures. If the Soviets had blockaded Berlin, would they stop letters being allowed out of their controlled parts of Germany too? And heaven forbid, people?

And all the while, Mia's story was still shut somewhere deep inside. No one but that little child knew what she'd endured, what she'd seen on her way from her grandparents' village to Berlin. She'd lost her mother, and her brother. But what had happened? And when?

By goodness, if Kate could do anything to help make the child's future story ten million times better than the one she'd already endured, she would leave no stone unturned to do so. Because that little girl was still bearing the weight of her own secret legacy from the war, and that little girl was now living under a regime that was blocking food to the democratically run parts of Berlin.

What were the communists capable of doing to the Germans who *were* living under their rule?

What would happen next?

Kate had a quick dinner of ham and eggs in her apartment that night, and then went out again to talk to a group of young aspiring women journalists at the New York Women's Club about her role as the only female reporter to cover the United Nations on a regular basis.

To supplement her income from reporting now she was no longer working at Albertina's, she'd reached out for opportunities to speak to organizations, conferences, clubs and societies where she could. The extra money was helpful, and she spent a deal of it on clothes for Mia, as well as the books she so lovingly sent.

Kate checked her reflection in her mirror, popped some lipstick on, and went out the door into the warm summer night. All afternoon, she'd followed up the news in Berlin. All afternoon, she'd not let news of the government under which Mia was living out of her sight. The crisis, as it now was, seemed to be escalating by the hour. West Berlin was totally cut off from the rest of the world, save for what passed in and out by air. Kate was certain that Stalin thought the US would back down if he confronted them with the threat of war. But President Truman was not Neville Chamberlain.

Stalin might understand recent history, and how Hitler had confronted nations with the threat of war, but Kate was certain he badly misunderstood the present.

Now, Kate removed her gloves, too hot in the warm summer air, and stepped into the Midtown building, greeted her contact at the New York Women's Club, walked down the aisle of the hall where at least two hundred women were waiting for her, stepped up on the podium, and once the host had introduced her, she stood up and leaned into the mike.

"Sometimes, I'm asked how come I'm doing this. Why am I, a woman, being a broadcaster since it's a man's job? Well, try hard as I can, I cannot split international problems into men's problems and women's problems."

A burst of laughter shot through the room, and someone started a steady clap. When the noise had died down, Kate went on.

"Tonight, I was asked to talk to you all about women's employment in journalism in post-war New York. Well, I thought about that and I have these things to say. I think women should be hired as reporters and journalists not based on their gender alone. I strongly believe that women should be educated so that we can offer information and understanding to our listeners and readers on an equal basis to men.

"I have no doubt that women have to put in twice as much effort as our male colleagues to win and hold a place in radio, or any form of print journalism, and I also believe that you have to be in the right place at the right time.

"I can tell you that broadcast news outlets are reluctant to hire more women, even though they are fully aware that women listen to the radio and women buy products offered by sponsors. You would think it would make good business sense to listen to women talk on the radio too.

"But that is not happening, because broadcasters in general think women are a species with limited abilities, who have brains too fragile to be concerned with the problems of the day."

The room was quiet. Kate scanned the faces, mostly girls in their twenties, a few years younger than she was. These were the women who had stayed in New York City, not been tempted by the mass exodus to the suburbs and the lure of domestic bliss and staying at home while husbands went out into the world, as so many women had. These were the girls who wanted to write their own futures, not have it written for them by men.

Kate paused a moment. A few years ago, Bianca had been the age of these young women too. Kate fought a stab of guilt that she'd not been in America when Bianca had made the momentous decision to marry into the Green family, to move out to Queens. Could Kate have stopped her? She still felt unsettled about the way Bianca had been so keen for Kate to move out to the suburbs too, but despite several attempts to talk to her younger sister, Kate had not gotten to the bottom of how Bianca really was coping out there with a child now. So, she'd forged on with her own career, doubts niggling away at her insides when it came to Bianca's situation, and her so-called domestic bliss.

"You might call my optimism and determination to make my mark in the male-dominated field of political journalism naïve, and indeed, I am well aware that I'm fortunate, but the seeds of my idealism were planted when I was growing up. And when I was covering the war in Europe, seeing embattled city after embattled city, I started to feel strongly that nations around the world could work together to bring peace.

"I began to feel strongly that the United Nations could do it.

"But there is a growing dedication in this country not toward brokering peace, but toward repelling communist diplomacy, and I think we are in danger of stepping aside from that assumption I made back in 1946, that the United Nations Charter, specifically, Britain, China, France, Russia and the United States, would work together in peace, as they had in war.

"We are starting to see hypocrisy and division between Russia and the western powers interfering with the goal of a happy world, and that, quite frankly, is starting to make me feel ill.

"As young women, don't be afraid to promote yourselves, don't be afraid to draw attention to your accomplishments. We need your voices more than ever right now, because I think we are poised, again, to enter a new and dangerous type of war."

*

At eleven o'clock, once she'd fielded questions from the many young women who wanted to work hard and contribute in a meaningful way to the world, Kate climbed back into bed, set both her alarm clocks, pulled her sleeping mask over her eyes, and lay in the darkness.

She turned on her side and tried to steady her quick breathing.

The time she'd spent with Mia would always remain as one of the most meaningful and purpose-filled of her life. Because it had felt, somehow, right. Taking care of a child. And she could not get away from the fact that she and Rick had done so together. Try as she might to forget him, Mia linked them together forever.

But now, the child they'd cared for was at terrible risk.

Chapter Twenty-Three

Kate

Berlin, July 1948

Kate leaned against the tiny window of the US Air Force C-47 Skytrain, traveling with a cargo of milk, flour, and vital medicines for the two million Germans stranded in the Allied zone of Berlin. As the plane descended, she craned around, keen for a first sight of the city. As they flew over, she could see that the rubble had been cleared at last. Now, the leftovers of war were raked into lumpy mountains in the gaping craters where handsome buildings had once lined the Berlin streets.

The military aircraft that had carried personnel and cargo during the war, and dropped paratroopers over this very country in combat, now flew low over a surviving group of apartment blocks. Kate looked out at the people standing on the high points in the streets, watching for the supply plane. She knew they were crowding together, three or four families to one small apartment since so many had lost their homes.

As the plane came in toward the runway, Kate's stomach turned afresh at the way the city had been transformed into a dust-ridden wasteland, with only burnt-out buildings, their windows like haunted eyelets, reaching up to the clear summer sky.

The RAF pilots landed the plane on the third and final round trip of the day. A trip for which Kate had negotiated hard with Harvey. She'd managed to convince him to allow her to cover the Berlin Blockade only because no male reporters wanted to come here.

Ostensibly, she was here to do her job. In reality, she was here to find Mia.

In the three days she had left after filing her report back to the US, she would have to travel behind the Iron Curtain, and try to convince Mia's grandparents to leave the village they'd always called home in order to save their granddaughter from a life lived under what was becoming an increasingly repressive regime.

The borders were still open between the Soviet zones of Germany and the Western Allied parts. But talk was that those Germans living under the Soviets might be forbidden to leave.

There was no doubt that the Soviets were becoming far more aggressive. Their demonstration that they were willing to starve the people of West Berlin was disturbing. Come winter, the citizens of West Berlin would not only need food, but fuel, unless they were going to freeze to death in their beds.

Leaving Mia to grow up under a government that could do this was impossible, and Kate had fought hard to get here because something needed to be done.

The aircraft landed at Tempelhof and Kate drew out her notes and unbuckled her harness. She'd been told she could get out on the ground at the airport, as long as she, like every aircrew member on board the flights to deliver food to the two million Germans stranded in Allied zones of Berlin, did not stray out of sight of the airplane where it had touched down on the airfield.

Two jeeps came rushing toward the airplane, and Kate helped a dozen men unload tons of bagged supplies. When they were done, another jeep rolled up with coffee, hot dogs and donuts. Kate wiped a hand over her sweaty forehead and accepted the offerings along with the RAF crew.

"They want us to unload the 'Gooney Birds' in six minutes flat, you know," a young man told Kate.

"Well," Kate said, grinning at the way he still used the old war term to describe the Skytrain, "I think we did that load in around seventeen minutes."

The man heaved out a breath, his forehead sweating in the July heat. "You've got that right. Now orders are they want the refueling done in eight minutes. At the moment, it takes thirty-three."

Kate watched the Air Force ground crew services as they checked out the props of the venerable plane. A makeshift scaffold rested up against one of her wings, and two men in caps were up on the wing, the sun beating down on their overalls and their faces shielded with caps.

"How many landings a day are we aiming for?" Kate asked, turning back to the young man who seemed to be happy to offer information to a reporter.

"The target is a landing every minute," her informant said. "You can imagine the flight orchestration and the ground operations that are going to go into this," he said. "They say it will be over in three weeks." He shook his head. "But out here, seeing the obstinate nature of the Reds, I think it could go on for months. Until we wear them down."

Kate shuddered.

When the orders came through to reboard the aircraft, she thanked the young man, downed the rest of her coffee, and returned to board the airplane, and to write the story that she'd file for WNYR.

Two days later, her story on the airdrop to Berlin filed, Kate had taken the train deep into the Allied zones of Germany. Now, she sat in the living room of Claudia's papa's house in Celle. Double sets of French doors were thrown open to the garden outside, and the filmy, sheer curtains waved in the soft breeze. Cherry-red chairs were arranged around a low coffee table, and faded Turkish rugs warmed the dark floorboards, while Claudia's father's favorite opera tunes played from an old-fashioned gramophone.

Outside, the garden was a riot of color, bees buzzed around the flowers where the winter had frozen everything in sight on Kate's other visits to the lovely old house. Kate accepted a warm cup of coffee from Claudia's sister, and rested her hands against the mug. Despite the summer heat, her body was cold after the journey to Celle's train station with its unspeakable memories of the devastating bombed trains and prisoners who tried to flee their persecutors during the war, only to be murdered by their countrymen. Memories that Europe must never bear witness to again, nor forget.

All the way here in the train from Frankfurt, Kate gazed out the window at the beautiful, aching landscape, now verdant and ripe with summer, but still haunted with the recent memories of the Nazi concentration camps and the horrors that were inflicted on the innocents.

Claudia spread a map of Germany on the low table in front of them, and by her side were the letters she'd received from Mia's grandparents in response to her offer, written in German on Kate's behalf, to bring the family out of the Soviet zone.

Kate, still overcome with relief at the fact that Mia's grandmother and grandfather's correspondence confirmed they too felt it was best for Mia to grow up in the Allied zones of Germany, leaned closer to the map. They would come. They would leave their home in the Soviet zone. And that meant she did not have to worry so much about Mia in the small hours of every night.

"The main Marienborn checkpoint is closed. However, we can still cross the border in several other places as is it not entirely sealed yet," Claudia explained.

But next to them, Claudia's papa shook his head. Kate shot a glance his way. *Please, do not hamper this journey. I know it is a risk, but it is a risk I have to take. The child fought so hard to live. She deserves the best chance in life.*

Kate broke down in tears when Claudia said she wanted to accompany Kate back to the small village. She wouldn't let her travel by herself, a woman alone crossing the Soviet border.

"It is too dangerous. For two women to travel alone, it is madness," Claudia's papa said.

Claudia traced her fingers, beautifully manicured, across the map. Her hair was curled, and even at home, she wore deep red lipstick and a fitted floral summer dress. "It is now or never, Papa."

Claudia's papa, Georg, sighed. He rubbed a hand over his chin. "Then I will come with you. I admit it, I am fond of the little girl. And I have passes to get us over the border. If need be, we will use them."

Kate closed her eyes in relief. She took a sip of the hot coffee, letting the warmth of it soothe her. Although she still hated to think what the journey ahead might bring. The last thing she wanted to do was place either Claudia or her papa in danger, but she feared he was right. The journey would be better with three of them on board.

"I shall say you are both accompanying me to Leipzig, where I am meeting with my musician friends. Goodness knows how long I will be able to continue doing that," Georg said.

Kate looked at the old man in surprise.

"Papa used to conduct in Leipzig," Claudia said, reaching a hand out to lay on her father's arm. "Back in the old days. He still goes there on occasion to see his old friends, and to play music with them. But the great musical city is in the Soviet part of Germany now. Papa goes there whenever he can, because we know that, sometime in the future, he may be cut off from those friends he holds dear in that city."

"Thank you," Kate breathed. "I cannot thank you enough."

*

The rudimentary checkpoint on the border of the Soviet lands was made of wooden huts. Georg produced his border passes and told the guards he was showing an American guest and his daughter the most beautiful city in Europe, he was showing them where the heart of music was, and that he trusted the Soviets would maintain the city's status, and that he had faith they would. He was the perfect combination of flattering and firm.

Kate hovered alongside him and only showed her passport. Her heart hammered in her mouth as they checked it, looked at her, took it into the hut for a moment, then came back. She'd left her journalist papers back in Celle. They were the last thing she needed.

Kate sat with her hands folded in her lap as they traveled out of the Allied zone, into the Soviet territories, the landscape achingly verdant, lakes glowing, forests reaching to the clear blue sky, nature pushing back after the devastation of war.

She drew deep into the car seat as they passed through the drab, rubble-filled villages. Many were almost empty, with no life in sight, only old signs in shop windows gathering dust, some still bearing the reprehensible anti-Jewish slogans that had littered this country during the Nazi regime. They were a blight on the faces of the now shabby towns. As they drove by, Kate felt as if watchful eyes were on her back.

When they finally rolled into the village where Mia lived with her grandparents, the town square was bathed in a haunting summer twilight. The village was eerily silent, the curtains in the surrounding houses all drawn against prying eyes.

Georg pulled up outside Mia's grandparents' cottage, offering to stretch his legs in the quiet square while Kate and Claudia helped Mia and her grandparents into the car.

But when Kate knocked on the door, it was opened with great caution, inch by inch. Kate drew her hand to her mouth, her heart beating double time in this strange place. *Had the Soviets discovered that Mia's grandparents were leaving and taken them away?*

When Mia's grandfather appeared, his head slightly bowed as he held the door open and stepped aside, Kate's heart bled for the old man who must have lived in fear of a knock at the door right throughout the war and beyond.

And then, Kate paled. She paled at the sight in front of her, in the pink frilly room with the last of the evening light pouring in through the cracks in the thin curtains, sending shafts of yellow sunshine onto Mia's blonde head.

Mia clung to her grandmother; the little girl's head buried in the elderly woman's skirts in the corner of the room. The child knelt down in front of her grandmother's wheelchair, and the sounds of Mia's muffled tears spoke volumes, indeed more than any siren in this hushed room.

Kate brought her hand to her mouth and stood there, helpless. Mia did not want to leave the home she'd settled into with her grandparents. After unspeakable turmoil in her young life that no child should ever endure, she'd only just found a home with family. Of course, the little girl didn't want to drag the only family she had left away from the village where they'd settled after the war. Mia would have friends here, children her own age at the local school. How could Kate have been so insensitive? How could she have read things so badly?

The rhetoric at home was all about life behind the Iron Curtain being brutal, about communist spies and Russian infiltration. About how the Russians were the new enemy now. Had she, Kate, become swept away in the anti-Russian propaganda and made an assumption about what was best for a child without giving the matter undue thought? Or worse, had she been selfish, pushing on to try and save Mia because she couldn't save her father? Because she hadn't been there to look after her little sister when Bianca was making the biggest decision of her life?

Kate gnawed on her lip, wrapping her arms around her body, not sure whether to go to Mia, or to stay put. "Mia?" she whispered. "Sweetheart? I'm sorry." She fought the sudden urge to bury her head in her hands.

But the child's grandmother only raised her head, her eyes meeting with Kate's, and in them, Kate saw the grief of a thousand years.

Mia did not move, and Claudia rested a hand on Kate's shoulder, the low murmur of Mia's grandfather talking to Claudia providing a counterpoint to the beating of Kate's heart in her mouth.

Kate wheeled around, slowly, to face Claudia. The room seemed to be spinning on an axis of its own. It was as if the entire world outside did not exist. None of it. All that mattered was this child, this family. The fact they were about to be ripped from their home.

And then she saw it. Sitting neatly outside the kitchen door was only one small brown suitcase. Not three. One.

Kate's eyes raked over Claudia's face, her head shaking in disbelief. Mia's grandparents were letting Mia leave, just as they had said goodbye to their grandson, Filip, just as they had let their daughter, Gisela, flee, never to lay eyes on either of them again? That would leave the elderly couple entirely alone, facing their old age by themselves, with no family in sight. It was unthinkable.

"They will not leave here," Claudia whispered, her eyes filling with tears. "And they have only just told Mia this. This is their home. They feel they are too old to make a new start elsewhere. They have lost their money, their farm, they are grateful," she said, "to be able to live in this village with food and a home. They cannot imagine a life anywhere else."

Kate's eyes dropped to the ground. *How could she be responsible for tearing Mia away from her grandparents?"*

"Kate?" Claudia's voice was a beacon in the fog of Kate's dark, troubled thoughts. "They want us to take Mia and give her the chances in life she deserves." Claudia reached out and gripped Kate's arm. "Kate, Rick has also been here to visit her."

Kate's head snapped up. "*Rick?*"

"Yes." Claudia nodded, her eyes searching Kate's face as if for understanding. "He has been here and brought her toys, Mia's grandfather says. And…" Claudia's voice dropped. "He also brought her a German passport from the Allied zones, in case she was able to get out. Her grandfather has it safely and will give it to us today to keep for her." Claudia's hold on Kate's arm tightened. "Please, Kate, don't think the family are not grateful to you both."

Kate's eyes swiveled from Claudia to Mia's grandfather, who stood with his eyes averted to the floor, fumbling in his pockets for his handkerchief. Despite the fact she'd had to write that awful letter to Rick, he still cared enough to come and visit their little friend. Kate fought the guilt at the way she'd hurt him and clasped her hands in front of her skirt. Rick's kindness aside, the fact was that the very idea that anyone would want to live under the Soviet regime was worthy of being hauled up and questioned at home.

Why? The word formed on Kate's lips, but remained unspoken, because at that very moment, Mia stood up, turning her solemn gaze toward Kate, and the little girl walked across the room, and silently placed her hand in Kate's own.

"She will come with us," Claudia whispered. "She will come."

And Kate closed her eyes, and she enfolded both her hands over the fingers of the brave young German girl by her side.

Chapter Twenty-Four

Kate

New York, summer 1948

Harvey appeared in Kate's office, just as she was leaving work after her first day back. Her hand brushed against the small bracelet that she'd bought for herself in Celle. It was one of a pair. One for Mia, who was starting school right where Claudia had studied, and one for herself. Kate had promised herself she would write to the child regularly, and one day, she hoped to be able to pick up the phone and talk to her, but apparently Mia had not said one more word since they left the village and her grandparents.

They'd considered bringing her back to America, of course they had. She, Claudia, Georg, sitting up late on that fateful night after they'd brought Mia to Celle. But in the end, they'd decided not to uproot Mia any further. And yet, the entire night, while she sat there in Claudia's papa's home, Kate had fought the dreadful, tragic knowledge, that if she and Rick were together, they could have given the child a loving home. They could have both looked after her. But the strings had been pulled and the dice rolled by Willard Shearer, and therefore Mia was to stay in Germany, Kate in New York, Rick traveling like some lost nomad in search of other people's stories.

"What can I do for you, Harvey?" she said.

He smiled at her, his expression as warm as ever, but the frown line between his eyes looked more pronounced these days. The fear swirling around communism was starting to take its toll everywhere.

People had to watch their backs. And everyone in the media was worried this new storm of fear would catch them up too.

"You okay, Harvey?" Kate asked, gathering her black jacket and holding it in her hand. It was too hot and humid out for jackets. She only carried one on her arm to look professional.

Harvey's smile held a little of his old enthusiasm, and he switched back to his usual enthusiastic self. "Sure, I am. You know, I've got something I want to talk about with you. I'm excited about it, and I hope you will be too. Can we go somewhere, have a drink and talk?"

She followed him out to Sixth Avenue, and he led her, jostling through the crowds, into a cocktail lounge, away from the bars that journalists were likely to frequent. Quiet booths were set against the walls, lamps cast a soft yellow light, and a pianist played Cole Porter at a grand piano whose lid was open wide.

Harvey waited for Kate to slip into a leather-seated booth, before sliding in beside her. He picked up the menu and studied it. "Well then," he said. "I'm up for a Gin-Gin Mule, how about you?"

Kate scanned the drinks offerings. The cocktail lounge was starting to fill up. Every other woman who entered was shepherded by a man as if they were on a date. A woman in a bright New Look skirt flounced by, giggling with a handsome boy, and Kate rolled her eyes. She avoided the wide skirts and hip-flaring dresses that categorized the New Look like the plague. She was too tall, and with no hips, she looked like a pumpkin in the latest fashions. Her slim-fitting skirts, trousers and blouses served to give her a professional, don't come near me air, and that suited her just fine right now.

Even though she was out with Harvey, and this was not a social occasion, she decided she may as well splash out and order something special. "I'll go for the Valencia," she said; sherry, orange oil, gin, garnished with flaming orange peel.

Harvey ordered some cheese gougères, the lounge's mini cheese puffs, and toyed with his classy drink when it arrived.

"Not my usual destination," he admitted. "But I wanted to ask you something quietly, give you the opportunity to consider it, as it's something I believe you could do. And to be honest, I'd like to have you there for WNYR." His eyes caught with Kate's. "We were impressed with your coverage of the first American mercy flights during the Berlin Blockade." He shook his head. "I think three weeks is going to extend into something much bigger when it comes to the blockade in Berlin, Kate. We've come to trust you, and I have a proposal to make."

Kate's hands stilled over her drink. Trust was becoming more and more a keyword in every organization across the country. "Of course, you can trust me, Harvey," she said.

Harvey lowered his voice. "The public are starting to place faith in your reporting," he said. "I was pleased with the write-up about you in the *New York Times* recently. The public need reporters they can turn to and rely on in these increasingly uncertain times."

Kate took a sip of her drink. "Yes, I saw that," she said. Privately, she'd been very happy about it.

"Being described as surprisingly intelligent, with a deep base of knowledge behind your womanly voice is something to be proud of."

Kate let out a chuckle.

"But I'm serious. We need to make sure your career is progressing, and to that end, I've got an idea."

"Oh?"

"I want you on television," Harvey said.

Kate nearly fell backward in her chair. *Television?* No one was on television!

"I think it's a wonderful opportunity for you. My other journalists, and this is across the board, are resisting assignments to cover the political party conventions, because radio is their medium of choice."

"The conventions are going to be televised," Kate breathed. She'd heard rumors of it before she left, but the reality of it... She pursed her lips. What went on at the political conventions was often best left under wraps. Some of the shenanigans beggared belief.

"I want you to go cover the Republican and Democratic conventions this summer in Philadelphia. No one has experience reporting in front of the camera, so I've convinced the other execs that you may as well go as anyone else."

Kate placed her drink down on the table. "*Me? On television?*"

Harvey's expression was serious. He nodded. "The other execs have agreed to it." He sighed. "But you'll need to go and find out about television makeup, what to wear, because how you look will be the most important thing."

Kate bit a cheese puff. So, that was the catch. "Seriously, Harvey?" she said, looking down at her outfit. "I dress like this to be *unnoticed*. And you want me to stand out like the brightest piece of candy in the store while covering the political conventions?"

Harvey's gaze was intent. "Television will be different," he said. "I don't like this, and you know that, but believe me, on television, folks will take in how you look first, and then they'll listen to what you say. With a man, it will be the other way around."

Kate glared at the table.

"Come on, Kate," he said. "The excitement of the political conventions will make for great television. You'll be one of the first ever television reporters to cover them, and just think, up until now, no one but the participants have been privy to the nomination of presidential candidates."

Kate raised a brow. "Well, I guess the truth is, this campaign could become a real horse race, but I know far more about the Republican tickets, Thomas E. Dewey, Earl Warren and of course about President Truman than I do about television."

Harvey sent her a trademark grin. "They are advising reporters to go to the library and borrow books on the new medium."

"Well then. I guess I'll have to take a trip to the library, won't I?"

A couple of unfathomable expressions crossed Harvey's face. "Listen. There's something else on my mind and I don't want to beat around the bush. When we were away, traveling together…."

Kate set her drink down and played with the straw.

"I thought you and Rick were… real good friends," Harvey said. "And that time we all went out to his sister's engagement? Well, I thought there might be something more going on between you. But I haven't seen you together since." His brows knitted together. "I'm afraid a couple of the other execs had their eye on you both. I thought I'd better warn you. You know, we wouldn't want you to be compromised in any way. Unfortunately, a woman's reputation needs to be squeaky clean in your position, and, well, if you were thinking about kids and settling down, that would cause a different type of complication for us. Oh, darn it, Kate. You know how I hate this for you. Both sides of the coin make things so difficult."

"Yes. Thank you. There's nothing to worry about when it comes to me and Rick, or me and anyone else, Harvey." Kate gathered her jacket. "I'll get prepared to report on television for you. I've plenty to do, so I'd better get going now."

"Kate…" His expression clouded.

"I must go. Thank you." She flustered about with her bag, her stomach fluttering.

"I'm sorry if I—"

Kate stood up. "I can assure you I'm not in a relationship with anyone," Kate said. "My entire dedication is to my career, Harvey. And I'll cover the conventions for you. You can rely on me. You know that." *Loose lips could destroy a woman's career.* "I can assure you, men are the last thing on my mind."

"I didn't mean anything by my question," he said.

"Goodbye, Harvey. And thank you. I'm off to work." She turned around and walked out of the cocktail bar into the heat of the Manhattan evening.

*

The next day, Kate stood at the Elizabeth Arden counter at Macy's with a couple of books from the New York Public Library on television tucked into her bag and three perfectly made-up assistants gathered around, peering at her with interest over the glass counters filled with lipsticks, compacts and perfumes.

The department store bustled with customers who were escaping the heat in the air-controlled store with its soft carpets and sparkling glass counters, where perfectly dressed women chatted over glamourous handbags and cosmetics. Kate felt like a giraffe among a sea of gazelles. Bianca would be so much more at home here.

Kate fought a familiar pang at the state of things between her and her sister, the unspoken words, the polite exchanges, even after the birth of her little girl, Sofia, even as she grew into a toddler, and Kate had no real idea about how Bianca was coping out in the suburbs by herself. Every time they met, which was not often, a well of underlying tension still hung between them. In the early hours of the morning, Kate sometimes even fought guilt that she'd not just accepted Bianca's invitation to move out to Queens so they could be proper sisters again.

Kate braced herself and faced the beautifully made-up cosmetics sales team. "Could you give me a list of dos and don'ts when it comes to makeup for television?"

"I don't know anything about television," one of the attendants said. "You are going on television?"

"Yes, it seems so," Kate said faintly.

"Heavy pancake with very dark lipstick," she said. The young woman turned and pulled a few slim wooden drawers open behind the counter.

"No, no, no, light pancake, with medium-shade lipstick." The older of the three women peered at Kate's olive complexion. "And no rouge. Nothing."

"Definitely, rouge." The first was back with a selection of Elizabeth Arden lipsticks and pancakes. "Here, let's try it on," she said.

Kate nibbled on her lip at the sight of the confounded makeup. She never wore it for radio reporting. She didn't need to and that was a blessing. Her eyelashes were naturally dark, her complexion was even, and the last thing she wanted to do was look like a clown.

What was worse, she'd heard a couple of male reporters snickering in the office at lunchtime that the light would go right through her on television and she'd be seen in all her glory!

"Honestly," the other attendant said, frowning at her colleague's selection of products, "I could give you advice on the movies, but not television. I don't know anything about that."

"Oh, go on," the first girl said. "You know I don't know either. At least I'm willing to guess!"

Kate blinked hard. The men at the station were not only snickering about her being seen right through, but they were also saying that she'd have to look like a beauty queen, or she'd be the laughingstock of New York!

"Well, if no one knows how to do television makeup for the modern day, I guess I'll have to experiment," Kate said. "I've read that the cameras they use these days are more sensitive than the old ones, and the pick-up tubes can reproduce gray tones as faithfully as on panchromatic film."

The women all stared at her, frowning at this and shaking their heads.

"I do know that we won't have to use green and red makeup, along with facial lines being emphasized in purple or yet another shade of green, as things have improved with the new advances in technology for television, but that's the extent of my knowledge, I'm afraid."

The women stood stock-still.

Kate sighed. "Can you sell me some small packets of makeup, so I can experiment with some of your ideas and see which work best? How would that be?"

The older woman nodded and popped a few small tubes and samples in a bag, handing them over, while her colleague whisked off to serve their more regular types of customers.

Kate paid, and stalked out with her little bag of tricks, heading for the department store Bonwit Teller, to try and determine what colors would look best on camera when it came to clothes. But, again, she had no luck. All she knew was that her favored trouser suits would most likely be looked down upon and dismissed. She would have to rely on dresses and skirts, but what colors? There was nothing about that in anything she'd read on the new medium that was going to make her look right when she was front and center stage.

She sifted through rack after rack of women's wear. Not only her makeup and outfit, but her hair would be scrutinized, along with every detail of her appearance that would go unobserved on a man. She'd heard the men today reinstating this fact again, laughing that all they'd need to do was shave cleanly, dress conservatively and be well groomed.

Kate threw a couple dresses over her shoulder and marched toward the fitting rooms.

"Do you know anything about clothes for television?" she asked the attendant, already prepared for the response.

"Black is all right," the woman said, eyeing the dresses Kate held.

"No, it's not," another woman in the queue for the fitting rooms told Kate. "You mark my words, don't wear black."

"Let's face it," the attendant said, handing Kate a wooden number and telling her to go into the fitting room, "no one has experience in television. It's all a guessing game, honey."

Kate stalked into the fitting room, clutching the dresses with no idea what would work. Half an hour later, she left with two navy dresses with austere necklines, and one more jazzy outfit, a light blue dress with a slightly lower neckline and a daisy pinned to the bust. Her preparation had been a guessing game, and all she could do was hope her guesses were correct.

When Hilary sat her down in her office that evening, she inspected Kate's dresses, nodded and gave her more news.

"Kate, management want you to wear glasses, because they'll make you look more like a newsperson."

Kate didn't need glasses. "I hope they don't make me blind."

"Just get a fake pair," Hilary said. "And your hair is too dark."

Kate lifted her head.

No.

"Before you leave for Philadelphia, we want you to dye your hair blonde, and tease it, to give it more coiffure."

Kate crossed her arms. "Heavens to Betsy, Hilary."

"Orders from the top," Hilary said. She was in one of her famous no-nonsense moods and she leaned forward and lowered her voice. "It won't be enough for you to be an astute reporter, or even a brilliant one. You'll have to be wholesome for the home audience, you'll have to have sex appeal, and you'll always have to look the right side of forty if you're going to have a career in television."

Kate snorted. She couldn't help it. Perhaps she should just don one of those new French bikinis instead!

Hilary took off her own glasses and placed them down. "We estimate that ten million Americans will watch the conventions, and they will be aired on three hundred and fifty thousand television sets. Pictures, Kate, are going to be just as important as words."

Kate folded her arms and looked to the side.

"Could you tint your eyelashes?" Hilary asked.

Kate's eyes rose to the roof. *Perhaps it would be a blessing no one would recognize her because she'd look nothing like herself!*

Hilary tidied a stack of papers on her desk. "There's one more condition," she said.

"I have to waltz with President Truman? Do the jitterbug in front of ten million viewers?"

Hilary frowned. "Please."

Kate fidgeted with her pen.

"They want you to focus on the women's angle at the conventions."

Kate flushed. She bit on her cheek.

"Put aside your knowledge of politics and cover the activities of wives and families of the candidates." Hilary kept tidying and did not look at Kate for one moment at all.

Kate tapped her foot on the floor. She cocked her head, then shook it. "Hilary?" she whispered. "You're sending me to cover women's stories? *What w*omen's stories are there to cover at the political conventions that are dominated by men? And was there a reason that I'm only being told this now, once I've agreed to cover the conventions for you?" Harvey had not told her this, but Kate bit back her frustration.

Baby steps.

She would have to climb them one by one if she were to get anywhere near the level of political television reporting that would be done by the men.

"You won't be the only woman journalist at the convention, Kate, but the others will be serving behind the scenes. I hope you understand," Hilary said. "This is a great opportunity for you, but we need to take things slowly."

Kate could only give her a glassy stare.

Hilary's hands flew around her desk. "Well, that's sorted then. Very good. Thank you, Kate."

Kate pushed back her chair, but as she did so, she heard the sound of footsteps behind her. Harvey took a step inside the room.

"Kate?" he said.

She stilled, her hands clenched.

"We flew Rick out of Germany yesterday, and he's covering the convention alongside you. He'll join you after the first few days."

Kate couldn't move. She looked straight through Harvey, the fingers of her right hand curling around her little bracelet, and staying there.

Hilary stayed quiet.

Harvey lowered his voice. "You know, I'd hate to see a *real s*ense of division between you and Rick, despite your assurances that things are fine between you. You're two of our best reporters. We don't want you at loggerheads."

Kate lifted her chin. "Like I said, there's no division, no *nothing,* between me and Rick."

"Good, Kate," Hilary said, her voice breaking into the quiet. "Now, I suggest you put your head down, and focus on the task at hand."

Kate stood stiffly. Her chest ached and the room felt heavy somehow. "Thank you, then," she managed. "I'll get myself to Philadelphia on Monday."

"Good luck, Kate." Harvey patted her on the shoulder.

She fought the urge to shrug him off and walked out the door.

Chapter Twenty-Five

Kate

Philadelphia, summer 1948

Kate took a last turn around Convention Hall, perspiration dripping down her forehead in the stifling Philadelphia heat. All around her, delegates and journalists sweated it out in shirtsleeves after the plan to have sixty large fans blowing across fifty-pound blocks of ice that were attached to the roof had failed when the ice was hauled manually up six flights of stairs and melted immediately.

The city was hit with a second scorching heatwave as the convention rolled on and the hall was oppressive. People started collapsing in the aisles and the first-aid station was constantly overflowing with victims of heat exhaustion. If that wasn't bad enough, the hall had been invaded with dive-bombing pigeons, and some delegates had taken to sitting with newspapers on their heads to protect themselves.

Kate had been boarding in a college dormitory since the Republican Convention began, because there were not enough hotel rooms to accommodate half the visitors to the city. Everyone was gobbling up all the suspense, the intrigue and the back-room dealing in smoke-filled rooms. Kate's male counterparts delivered political reports to thirteen eastern seaboard states and viewers invited friends and neighbors into their living rooms to watch the escapades for the very first time.

One day, a baby elephant was paraded through hotel lobbies. Despite the heat and the exhaustion, everyone wore political buttons and silly hats. Every poll predicted that Thomas E. Dewey would win the election outright if he was nominated as the Republican candidate, and the Republicans were confident they'd take the White House now the war was done.

Meanwhile, Kate had become used to days spent pushing her way through the crowds to secure interviews with delegate's wives, clutching a walkie-talkie to alert the program manager if she had secured an interviewee, only to begin the soul-deadening process of asking the women about their fashion choices, why they thought their husbands made good politicians, opening the way for the same old chitter-chatter about their children and their home routines.

But, to her surprise, television audiences had become glued to Kate's interviews, they were fascinated by the chance to actually see congressmen and senators' wives wax lyrical about the way they lived at home. Kate was receiving fan mail and the station had been bombarded with phone calls from women of all ages wanting to know more and more about what wives cooked for their husbands so that they could emulate them for their boyfriends and for their husbands, fathers and brothers at home.

With gritted teeth, Kate smiled her way through revelations about the current fascination with gelatin. She was the most informed political correspondent in the room on how many variations there were for Jell-O salads and jellied chicken. She'd adjudicated mock debates about the best hot dog to jazz up a potato salad, along with countless wives telling her they had, hands down, the best recipe in the country for coconut cream pie or gold nugget cake.

The wives never failed to tell Kate how their men were good fathers, and especially, they emphasized, they were loyal patriots to the United States who would not let the country down.

Behind the scenes, Kate had built up quite the reputation as the reporter who knew how to put makeup on any woman and make her look good on television. She'd been sent sample bags from nearly every cosmetics brand in the country and knew how to make up her interview subjects to their best advantage before they graced the screen. Despite the indignity of the topics on which she had to report, she was coming to appreciate having the audience *see* her interviewees live.

Being able to react to the way her subjects delivered their answers in an interview while viewers were watching was exciting. There was no doubt in her mind that television was going to open up a whole new way of communicating between people, once they could see moving images showing what was really going on in the world, right in the comfort of their homes.

And often, she wondered, if ten million Americans had been able to see the reality of war playing out into their very living rooms each night, would that have stopped folks from glorifying war?

Now, Kate was resigned to being blinded on a daily basis by the floodlights in the broadcast booths. After nights spent tossing and turning with no fan and not a whisper of a breeze in her tiny college dorm, she had to be on set an hour before her male counterparts, while her skin was coated and her newly dyed blond hair was fluffed up and sometimes her color tweaked. She was told that her subjects needed to relate to her, and to achieve that, she needed to look like them.

All throughout the convention, Kate had to set up her own makeshift broadcasting booths for herself wherever she could find a tiny space. The camera's merciless eye peered unblinkingly at her, and Kate was warned by her program managers that television made good-looking women look like witches, and that it would catch every one of her expressions, boredom being chief among them.

And all the while, she and Rick had avoided bumping into each other, like a pair of tigers pacing in a zoo, avoiding eye contact, turning the other way the moment they came face to face.

Now, she jolted at the sound of a loud bang somewhere in the hall. Another monitor had blown up. Earlier that morning, one network's giant floodlight was so bright that when it honed on a broadcast booth all the images were killed. The high temperatures at the convention were causing the largely untested video machines to overheat, forcing technicians to pack bags of ice around them.

Kate came to a standstill outside the official WNYR booth. She was stuck in a line of folks who'd stopped to watch Rick delivering a broadcast. When his eyes met hers, he only showed a hint of recognition. She could see it in the way he inclined his head and narrowed his eyes. She lifted her chin and looked the other way.

But she was stuck as the crowd thickened. She stood there and folded her arms. And she had to hand it to him. He was mesmerizing. Playing the camera with that intimate smile, his brown eyes kindling and always, always speaking as if to one person.

At last, he drew to a close. "You've been watching Rick Shearer, signing off for *Evenings with Rick* on WNYR."

Once the show was done, the crowds started moving, and Kate put her head down and pushed her way out. The memories of their brief time together hurt so much they sometimes threatened to break her in two.

"Kate."

She came to a shuddering halt and jerked her head backward to stop herself from walking smack into the man in front of her.

Folks moved around her, and she gathered herself before turning around. And yet, as she looked up at him, standing there, brown eyes brimming with that unfathomable expression she used to love, her already torrid body temperature soared, and her stomach quivered, along with her resolve.

He searched her face, and the hot, crowded hall shimmered and swayed. "Can we go someplace and talk?" His voice cracked on the last word.

Kate swayed, her mind racing. *No, they could not. And there were a million reasons why.*

She managed to lift her hand to wipe her perspiring forehead. "I need to go."

"*Katia*. Please." His brow furrowed and his expression held everything. Every cold, dark evening they'd spent talking in rusted old hotels across the continent, every moment filled with joy that they'd shared during their brief interlude together in New York. Every heart-piercing regret that Kate had endured since Rick's father had forced them to break up.

Her hand floated up to fidget with the plain silver necklace that she'd bought for herself to wear at the conventions, the new necklace that sat against her sweat-beaded throat. "It's best we don't talk."

"Best? *Whose best?*" He reached out and tucked a tendril of hair off her sweating face.

Kate jolted at the feel of his touch. The distance between them tore at her, at every part of her being.

"One drink, please, Katia. Just one drink. It's all I ask," Rick said, and Kate was pushed by the crowds, had no choice but to move through the swathes of folks who'd come to witness men becoming famous, and the women who supported them no end.

But just for a moment, instead of Rick, she saw Willard Shearer, and his terrible words, *I will ruin you,* rang in her ears. Kate moved with the surging people toward the exit sign that led out into the searing, hot Philadelphia afternoon. And behind her walked the famous reporter. The famous reporter who was escorting that woman who interviewed delegates' wives about baked Alaska and cheese fondue.

She stepped into the blinding sunshine, acutely aware of Rick walking next to her as they wove their strange, urgent way through the crowds that milled around under the flags and the sign emblazoned with the words: Republican National Convention.

When they came to a standstill on the sidewalk, a steady stream of cabs and cars pulled up to deliver men dressed in pristine, pressed suits.

Slowly, inevitably, she turned to face him, her mouth working. "*Rick—*"

His brow darkened. "Please, Katia. I can't stand this. Come with me. We need to talk."

A taxi pulled up right in front of them and the driver leaned out. Rick held open the door. "Just a few minutes. A drink. Kate, please."

She ran her hands down her navy frock and even though the heat was overpowering, she wrapped her arms around her body.

"What harm can one drink do?" He whispered the words, and the car behind the taxi honked, and without hesitating to think, Kate slipped into the hot, sweaty, back seat of the cab, and Rick was in front next to the driver, and she knotted her hands in her lap.

"The Bellevue Hotel," Rick told the driver.

The car was stifling. Kate's legs sweated against the hot leather seats and as the taxi wound its way through the streets of Philadelphia, crossing the river, pausing on the other side behind a couple of trolley cars that were trundling down Market Street past Wannamaker's Department Store, Kate asked herself four thousand times what she thought she was doing. She hadn't worked this hard to throw it all away.

Would Willard Shearer's spies know she'd taken this ride with Rick? *It was worse, this, than riding through communist Germany.* Her heart in her mouth, she knew the moment they stopped, she'd have to make her excuses and run. It was impossible. The situation was impossible. Rick's father had given her no choice.

Kate took in a shuddering breath and fanned her face with her hand.

When the taxi stopped on the corner of Broad and Walnut Street, she gawped out of the window at the French Renaissance-style building that loomed up ahead.

A doorman came and held open her taxi door, while Rick paid the driver, pulling several crisp notes out of his leather wallet.

Kate gazed upward at the grand façade with its arched windows and sets of French doors leading out to terraces where folks smoked and had drinks on balconies. Carefree laughter filtered down to the boiling sidewalk and a broad stairway led up to the brass and glass rotating doors.

The Bellevue Hotel looked more like home to high society than a place of residence for some mere journalist.

But then, Rick's family were high society.

She was the mere journalist.

And Rick's father had made that crystal clear.

Rick waited for her to go up the stairs first.

"I'm not dressed for this." She turned to him, pleading. "And I can't talk with you." She scoured the street for a train station. She did not belong here.

"*Can't?*" His eyes flickered with hurt as a doorman swung open the doors.

"Welcome back, Mr. Shearer," the doorman said.

Kate's heart almost stopped. A few minutes. One drink. The dark voices inside her that told her this would make things worse. Ten thousand times worse, and harder and more complicated, and she'd be set back all the time she'd spent getting over him, telling herself it didn't matter, telling herself she was better off on her own. But she ignored them all and nodded at Rick.

Inside the blissfully cool lobby with vast marble floors, and elaborate chandeliers throwing sparkling light over the wide reception desk, she almost fainted with relief from being out of the heat.

"Good evening, Mr. Shearer," the man behind the reception counter said, his lip curling at Kate's simple dress.

Rick led her through the marble lobby and into a glorious domed room, where a chandelier cascaded down from the ceiling, its glass baubles dripping above the few diners' heads. Soft chairs sat atop rich carpet and small tables were set with white linen napkins and sparkling silverware.

Rick spoke to a waiter, who held out a chair for her and she sank into it. Everything seemed surreal. This couldn't be further from the drab single bedroom she'd been allotted on campus, with no fan for the heat, the window stuck closed, worn linoleum on the floor and a shared bathroom down the hall. Rick ordered a bottle of champagne on ice, and a selection of the hotel's best sandwiches, pastries, and mini cakes.

Kate bit on her lip and waited while he poured her a glass of champagne. His hand stilled, and his dark eyes caught with hers. "Claudia tells me that Mia is starting school in Celle in September."

Her stomach lurched with guilt again. Had they done the right thing by Mia? It was so hard to tell if the child was really doing okay when she still would not speak.

He offered her the plate of food, and like a clockwork doll, Kate took some delicacies out of politeness. She sipped at the cool champagne.

Silence hung between them like a hangman's axe, and Kate made an attempt to eat a chicken sandwich, but it stuck in her throat, and she toyed with her hands.

"Tell me you don't love me," he said, his words barely above a whisper. "And I'll never bother you again."

Slowly, Kate raised her eyes to his face. His fedora sat on a seat nearby. She hadn't realized he was carrying it, but then, he'd kept it all those years.

"I don't love you," she lied.

Chapter Twenty-Six

Bianca

New York, summer 1948

Bianca took the long route through the forest path to Riley's Lakeside Lodge for breakfast. She strolled slowly, savoring the chance to breathe in the clear country air before the endless daily activities in the Catskills began. Swimming, sailing, cruising on the lake, tennis, ping-pong, golf, horseback riding, dance lessons, dance teams, and Simon Says. One of the resort's nurses had arrived at half-past six to collect Bianca's little daughter Sofia, and Bianca wouldn't lay eyes on her again until Sofia was safely deposited back to her tonight.

Tonight, Marshall's mom, Florence, had organized a moonlit dinner on one of the verandahs overlooking the lake in the lodge, followed by an evening watching the entertainment in the ballroom and dancing until late. She'd told Bianca a babysitter would be arriving at the cottage Bianca shared with Marshall and Sofia at half-past six on the dot after Sofia was brought back from the nursery. Marshall had just gone back to New York for the working week.

He'd driven off early, rushing with his father to make it to the factory by nine a.m. sharp, both of them with hats perched on their heads and cigarettes pressed between their lips, talking shop and quickly pecking Bianca and Florence on their cheeks by way of a farewell. Marshall had been restless all of last night, continually getting up and checking his travel alarm clock and disturbing the double bed, while Bianca tossed and turned, moonlight pooling on the bare floorboards of the cottage by the lake, and cool breezes filtering through the open window, the gauzy curtains blowing softly in the dark.

Now, she hesitated where the path widened out at the edge of the forest, the vast lawn that surrounded the white wooden Lakeside Lodge spreading before her. Already, guests were seated by the water, women in halter-necked swimming costumes with their legs stretched out in the sun, their heads tilted back, big black sunglasses shading their eyes. The sounds of the jazz band filtered out from the lodge, and bursts of laughter punctuated the endless commentary on the loudspeakers from inside the ballroom.

Bianca's espadrilles pressed into the soft green lawn as she made her way across to breakfast on the verandah. She had lingered after Marshall had left this morning and Sofia had been collected for the nursery. With a tiny moment to herself, Bianca had curled up and read a novel on her bed. She couldn't sit outside on the front verandah of their cottage without getting found out. Florence and Patricia and her family were staying in cottages either side of her, and they'd be sure to see her and get her to come help them fix their hair, or mind Patricia's children before her four kids went off for their sailing lessons for the day.

"Good *afternoon*, Bianca." Florence was at the top of the short wooden stairway that led to the verandah where breakfast tables were set out. She looked Bianca up and down, turned around, and led her right to the front, her trim hips swaying and her long legs shapely beneath her swinging shiny skirt. She stopped at a table that overlooked the lake.

If she were honest, Bianca had watched Marshall leave longingly, wishing she could go home to the Village for a holiday rather than stay here with her in-laws and all the organized sport.

Now, at breakfast, Bianca felt on show. Patricia had already laughed away Bianca's petite, dark figure and her flashing black eyes to her friends, saying that she probably had gypsy blood.

Bianca had not contradicted that. *If only she had Kate here standing up for her as she used to do.* Bianca was more aware than ever on this vacation that she'd lost that person who used to watch her back.

As time wore on, the days, weeks and months had bled into each other, punctuated by the pills her doctor had prescribed to calm her down and hours spent dusting and cleaning, changing diapers and preparing Sofia and Marshall's meals, and Bianca had plenty of time to think.

Plenty of time to realize she'd had no right to blame her sister for their father's death, and no right to try and suggest that marriage and a ticky-tacky home in the suburbs was the answer for Kate. Bianca knew now, only too painfully, that her idea of bringing Kate out to Queens was desperate. She'd wrung her hands over her hopeless attempt to match Kate up with Roy Hammond. What had she been thinking?

It had taken her months to realize that, underneath the bravado she'd put on about being married, about having what every girl dreamed of, she'd been afraid of feeling alone for the rest of her life. There seemed to be an irony in that, despite being married, she felt more alone now than before.

Patricia and her friends all wore pastel-colored sun frocks for breakfast with little hats perched on their heads. They'd all make at least four changes of outfits for the day, just like women used to before, Bianca knew, the First World War. Florence and Patricia had arrived with a veritable collection of luggage for themselves.

Bianca ran her hands down her own simple cotton frock, gritted her teeth.

But when she sat down at the table, the half slice of grapefruit and the orange juice neatly poured out for her, she grimaced. Her stomach roiled, as it had done every morning for the past month, and she gently pushed the plate further away from her nose.

"Is the food not good enough for you, Bianca?" Patricia said, her pretty face scrunching up into a confused frown. "This resort doesn't serve salami, latkes, or toasted challah, you know, dear."

A titter spread around the table and some of the women covered their pink-painted mouths.

I'm Italian, not Jewish. I know this isn't a Jewish resort, or one frequented by Italians. She closed her eyes at the way they patronized her. If she stood up for herself, they'd laugh, call her bossy, or difficult. They'd make her life even worse. No, she'd have to deal with another month of this vacation, and then she could go back home, perhaps ask the doctor to up her prescription for tranquilizers.

Bianca swayed a little and placed her napkin on her lap. She waited for them to start another conversation and reached for a slice of white toast in the silver toast holder in front of her plate.

"Let's go play Simon Says." Patricia eyed her friend's empty plates, and smiled, showing her pearly white teeth. She ran a hand through her soft blond hair, that hung in waves to just below her shoulders, pinned back with a tortoiseshell comb. "That is, if you are ready, Bianca?"

"Sure," Bianca said. She finished nibbling at her piece of toast, her stomach unable to take any more. A salty, strong taste brewed in her mouth that was as much a portent of the future and what life had in store for her as anything else in front of her eyes.

And she'd chosen this life. She reminded herself of that every single day. The cardinal rule was not to bother your husband. *He was the one slaving away and working so hard every day, so you could have pretty clothes, so your children could be fed, educated, brought up in the proper way.*

Inside the ballroom, a host leered into the microphone on the stage, while a hundred guests stood in lines on the gleaming floorboards, and sun beamed in through the high windows that lined the tops of the walls.

"Well," one of Patricia's friends said, "I always say a game of Simon Says is the perfect way to work off breakfast! It's like calisthenics!"

Patricia and her friends all let out a delighted laugh and Bianca hovered on their edge.

Her mother-in-law, Florence, waved her over to come into the group, her eyes rolling to the ceiling. "Come on, Bianca," she whispered.

The host, a middle-aged man in a cream T-shirt with a brown collar and matching brown trousers, led the game. "Simon says put your hand over your head!" he called into a microphone. "Simon says put your hands by your side. Wave your hands! Bye."

A woman reddened and doubled up with laughter. She walked off to sit on the side of the room while the game went on.

"Simon says bend forward." The host bent backward, and Bianca, flooded with dizziness—was it the medication, was it morning sickness?—copied the host. She bent backward and Patricia let out a shriek.

"You don't copy him! You listen to him! He said bend forward, silly girl!"

There was an awful noisy buzzing sound, and everything went black.

"She was late to breakfast and didn't eat." Patricia's voice pierced the room.

Bianca opened her eyes. She lay on the wooden floor of the hall and several faces peered down at her, moving in and out of focus, blending and fading away.

"Since she had Sofia, she's looked like a twig. Goodness, darlings, that name. I never could abide it. Poor Marshall, having to put up with it. The foreignness…" One of Patricia's friends clicked her tongue.

Now, Florence spoke: "The nurse is here. Move away, girls."

There was a sound of shuffling.

Bianca blinked, and tried to prop herself up on one elbow.

"Little stick legs. Not a good look," Patricia sighed, and Florence's face filtered in and out of focus.

Someone was holding her wrist, taking her pulse, and Bianca turned to see a uniformed staff member.

"She'll be fine," Florence said. "Silly girl. I told her to be here on time, and this is what happens when you're late."

Bianca clutched at her throat. She tried to open her mouth, but nothing would quite come out.

"Poor dear, you fainted in the heat," the young nurse said. "You're quite hot. You should take a rest."

Bianca peered up into a concerned face. Owl-like spectacles framed a pair of serious brown eyes and the woman, who looked to be about Bianca's age, had her hair cut short in a bob around her face.

Bianca lay there for a moment. Gradually, the sounds of Marshall's mom and sister drifted off into the distance.

The hall was empty.

They'd gone and left her here.

Bianca eased herself up. She sat up; her legs folded in front of her.

The woman handed Bianca a glass of cold water, which she sipped, took her by the arm, and led her to a chair to rest.

"Thank you," Bianca said.

"My pleasure. Your family seems to have left," she said, concern flickering through her eyes.

Bianca nodded. "Yes. Yes, I think they have." She curled her fists tight, her breath coming in short bursts. Her hands rested on her flat stomach. What if she was pregnant? What if she was having another daughter? If anyone ever treated Sofia, or any unborn child, in the way she was being treated right now, well then… what sort of role model was she being for Sofia, putting up with the way Marshall's family bullied her?

Bianca folded her arms.

"Let's get you back to your villa. Can you walk, or would you like a wheelchair?"

Imagine. The embarrassment of being wheeled back to her room in front of all Patricia's athletic friends.

"I'll be fine to walk," Bianca said, hardly recognizing her own voice.

She looked at the empty room. Empty room, empty heart.

She sat up. "Yes. In fact, I'll definitely go by myself."

A couple of hours later, Sofia scooped up and resting on her hip, a short note left on the kitchen table of the cottage she would never be returning to, Bianca stood on the driveway outside the Lakeside Lodge, the one suitcase she had brought for the holiday by her side, along with Sofia's things in a neat brown bag. She'd fixed herself a cool drink and managed to down two pieces of toast back in the villa, had packed lunch for herself and Sofia, washed and dried the dishes, and left the cottage immaculate.

Enough was enough.

When the trolley car came to drive her to the train station back to New York, she climbed in, stored the luggage up front, and sat down, looking straight ahead, not backward. Never would she do that.

As the trolley car drew out of the resort to the tree-lined main road, Sofia turned to her, her own black eyes lighting up.

What now, my darling?

Bianca intertwined her fingers through her daughter's chubby ones and faced resolutely forward. *We are going to talk to your daddy, because I don't want you growing up seeing your mommy treated like that.*

*

That evening, Bianca stood on the front porch of her Forest Hill Gardens home. The street was silent and blessedly empty. Twilight muted the vivid green lawns and turned the trees that surrounded the house into soft shapes. The click of cicadas was the only noise to break the quiet. She thanked the taxi driver who'd driven her and a sleepy Sofia home, and gave him an extra tip out of her weekly allowance from Marshall, for carrying the luggage to the front door for her.

Sofia's sleeping head lolled on Bianca's shoulder, thumb in her mouth, dark eyelashes splayed across her cheeks. Bianca sighed and thanked goodness Florence was not here. The thumb in the mouth would result in Bianca's mother-in-law placing mustard on poor Sofia's fingers and slapping her hand. The last time she'd done that, Sofia had let out a righteous roar.

Bianca turned the key in the lock, and holding the front door open with her foot, she maneuvered the luggage inside. Sofia's soft breath flickered against her cheek.

Bianca came to a sudden halt in the foyer and drew her hand up to her mouth.

"*What...?*" she whispered.

Exhaustion from the journey aside, Bianca pushed back the nausea that threatened to inundate her stomach all over again and raised herself up to her full height of five foot three.

From the living room which she'd polished and vacuumed every single day since she'd married Marshall, carefully primping cushions and changing flowers so that her husband would come home to perfection every time, there came the distinct sound of laughter.

A woman's voice, tinkling, light, with that distinct twang that Patricia's friends always adopted when they were talking intimately among themselves.

And Marshall's deeper tones, soothing. Intimate as well.

Bianca froze. Heat flushed through her body, her muscles quivering. Her forehead was laced with sweat, and a flutter of pebbles danced through her stomach.

Step by heartbreaking step, she edged toward the living-room door.

And stood there, framed with her baby on her shoulder.

"Marshall?" she said.

But he'd seen her. In an instant, he was up off the sofa, moving toward her, rolling down his sleeves, tucking his shirt, which was hanging loose over his trousers, in again, until he came to a stop.

It was too late. In that split second before his eyes had met with his wife's, Bianca had seen the way the woman's legs were intertwined with her husband's on the couch. Her furniture. She'd seen the way the woman's blue eyes had rounded at the sight of Bianca, seen the way she'd lifted her chin and tossed her hair in that defiant way that Patricia's friends favored.

Bianca's house, Bianca's husband, Bianca's life.

But the woman's confidence said it all. She belonged here.

And Bianca did not.

Two hours later, Bianca paid another taxi driver outside her mom's house in MacDougal Street. She stood on the sidewalk, a grizzly Sofia balanced on her hip and their luggage, still packed from the Catskills, lined up. Frowning with concentration and forcing herself to focus heroically on the task at hand, Bianca fished in her handbag for the house key she always kept to her childhood home.

She pulled it out and turned it over in her palm.

Had she always suspected she might need to come home? Was that why she'd never stopped carrying it with her?

Bianca had been putting up with Florence and Patricia's snubs and patronizing attitude toward her for an age. Ever since Sofia had been born, they'd compared the little girl's progress with that of Patricia's children, sniped at the way Sofia's black eyes flashed like her mother's, told their friends that Sofia was nothing like the Green side of the family.

Now, Sofia placed her chubby fingers over her mother's lips. "Gran?" she said, her little face lighting up into a smile.

"Yes," Bianca said, taking the little girl's hand and squeezing it, before pressing it with a kiss. "Yes. Gran."

When Livia opened the door, her eyes flitted straight to Bianca's suitcases, her hand rose to her throat, and her black eyes narrowed.

"Mama," Bianca said, reverting to the name she'd always called her mom when she was little.

And then Livia held her door wide open, and stepped aside for her daughter to come in.

That evening, once Sofia was bathed, fed and in bed in Kate's old room, and the soft sounds of the little girl's chatter had fallen quiet, Livia pulled up a chair to her kitchen table, offered that Bianca sit down, and rested her chin on her elbow. "*Santa Maria*, my love."

Bianca lifted her chin. "I will go back to teaching, Mama. I can manage two kids and a job, just like you did."

Livia's small fingers tapped on the table. "*Two* kids?"

"I can't go back there. And yes, I think so. Two, Mama." Bianca looked out the window at the twilight, the capturing of that halfway moment between day and night, past and present. The dying day. "I thought it would last. I thought it was real, you know, I truly did."

Livia stood up, went to her kitchen bench to make coffee and leaned on the bench, her hands reddened from gardening and decades of honest hard work. "I'm sorry, sweetheart. I'm sorry for everything." She turned slowly.

Bianca looked up. "No," she whispered. "It's not your fault."

But her mother's sadness pierced at her heart, and she folded her arms as her mother came back and sat down heavily.

"I'm sorry you felt left out. When you were a girl. Your papa...
Kate." She lowered her voice. "*Me.* I should have noticed more. So
much more. But your papa died, and I was inconsolable... I'm sorry
it had to come to this." Livia's voice shook. "It wasn't fair on you."

Bianca raised her head to meet her strong Italian mama's eyes.
The honesty, the raw honesty of her mom's words, struck at her
heart. Had she run into this mess entirely because she'd never felt
part of the circle her sister and father had created for themselves
once her older sister's talents had become so blindingly obvious
to everyone? And had the focus on Kate, the intelligent daughter,
the daughter who would cement the Mancini family, make them
successful in America, left Bianca roiling around without a compass?

And now, she and Kate were so far apart in their two worlds,
in their opposing attitudes, that there seemed no way back, and
Bianca was going to be a divorced woman.

All she'd wanted was to feel part of a family. How had it all gone
so terribly wrong? She'd fought so hard, but she'd unknowingly
put herself into the exact same pattern with Marshall's family that
she'd known growing up with her own.

Livia looked at her daughter with worried eyes.

Bianca placed her hand over her mother's.

And outside the window, the sky was stained pink as a blood
rose.

Chapter Twenty-Seven

Kate

New York, summer 1948

Kate shook Harvey Milton's hand at eight o'clock sharp in the morning and sat down opposite him at his desk in Radio City. Behind him, the sun beat on the picture window that looked out over Manhattan's skyscrapers, and Hilary Winthrop hovered in a pale blue summer suit. Kate bit back a yawn. Insomnia had troubled her ever since that awful encounter with Rick. When he'd stood up and walked away from her after her distressing lie to him in that confounded hotel, she'd known it was the end.

"Well done, Kate," Harvey said. "The television department was inordinately happy with your coverage for the political conventions. You made quite the splash across the nation, and you are continuing to receive calls and fan letters from your new audience."

Hilary's expression held a warm glow.

"Thank you," Kate said. It was all she could say. *Interviewing politicians' wives?* Was that what she'd studied four long years at university to do?

Hilary leaned on Harvey's desk. "Exposure is exposure, Kate, and like I always say, women listen to radio, and women *will* watch television. They want to know that their stories are being told."

Kate held Hilary's gaze and nodded, up and down, up and down.

Harvey leaned forward. He held strong eye contact with Kate. "I spoke with the other execs while you were away." Harvey's sleeves were rolled up. "You converted your talents in radio effortlessly onto the television screen."

"I'm glad you are pleased."

"Oh, we are," Hilary said. "Go on, Harvey."

Harvey lowered his voice. "*Vogue* are doing a story on you in their August issue, focusing on your appearance, and the role of cosmetics."

Kate drew in a breath. *Oh, my.*

"The editor-in-chief called me yesterday," Hilary said. "She told me so many of the men at the conventions looked too haggard—blanched was the word she used—but you with your dark bronze foundation, heavy pancake makeup and moist reddish-brown lipstick, with no rouge, no eyeshadow, but heavy mascara, looked fantastic. They congratulate you."

Kate sat back in her seat and sighed.

"Kate, there's no point beating around the bush," Harvey said. "We want to offer you a full-time contract."

Kate covered her mouth with her hand. "Say that again?"

Harvey's toothpaste grin widened, and he pulled a piece of white paper from his desk. "We want the only female broadcaster in New York to work full-time for both our radio station and our television station. We want you on a television show called *Kate Mancini's Guestbook*, which will air on a Sunday evening. We're going to have you conduct in-depth interviews on political news from the previous week. What's more, you'll have an additional two broadcast news shows on radio, called *Kate Mancini Reports*, every evening, and we want you on another political daily feature, a fifteen-minute television show airing every weeknight on television."

Kate squeezed her hands by her sides. This was not what she'd expected. She had to force herself not to punch the air. *So, no more makeup and cooking?* She didn't hate women, only the way men viewed them, and the way men thought women had no interest in the outside world. "And these shows will all be politically based?"

"Indeed," Hilary said. "Congratulations, Kate."

Harvey flipped the contract around, and Kate forced herself to scan it carefully.

"Your salary will be $158 a week. As a full-time employee with the network, you can write your own feature articles for your shows."

Kate eyed it. She knew male reporters earned more than that.

"If things heat up between the United States and the Soviets," Hilary said, "demanding increasing coverage, we may put you on air for another show as well."

She folded her hands in her lap. "And in that case, could we review my salary so that it might be in line with our male reporters who have their own shows?"

Harvey cleared his throat. "We are willing to consider that. Yes," he said.

Kate nodded.

"And down the track, we are considering having you hosting a couple more shows on television, so you can demonstrate that you're not only a political soul. We're thinking about a travel program about why people come to America, and what they expect to find here."

"That sounds interesting," Kate said. "I'm already intrigued to find out what travelers to America do expect!"

"Well," Harvey said, "someone told me recently they expected all of our cities to be filled with skyscrapers and gangsters everywhere. They also thought all Americans lived in luxurious homes." He drew his brows together. "There are also those who mistrust and fear us."

Kate held his gaze. Now, the idea was getting mighty interesting.

"Don't snap your cap, Kate," Hilary said, "but I still want you to appeal to my female listeners and viewers. We're going to take compelling publicity shots of you and use them to advertise our station. You'll be one of our lead television journalists."

"Well, thank you." Kate wanted to hug Hilary and Harvey. The dull ache in her chest might never quite go away when she thought about Rick, but this was what she'd worked for. This was her dream. And her papa would be so proud of her. She had to let herself celebrate. "I simply can't wait to get started," she said.

Harvey scuffed his chair closer to the table. "Three hundred and fifty thousand homes in eighteen cities now have television sets. Folks are spending four hundred dollars on average for the privilege of having television in their homes. And you are about to air in these folks' living rooms every night of the week. You have to see how excited we are."

"And we're putting you up against top-rated shows, airing on other stations," Hilary said, quirking an eyebrow and smiling at Kate. "You'll be on against *I Love Lucy* every night of the week."

Kate chewed on her lip. "Well then," she said, her eyes dancing, "I'm no Lucille Ball, but I sure am keen to stay on the beam, and I hope I've proved to you that I've got what it takes to stick around."

"Oh, you have," Hilary smiled.

Harvey pushed the contract across the desk.

Kate took it, told them she'd show it to her attorney this afternoon, shook their hands and walked out of that studio. She'd fought so hard to get here. As for love? She'd always known, deep in her heart, that it wasn't ever meant to be for her.

Part Three

Chapter Twenty-Eight

Kate

New York, spring 1951

New York Times, March 1951

This week, we are profiling the extraordinary and determined female journalist Kate Mancini, the woman who continues to defy the notion that women are not suitable for radio and television broadcasting. Ms. Mancini, who hosts both weekly radio and televised news shows on WNYR, has become well known to viewers across the nation, with her innovative broadcasts featuring both news and views. Her offerings include a variety of commentary, feature stories, and even short documentary projects, unusually for a woman, centered around international politics.

Ms. Mancini first came to television three years ago on the back of a career in radio and print journalism, a career that, again, remarkably for a woman, involved a ten-month tour of post-war Europe with an all-male contingent of journalists reporting on the devastation across that continent, followed by extraordinary coverage of the Nuremberg trials. Competing with top-rating television show *I Love Lucy*, Miss Mancini held her ground and forged onwards after a stunning television debut reporting on women's interests at the Philadelphia political conventions in '48.

Her Sunday-evening broadcast, *Kate Mancini's Guestbook*, for WNYR, remains one of the most highly rated shows on television, in which she has interviewed politicians, leading businessmen and international figures in depth.

Her feature show airing on weeknights also remains a hit, in which she delves into one feature news story of the day. Ms. Mancini earned nationwide recognition for her coverage of such major world events as the lifting of the Soviet blockade of Berlin, and the communist armies of North Korea swarming south of the 38th parallel, invading the Republic of Korea, to launch the Korean War.

Ms. Mancini is a woman who has forged ahead in the business world, running her own career with complete aplomb, when most women in modern America have no desire to succeed in business, preferring to focus on raising children and staying home. These days, the majority of American women spend their leisure hours focusing on the domestic arts—canning, preserving, and interior decorating the home is the central focus of their existence when they are not with their children and seeing to domestic tasks.

In fact, in a recent survey, the majority of women would list becoming a gourmet chef as the height of their ambitions, with the higher role of wife and mother being the pinnacle of female success after the era of discontent brought about by the war and the upset caused to women's lives when all our men were called away and feminist notions took sway across America. However, Ms. Kate Mancini admits she is hopeless when it comes to the domestic arts. Rather than cooking gourmet meals, she prefers to come home to a dinner of ham and eggs.

So, what is the secret to the extraordinary Ms. Mancini's success? Sources who have worked with her report that she is not temperamental, and above all things, she

cultivates composure. Underneath her serenity, there is a
fine ruminating of ideas and thought.

    With women making up twenty-eight percent of the
total employees in broadcasting, few women cover news
or even talk about it, preferring to work behind the scenes,
with only a handful working as local news correspondents.
Ms. Mancini does not brag about her ideas unless it is
to provide the country with an answer to the biggest
question in television today—how can the medium best
handle news?

Kate stirred. Soft morning light filtered through the curtains at
the window of the two-bedroom apartment on Sixth Avenue she'd
moved into a few months back, and yesterday's *New York Times* lay
open on the other side of her bed.

She'd only had a chance to read the article about herself right
when she was about to fall asleep, and now she folded up the paper
that she'd been too tired to tidy away last night, stretched and
yawned and slid out of bed. It was Saturday. All she had to think
about was wandering down to Café Reggio in the Village, where
she'd sit and catch up with today's newspapers while she sipped
one of their famous espressos and the locals strolled in the sunshine
outside the stained-glass windows that overlooked the street.

Afterward, she'd wander across to MacDougal Street to visit
Livia. Kate pushed aside the feelings of guilt that bit at her about
Bianca. Her little sister and her two children, Sofia and Lara, were
crowded into Livia's apartment while Bianca's divorce was being
finalized. Every time Kate went to visit, Bianca and she still skirted
around each other, polite, stilted, eyes never really meeting and
their conversation never opening up. Today, Kate knew that Bianca
was taking her kids to see their father, Marshall, out in Queens,

and she felt ashamed of the relief that washed over her because she wouldn't have to feel awkward around Bianca.

But there was nothing she could have done. When Kate tossed and turned at night about her sister, she always came back to the same conclusion. She couldn't have saved Bianca's marriage by moving to Queens. She would have destroyed her own career in the process. But somewhere, deep inside, she felt remorse that she hadn't stepped in and done more to help when Bianca needed her. Now, she only wished she'd seen Bianca's attempt to match her with Roy Hammond as the cry for help it was.

When the phone rang, she moved into her living room with its pale blue sofa and desk set up against the window where her typewriter took pride of place.

"Mama?" she said, picking up the black receiver on her desk, and opening the curtains to let the sun spill into her living room. No one else would call on her on a Saturday. Livia probably wanted her to nip into Albertina's deli and buy some of her favorite pecorino cheese to have after lunch. But at the sound of a different voice on the other end of the line, Kate stopped, her hand poised in mid-air. "Hilary?"

Something must be wrong.

"Kate, I won't mess with you. I need you to come up to the station at once. Now, please. I'm sorry to disturb your Saturday morning, but—"

"It's no trouble," Kate said, hurrying out the words. Hilary never called her on a weekend. "Is everything all right, Hilary?"

Kate's boss was quiet down the line. "All I can say is I'd get here as soon as possible, Kate," she said. "I don't want to say anything over the phone."

Kate held the receiver away from her face a moment and examined it. Was Hilary worried she'd been bugged?

"We've scheduled a meeting for half an hour's time."

"I'll be there."

Kate washed and dressed in a hurry, discarding the pair of navy slacks she'd planned on wearing and throwing on a belted dress instead. She strode up Sixth Avenue, her brow furrowed and her head down, rushing past Bryant Park, where folks sat on park benches and leaned against the terrace overlooking the neatly mowed lawn, while others sat outside sunning themselves and strolled along the gravel paths. As Radio City loomed closer, the neon signs a beacon on the street, Kate moved through the crowds stopping to stare, and the doorman swung the glass doors open for her as she approached.

Kate made her way to the staff room, where Hilary stood in one of her famous navy suits, her expression strained. Kate's boss sent quick glances toward Harvey Milton, who rubbed his hand over his chin and looked over the small group gathered in the staff room. Kate took a sip of the station's coffee, which was no substitute for the usual strong espresso she enjoyed at Café Reggio.

"There's no beating about the bush," Hilary said. "What I'm about to tell you is something that disturbs us all greatly. It goes without saying that we would not have called those of you who are not working today in unless it was vital you were here."

Kate flicked her gaze around the room. The station's contracted reporters, from those who covered politics, to general news, and even the couple of newer female announcers who dealt with women's stories all watched Hilary, while Harvey leaned against a table wearing a white jumper and a pair of camel trousers. His face was ashen, and he looked down at the ground.

What had gone wrong? Was the station in trouble?

"We have bad news concerning one of our employees," Hilary said.

Something dark stirred in Kate's insides. The McCarthy trials. Surely, someone had not been indicted, accused of being a communist sympathizer. She focused hard on Hilary, but her mind whirled with dark thoughts. And one crept to the surface, and she grimaced.

"As you are aware, Rick Shearer has been producing an in-depth series of feature shows and articles on Senator McCarthy."

No. Kate placed her cup of coffee down with a thump and splattered brown liquid all over the table. Her hands shook as she frantically scrabbled for the napkin holder to wipe it up.

"Rick's stories," Hilary went on, "are widely regarded to be some of the most read on McCarthy in the entire nation. Ever since McCarthy stumbled on his moment of destiny during that Lincoln Day dinner speech in West Virginia, when he claimed to possess the names of two hundred and five known communists in the State Department, Rick has covered McCarthyism on his shows."

Kate, her stomach roiling, hugged her bag to her chest.

"Rick's covered the House Un-American Activities Committee hearings and has worked himself to the bone for our listeners. Indeed, he's been receiving daily mail from his fans, thanking him for educating them on the terms that have become catchphrases in this country—New Deal Democrat, Popular Fronter, fellow traveler, Soviet Dupe, Pinko, dyed-in-the-wool red, card-carrying communist."

Please, let him be safe. Kate had to stop her head from shaking from side to side, and she held her hands in vice grips at her sides.

"Rick has interviewed countless folk in the entertainment and media industries, asking them how they felt when their phone stopped ringing and they stopped getting work, and they were faced with the scenario everyone dreaded."

Kate's stomach churned. Every journalist in New York had built their career on personal contacts, lucky breaks, and gut instincts, and the industry was already laden with job insecurity and performance anxiety. She herself had read, with her heart in her mouth, of the unspeakable panic that reporters felt when they got that knock on the door, and that question that everyone dreaded. *Are you, or have you ever been, a member of the Communist Party?*

"Rick, on our behalf, became engaged in the debates that raged in the press galleries. He covered on radio, on the hour, every hour, the House Un-American Activities Committee's sensational nine days of hearings into alleged communist influence in the motion picture industry, the face-offs, shouting matches, and ten witnesses going to jail, while in turn, accusing the HUAC of legal lynching." Hilary lowered her voice. "He famously called the process a witch hunt. And I'm afraid, now, that witch hunt has turned on him…" Hilary's voice faded out. She sat down on a chair with a thump.

A murmur whipped through the room. People started asking questions, and voices were raised and riled up.

She'd told him she didn't love him. Now, he had to face this alone. Kate sat, poleaxed, unable to move, unable to speak, knowing her face was as white as the ream of paper she'd asked her papa to go out and buy for her the day he was killed.

Her papa, Bianca. *Rick.*

Harvey held up a hand. "Rick's been identified as a controversial personality and accused of being a communist because he visited the communist-controlled areas of Germany while ostensibly working for us, in the late forties, and we don't know why."

Kate's brow tightened. But then, she gripped the sides of her chair.

"HUAC say he's got contacts behind the Iron Curtain, with whom he'd been corresponding regularly, and they are accusing him of traveling there for nefarious purposes. They are even going so far as to suggest he's a spy."

A stir rippled through the room again.

A realization bit with surprising force. *Mia.* Mia's grandfather had said Rick had been to their village to visit her. And this was the price Rick had to pay for his kindness to the child Kate loved, even though Kate had treated him in such a horrible way?

It was her fault. She had wrecked his career.

"It will be all over the news tonight, and as a station, we ask you not to comment," Harvey said.

Hilary sat with her hand over her mouth.

Kate flushed, but a deep coldness hit at her core.

Kate stumbled back to her office, flicked on the lights and sank down behind the desk she'd worked so hard for over the past decade. All around her, pictures of her achievements loomed on the walls: enlarged photographs of her standing at Lake Success with the flags of all the countries of the United Nations billowing behind her, smiling at the cameras despite the sweat trickling down her face in Philadelphia in front of a makeshift television booth, reporting on Goering's trial in Nuremberg, earphones over her glossy curls, standing out front of the bombed-out shell of the Reichstag, its pockmarked walls and collapsed roof a symbol of the city's utter destruction.

How was she supposed to stand by and let Rick's career be decimated, bombed and destroyed until there was only a shell of the man she loved left? And how could the country she adored, which had afforded her such wonderful opportunities, turn on a good man like Rick and drive his future into the ground?

Kate picked up the silver fountain pen she'd bought herself when she'd finally won her full-time contract at the station after all those years of instability and darned hard work. She tore a piece of paper from her notepad, and, tucking her hair behind one ear, drew a line down the middle of the page.

On the one hand, she could leave Rick to fight his own battle, and watch from the sidelines, safe in the security of her stable career, and let fate take its course with the man she'd always love.

Or the other option. She'd fight for him. Prove that he went to Soviet territories to visit a little girl whom Kate knew he would have been deeply worried about, growing up under the very regime he was being wrongly accused of supporting. She'd do everything within her power to supply his testimonial hearing with facts about how he'd risked his reputation at home to visit a child, to provide her with a passport and to help give her the opportunities that living in a democratic country could bring.

And then, she placed her pen down, the idea that burned in her mind that seemed absurd at first becoming more and more like the only answer in the world.

The best answer.

What if she were to ask Mia to come to Rick's testimonial?

Ask her to save Rick as Rick had saved her. Tell Mia that, despite her years of silence, despite that, as far as Kate knew, the child still had not told her story, and had not revealed what happened to her on that dreaded flight to Berlin, she had a voice like every woman in this world, and that it was her right to use it, and it was her right to speak out for the greater good.

Because Kate's government had it wrong.

Kate screwed the lid back on her fountain pen. She stood up, went to the window and surveyed the crowds surging down below the building on Sixth Avenue. Her view stretched right to Central Park.

She'd made it. She had all she'd ever dreamed of.

But her love for Rick was laced into the fabric of her heart, and if he lost everything, then what she had fought for all this time was worth nothing.

Perhaps that was the definition of love.

She couldn't live with herself and see him suffer so badly.

And right then, she knew she'd made her choice.

Chapter Twenty-Nine

Bianca

New York, spring 1951

Bianca curled her fingers over her new key. Her very own home. Gia Morelli and Livia stood like a pair of gentle doves in the narrow hallway outside the front door.

"Go on, open it, dear," Gia said.

Bianca turned to her mom's oldest friend, doubt seeding in her stomach for the millionth time since she'd signed the papers to buy the apartment where Gia had raised her own two children, Tom and Natalia. The home was filled with such wonderful memories for them all, and it seemed so much a part of the Morelli family that Bianca still felt slightly intrusive, as if she needed Gia's approval to put her own stamp on her new home.

"You must decorate it as you please," Gia said, sensing her doubt as only Gia knew how to do. "No looking back to how it was when I was here." Gia folded her arms in front of her cotton frock, her expression serious. "I couldn't bear it if you felt constricted, or that I was somehow looking over your shoulder."

Bianca sent Gia a warm smile of relief. Next to her, little Sofia tucked her hand into Bianca's own. And her other daughter, Lara, rested her sleepy head on Bianca's shoulder, her chubby legs hanging down toward the ground.

With a great heave of anticipation, after a two-year divorce process, heated negotiations during which Livia had fired bullets from guns Bianca never knew her mom possessed, Bianca had walked away with enough money to be able to buy her own apartment. And Gia and Livia had cooked up their brilliant plan. Bianca would buy Gia's apartment, be near her mom and the family she'd always known and loved in the Village, and Gia would move in with Livia, because both of them, warm mothers who'd both lost beloved husbands, fancied not being on their own.

Bianca turned the key in the lock. The dear old floorboards stretched in front of her, the small living room was perfect and cozy for long winter New York nights, when she'd read to her children, and have them fall asleep on her shoulders, tucked up warmly while the snow fell outside, and the kitchen was already the focal point of the home. Bianca, staying with her mom these past two years, had rediscovered her passion for cooking, and for painting and decorating rooms. She'd gotten herself a job three days a week at the local grade school, and when she wasn't playing with Sofia and Lara, she'd put on a pair of dungarees, tied her hair up in a turban and repainted her mom's entire apartment, giving the place an entirely new breath of fresh air.

Now, Lara marched into her new home, her little feet going a dime a dozen, her fat little legs certain as she waddled down the hall. There were three small bedrooms, and Bianca had already chosen the fabric she was going to use for curtains; lace for the summer and thicker material for the freezing winters, and she'd bought pots of paint which now sat in pride of place in the living room.

The children ran and tumbled around the empty space, and Bianca turned and pulled Gia and Livia into a hug. "Thank you," she whispered. "I don't know what I would have done without you."

"Nonsense, darling," Gia said. "You did it all yourself. We were just a pair of old birds helping a young one to fly." She held Bianca at arm's-length. "And we know you will soar."

Bianca grinned at the floor. "Well, I'm not going to tie my dreams to another person, that's for sure," she said.

"Although…" Livia nudged her. "You're not wanting for suitors."

She was right. A couple of the young teachers at school had asked Bianca out, and a neighbor who owned a thriving fruit and vegetable store on Bleecker Street had taken to carrying Bianca's boxes of produce home.

"In time," Bianca said firmly, her eyes roaming to her gorgeous girls. They needed stability. And so, goodness knew, did she. "In good time, Mama."

Livia's eyes crinkled into a smile.

Bianca stepped right into her new living room. She'd learned to push back the slight ache in her heart that her dream had not worked out. And she'd learned to accept that she had a new life now, one, albeit different than what she'd ever imagined, that was perfect for her. Her daughters were the most important thing in her life. And the thought of what the future might bring filled her with anticipation, not that old sense of dread she felt out with Marshall, where she couldn't have felt less at home if she'd tried.

Only one thing was left unspoken: her broken relationship with Kate. Her sister. Try as she might, she had no idea how to resolve things. They were so different, and yet neither of them was willing to open the floodgates that held in old blame and jealousy and resentment, that, if let out from the place where they were locked away inside, might turn their silent war into a full-blown battlefield; and Bianca knew, and she knew Kate knew, that if that happened, it would break Livia's heart. And worse, there could be no turning back.

So, they pushed on without speaking, and the longer this went on, the more impossible it seemed that things would ever resolve.

Bianca sighed, turned back to the door, and made her way down to the street, where a van filled with the furniture she'd claimed as her own from Marshall waited to be unloaded.

Chapter Thirty

Frances

New York, spring 1951

Frances lifted her face to her reflection in the pristine mirror. The skin under her eyes was red and puffed, her cheeks sagged, and her eyes looked dead and dull. Worry draped her like a blanket and ate away at her insides. She'd still not confronted Willard.

Her surge of confidence and resolve had fluttered away when she saw her daughter trying on her beautiful bridal veil. Ellie deserved to have her father walk her up the aisle, and she deserved to have her mother sitting in the pew right next to her dad. So, Frances stayed quiet, and yet she sickened at the stories of Willard and Daisy McKinnon. And like a woman steering a boat with no tiller, she forged on, putting off her day of reckoning until Ellie's wedding, lying awake night after night, trying to get through life in twenty-four-hour doses.

But now. Nothing had prepared her for this. What they faced now as a family eclipsed Willard's philandering because it could turn out all the lights in her life in one fell swoop.

The sensational Saturday evening papers shouted about the journalist son of one of New York's wealthiest bankers, accused of communist sympathies, likely to lose his burgeoning reporting career. And with it the entire Shearer family would be dragged into disgrace, discrediting the generations of ancestors who had preceded her son.

A Controversial Personality? She'd stood by in silence while, white-faced, lips pale, Rick had strode around Woodlands with all the purpose of a man who was about to fight on that terrible weekend they'd found out.

But Frances had known better. She'd seen how defeated he looked.

While she and Ellie had gathered in the entrance hall to hug him, Frances had fought tears at the expression on his face. Deathly pale as he gathered his keys, his wallet, his briefcase, and drove back to New York to face the accusations that were being leveled at him by his own countrymen. The country for whom he'd fought during the war, risking his life and sacrificing six years of his youth, like so many other young Americans had done.

He knew too much of this new war against communism. Knew what this meant. Knew because he'd been in the thick of it, reporting on the blacklists, reading in great depth about who they were looking for. Knew that many innocents had lost everything and ended up in jail.

Knew it was all totally ridiculous. But threatening. A terrifying farce.

And Frances understood too much as well. Now, she fretted, blaming herself. Blaming herself for encouraging him to have a voice, encouraging him to break free of the confines that weighed down upon him as a result of his birth into one of the wealthiest families in America, inciting him to think for himself, to get into the thick of things, not to stand on the sidelines, and not to follow the rules.

As Rick's career had gone from strength to strength, Frances, too, in some sweet desire to keep up with what her famous political journalist son was doing had read everything there was to know about the investigations. She'd always taken a keen interest, but in order to keep up with Rick, she knew far too much now.

Frances knew that those accused of communist sympathies were automatically guilty of a flurry of alleged sins. All had lost their jobs, families destroyed, businesses closed. A black cloud hanging over their futures as they were shunned and feared by their communities and the business world, all the same.

So, why him?

She walked out of the bathroom into her bedroom in the family's New York apartment where she'd come to be near her son. On the bed lay a drift of outfits. So, unlike her. Today, she could hardly choose what to wear.

Guilt stabbed at her again when she passed a photograph of Willard and Rick on a sailing boat in the Mediterranean as she moved through the hall to the front door. Not a care in the world. Was it better to be oblivious? To live in the cocoon of wealth as Willard did?

Clearly, he preferred Daisy McKinnon's carefree attitude to Frances' constant tuning into the events of the world.

But she had lived through such tumultuous decades, and Frances could never have sat by, draping herself in fur coats and drinking expensive cocktails. The Great War, the Great Depression, the Second World War, and now a war of ice threatening not only to divide the world into two, but, terrifyingly, to destroy the planet in a way that had been beyond the imaginations of all Americans until relatively recently.

Because on the morning of February sixth this year, Frances had sat in horror as Los Angeles had beamed an image of an atomic bomb test. For the first time in history, Americans at home had listened to the call "*Bombs Away!*" they'd listened to the counting down of the seconds, while play-by-play commentary had beamed a mushroom cloud into the homes of Americans, which had been clearly visible from the tops of the hotels in the desert oasis. It was no longer just about military defeat, no longer about cities laid to waste. The prospect of species annihilation loomed over America as a decided possibility.

And Willard was out dancing with his girlfriend in Manhattan.

Frances pinned her hat to her head, smoothed her hands down her blue costume. She walked out of the front door into the bustling Upper East Side.

If she could represent Rick at his hearing and attest to his good character herself, she would. She would lay down her life for her son. She would do everything in her power, whatever it was, to stop him from losing everything he'd fought so hard for all his life.

An hour later, Frances knocked on the front door of Rick's apartment across the park. She'd walked the entire way to the Upper West Side, oblivious to the heat, tracking the well-worn path through Central Park that she knew well, finding the shady walks, instinctively avoiding the burning sun.

Now, her throat was parched, even though she had drunk a large glass of water before leaving home. But she stood up straight, shoulders back, ready to face her beloved son.

Rick opened the door, dressed in a white shirt and blue jeans. Despite the fact he had no work and his phone had stopped ringing with assignments, he had still brushed his hair, bless him, and when he pulled Frances into a hug, she smelled the comforting scent of soap. She closed her eyes with relief. *He had not given up.*

But even the strongest will could break and bend, she knew that. And as he led her into the kitchen of his three-bedroom apartment, he poured her a glass of water, sat her down on a bar stool at the kitchen bench, and rested his head in his hands.

When he looked up at her, his eyes were hollow, his cheeks sunken. "I have two choices: I suffer in silence, or I defy the accusations publicly. Mom, this is life-altering. The fallout after being stained with the brush of controversy over communism will change everything." He looked at her. "I think the family would be better off without me."

Silently, Frances reached across the wooden kitchen bench, and she placed her hand over her son's, while sending him a brave, if watery smile. "My darling, you will always be part of my family. Always. No matter what." And she squeezed the hand that had slipped into hers so trustingly when he was a child. The years peeled back, and she only saw the face of the little boy whom she'd been blessed to call her son. That tawny-eyed, bright little boy. She would always adore him.

But now, she only hoped her adult son could trust his homeland to do the right thing by him.

Because the fact was, she was losing faith in the political systems she'd been fascinated with for so long.

Chapter Thirty-One

Kate

New York, spring 1951

On Monday morning at nine o'clock precisely, Kate made her way down the stairs from her office to the ground floor of Radio City, the number she needed in her hand. She went to the receptionist and showed her identification card to the woman behind the window.

"I need to send a teletex, please."

The young woman behind the counter blinked, her fashionable upswept hair glinting under the bright reception lights. "Very well," she said, eyeing Kate's pass, reddening slightly at Kate's tone of authority.

"Thank you," Kate said, keeping her voice utterly reasonable, her heart hammering a drumbeat in her chest.

The girl held out her hand for Kate's message.

"No," Kate said. "I need to send it myself. It's breaking news and I am reliant on my source for some particulars before it goes to air."

The girl's eyes widened.

"Thank you," Kate said. "I can't stick around much longer."

The girl came around to the side and opened a half-glass door that led to the main offices behind her. A stream of young women sat in the typing pool, many of them working on just the sort of teletypewriter that Kate wanted to use right now.

"Would you like any assistance sending your teletex, Ms. Mancini?" the girl asked.

"No, thank you," Kate said.

When the girl had disappeared, leaving Kate at the back of the room on a spare machine, Kate drew in a breath and typed Claudia's address into the teletypewriter: 6860 CLAUDIA D. She placed the verification code that belonged to Radio City, rather than her own personal code, at the beginning of the message, which she would also place at the end, then typed her message onto the round keys, so that Claudia, in Germany, could also type on her keyboard when she replied, and the characters would be printed on Kate's machine.

Tickertape punched with little holes poured out of the machine beside Kate as her message sent.

And then, she began to wait.

Until, a few moments later, paper started flowing from the receiving machine with neatly typed words. Kate sighed with relief, pulled Claudia's response out and moved back out to the reception area. She stuffed the paper in the pocket of her shirt-waisted dress and pushed the glass doors open out into the humid morning.

In a diner, twenty minutes away, Kate ordered an orange juice and a piece of plain toast, which she managed to stomach, read Claudia's message, frowned, carried out a deal of mental calculations in her head, tore up the message into tiny shreds, and strode with purpose back out into the street, blending effortlessly with the folks on the sidewalk.

Then she went into a hotel, asked if she could use their telephone, and dialed Rick's number.

"Rick," she said.

"*Kate?*"

She took in a deep breath. "How are you?"

There was a silence. "Kate," he breathed. "You shouldn't call me. Please. Hang up. I can't talk to you and I don't want to put you at risk. If they find you are associating with me…"

He turned quiet and she leaned her head against the wall, the usual sounds of the hotel piping away behind her as if nothing was wrong at all, porters pushing trolleys filled with luggage, holidaymakers giggling with excitement about their first time in New York. Already the investigations into communist activities in America had led to imprisonments. Just recently, Kate had read how being found guilty of passing information to the Soviets could result in up to twenty years in jail.

"When is your hearing?"

"I don't want to hang up on you, but you need to leave this alone."

She clung to the receiver. "How long have we got to prepare?"

"No." His voice lowered. "Not we."

"Yes," she insisted. "I'm not leaving you to deal with this alone, Rick. I'm not going to say what we both know, but I'm going to leave no stone unturned, because I know as well as you that you are no communist. And you know I can prove it."

Down the phone line, there was a silence, a hitch of his breath. If she closed her eyes, she could see him, his brow furrowed, shirtsleeves rolled up, running a hand over his forehead.

"Tell me how long until the hearing."

He murmured the words. "Two weeks."

And right then, in the middle of a busy Midtown hotel lobby, Kate closed her eyes and forced herself not to reveal how she felt for him. Forced herself to hold in her feelings, because she couldn't bear to put the man she loved under a smidgen more pressure. She couldn't bear to complicate his life with her own.

"Good," she said. "Take care."

And silently, she placed the receiver down. And her whole body shook as she walked back out into the Manhattan sunshine, while her mind threw up pictures of a cold March afternoon in Berlin, where, among the strangled pipes and the burnt-out houses, she and Rick had found a little girl.

*

Kate surveyed her second bedroom. The single bed was covered with a fresh gingham bedspread, and a cluster of cushions decorated with tiny flowers sat on the coverlet. The walls were newly papered with a tiny floral print and a blue ceramic jug was filled with daffodils. On the floor, a new white rug was soft underfoot, and a pretty second-hand wardrobe was painted crisp white.

Bianca had been responsible for all this. Quietly, Livia had suggested when Kate was panicking about having Mia come to stay with a bland second bedroom and nothing for a sixteen-year-old, that Bianca would probably be honored to help if Kate asked.

If she simply asked.

Kate had worried profusely about this. Every time she and Bianca met, they hardly exchanged more than a few words. They'd kiss each other politely on the cheek at occasions in the Village, for Livia's sake more than their own, Kate knew, and then get as far away from each other as they could.

Now, Bianca hovered in the doorway while her daughter, Sofia, played with a jigsaw puzzle on the living room floor, and her little child, Lara, waddled around, her fingers reaching for anything Kate hadn't put out of sight.

Kate turned slowly to face her sister, honestly grateful for all she'd done to help. Bianca had not hesitated, had not asked any questions, and had simply stepped in.

Now, Kate took in a shaky breath. It was as if the tables had been turned. Bianca was helping her, not the other way around. And willingly. It was not something they were used to and they'd both moved around each other awkwardly while Bianca got on and did what she knew how to do. Make something beautiful out of something plain. It was a gift her sister had always had, and it had gone unrecognized, both by the family she'd grown up with, and her husband's family. And now, out of the mire of separation, she'd had a chance to prove herself.

Bianca was hard-working, independent and strong.

Kate lifted her gaze and met the eyes of the brave woman her younger sister had truly become.

Kate was more than aware of her own limitations; home decoration and the domestic arts were not her forte. She'd watched, touched, as her sister had spent the little free time she had, sourcing fabrics and fighting over prices with suppliers, when she was not busy with the children or teaching part-time at the local grade school. Over the past couple of years, Kate had come to admire her sister's fortitude, the strong determination that had seen her through a nasty divorce from Marshall, the strength of purpose Bianca had shown when finding practical solutions for herself and the children, buying Gia Morelli's family apartment when Gia decided to move in with her dearest old friend Livia, now their children had all left home.

And Kate had heard whispers on the Village grapevine that Bianca was seeing a local Italian man, and that he was terrific with Bianca's girls.

Kate's eyes softened. "Thank you," she said simply. "I could never have done this without you. I don't know what sort of a host I'm going to make, but at least Mia will feel welcome, and she'll have a charming room to call her own while she's visiting here. This is beautiful. You know, you have a real knack for decorating. It's a gift."

Bianca let out a sigh. "Well, you know as well as I do that the perfect home was always part of my big dream and I spent hours conjuring up plans of my own." Bianca folded her hands in front of the red dress she wore. "I wasted my youth dreaming up rooms like this one. If you want magazines on how to decorate, I've got boxes full of them!"

Kate sent her sister a genuine, admiring smile.

Bianca lowered her dark eyes to the floor. "I'm happy for you, Kate. Happy that one of us, at least, got what we longed for. You have realized your dream."

Kate sat down on the bed that Bianca had done up so beautifully for Mia. "Oh no," she said. "I haven't, Bianca. Don't believe that in the least."

Bianca's head lifted. She waved a hand around the apartment, sent Kate a rueful smile. "Oh, but you have, Katia," she said. Her voice cracked, and suddenly, she blurted out what needed to be said, "I'm sorry I was so hard on you when Papa died."

Kate pressed her hands into the bedspread. "No," she whispered. "I'm sorry that I took him over, Bianca. I'm sorry that he and I were such a team and that we excluded you."

"But he was proud of you. And for good reason. You know," she said, her voice softening, "I had no idea how hard you'd worked. How hard you'd always worked to do something exceptional. Until I was thrust out of my home, without Marshall to do everything while I didn't worry about money at all. I had to fend for myself just like you do. That's when I came to appreciate all you've achieved." She leaned against the white doorframe. "I'm sorry I didn't understand before. But I've learned what you always knew: to rely on myself, see that the approval of any man was not necessary if I approved of me."

Kate couldn't help it. She tilted her head and smiled. "Come here," she whispered to her sister.

And in a flash, her warm, passionate sibling was across the room and enveloping Kate in a hug, and as Kate clung to the sister she'd thought she'd lost for good, Bianca whispered more words.

"I know it wasn't your fault he died, Katia. And I know he would have done exactly the same for me." She wiped her eyes. "But I was angry. I had to *blame* someone, you know?" She took a deep breath and closed her eyes. "I needed the loss of Papa to make sense. And blaming it on you made sense to me at the time. I'm sorry."

Kate held Bianca at arm's-length, the flood of emotion she was feeling threatening to cut her in two. "I'm not half as warm as you are, Bianca. You have loved and lost, and now, you've taken another chance with love again. But me?" Kate beat her hand against her chest. "I'm just a fool where love is concerned, and try as I might, since Papa died, I just clam up and walk away when things get too difficult. No matter how I might feel, no matter how much I really care. I haven't fought like you have, not in the way you have. For my career, yes. For love, no." Kate knotted her hands at her throat. "I was even willing to let you go."

Bianca's gaze flickered to the open door into the living room, where Sofia was placing large pieces of jigsaw in Lara's pudgy little fingers and showing her where to put them on the board. "Well," she said. "I take it you don't want to walk away this time; you want to fight for something, or someone? You feel that passion inside you that you thought you'd lost for good?"

Kate eyed her sister, as if she had all the answers in the world. "Yes," she breathed. "I have to. I want to fight for my little German orphan, for her to be freed from whatever she's locked away inside, and I want to fight for... Rick."

There, she'd said it. His name.

She looked in wonder, eyes round at her sister, startled at herself.

"I want to fight for his freedom, Bianca, and then I want to tell him how I feel." Her throat thickened. "But I'm pretty certain he wants to shut the memory of me out. I think I've messed up far too badly." She shook her head.

And then Kate felt something. She felt Bianca's hand suddenly landing on hers. And Bianca gave it a squeeze.

"Then you shall fight for him," Bianca whispered. "Because I don't know anyone who is braver than you."

Kate tilted her head. "Thank you," she whispered. "I only hope I can be as brave as you've been, my sister."

And Bianca smiled at her through tear-filled eyes.

Chapter Thirty-Two

Frances

New York, summer 1951

Frances sent a nervous glance toward Rick. A soft knock had sounded on his front door. Every time she collected the mail, answered the telephone, or ran into one of Rick's neighbors, her stomach churned.

Ever since he'd been accused, Rick had suffered in silence. It was his way of coping, Frances knew that. Whenever things had gone wrong since he was a little boy, he'd withdraw into himself, set himself away. Now, her adored son sat at his desk on the far side of his living room, a pencil stuck behind one ear and his shirtsleeves rolled up. The steady tapping of his fingers on the typewriter stilled as he lifted his head.

Frances turned from her vigil by the window, took in a breath, opened the door, a deliberately composed expression on her face.

When she stood face to face with her husband, she blinked hard.

"Willard," she said, her hand floating to her mouth. Willard hadn't visited since Rick was accused of being a "controversial personality."

And now, here he was.

Rick, his eyes hollow, a flicker of annoyance passing across his features, stood up and came forward to shake his father's hand.

Frances closed the door behind her with a soft click.

When both Rick and Willard sat down, the morning sun threw a shaft of light across their features, highlighting the fact that Willard's handsome face was ashen, his blue eyes red-rimmed.

"How are you both?" he asked.

Rick glanced at Frances. "As you see,'" he said to his father, "fine."

Frances, fretting, circled around the room, intertwining her fingers, lacing them up until her fingers hurt. She brought a hand to her mouth. Couldn't help it. It was the sight of Willard, walking in here, sitting here when she had not laid eyes on him since the confounded accusations had been hurled at Rick.

Where had her husband been? She'd laid awake countless nights with an untold ache that she and Willard were not dealing with this together. That their son was being accused of what amounted to a crime—his future, his wellbeing, his hard-won career all at great risk. *And where was his father?*

The man who used to pull strings and solve all their problems as if the security of family them untouchable.

He was with a Broadway actress.

She shot Willard a level gaze, but he did not notice her, he was staring straight ahead.

"At least you saw sense about that woman. The reporter." Willard spoke to Rick. "I'm only relieved you don't have her sniffing around this story."

Frances cleared her throat and folded her hands in front of herself, assuming the position in front of the fireplace that Willard usually took at family conferences.

Rick's nostrils flared, but only for a minute, before Frances' beautiful son stood up, and came to stand right next to her. Sagging with relief, emotion, she knew not what, Frances fought the urge to reach out and rest a hand on his tired shoulder. Instead, she almost fell to her knees with gratitude for Rick's simple gesture. A gesture of solidarity.

How many times had Willard assumed this position of power, standing over them all as a family, while she listened, allowing him to have his authority? Not questioning him. The authority a man was supposed to have over his family.

"Dad," Rick said simply, "despite everything, Kate is fighting for me. She's fighting to prove that I'm no communist, and to be brutally honest, I think she's the best chance we've got. The best chance we've got of saving my reputation, and in turn, of saving the entire family's standing in New York. Because she's the only person who can prove anything, darn it."

Willard's gaze flew from Frances, to Rick and back. His mouth was working. "No," he said. "That cannot be."

But Rick went on, his tone assured, confident.

Frances turned to him in wonder.

"You see, the person whom you assured me was chasing down my money is, in fact, doing this without expecting a thing in return," Rick went on. "Nothing in return, in a way that you, or any other man, even such as myself, from our background of privilege would ever begin to comprehend."

"Don't be absurd. She can do nothing."

But Rick held up a hand. "Father, I will thank you never again to put her down or question her integrity, her honesty or the sincerity of the feelings she once had for me, that I suspect you put a swift end to by blackmailing her at Ellie's engagement party. As you blackmail and bully everyone else. If you denigrate Kate once more, either behind her back or to her face, or if you ever threaten her again, you will never be welcome in my home as long as I live."

And right then, Frances gasped. Her husband started shaking uncontrollably.

"*Willard?*" she said, her voice hysterical. "Is there a grain of truth in this? Blackmail? What did you say to that poor child?"

But something had broken in Willard at last. Her husband stood up, stumbled across the room, staggering, his hands flailing out as he gripped for sofas, the dining table, anything to stop him from falling, until he came to a juddering stop in front of Rick, his eyes dull and lifeless. Then roughly, he pulled Rick into his arms. "Sorry," he said simply. "I'm sorry."

And over Willard's bowed body, his head resting on the shoulder of his son's, Frances' eyes locked with Rick's, and she saw a silent tear slide down his cheek.

After a hastily put together lunch of ham sandwiches and salad, during which Willard had, embarrassingly, broken down into tears twice, Frances, seeing the strain this was putting Rick under, insisted that Rick return to his vigil at the typewriter while she took her husband away for a walk in Central Park.

Instinctively, she led the silent Willard to the most secluded and peaceful area of the Park, the North Woods, where she always felt most at home, as if she'd returned to her beloved Connecticut. She'd rambled through here on many an afternoon lately while she was worried sick about her son.

Now, she walked toward the pool, finding a rustic bench beside a quiet, weeping willow. She sat down, and waited for her husband to join her, to sit by her side.

He was quiet for a few more moments, and Frances occupied herself by staring long at the still, serene water, which sat like a blue-green millpond in front of them, deep, tranquil and undisturbed.

"I was scared of dying," Willard said.

Frances stayed quiet.

"Of growing old," he went on. "Fran, I…"

She gasped. *Fran.* He'd always called her Fran when they were together. Before everything had fallen apart.

She reached for the string of pearls around her throat.

"I was never having an affair with Daisy McKinnon, for what it's worth," he went on.

She hardened her gaze, focusing on the water, a slight ripple as a dragonfly coursed across the surface. *What* did he just say?

"I met Daisy backstage at some charity event." His words murmured on, and Frances focused on the water, as if the deep pool held the answers that she sought. "From the start," he went on, this new version of her husband, this man who she felt was more a stranger to her than the Willard she'd known for decades, whom she'd been married to, for goodness' sake, "I knew deep down that Daisy wanted a patron, someone to help her get onto the Broadway stage. She was introduced to me, and I offered to help her. Pull a few strings. She's smarter than to have an affair with an old man like me. But I was flattered. I was stupid. Thinking she liked me for who I was, not for my wealth or for what I could do for her."

The trees whispered and Frances remained still.

"I was possessed with some sort of madness, Fran," he went on, his voice husky. "I don't know what happened… but I had this overwhelming urge to live, as if for one last time, I could capture the elixir of youth. Until I realized it meant nothing," he said, folding his hands in his lap. "Without you by my side."

Frances pressed her lips together. *Had he just said the words she'd wanted him to say for months?* No. That would be impossible. She was imagining it. Years of agony, of wringing her hands in despair over the loss of his love, their relationship, worrying about how her life was going to be if he decided to leave their marriage, break up the family for good. She'd lost weight, could hardly eat, had not slept properly since he'd by all accounts left her. Her thoughts were in a swirl. *Was he really coming home to her?*

She took in a jagged breath.

And then, a darker question: *would she take him back?*

He hunched back further onto the bench. "I was ashamed. Ashamed of what I'd put you through, and now, with Rick facing those terrible accusations. I don't know, I almost ended it all."

Frances sat up, turning to him blankly, wanting to crumple onto the ground herself now. "No, Willard," she whispered.

And in that instant, his eyes searched hers and their gazes locked.

After a long moment, Frances let out a moan. In his eyes, she saw that he was just the man she'd fallen in love with, the man who had danced with her, slow waltzes on moonlit evenings, the gramophone playing by the lake at parties at Woodlands before the Great War, their war had ripped their own generation apart.

She started to shake, tears threatening to fall down her cheeks. How could someone you thought you knew so intimately become a perfect stranger? How had they grown so very far apart?

"I was so angry with Rick," Willard went on.

Shock at the change in him today still coursed through her system in rippling, stomach-roiling waves.

"I was angry with him for choosing what I saw as the wrong kind of girl." His mouth worked. "While deep down, I knew she was exactly the *right* kind of girl, like you always were for me. I'm sorry." He buried his head in his hands. "I sensed that this woman, too, might eclipse me in brains, and integrity, and… well, everything. Just as you do, my dear. I felt threatened and useless, and it was pathetic." He looked at her. "I had to find my own way."

She stood up, and went to stand by the water, her hands shaking.

"Darling Fran," he said, his voice cracking now behind her, and she looked down below the surface of the water, watching the shimmering, almost indiscernible activity in the water's depth, the shifting, constant movement that was not theirs to see, but was happening all the time. "Darling, I was scared of him being with Kate because I knew she was real—a real, authentic woman who would treat him well, just as you have done with me, my dear."

She squeezed her eyes shut, clenched her fists hard.

"And I also realized what a terrible, stupid mistake I was making, trying to flatter myself that I could defy what happens to us all. Old age. Growing old. The children marrying, us becoming grandparents."

"That will happen, old age, us becoming grandparents—we cannot deny it," she whispered, but perhaps, he didn't hear.

"Fran, I want to grow old with you. I always did. If you can forgive me, darling girl."

Frances gazed over the water, and it seemed to cloud a moment, the surface thick and gray, before the sun shot through the trees and everything became perfectly clear. She brought her hands—hands that were aging just as Willard's were—and wrapped them around her waist. And then, horribly, for the first time in decades, her shoulders started to shake, and tears coursed down her cheeks, salt licking her lips. And she let them fall.

In a trice, he was next to her, his arm around her shoulders. "Darling," he said. "I'm sorry." He lifted her chin so that her brown eyes looked straight into his tired, blue eyes. "Sweetheart. Please. We *have* to talk to one another. We have to be open. Both of us. I had no idea what to say to you about this. Please, in turn, don't you hold things in. If I annoy you, tell me so. And, when I'm feeling old, or I'm tired or just sad, I promise that I will talk to you, but, darling, please, know that you can tell me anything, always, in return."

Willard pulled her into a hug, and she closed her eyes, resting her head against his shoulder. The father of her children. A man who was human. A man who had the grace to admit he was wrong.

"Yes," she said simply. "Yes. I'll talk to you too." She lifted her head a moment, and for a fleeting second, standing here, in his arms, she felt all at once, and all over again, like that girl who had fallen in love with the most handsome man in New York. "But the first thing I will say is that I think you're an idiot," she began, sending him a watery smile. "You are good at what you do, and this comparing yourself to me, or to Kate, has to stop."

"Thank you, darling." He leaned down, his eyes warming, and crinkling into that long-remembered smile, his lips brushing against hers, and through her own tears of joy, she let out a chuckle that rang through the air, forever to linger among the trees.

She'd waited. And he'd returned to her.

Now, they could support their son, and they'd do so together, and that way, they were far stronger than if they were apart.

Chapter Thirty-Three

Kate

New York, early summer 1951

Kate took Mia to Livia's house the night after she'd arrived at the airport. She led the beautiful, quiet German girl up the old rickety stairs of the tenement house in MacDougal Street and she rattled on with a bevy of conversation about Mia's long journey to America, the plans she had for them both in New York, and how much she hoped Mia would enjoy staying here.

At the top of the staircase, Kate turned to her. Mia's cornflower blue eyes gazed at the closed front door of Livia's apartment, and she clasped her hands in front of her belted dress.

"You are taking me to meet your mother?" she asked, the English she'd been taught in the Gymnasium, the high school in Celle, like cut-glass crystal, each word enunciated with perfect precision.

Kate still marveled at the sound of Mia's voice. Every time she heard the girl utter a word, she sent up a prayer of thanks that Mia had gained the confidence to speak again, even if no one knew what terrible secrets she harbored, what she had witnessed during the war.

The war seemed like an age away now, here in New York, but Kate knew that its memory burned deeply in the hearts of so many, and she felt almost in awe of the stunning girl who stood next to her, so poised, so mature.

Mature, Kate knew, beyond her years because of all she had endured. For Claudia's telegram had sent Kate into a frenzy of activity, not only did she want to ask Mia for the biggest favor of her life, but Kate's heart had also gone out unreservedly to the child when Claudia had told Kate how Mia's grandparents had died. First, her ailing grandmother, and then, her grandfather soon afterward. He'd died of a broken heart. Even now, Kate felt a stab of guilt that she'd taken his granddaughter away, and in turn, his death had left Mia with no family.

Now, Kate pressed her ear to the door of Livia's house. Inside, the cacophony of voices that always rang around this building leached out into the corridors, belted through walls, broke down barriers for all the Italian newcomers to this part of New York. For decades, Italians had ended up here, and this house had gotten folks through the darkest days of the war.

Kate raised a brow at the sound of several distinct voices. Gia Morelli, Livia, Bianca, her children's high-pitched chatter and nonsense, and Gia's daughter, Natalia, along with Kate and Bianca's old friend Elena. Kate paused at the sound of a deeper voice, that of Tom Morelli. Kate's face lit up. Tom. She wondered if his sensational wife, Lily, the famous chef, would be here.

"I think you have quite the welcoming committee," she told Mia.

"A committee?" Mia said, her face dropped.

"No!" Kate grinned at the girl. "No. Sorry, just a silly expression. It is my family." She tilted her head to one side. "Mia, you are my family. My family always will be yours. You know that."

"And Mr. Rick?" Mia asked.

Kate smoothed down her dress. "Rick will always be inordinately special to me," she whispered. "And when we support him tomorrow, I know he will be honored that you have come to be here for him."

The girl suddenly sent Kate a quiet smile. "What are we waiting for?"

Kate's pulse rang with excitement. "What are we waiting for indeed!"

*

When they had feasted on Livia and Gia's risotto rice balls, crisp and delicious on the outside, and creamy inside, Gia's famous caponata with eggplant, pine nuts and raisins, and then a course of pasta with tomatoes, garlic basil and ricotta, followed by Tom Morelli's sardines stuffed with raisins and pine nuts, and baked with breadcrumbs, and then his swordfish rolls topped with capers and lemons, Kate couldn't help but grin at the way Mia's face lit up at the sight of Lily's take on Torta Setteveli, the rich Sicilian seven-layered chocolate and hazelnut cake.

Every now and then, Mia's eyes had drifted to Kate's as if asking her approval to speak, to eat, to help herself to the rich bounty of food that Gia and Livia produced, a pair of buzzing birds, reveling in the fact that they had all their children together in one room, along with partners, and grandchildren.

Kate even found herself throwing sidelong glances at Tom's dark-haired wife, Lily, who held her baby girl on her lap. Little Isabella had charmed everyone, and her brown eyes flashed just as her grandmother's did.

But when the two younger generations all piled into Livia's little living room with their coffee, Kate waited until only she, Mia and Gia Morelli were left in the dining room with Livia.

"Shall I help tidy up?" Mia asked Livia.

"You must be exhausted after your flight," Gia said. She sent the girl one of her thoughtful looks. And when Livia went off into the kitchen, she touched Mia on her shoulder. "Dear, I know what it is to lose those you love during the war. During the First World War, I lost my papa, and my two brothers. I do feel for you. But there is a way forward," she whispered. "There is light after the darkness. And coming here, I know you will find it, as we all have," she said. "I have found that I have to strive for it," and she looked at Kate. "And always, I have followed my heart."

Kate bit her lip, but dear Mia did something Kate had not seen her do this visit, had not seen her do since the death of her grandparents had dealt her another blow. She reached out, and she hugged Gia Morelli, and the older woman held her in her arms, and a single tear rolled down Gia's cheek.

The following morning, Mia sat on her perfectly made-up bed. Her hands were folded in her lap and she wore a simple navy frock, belted with a red belt, while a pair of red pumps graced her slender feet. Her hair was tied back with a navy-blue ribbon, and she raised her luminous eyes toward Kate.

"Come and have some breakfast, dear," Kate said. Her hand rested on the door of her second bedroom.

"This is okay?" Mia asked, indicating around the immaculate bedroom.

Kate drew her hand to her mouth. "Oh, darling Mia. You don't have to impress me in any way. You know you can make yourself utterly at home here. Come and have some breakfast. I have cooked eggs and bacon for fortification."

Although as Kate led Mia back to her kitchen, where she made a great show of serving up the breakfast she'd cooked, while pouring orange juice into glasses, her own stomach churned with nausea.

Was she insane? Relying on a child to vindicate Rick against HUAC? To save him from imprisonment? The more she glanced at the young girl sitting opposite her, silently eating her breakfast, the smell of which made Kate swoon, the more she realized how difficult the task ahead was going to be.

And if she'd stood up to Willard? Told him she would not accept his bullying and defied his orders to stay away from Rick? Well then, at least she would have gone to Germany with Rick, and they'd be in this together. The fact that Rick was taking the fall after being so badly treated by his own father, and, in all honesty, by Kate, broke her own heart into a thousand pieces.

And HUAC were not going to be sympathetic to the son of a banker. If they could use him as proof that no one was immune to their investigations in America, then Kate knew they would relish the chance.

She'd explained the situation to Mia last night, and the girl had simply said that of course she would help. Of course, she would speak up and say what Rick had done for her.

Mia placed her fork and knife down neatly on her empty plate. And Kate sent her a brave smile but refrained from reaching her hand across the table to rest it atop the girl's. The girl's formal politeness, the loss of the spontaneity she'd shown as a young child toward Kate, hid, Kate knew, some terrible story, and Mia was holding her secrets close.

Doubt snaked its way through Kate's insides as she stepped out onto Sixth Avenue with the sun gleaming down on New York, and folks rushing about as usual, weighed down with shopping bags and briefcases and toddlers in tow, but Mia glanced around the bustling, sun-drenched city, her arm linked tight with Kate's, her silence saying more than all the chatter of the New Yorkers on the street.

As they approached Radio City, it was Kate who tightened her clasp on Mia's arm. They drew closer to the building and Kate reminded herself that this was a girl who had found her way home through the forests of Germany. Mia was a survivor. Kate had to trust her instincts. She'd surely made the right decision to ask her to testify.

The doors swung open to Radio City, and it was too late for doubt or misgivings or panic. They climbed the flight of stairs to the room where HUAC were carrying out their committee hearing for Rick, to determine his guilt or innocence, whether he'd be able to return to journalism or be fired, and whether he'd spend the coming years in the safety of his home, or in prison, with the ignobility of having been judged.

Kate stood a moment in the doorway to the room where Rick was going to be heard, looking around at the familiar space, lined with exhibits and photographs from WNYR, the faces of all the people who worked here in this industry, the scriptwriters, the producers, programmers, actors, journalists and the telephone girls at the switchboards, the musicians composing scores to play on the radio and the television. These were the people who represented this industry. But now, the room was being used for a case in which the life and the reputation of a single human being depended.

Rick.

The American justice system, even for an accused murderer, demanded a judge trained in law, a defense lawyer, a carefully chosen jury, and all the evidence on both sides of the case. Yet Rick was about to appear in front of a committee that had been selected arbitrarily to hear him, and he had been afforded no lawyer, and there was no elected judge.

Kate searched the room for him. Her eyes locked with his for one long painful moment during which all the things that hung between them remained unspoken, unsaid, locked away, perhaps for good, until his gaze strayed to Mia and his brows drew together in a frown. He was wearing a dark suit, his tie neatly knotted, his hair brushed. His face was ashen, and even from a distance, Kate shivered at the way his posture was stooped.

She dared to send him a brave smile as the queue moved forward. She told an official that Mia was going to be a witness, pressing her hand against Mia's arm one final time, and the girl was taken into the front row of the room where chairs had been set up facing the table where the inquisition would be carried out.

Inquisition. The word was apt.

Kate sank down into her chair and folded her shaking hands in her lap. Up front, Mia signed in as a witness. Kate focused on the back of Mia's blond head. What was going on inside there? Would she be able to articulate how her life had become intertwined with Rick's?

When Harvey slipped into the seat next to Kate, and a line of other executives followed him, and Hilary appeared to sit by Kate's other side, Kate, heat flushing through her system, started to fan her face with her hand. And when Frances Shearer walked, solitarily, down the aisle and slipped into a seat a couple rows ahead of Kate, her mind flew to the worst possible scenario. Was Frances about to lose her only son to the machinations of her own government, when he'd fought for America and faithfully reported back home, traveling all over Europe, only to return and have it turn on him?

The committee chairman called for order. Hilary folded her hands neatly in her lap and Harvey crossed his legs. Kate drew on all her inner strength, her heart beating hard against her dress.

She scraped a hand over her hair when a member of the subcommittee, a man holding a cigar in one hand, read out the allegations against Rick.

A flash went off somewhere in the room. A photographer.

Whatever the outcome, Rick was going to be front-page news tonight.

Sweat beaded on Kate's upper lip.

"Today, we are at the trial of a man who clearly had associates who were communists, socialists, and crackpots. Rick Shearer traveled to communist-run territories in 1948 with no clear reason relating to his work as a journalist, and, without a shadow of doubt, had ulterior motives for his travel to the Soviet zone."

The man could have been saying anything. His words filtered over Kate like mist.

She sat bolt upright when Rick moved to sit in front of the committee.

Rick requested the right to make an opening statement, but he was rejected.

"Mr. Shearer," a member of the subcommittee asked, "are you now, or have you ever been, a member of the Communist Party of the United States?"

"I have not," Rick said.

The room was silent.

Rick's features were pale, and his hands were folded on the desk. A sudden memory from the Nuremberg trials bore down on Kate, those hands of his making notes, those hands of his now stilled. Goering. Rick couldn't be less like that monster if he tried.

"During your travels in Europe in the last decade, we believe you attended a peace conference in Stockholm," a member of the subcommittee said.

"I have never been to Stockholm." Rick was implacable.

Kate bit deep into her bottom lip. She hated that they were trying to divert him with irrelevant questions, no doubt to catch him off guard.

"During the ten years or more that you have traveled throughout Europe as a foreign correspondent, being in close contact with a situation in which communists are operating in multiple countries that you have visited, you did not know or have personal knowledge of, a member of the Communist Party?"

Kate took in a shuddering breath.

"I can say fully and without any reservations before the committee that I have nothing to be ashamed of, and nothing to hide. I am not a communist. I am a liberal by inclination, and a loyal citizen of this country by every act of my life."

A committee member shuffled papers and whispered into his neighbor's ear. Kate's eyes flew from one of Rick's accusers to the next.

The man with the cigar waved it in the air. "I do not believe you are telling the truth."

Kate, hands wanting to flail and her lips fighting to utter a sharp protest, wound the straps of her handbag around and around her fingers. *If they wanted to incarcerate him, they would.*

"Communist influences can work in many ways," the man with the cigar droned on. "The opinion of a journalist can make the difference as to how a subject is reported. I can see, from my standpoint, how easy it would be for an underground movement to use influence on a correspondent such as yourself, in such a way that an individual such as yourself would be used to their advantage."

They were making up a narrative to suit themselves.

"I should like to emphatically state that I am not a member of the Communist Party. I am not sympathetic with it, nor with its aims," Rick said.

Kate sat taller in her chair, but the man with the cigar leaned forward in his seat, his eyes narrowing. "I know that there is a traditional dislike among Americans to be an informer, but at this moment, it is absolutely vital that you tell us exactly why you visited the Soviet territories in Germany in 1948, and whom you were with. Whom did you consort with in Russian territory, and why were you there?" He lowered his voice, addressing the room in general. "The communists are as ruthless with their own people as they are with their enemies, and today it is necessary for Americans to be equally ruthless."

There was a murmur through the room, and all of a sudden a great commotion at the back. The doors were thrown open, and the ushers let out useless protests. Useless, because in the face of them, a man thrust himself into the aisle between the neat rows of chairs.

"This is a farce!" The words burned into the room before Kate had a chance to turn her head. Until everyone in the room turned around as if woken from a spell. And there, right in the center of the room, Rick's father stood in the aisle, his blue eyes blazing, his chest heaving up and down.

Willard Shearer.

Kate drew her jacket closer around her at the sight of that odious man.

But Willard was not taking any notice of anyone, save the committee, and he strode right down to the front of the room, not caring for protocol, not asking anyone's permission, just marching like a man on a mission.

"This," Willard said, jabbing his finger at the committee, "is ridiculous! My son is no more a communist than anyone in this room." He came to a shuddering stop at the committee's table. And he pulled the cigar right out of that man's hand and stubbed it out, grinding the cigar into the ashtray as if he handled the things every day of his life. "You," Willard said. "You disgrace of a man. A throwaway comment? At the club, for pity's sake? I tell you that my son won't take on an executive role and is behaving like a darned Red and you repay me with this?"

Kate sank down in her chair. *The careless words of an American father had led to the indictment of his son. What madness was this?*

Willard jabbed a finger in the man's face. "How *dare* you. How dare you take that as some…" Willard turned around, clearly enjoying playing the room right now. "As some excuse to haul my beloved boy up like a scarecrow!"

"Willard!" Frances stood up; her face as red as a beet. "There's no need—"

But Willard shook his head and lowered his voice. He studied the ground; his hands gripped in front of him. "Rick is one of the most dedicated and hard-working journalists I know. It is I who misjudged him." He ground out the words.

Kate's gaze flew to the front of the room. Was she hearing right? Was this the man who had derided journalists, who had dismissed her entire profession as scheming interlopers looking for a story, no holds barred? The man who had threatened her into leaving his house?

"My son was never in any way fraternizing with Russians."

Harvey sat taller in his seat next to Kate, and she sat on her hands, her eyes glued to Willard. What had happened to him?

"He just wants to write darned stories," Willard rolled on. "Goodness knows, it's more than I've ever done. He's reached more folk than I ever have. And if any of you dare suggest he's a communist, then you will all answer to me, and I shall report you to the FBI, the police, I'll take every proper measure, every legal and right measure in the United States, to investigate the grounds upon which you make your insidious, ill-founded and preposterous claims!" Willard turned, towering over the crowd, daring anyone to defy him.

Kate drew her hand to her throat, and next to her, Harvey let out a shuddering breath.

"Sit down, Mr. Shearer," one of the committee members said. "You have not explained why your son visited communist territories; therefore, you have not saved your son. We are a civilized organization, and we will not press charges against the outburst of a man who is so clearly devoted to his family."

Kate rolled her eyes. *What?*

But then, Rick spoke, and the whole room seemed to turn their heads to him. "I have a witness who is here to testify why I visited communist territories."

Kate, wide-eyed, heart thumping, watched as Frances bustled up the front, her face burning, and pulled Willard down into a chair, despite his protests, and the committee eyed him, passing notes to one another, while, incredibly, in the middle of all of this, Mia, darling Mia, Kate's little orphan girl, tremulous, made her way to the table next to the committee. Rick pulled out a chair for her, and she sat down, her hands neatly folded in her lap. A stir went around the room, and Kate grimaced as the men on the committee leered at the stunning girl, her blue eyes as bright as the day Kate had met her.

"Tell us who you are," one of the committee members said.

"My name is Mia Stein. And I am German."

Something in the room shifted. Was it the way the girl sat there, a living embodiment of what everyone feared, with her German accent and her background in Soviet zones?

The room was silent as midnight. Midnight over some old battlefield, where only the ghosts lingered, and memories hung like shadows in the dark.

"I was born in 1935," Mia continued, and the audience was riveted. "I was born under the regime of Adolf Hitler, a man whom my family hated. His name was spoken with revulsion in my house."

Not one committee member said anything, and Mia took a deep breath.

"I was four years old when the war broke out. My mother, myself, and my little brother Filip went out to live with my grandparents on their farm north of Berlin." Mia lowered her eyes. "We fled after the Russian campaign, when my father was reported missing, and then dead, in a Russian prisoner of war camp. He'd been sent to Siberia." She raised her extraordinary eyes to the room, locking everyone in. Entrancing them, taking them all to the old countries, the places that Americans only knew of in their dreams. "So, believe me, I know about life with the Soviets."

A man on the committee raked his hand over his hair and regarded Mia through his hooded eyes.

"I remember the Nazis taking things from the farm, the wheels from my grandfather's car, then the car itself, and my grandmother yelled at them, and they struck her down. She was in a wheelchair after that."

"The Nazis are not who we are here to talk about," the man who had lost his cigar growled.

Kate's eyes burned into him.

Mia shot a glance to Kate, her eyes flashing with worry for a millisecond, and quickly, Kate nodded. *Don't let them intimidate you. Go on.*

Mia took in a deep breath. "My mother wanted to get away before the Soviets came through. We had waves of refugees staying in the farm, sleeping in the outbuildings, lumping their worldly goods west on the backs of wagons, and my grandfather fed them with potato gruel from the farm. I remember the smell of those potatoes cooking, the families who came through."

The room was silent. Silent because everyone was hearing a story from the other side of the war.

"But my grandmother was infirm and injured already by the Nazis. The refugees told us how Nazis were shooting and threatening Germans who deserted and did not stay back to protect the Reich. That you had to be able to run, to get away from the remaining Nazi soldiers, what was left of them." Mia lowered her head. "My grandparents left it too late and the Soviets, they came all of a sudden."

Not a breath could be heard in the entire room.

"An entire battalion of them. They swooped into our farmyard, yelling *'Women! Women!'* And while my mother, who was beautiful and only thirty-five years old, tried to disguise herself, tried to powder her hair so it looked gray, but she was still a desirable woman." Mia's voice was low and cold. "The Soviets wanted to take revenge for what they had suffered at the hands of the Nazis on the women and children and the elderly they found still living in the ruins of Hitler's Germany."

A sour taste spread in Kate's mouth.

"The Soviets pushed my grandmother, me and Filip upstairs into the farmhouse attics at gunpoint, and while my grandmother stuffed my face into her lap, nothing could muffle the sounds of my mother's screams as the soldiers, the entire battalion, raped her repeatedly. They took my uncle, my mother's brother, who had come back from the war with a lame leg, out in the woods and they beat him to a pulp, and then they decapitated him and left his entrails all over the forest floor."

Kate's stomach rolled. She fought the urge to run to Mia, to hold her in her arms and tell her she'd take care of her for good. But nothing could still those memories, memories that must swoop around like treacherous winds in the child's head.

"They beat my elderly grandfather until he was on his knees and begging for mercy. Having butchered his son and raped his daughter on that first day, another three men blasted into the house the next day, and the next, raping my mother again. I will never forget her screams, her body, hunched in two with agony, the way she sobbed for my dead father, her dead brother. The Soviets smashed my grandfather's farm. My house became a war zone. They slaughtered my pet dog, and my kitten, destroyed our mattresses until only the bedheads remained, smashed our glass photograph frames, ripped the pictures to shreds. They took all our food, and they pissed on the floors and started a fire in the living room, using my grandmother's crutches for kindling. It was me who put out the fire, because I was the only one who could walk."

Kate leaned forward, her head in her trembling hands. The room was silent. *If Mia had been left with the Soviets, she would never have been able to talk. They had saved her, thank goodness. And in her own way, the young Mia had saved Kate. Had brought feeling back into her life. But, oh, at what an unthinkable price.*

"In the following days, I walked to my uncle and aunt's house in the nearby village, but the village had been burned down. The stench of it, I will never forget. And I will never forget the sight of light and fires on the horizon. I hid in the forests whenever I heard anyone approaching. I had learned to trust not one soul, German or Russian."

Mia focused straight ahead. "In the village, there was one old woman, the postmaster's wife, scrounging in the ruins. She told me that my uncle had taken my aunt and his two girls, my cousins, Dina and Heli, with whom I used to play and with whom I walked to school, out to the lake and he had drowned Dina and Heli and shot my aunt in the head before shooting himself in the mouth. He didn't want them to face the Soviets, he knew what they would do."

The room was silent.

"Finally, after the Russians showed no more interest in our desecrated farm, my grandfather and grandmother managed to get to their neighbor's farm with dozens of other refugees. My mother said that she, Filip and I would walk to Berlin with these refugees. We would go home to see if our Berlin house still stood and send back a wagon for my grandparents. I went along with my mother's idea, but I worried that leaving my grandparents seemed a foolhardy plan."

"But barely had we started to walk when we were surrounded by the Russians. Only three miles away from my village, Russian planes, piloted by boys grinning and yelling, began shooting at our bedraggled party. And the last thing I saw of Filip was his body, blown to bits by Soviet guns. And the last I saw of my mother was her body, thrown over his, where she'd tried and failed to protect him, her blood spreading over the dark soil. And what wakes me up every night is the picture of body parts, of the arms and heads and legs of my fellow refugees, while I watched, curled up in the forest, where I had run to protect myself." Mia's eyes locked with Kate's. "And I will never forgive myself. Because I could not save my mother or my little brother."

Kate rocked in her seat, she let out a moan, and Harvey leaned toward her. "Kate?" he said.

She nodded to let him know she was okay. She and Mia, both locked in by their own heartbreaking scars and yet drawn to each other, Kate battling guilt after her father's tragic death, Mia imprisoned in a dark silent place after witnessing these unspeakable acts, tormented because she'd lived and so many of her family members had not.

It was not your fault! Kate wanted to enfold Mia in her arms.

But the committee sat, formidable. The men who still had the power to choose Rick's fate, despite Willard's confession, despite the testimony of the little girl, so bravely sitting at the front of the room.

"I was in the forest, alone." Mia was almost whispering now, her eyes straight ahead, her hand clasping at a necklace she wore around her neck. "And I had to make it back to Berlin. I scrounged through the forests, occasionally finding a bed of straw at farms along the way, stealing food scraps from abandoned German farmhouses. Constantly in fear of the Russians.

"Once, I was at the window of a farmhouse. I was so hungry, and inside, there were Russians eating food that had been stored by German farmers during the war. They saw me and shot at me and I scrambled back out to the woods." She lifted her chin. "Another time, I found a German man, hung dead on a rope in a barn, and while there was food in the farmhouse, I could not bring myself to steal it, I could not stomach doing so.

"I was a child of the forest for months. What kept me alive was the idea of getting to Berlin, finding our house and sending for my grandparents. But when I finally arrived and did find my parents' house, it was all gone. There was nothing left. It was an empty shell. By then, my journey had taken me six months. I was cold, alone, freezing, ready to give up. And Rick Shearer and his friend, Kate Mancini, found me. They, these kind Americans, brought me to safety. If they had not done so, after all my efforts to get home, I would have been placed at the mercy of the Russians. In an orphanage. And if that were the case, I think I would have died."

Mia lowered her head. "I would rather die than live under the Soviets. But when my grandparents were found in a tiny house in a nearby village, I went back there. And Rick Shearer came to visit me on several occasions, bringing me toys, clothes and treats from America, talking to my grandparents about his concerns for us living under the communists, and finally bringing my grandparents the documentation I needed to get to the British zone of Germany right before the blockade of Berlin in 1948.

"He also brought us a passport for me to come to America if I wanted to. He told my grandparents that he suspected things would get worse, and then when the blockade indeed took effect, his friend, Kate Mancini, came and finished what Rick had started. She rescued me, a German orphan, from the clutches of the Soviets. Still my grandparents refused to leave the part of Germany they had always known. And now, they are both gone too. My grandmother died in the winter of last year. And my grandfather died soon after of a broken heart. The Soviets killed my parents, my brother, and now my grandparents are dead, having lived under their regime. I have no family left. But the two people who saved me are sitting right here in this room."

Kate's cheeks burned. Heads swiveled toward her, then back to Rick, and she could hardly swallow the bile in her throat.

"Mr. Shearer is not a communist," Mia went on. "Mr. Shearer protected me from the communists. And if it weren't for him, I would have had to walk back to Berlin again when my grandparents died. I would have had to make my own way out of Soviet Germany, and most likely, I would have been caught and sent to Siberia, or I would be dead."

And with that, Mia stood up, ran her hands down her dress, and carefully stepped back to her chair.

The room was silent, save the soft sounds of people crying.

Tears were falling unchecked down Kate's cheeks. She accepted the white handkerchief that Harvey handed to her, and blew her nose noisily, not caring right now who heard. The poor, darling girl. Poor Mia. That little girl who had tucked her hand into Kate's and trusted her. What she had endured, what her mother had endured! It was unthinkable.

The committee members slid papers along the desk to one another, and everyone in the room seemed to be holding a collective breath.

There was a mighty pause, and then a man in the front row started a slow clap.

Kate wheeled her head around, and behind her, folks were standing up.

Kate stood up too. And someone sent a cheer through the room.

"Mr. Rick Shearer is acquitted of the accusations leveled against him. He is free to return to work as a practicing journalist." the committee member shouted over the noise.

And the room erupted. And flashbulbs went off.

Kate ran to the front of the room and, shoving her way past folks in the aisles, she threw herself into Mia's arms, and as she stood there, hugging Mia and sobbing into the girl's dress, she felt a warm pair of arms around both of them, and she looked up. And her eyes caught with Rick's.

"*Katia,*" Rick whispered. "My darling, Katia, and dearest, dearest Mia, our girl."

Uttering a cry of relief, Kate drew him close. In front of his parents, who stood right behind him, in front of Hilary, in front of the entire executive team at WNYR, she made it abundantly clear that not only was she a proud, independent journalist, she was a woman who would fight to protect the man she loved. And despite trying to block love out due to awful, tragic circumstances that were beyond her control, one orphan girl had stopped her from shutting herself off, and that was the best thing that could have happened to her.

And thanks to the bravery of this girl, this young girl who hailed from the other side of a brutal war that had turned Europe into a graveyard, Rick's life, in turn, had been saved.

Kate buried her face in Rick's shoulder, her pulse racing, not caring that Harvey, and the other executives had turned silent, and their eyes were glued on her, come what may, she'd deal with it. Her career? Let them try and take it away from her. Just let them try!

And with one hand encircled in Mia's, she leaned up to give Rick a heartfelt kiss.

Chapter Thirty-Four

Kate

New York, summer 1951

Rick was already seated at the long bar that ran the length of Josephine's, flicking through a newspaper. An overhead fan whirled above his head. Kate slid onto the bar stool beside him. All around, the restaurant buzzed with the chatter of guests, and in the corner of the room, a jazz band were setting up to play.

Rick stood up and leaned down to kiss Kate on the cheek. His aftershave smelled of cinnamon and citrus, along with smoky patchouli. His lips brushed her skin, and when he stepped back, his brown eyes searched her face, and for a long moment, she fought the urge to reach out and trace her fingers across his freshly shaved chin. Her senses fired at his close proximity and her stomach gave a little lurch.

When the bartender came to ask for their order, Rick asked for a coffee, and Kate ordered a soda and lime.

"I've got marvelous news," she said, unable to contain her excitement, batting away the old attraction that fired between them every time they met.

Rick moved a little closer to her. He picked up her hand a moment and squeezed it gently. "Tell me, Katia."

She bit on her lip but couldn't contain her wide smile. "Mia is staying in New York. She's been granted a visa and—"

But she didn't get to finish her sentence. Rick pulled her into his arms and swung her around like a girl on VE day right in front of the crowded bar, only letting go of her when their waiter appeared, holding their drinks on a tray. Rick's eyes danced and he looked fit to shout the news to the world while the waiter put their drinks down and ducked out of the way.

"How are you feeling about that, Katia?"

"Wonderful, as you say!" Kate's eyes sparkled, and she slipped back onto her bar stool with a fluid grace. She raised her glass to him and took a long cool drink.

"I don't know how either of us will ever repay you," he said, his eyes serious.

The band struck up "Love Somebody" and, while Kate sipped her soda, Rick took her free hand in his. He leaned in close again.

"Katia?" he said. He picked up his jacket from the bar stool, flicking it over his shoulder. "Are you free for the rest of the day?"

Kate's pulse raced.

"Sure, I'm free," she said.

His hands rested on the bar. "And Mia?" he asked, his voice soft. "Might she be able to join us?"

Kate's cheeks glowed. She couldn't help it. "Sure," she said. "Let's go ask her."

Right now, after Mia's stunning revelation, after Willard Shearer's sensational confession, and after he'd written to Kate and apologized, point blank for any harm he'd caused her and with Mia staying in New York, anything seemed possible, and that was a heady thing.

Just over an hour later, they were driving through the heart of Connecticut, Mia sitting between Rick and Kate in the front seat of his Alpha Romeo, the roads dappled with summer sunshine and lined with majestic maple trees, apple trees, and manicured gardens framing New England farmhouses. The air was fresh and still, and the scenery reminded Kate so much of that around Rick's family home near Farmington, but they were closer to the town of Wilton, and Rick had told her not to ask any questions and he wouldn't tell any lies.

An hour and a half out of New York, Rick turned down a driveway and came to a stop outside a white-painted house with a shingle roof, its two stories of windows framed with black shutters and a polished front door underneath a dear little porch. A pair of tall trees framed the entrance, and all around were shady lawns set with more English trees, while neat box hedges and white roses formed a border along the front of the house.

Rick turned off the car engine, and turned to Kate and Mia, his expression almost shy. "What do you think?" he asked softly.

Kate drew her sunglasses back and sat them atop her head. "Wow," she breathed. She turned to him. "*Rick?*" she asked.

He opened his door and came around to open Kate and Mia's car door for them, scraping a hand through his hair.

When Kate stepped out onto the driveway, she had to catch her breath because she might have stopped breathing altogether. The house was gorgeous. A dear house, not pretentious or grand or anything showy, just a lovely old farmhouse with two tall chimneys in a New England setting that may as well have been paradise.

"It's called Maple Farm and I fell in love with it," Rick said. His voice cracked on the last words. "Want to come and have a look inside?"

Mia gasped next to her, and Kate found herself rooted to the spot. "Wait," she murmured. "You're telling me…" She turned to him, and he searched her face, his expression serious, his chest rising and falling as if he were nervous.

Dear Rick.

"Yes," he said softly. "I decided to sell the grand apartment in Manhattan that my family bought for me." He screwed up his nose. "It wasn't really my style, you know."

"No," Kate said. The place had been grandiose. The views over Central Park were heaven, but it was a prima donna compared to this lovely old home.

He took in a breath. "Well, the truth is, I closed on Maple Farm just a few days after the trial, and you're the first people I've told."

Kate was speechless. She simply stood still and bit on her lip.

"It is very lovely," Mia murmured.

Kate reached out and clasped Mia's hand in her own.

"I want somewhere to go on the weekends, somewhere to escape and rest. Somewhere, perhaps, down the track, where..." Rick fell silent, and jangled his keys, cleared his throat. "Well, you, me, Mia..."

Kate shaded her eyes from the sun that dappled down through the green leaves. It was so quiet out here.

Mia took in a little breath, and Kate squeezed her hand. Darling girl.

Rick still looked a little shy. He stood in front of them both, hesitantly.

"Well," Mia said, "I would like to see inside, please."

Kate let out a giggle.

Rick's eyes finally danced, and his shoulders seemed to drop in relief. "Well then," he said. "Shall we?"

Kate stumbled up the front steps after him, Mia already waiting on the front porch, exploring the wooden verandah with its pretty, intricate wooden railings overlooking the soft green garden. Kate's heart thumped something wild. Mia seemed at home here already and when Rick reached out to stop Kate from falling, catching her in his arms on the threshold, right in front of the elegant front door, she looked up into his eyes, and hardly could breathe he was so close to her.

"*Katia,*" he murmured, his eyes darkening. "It means the world to me that you like it. That you like Maple Farm." He held her shoulders in his hands, and he sent her one of his sudden, warm smiles. "Are you okay?" he whispered. "You didn't hurt your ankle."

All she could do was shake her head, and gently, he let go of her, running a hand down her arm, before taking the key on a great old silver key ring and turning it into the lock.

When he swung the old front door open, he stood aside. Mia strolled over to peer inside the front door, and Kate's hands trembled, her eyes sparkling at the sight in front of her. Sunlight flooded the entrance hall, lit from a big window atop a flight of stairs that led to a landing. The floor was made of polished wood, and the stairs were wooden and charming. The house smelled of beeswax and everything gleamed.

Kate hugged herself as she followed Rick and Mia upstairs, both of them chatting easily, Mia laughing at a couple of jokes Rick made. But Kate wandered, speechless, through seven beautiful bedrooms, each with large paned windows overlooking the English park-like lawns that seemed to spread as far as the eye could see.

Downstairs, there was a gracious old living room with a stone fireplace, a dining room, and a sunroom, next to another living room and a huge country kitchen. The whole house was flooded with light, and potential, and the more Kate walked through it, the more at home and welcomed she felt.

Rick threw open the back door and stepped out into the warm sunshine. He turned to Kate and Mia. "The best part," he said, lowering his voice, and taking Kate's hand as naturally as could be, tucking Mia's hand into his free arm, "out here, there's a private cottage, for writing, or reading. It's such a wonderful retreat."

They came to a stop at the edge of the wide lawn, outside a perfect little white cottage, with a dear staircase winding up to a half-glass door on a tiny balcony. "Oh, it's sweet," Kate breathed.

"Come on," he whispered. He led them up the wooden staircase and unlocked the little door.

Inside, Kate drew her hand to her mouth. A desk was set up overlooking the window, and already, a typewriter just like the one she'd taken all over Europe with her sat on it, a fresh piece of paper peeking out from above the keyboard. Next to this, someone had placed a crystal bowl full of roses and a set of silver biros, along with a stack of snowy white paper. A Turkish rug lay across the floor, and against the window on the other side, there was a faded old leather sofa, and a charming armchair. Both were piled with plump cushions, and there was a fireplace filled with pinecones. A tall lamp sat above the sofa, and in here, Kate felt immediately at home.

"Rick?" she said, turning to face him.

He looked down at her, and his expression was filled with such tenderness that she found herself unable to speak for a moment. "Kate, Mia, come over here," he said.

He led them over to the desk and pulled out the piece of paper from the typewriter. Kate scanned the document, at first frowning at the fact that the page was covered in neat script, but it wasn't a story, not something Rick had started, this was a document. An official script. Her eyes moved at the lightning speed she was so used to when she read, and she couldn't help it, she bounced from foot to foot.

"Oh, Rick," she said, turning to him. Her eyes glowing, she pulled gorgeous Mia into a close hug. "Darling," she whispered.

The girl lifted her face to Kate's, her beautiful eyes shining, still, bless her, looking a tiny bit lost.

Well. Rick had just put paid to that for good.

"These are adoption papers, for you," she whispered. "For you, darling, so that you can be family, a daughter. So that you will never be alone, ever again in your life. It seems while we were getting a visa, Rick was working behind the scenes too. Just like he did when you were in Germany." She turned, eyes shining to Rick. "What a good team we make."

And right then, Mia's mouth opened and closed, and she let out a squeak and turned to Rick. He nodded his confirmation, and Mia fanned herself, her blue eyes sparkling as if all the lights had just been turned on over Berlin itself again. "You are kidding me?" she asked. "Me, you, Rick, a real family? And us, living together here?"

Kate nodded, and she pressed Mia's hand gently in her own. "Yes, here and in New York…" And suddenly she stopped. She turned to Rick. *Hang on.* She was making a big presumption there. The adoption papers had Mia's name on them, and hers, and Rick's, but… they weren't exactly a family.

And then Mia did something, she danced across the room. And she turned, her big blue eyes brimming with excitement. "Rick, Kate? Do you mind if I run outside? I am so excited, I think I will break in two if I do not get some fresh air!"

"Of course, sweetheart," Kate said, and she watched, her heart filled with every emotion as Mia made her way down the stairs to the garden, where she walked around, hugging herself. Simply hugging herself.

Slowly, Kate turned back to Rick. He was standing right behind her, and he drew his hand under her chin, lifting it and bending down closer to her, tentatively at first. She let out a little cry and his lips were on hers, and she wound her arms around his neck, and closed her eyes, reveling in the way she felt at home, here. With him, in his arms.

"Darling," he murmured, finally. "I want both darling Mia and you to be happy here. Katia, I'm in love with you. I can't bear being apart from you. And I swear I won't let anyone stop you from having that career you love, nor from being the person you want to be."

She looked back up at him, her eyes running back and forth over his dear features. And finally, she let out a huge breath. "I love you too, Rick," she whispered. "And I know how to fight for my career. Don't you worry about that."

He reached forward, tucking one of her curls behind her ear. "I can't believe this is real," he said. "I've dreamed of this for so long."

She nodded, her eyes threatening to fill with tears. "Yes," she said simply.

"Marry me," he whispered. "Marry me and we will work this crazy thing out together. I adore you, and, Katia, please know, one thing is absolutely certain. I always will."

Kate closed her eyes, and with the sun shining gently down on them, she nodded, her throat too thick to be able to speak, and she drew herself closer, resting her head on his shoulder. Finally, after so many years wandering, trying to find meaning after the tragic death of her beloved father, in the face of a terrible, heartless, sordid war, after months spent scouring war-torn Europe trying to find more answers and failing, and then years fighting for the career she'd always dreamed of, she felt as if now, she'd come home.

Kate laid the weekend newspaper down on the wrought-iron table on the terrace at Maple Farm. All around her, the lawns spread out in a glorious rich, green, and her niece, Sofia, was sitting on a picnic rug under one of the shady trees, the sun catching on her dark hair, the child's striking black eyes were purely Bianca's, as was her honey-colored skin. Sofia's little sister, Lara, was toddling around in the grass, while Bianca lay on her back, her elbows spread wide, a look of contentment on her face, dappled by the sunlight that filtered through the shady trees.

And next to Bianca was Mia, stretched out on the rug, her beautiful face turned up to the sun, her own, blessed sun out here in Connecticut, where they'd spent the rest of the summer, swimming in the pool, reading, and laughing late into the night, cooking together, horse riding with Frances, healing. And behaving just as a family ought.

A handful of friends and family had witnessed Kate and Rick's marriage in a private ceremony in a little church near Wilton. Afterward, they'd come back to Maple Farm for a feast fit for a kingdom, prepared by Livia and Gia Morelli, and they'd held a small party to celebrate. It had been a wonderful wedding and Willard Shearer had made everyone laugh until they cried with his speech.

Now, Frances wandered out onto the terrace, her husband right by her side.

When the door to Rick and Kate's writing cottage opened, and Rick appeared at the top of the flight of wooden stairs, stretching and facing up to the warm sun, Kate waved at him, and held up the jug of iced tea she'd brought out. Even from a distance, she could see the way his eyes crinkled warmly in response. He trotted down the wooden staircase, his long legs going a dime to the dozen.

Kate rested her chin in her hands and watched her husband come toward her, stopping a moment to pick Lara up from the picnic blanket on the lawn, and showing her a daisy that he'd found. The little girl's face lit up, and so did Rick's as he gently tickled Kate's niece's nose with the flower, sending her into rafts of giggles, and causing Sofia to dance around him, clinging to his legs, laughing up at her adored uncle.

And when Mia reached up a hand to him, Rick held it a moment, and they smiled at each other, Mia in the knowledge she was safe, and would always be safe with Kate and Rick by her side, and Rick knowing that the strange little orphan they had met in Berlin was growing to be one of the bravest women he knew.

Tenderly, he placed little Lara back down on the rug, swung Sofia around in the air a few times, and laughing with her, handed her back to her mom.

As he wove toward Kate, his face tanned, and his handsome face splitting into a happy grin, she reflected again on how much she loved him.

As he came to a standstill at the small table where Kate sat, he stroked her cheek and leaned down to drop a feather kiss on her lips.

Kate leaned into his shoulder, closing her eyes, her head resting against the soft, steady thud of his heart.

A new family to protect and love. She, Rick and beautiful Mia. War may have brought them together, but nothing would tear them apart.

A Letter from Ella Carey

Dear reader,

I want to say a huge thank you for choosing to read *The Lost Girl of Berlin*. If you did enjoy it, and want to keep up to date with all my latest releases, just sign up at the following link. Your email address will never be shared and you can unsubscribe at any time.

www.bookouture.com/ella-carey

This book was such a labor of complete love for me. There was a wealth of material to work with—women's lives in post-war Germany and America, the battles female political correspondents had to wage in order to find any sort of recognition in the late 1940s and early 1950s, the rise of radio and television, McCarthyism, and the stories of the war orphans. I struggle to put my feelings into words about these children, even here.

I am so fortunate to have a career which I love. I wake up every day and cannot wait to get cracking, and I am only appreciative of the women of past generations. Kate, Bianca and Frances came so fully alive to me, I adored telling their story, and I thank you for your time reading the book.

I hope you loved *The Lost Girl of Berlin,* and if you did, I would be very grateful if you could write a review. I'd love to hear what you think, and it makes such a difference helping new readers to discover one of my books for the first time.

I love hearing from my readers—you can get in touch on my Facebook page, through Twitter, Goodreads or my website.

Thanks,
Ella

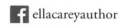 ellacareyauthor

 @Ella_Carey

www.ellacarey.com

Author's note

I would like to acknowledge that parts of Kate's professional journey are inspired by the life of Pauline Frederick, the pioneering American female broadcast journalist who was the first woman to become a network news correspondent and who also once covered a forum on "how to get a husband," after reporting on the Nuremberg trials of Nazi war criminals at the end of World War Two. In 1976, Pauline Frederick became the first woman journalist to moderate a presidential candidate's debate, and she was the first woman to receive a Peabody Award, the radio industry's equivalent of the Pulitzer Prize.

Acknowledgments

My sincere thanks to my editor, Maisie Lawrence, for your support for this story from the outset, for your belief in my ability to tell it, and for your wonderful guidance during the entire process from beginning to end. My heart is filled with gratitude to you. To my wonderful agent, Giles Milburn, thank you for being there during the birth of this idea, for helping me to develop it, and for all your fantastic ongoing enthusiasm and support for my work. I am truly blessed to work with you both.

Thank you to the entire team at Bookouture; to the publicity marvels, Kim Nash, Sarah Hardy and Noelle Holton, who work tirelessly to promote every one of our books, every day. Thanks to the entire marketing team, especially Alex Crow, for putting together such wonderful strategies to reach lovely readers with each new book and, especially, for your ongoing support of my entire backlist. Thank you to copyeditor, Jade Craddock, for all your meticulous work reading and line editing my work, to proofreader, Anne O'Brien, for carefully checking the final draft, and to Lauren Finger for coordinating the copy edits and proofreads. Special thanks to cover designer, Sarah Whittaker, for creating such beautiful and evocative covers for this new series, Daughters of New York.

Thank you to the foreign rights team at the Madeleine Milburn Literary Agency, especially Liane-Louise Smith, and Georgina Simmons, for selling this new series into so many languages other than English. I am enormously appreciative, and in awe.

Thank you to all the lovely authors at Bookouture, who are the most supportive group of writers I know. I am so privileged to be a part of it all and thank you for your chats and friendship.

This book is the culmination of many years of research, of several visits to Germany, to Berlin, and to New York, and I send my thanks to all the kind people who talked to me during those journeys, and helped me bring the past alive as best as I could in this book.

Huge thanks to my family and friends, to my children, to Ben, who has loved history and has shared my fascination with the past since he could pick up a book, and who also has a passion for politics, to my daughter, Sophie, for all your wonderful support.

And finally, my deepest thanks to my loyal, wonderful readers, many of whom have been with me since my first book, *Paris Time Capsule*, was published back in 2015, and to my new readers, thank you for your lovely emails, messages of support and love for my books. You keep me writing. Thank you. xx

Made in United States
Orlando, FL
28 December 2021

12585797R00195